1

The Darkest Place: A Surviving the Dead Novel

By:

James N. Cook

Also by James N. Cook:

Surviving The Dead Series:

No Easy Hope

This Shattered Land

Warrior Within

The Passenger

Fire in Winter

I had a dream, which was not all a dream.
The bright sun was extinguished,
and the stars did wander darkling in the eternal space,
rayless and pathless, and the icy earth swung blind
and blackening in the moonless air.
Morn came and went and came, and brought no day.
And men forgot their passions in the dread of this,
their desolation.
And all hearts were chilled into a selfish prayer for light,
and they did live by watchfires,
and the thrones, the palaces of crowned kings, the huts,
the habitations of all things which dwell,
were burnt for beacons.
Cities were consumed,
and the men gathered round their blazing homes,
to look once more into each other's face.

-Lord Byron
Darkness

ONE

Hollow Rock, Tennessee

Caleb Hicks awoke to the sound of bells ringing.

This is getting to be a habit, he thought as he sat up and reached for his gear. Everything was exactly where he had left it the night before, which was the same place he always left it. If an alarm started ringing in the middle of the night, there was no fumbling around trying to locate his MOLLE vest, rifle, assault pack, helmet, and spear. It was always in the same spot, ready to go.

"For Christ's sake, what the hell is it this time?" Specialist Derrick Holland moaned as he tugged on his boots.

"Probably more walkers," Sergeant Isaac Cole said groggily. "Been getting a lot of those lately."

Staff Sergeant Ethan Thompson, Caleb's squad leader, stood up and addressed his men. "Whatever it is, it's our job to deal with it. Let's get moving, ladies. Time to go to work."

The other men in Hicks' squad quickly dressed and armed themselves. He looked across the VFW hall that had served as his platoon's quarters for the last few months and saw forty-eight soldiers lining up for inspection. As usual, the platoon's commanding officer, First Lieutenant Clay Jonas, a forty-something former master sergeant given a field commission

11

after the Outbreak, was the first to be ready. His men stood at respectful attention as he looked them over.

"All right," he said, satisfied with what he saw. "Squad leaders, form your men up and get ready to move out."

The four staff sergeants of First Platoon answered with a chorus of yes sirs and turned to their men, barking out orders. Thompson took a few extra moments to make sure his squad's gear and weapons were squared away, then had them form up with the rest of the platoon. Jonas took his place at the head of the formation and nodded to his platoon sergeant.

Master Sergeant Damian Ashman—all six-foot-six, two-hundred-seventy pounds of him—towered over the men behind him as he turned and addressed his troops, the hilt of his massive broadsword protruding over his right shoulder. If they had been back home at Fort Bragg, he would have given a crisp *FORwaaaard, MARCH*. But Ashman had been in the Army long enough to know that out in the field such things weren't necessary. Instead, he simply tilted his helmet toward the door and said, "Let's go."

Hicks adjusted the tactical sling on his rifle as he emerged into the chilly morning. The sun was just beginning to burnish the eastern sky in shades of crimson and copper, a clatter of birdsong echoing through blooming tree-lined streets. If not for the urgent bronze cacophony rattling from the south side of town, the morning would have been idyllic.

Caleb felt an elbow nudge his side and looked to his right. "How much you wanna bet it's walkers again?" Holland asked.

Hicks shook his head. Holland would bet on anything.

"I'll take that bet," Private Fuller said from behind them. He was almost as much of a gambling addict as Holland, and that was saying something. Hicks had a theory the two of them never actually gained anything over one another in their constant wagering, but instead simply traded their personal fortunes back and forth two or three times a month.

"I'll put up two mini-bottles of Bacardi," Fuller said. "How about you?"

Holland thought about it for a moment, then said, "Three MRE packs of instant coffee."

"Make it four."

Holland spun around and marched backward while he shook hands with Fuller. "You're on."

As his platoon marched closer, Hicks looked up at the towers on the south wall. The guards in the towers and along the walls did not look more agitated than usual, which was a good sign. Their attention was focused toward something on the ground below, outside the palisade of telephone poles and tree trunks. They gestured, and pointed, and spoke into handheld radios. Hicks recognized the shapely silhouette of Deputy Sarah Glover as she walked back and forth organizing the response to whatever crisis was occurring.

"That cop is a sweet-looking piece of ass," Holland said, eliciting a few chuckles from the men around him. "Kinda MILF-y, but I'd still hit it."

Hicks felt heat rise in his face, and before he realized what he was doing, he had seized two of Holland's fingers and twisted them together, grinding nerves between bones. Holland gave a surprised squeak and stumbled to keep up as Hicks kept walking. The tall young soldier leaned over and said, "Her name is Sarah Glover, and she is a good, kind-hearted woman. So I don't *ever* want to hear you talk about her like that again. Understood?"

Holland nodded quickly, unable to draw a breath against the pain. Hicks released his hand.

"Jesus Christ, man," Holland complained, trying to work feeling back into his fingers. "Half my arm is numb. What the fuck did you do to my hand?"

"Don't worry," Caleb said. "It's not permanent. This time."

Sergeant Ashman brought the platoon to a halt while Lieutenant Jonas proceeded ahead to speak with Deputy Glover. The soldiers around Hicks shifted restlessly, grumbling quiet complaints as they awaited orders. After conferring with Sarah and the watch captain, Jonas turned on his heel and walked back to his platoon.

"We've got another horde on our hands," he announced. Fuller groaned. "We're headed for the north gate to meet up with the Ninth TVM and Second Platoon outside Fort McCray. Then we'll proceed south and encircle the horde at company strength. Same drill as last time. You men know what to do." He nodded at Master Sergeant Ashman.

"You heard the man," Ashman bellowed. "About face, let's go."

Holland muttered, "I sure am glad we marched all the way down here."

Caleb ignored him. He had long ago given up expecting life in the Army to make sense. Everything was hurry up and wait, and contradicting orders, and marching for miles to take position on a hill, wait there for days, and then get orders to march to another hill and wait a few more days for an enemy that never showed up. Hicks no longer complained. It was pointless, and changed nothing. He simply accepted.

The platoon crossed town, emerged from the north gate, and turned eastward. When the wall surrounding the town of Hollow Rock passed behind them, there was a subtle shift in the soldiers' demeanor. Behind the wall, they had been poised and confident, marching with casual ease, hefting their weapons with the surety of long practice. Now, without the wall separating them from the wasteland of horrors their country had become, they grew tense, eyes shifting, hands tightening on weapons, helmets turning as they scanned the fields around them and the treeline in the distance. The designated marksmen in each squad raised their sniper carbines and peered through scopes, searching the landscape for walkers or signs of an ambush.

Raiders, marauders, and insurgents were fond of using hordes as a distraction while they launched an attack. The soldiers of First Platoon had long ago learned how devastating such tactics could be, so they watched, and fidgeted, and worried.

Except Hicks.

He observed his surroundings closely, dark-blue eyes constantly on the move, searching for signs of living people having disturbed the tall grass around him. He did not allow himself to worry. One of the first lessons he had been taught, so long ago the memory was dim and hazy around the edges, was to master his emotions. To not let worry and anxiety dictate his actions. *A panicked man makes mistakes,* his father had said. *Mistakes get you killed.*

Furthermore, on long marches, when faced with an unknown number of walkers and the very real possibility of an ambush, tension burned energy best used for fighting. By staying loose and relaxed, he could stave off exhaustion far longer than someone with less self-control.

Master Sergeant Ashman called the platoon to a halt at the rendezvous point, a Y-shaped intersection between Hollow Rock's main gate and Highway 114. The men and women of the Ninth Tennessee Volunteer Militia were already waiting for them.

The militia was a stark contrast to the regular Army troops. Where Hicks and his fellow soldiers packed nearly sixty pounds of gear each time they ventured into the field, the militiamen carried hardly any equipment at all. Just a rifle, sidearm, melee weapon, MOLLE vest, spare ammunition, and a light assault pack. They even eschewed helmets in favor of ball caps, boonie hats, and in most cases, headscarves.

Since the other two platoons in Echo Company—2nd Battalion of the 1st Reconnaissance Expeditionary Brigade out of Fort Bragg, NC—had joined First Platoon, the Ninth TVM, who had once been the town's primary defense force, had been repurposed as scouts and guides, working closely with the

15

commanding officers of all three platoons to teach them the terrain, point out chokepoints and ambush sites, establish patrols along critical trade routes, and generally provide expertise and advice on how best to defend Hollow Rock and the surrounding area. The newly arrived soldiers had, at first, looked upon the militia as little more than civilians playing at being soldiers. This perception faded quickly when the militia demonstrated a level of training, discipline, and combat effectiveness rivaling that of Echo Company's best soldiers.

Over the course of hundreds of patrols, dozens of skirmishes with marauders, and countless battles with the walking dead, the soldiers fighting side by side with the militia had found them to be tough, resourceful, stalwart allies. Gradually, the soldiers' disdain faded to grudging respect, then acceptance as equals, and finally outright admiration.

At a gesture from Lieutenant Jonas, First Platoon broke ranks and walked out to greet their friends and allies. Sergeant Manuel Sanchez and his people made their way over to Caleb's squad and exchanged a round of greetings.

"Man, I'm getting tired of all these attacks," said Vincenzo, one of Sanchez's men, as he bumped knuckles with Hicks. "It's cutting into our salvage work."

"It's the weather," Hicks replied. "The walkers trapped under ice during the winter have thawed out. With all the noise going on around here, we're attracting them like flies to a pile of shit."

Vincenzo looked toward the wall surrounding Hollow Rock. "Yeah, but life is loud, you know? What else are we supposed to do?"

"Aside from killing them? Nothing at all." Hicks clapped Vincenzo on the shoulder and ambled away, casually stepping closer to the cluster of lieutenants and squad leaders near the edge of the clearing. He stopped a few yards away, back turned to them so as not to draw their attention, and listened in on their conversation.

"Where the hell is Second Platoon?" Lt. Jonas asked the Ninth TVM's commanding officer, Lieutenant Marcus Cohen.

16

Cohen was a former Marine infantryman who had been home on leave when the Outbreak hit. Rather than return to his unit, he had stayed in Hollow Rock to protect his family. There were a few soldiers in Echo Company who looked down on him for this decision, but they did so quietly. The last soldier to voice open criticism accepted a challenge from Cohen to disregard rank and settle things out behind the mess hall. Said soldier went to bed that night with two black eyes, bruised ribs, a missing tooth, and a broken nose. The rest of the company got the message.

"They're on their way," Cohen replied. "Lieutenant Chapman just radioed in. ETA five minutes."

Jonas looked confused. "Well how the hell did you get here so fast?"

"We were already out on maneuvers," Cohen said, grinning. "Unlike some people, my militia doesn't hold banker's hours."

Jonas chuckled. "Keep it up, smart ass."

"Sir," Sergeant Ashman broke in. "Should I radio Lt. Chapman to catch up with us?"

There was a moment's pause while Jonas thought it over. Ashman had a way of couching suggestions in the form of questions, a very effective technique when dealing with officers. "Yeah, go ahead," Jonas replied. "We'll assess the situation and instruct him where to set up."

While Ashman got on the radio, Jonas shouted for the two platoons to shut their yaps and listen up.

"We're moving out," he shouted. "We'll march south toward the railroad tracks and set up a perimeter around the southern wall. Standard crescent formation. SAW gunners and designated marksmen, grab one volunteer each and make your way to the woods past the tracks and conduct a thorough sweep. I don't want any surprises while we're dealing with the horde. Sergeant Kelly, turn your squad over to Sergeant Ashman. I want you to lead the recon detail. Any questions?"

Silence.

"All right then. Form up and move out."

As they turned southward, Caleb felt Cole's massive hand on his shoulder. "You ready to go huntin'?" the big gunner rumbled.

Hicks showed his teeth. "Always."

The two men broke off from the platoon and headed to the edge of the woods where Sgt. Kelly was mustering the recon detail. They were joined by Holland, Fuller, and the other heavy gunners and designated marksmen from both First and Second Platoon. As for the the Ninth TVM, since they were not regular Army, it was standard procedure to remain with their federal counterparts during a walker attack.

"All right, men," Kelly announced when everyone was assembled. "You all know the drill. Maintain five-yard intervals, radio silence, hand signals only. Move slow and quiet, and if shit gets real, stay in your lane. Questions?"

There were none.

"Let's move out."

Cole looked over at Hicks and grinned, his white teeth contrasting starkly with his dark brown skin. "Let's do this." He held out a huge fist, which Hicks bumped with his own. The young soldier felt the old familiar anticipation begin to course through him.

"You know me, brother. I live for this shit."

TWO

The only reason Holland was Delta Squad's designated marksman was because Hicks had never volunteered for the task.

Holland was well aware Hicks was the superior rifleman, but kept his mouth shut because he didn't want to lose the prestige of his position. Despite this, from time to time, Hicks found it necessary to flex his muscle on the subject.

Walking out on point, he peered through the scope of Holland's sniper carbine—which he had traded for his M-4— and held a closed fist over his shoulder. The men behind him repeated the gesture until the recon detail came to a halt. Hicks turned slowly and made a few hand signals toward Sgt. Kelly.

Possible hostiles sighted. Hundred meters ahead. Dug in.

Kelly raised his hands. *How many?*

Three fire teams. Two straight ahead, one to the east.

Kelly acknowledged, carefully backed off until he felt confident he would not be overheard by the enemy, then keyed his radio and relayed Hicks' information to Lt. Jonas.

"Very well," Jonas said. "I'll have First Platoon switch directions and cut them off to the west. You circle around eastward and make contact. Remember our ROE: do not fire unless fired upon. Over."

"All right, you heard the man," Kelly said over the radio. "Maintain the line, but swing it around eastward. We'll come at them from behind. Be on the lookout, fellas, there could be more of them out there. And don't forget to keep your eyes peeled for walkers. Two clicks to acknowledge, and for God's sake, maintain protocol."

Hicks listened to the clicking of radios until it was his turn, then pressed the button twice. When all fire teams had checked in, Kelly gave the order to advance.

Hicks threaded his way silently through the forest, Cole's heavy footsteps close by. The big gunner stayed behind Hicks and a few meters to his right, scanning the forest with his SAW light machine gun. Hicks led the team on a wide arc behind the hostiles, moving within a hundred meters of the farthest targets and taking position under a cluster of cedars. He and Cole dropped to their bellies, positioned their weapons, and waited.

A few minutes later, the fire teams behind them moved into position and began passing signals down the line. Not for the first time, Hicks was grateful there weren't many new people in Echo Company. All of the men on the recon detail were experienced veterans, many of them with pre-Outbreak combat experience. They moved swiftly and efficiently, staying low and quiet. There was no arguing or confusion. These soldiers knew the importance of stealth when closing in on an enemy position. One wrong footfall, one cough or sneeze, one dropped rifle, and the element of surprise would be lost. No one wanted that, and they were appropriately careful.

Hicks watched the other fire teams pick targets and signal each other their lanes of fire. Since he and Cole were on point, they were covering the easternmost group of targets with Holland and Fuller providing crossfire.

As he lay silently among the husks of dead cedar boughs, right eye an inch away from his scope, Hicks heard his radio crackle in his ear. "All stations in position," Kelly whispered. "Remember, fingers off the trigger until they give us a reason to shoot. Engaging now. Stand by."

From the corner of his eye, Hicks saw Kelly stand up and level his rifle. "You're surrounded," he shouted, voice echoing down the embankment. "Stand up and put your hands over your head. Do it now!"

One of the bundled shapes ahead of him responded by rolling over onto its back and opening fire in Kelly's direction. The veteran sergeant dropped to his belly and returned fire as the men around him let loose with their M-4s. The offending gunman died in a hail of bullets, a few stray rounds striking the man next to him and eliciting an agonized scream.

"Okay, he's down. Cease fire," Kelly said calmly over the radio. The chatter of rifles ceased.

Kelly shouted, "Unless the rest of you want to die too, I strongly suggest you stand up and keep your hands where I can see them.

A moment passed as the gunmen looked around and realized how badly outnumbered they were. Heated whispers passed between them.

"We don't have all day, kids," Kelly said. "I'm going to count to five, and then my men are going to open fire. One. Two. Three-"

"All right!" a voice shouted. "We surrender. Everyone, on your feet."

The remaining insurgents obeyed the command, rising to their feet and raising their hands.

"Move in, but be careful," Kelly radioed. "If they try anything, shoot them."

Hicks, Cole, Holland, and Fuller approached the two men nearest them. Hicks pointed at the man on his left. "Step that way until I tell you to stop," he said.

The man complied, his ghillie suit dragging the ground in his wake. When he was far enough away from his companion, Hicks ordered him to a halt.

"Turn around and put your hands on top of your head. Good. Now get down on your knees and cross your ankles." He moved forward until the barrel of his carbine was a few inches from the insurgent's head, then nodded to Cole. The big man slung his SAW behind his back before quickly and firmly zip-tying the gunman's hands. Holland and Fuller did the same with their prisoner.

Kelly keyed his radio and told the recon detail where to bring the detainees. Hicks kept his gun trained on the back of the insurgent's head as they marched him over and ordered him to sit. Two other fire teams brought his surviving comrades to join him.

"What about those two," Kelly asked, pointing in the direction of the men who had been shot.

One of the SAW gunners from Second Platoon shook his head. "Sorry, Sergeant. Both dead. The guy that shot at you looks like Swiss cheese, and the other guy took a bullet to the femoral artery. Bled out before we could do anything about it."

Kelly let out a sigh. "Oh well. Two less assholes in the world." He looked over at Hicks and punched him in the arm.

"Man, those guys were camouflaged like a motherfucker. How'd you spot 'em?"

Hicks pointed behind him. "Picked up their trail while I was out on point. Saw there were at least six of them, passed through not long ago. So I asked myself where would I set up if I wanted to use walkers as a distraction and snipe me some federal types. I'll give 'em credit, though, they picked a good spot."

Kelly looked in the direction the insurgents had been aiming and stepped closer to the treeline. There was a low knot of dense vegetation where the field met the forest, and then a broad, flat plain beyond. He knelt to stare through the brush at the undulating knot of infected pressed against the south wall.

"I see what you mean," he said. "If First Platoon and the Ninth had set up in that field, those assholes would have had them dead to rights." He cast an angry glare toward the prisoners. "Sneaky fucks."

"Well, we stopped them," Hicks said. "That's the important thing."

"Yeah." Kelly inclined his head toward the horde. "Now for the fun part."

*****

Hicks didn't need the Y-shaped stand under his weapon's foregrip, but he didn't mind using it either.

It was a simple thing, constructed of three lengths of slender, interlocking aluminum pipe with a thin bungee cord holding them together. When not in use, it could be broken down and lashed to his pack, similar to the red and white collapsible canes used by blind people. Every soldier in Echo Company—and the Army, for that matter—had one. They were modular, making them adjustable to a particular soldier's height. The stands increased accuracy rates so much that Central Command had made them mandatory equipment.

"You know, Hicks," Holland said between shots, "you can give my rifle back any time you want."

Hicks grunted and lined up another shot. The walker in his crosshairs had been a woman once. Her clothes had long since fallen apart, leaving her mottled gray skin exposed to the elements. Only her back was visible, but Hicks could tell she had been attractive when she was still alive. Early twenties, slim physique, well-muscled legs and buttocks, probably a runner or a fitness nut. He squeezed the trigger, felt a light jolt against his shoulder, and the walker fell.

"I don't know, I kinda like it," Hicks said. "It's a little heavier than my M-4, but the extra weight reduces recoil. Scope's not too bad either."

"Very funny." Holland shifted his aim, let out a breath, and fired another shot. "You want to take my job, go right ahead. I'm tired of crawling around in the dirt anyway."

Hicks let out a sigh and raised his right hand. A militiaman behind him tapped him on the shoulder and took his place on the firing line. Holland followed suit.

"Here," Hicks held the sniper carbine at arm's length. Holland took it and gave Hicks back his M-4.

"Thanks," Holland said. He looked toward the line of soldiers firing upon the horde forty meters in the distance. "I'm still pissed at you for fucking up my hand, but I have to admit that was good work you did earlier. You're a hell of a tracker."

"Thanks." Hicks slapped him on the arm. "You might be annoying as hell, but you're a good man to have around in a fight."

Holland grinned. "Fuck you."

Both men jumped a little when they heard Sergeant Ashman's voice amplified by a bullhorn. "Cease fire! Cease fire! Weapons safe on the firing line!"

"Fuck me running," Holland mumbled.

The next command was predictable. "Draw hand weapons and prepare to advance."

"Here we go." Holland drew his twin tomahawks and gave them a little twirl. Hicks reached over his shoulder and grasped the handle of his short, heavy bladed spear and drew it from its makeshift leather-and-para-cord sheath. Ahead of them, Cole stepped away from the firing line and gave his massive bar mace a few warm-up swings.

The commanding officer of Second Platoon turned to his men and raised his bullhorn. "Draw blades!"

Second Platoon, who had spent the winter exterminating infected in Kansas, all drew the Army's new standard issue melee weapon: the MK 9 Anti-Revenant Personal Defense Tool. It consisted of a heavy twenty-inch blade forged from

24

high-carbon steel, similar in shape to a bolo machete, and a twelve-inch plastic composite handle.

Designed to be wielded two-handed, the MK 9s could split a walker's head in twain with a single overhead chop. Hicks had seen them put to hard use many times, and although he preferred his spear, he had to admit the big, ugly weapons were effective.

He watched Second Platoon warm up for a few moments, then turned to Holland. "Stay behind me and to my right," he said. "Make sure any walkers you kill fall away from me."

"Yeah, yeah, I know. Same thing we always do."

"Makes me feel better to say it."

To his left, Hicks saw Ashman raise his bullhorn. "Drop your gear except hand weapons and water. I don't want to see anyone with a rifle except squad leaders. Don't forget to don your gloves and PPE. When the fighting starts, make sure you pace yourselves. Remember to take long, deep breaths. We're in for a long fight, boys, so be smart and look out for each other."

Hicks and the other men in First Platoon put on goggles and wrapped thick scarves around their mouths and noses. Second Platoon switched from their Kevlar helmets to the Army's new plastic helmets designed specifically for fighting revenants. Hicks thought they looked like the offspring of an aviation helmet and a plastic face shield, and from everything he had heard, they were horrifically uncomfortable. Hicks preferred the scarf-and-goggles method.

One of the Army's new innovations he did like, however, were his armored gloves. Sewn from dense nylon with hard plastic plates woven around the knuckles and forearms, they extended from his fingertips all the way past his elbows and had a Velcro strap at the top to secure them in place.

The Army, after conducting research to assess how they could better protect troops from revenant bites, had discovered over ninety percent of bites were inflicted on the hands and forearms. Subsequently, after using one of their few remaining manufacturing facilities to turn out over a hundred thousand pairs of armored gloves, the casualty rates directly attributable to walker attacks fell to a fraction of what they had been before. Hicks flexed his hands a few times to loosen them up, adjusted the position of his plastic armor, and double-checked the straps above his elbows.

Good to go.

"All right," Ashman shouted, holding his custom-forged zveihänder over his head, poised for a skull-splitting chop. "Form up."

Hicks ceased his warm-up routine and fell in line. Cole stood to his left, Holland to his right. He brought his spear to the ready position and adjusted his stance, weight centered over the balls of his feet, legs braced at the proper angle.

The people on the catwalk in the distance continued beating pots and pans together and shouting at the infected, keeping them packed against the wall. Ashman stepped in front of the platoon, raised his sword, and opened his mouth to give the order to advance. But before he could, Lt. Jonas' voice cut across the field.

"Hold up, Sergeant," he shouted, radio in hand. "I have a better idea."

Ashman, somewhat crestfallen, lowered his sword. Hicks watched him walk over to their CO before turning his attention back to the wall.

On the catwalk, Deputy Glover stood with her hands cupped around her mouth shouting something unintelligible at the people making noise. After a few seconds, the clamor stopped and the townsfolk slowly began climbing down.

"The hell they doin'?" Cole muttered.

Hicks shook his head. "No idea." He kept his place in ranks, shifting restlessly, until a few seconds later the throaty rumble of a tank engine echoed across the field.

"All right, kids," Ashman called out, grinning. "Make some noise."

Hicks took off his right glove, pinched his fingers between his teeth, and let out a piercing whistle. The men around him began shouting a colorful tapestry of insults, threats, and general obscenity. Holland joined them by loudly clanking his tomahawks together. To Hicks' left, he watched an M-109 Howitzer round the corner of the wall and roll into view.

Jonas gave the order to pull back but keep the infected bunched together. With the front ranks of infected only fifty yards away, the troops slowly led the undead toward the self-propelled artillery piece. When Jonas gave the order to break ranks and run, the horde had reformed into a teardrop shape pointed straight at the barrel of the Howitzer's 155mm cannon.

Once safely out of the way, the soldiers and militiamen put in their earplugs and waited. Hicks watched the Howitzer's six-man crew lower the vehicle's spades and back up over them. Once the massive gun was stabilized, the crew loudly exhorted to their audience to get ready for a little Killer Junior action.

"Oh, this is gonna to be good," Holland said, rubbing his hands together.

Vincenzo tapped Hicks on the arm and leaned in close. "What the hell is a Killer Junior?"

"Direct-fire fragmentation round. Nasty shit. Just watch."

The horde was less than a hundred meters from the Howitzer. The soldier manning the .50 caliber machine gun held up a hand and counted down three, two, one…

BOOM.

The backwash from the blast slapped Hicks in the chest like a giant, invisible hand. A cloud of white smoke obscured the horde, then quickly dissipated. The shot cut a swath through the infected, reducing more than half their number to a maroon-colored mist. Hicks listened to the artillery crew shout back and forth while they reloaded, and then, when the horde recovered and resumed its previous teardrop-shaped approach, the

Howitzer thundered again, leaving only a few dozen walkers in its wake.

"Holy Mary, Mother of God," Vincenzo whispered. "Why didn't they just do that to begin with?"

Hicks laughed. "Why does the Army do anything?"

"Good point."

Sergeant Ashman stood up and turned to his men. "All right, fellas." He raised his sword and pointed it at the few remaining infected. "I don't know about you, but I could use a bite to eat. Let's mop up and get the hell out of here."

Hicks took up his spear and went to work.

THREE

The rest of the day was routine.

First Platoon returned to their barracks and cleaned their weapons. A short time later, the civilian contractors showed up and cooked them breakfast. Then came PT—led by Sergeant Ashman—followed by an equipment inspection carried out by the platoon's squad leaders. After inspection came the filling out of requisition forms to replace anything worn beyond usefulness.

These events preceded a patrol of the town's perimeter, which was really just an excuse for Ashman to lead his men on an eight-mile road march in full combat gear. Consequently, when they returned at 1300 hours for lunch, they were ravenous.

The afternoon consisted of cleaning their barracks, digging new latrines, and expending a portion of the company's training ammunition in the urban combat facility just outside Fort McCray. Then they cleaned their weapons again, marched back to the barracks, and ate their evening meal. At 1800 hours, Lt. Jonas told his men to check the watch bill and keep their ears open for alarm bells, but otherwise, the rest of the day was theirs.

Hicks wasn't worried about having to stand watch. He had drawn the mid-watch the night before, and he knew Ashman was a sensible sergeant who knew better than to wear his men out with unnecessary sleep deprivation. Still, he checked the bill just to be sure. He wasn't on it.

As Hicks was stowing his gear and preparing to leave, Holland sat down on the bunk across from him. "Going to see Miranda?"

"Yep."

"I'll never understand how you landed her. Half the platoon tried and failed. Even Cole struck out, and that guy is a bona fide pussy magnet."

"Just lucky, I guess."

"Everybody's in love with her, you know. We all hate you because she picked you over the rest of us. I'll never understand why. You barely talk, you're not intelligent or charming, and your face looks like a bowl of smashed assholes. I don't get it. What does she see in you?"

"Must be my southern charm."

Holland began unlacing his boots. "You must be hung like a horse. That's gotta be it. How big is your dick? Eight, ten, eleven inches? It's the only explanation."

Hicks found himself laughing. "Tell you what, Derrick. You enjoy spending the rest of the evening pondering the dimensions of my penis. I'm gonna go see my girlfriend."

"I hate you, Caleb. I'm gonna kill you in your sleep and *steal* your girlfriend."

"Stay out of trouble, amigo."

"Never in life. You coming by Stall's for drinks tonight?"

"Probably not."

"Can't say I blame you. All right, man, have fun."

"Adios."

*****

The Hollow Rock General Store was a short walk from the VFW hall, which was one of the many reasons Hicks was grateful his platoon was garrisoned in town and not with the rest of Echo Company at Fort McCray.

The afternoon was warm, the springtime sun still well above the horizon, leaving a few more hours of daylight before nightfall. It was a welcome reprieve from what had been a long, dark winter. As he walked, Hicks thought to himself that given the choice between another winter like the one just passed, and dealing with marauders and infected on a daily basis, he would take the extra combat action any day of the week.

Besides, he liked combat. Being close to death made him feel more alive, although he would never admit it out loud. Especially not to Miranda.

The CLOSED sign hung in the window when he reached the general store. Undeterred, he went around back and knocked three times, paused, knocked twice more, paused again, and knocked three more times. There was a shuffling sound, the clicks of locks disengaging, and the door opened.

And there she was.

If he could have seen through Miranda's eyes, he would have beheld a subtle shift in his features. A brightening of the eyes, a slight curving of his lips, a gentle gaze that held Miranda's and said much without saying anything at all. Caleb was not a terribly expressive young man, but Miranda had learned to read him. She stood in the doorway for a moment, hand on outthrust hip, head slightly tilted, smiling sweetly, and let him take her in. She had lived in her own skin long enough to know what men saw when they looked at her, and in most cases, she hated being stared at. But with Caleb, it was different. She liked it when he looked at her. And touched her.

Among other things.

"Mind if I come in, pretty lady?" Hicks asked.

She reached up, grabbed him by the front of his shirt, and pulled him down for a kiss. It was only when she stood close to him that she realized how tall and broad he was. He had a slouching, lazy, head-lowered manner that made him look slender, narrow, and a little awkward. It was deceptive until you looked at the thickness of his forearms, the breadth of his shoulders, or the understated springiness in the way he moved. He looked thin and light, but in truth, he was six-foot-two, two-hundred-ten pounds, and very good at concealing his physical prowess. And she loved every inch of him. Scars and all.

"How was work?" she asked.

Hicks shrugged. "Dug a latrine. Cleaned my gun. Shot some infected. Captured a few insurgents. Same old, same old."

Miranda shook her head. "You're crazy."

"It's part of my mystique."

The heel of her palm rebounded gently against his forehead. "Get in here, soldier boy."

Hicks stepped into the back room of the store and looked around. Several rows of metal shelves dominated the space, bearing inventory stacked to the roof. Sunlight filtered in through a window near the ceiling, highlighting dust motes floating in the air. Hicks reached up and passed his hand through a golden ray, sending the little white flecks swirling. He watched them turn and shift while Miranda shut the door and locked it.

"I just have a few things to finish up. Why don't you have a seat?" she said.

"Don't mind if I do."

He took a seat on a stool under the window and watched her work. She had tied her light blonde hair back in a loose ponytail, a few errant strands framing her pale, oval face. She wore no makeup. Her clothes were loose, designed for comfort, and durable. Her boots had steel toes.

Hicks couldn't take his eyes off her.

He remembered the first time, at her invitation, he had gone to visit her at her trailer. She had answered the door with her hair styled in loose curls, slender body clad in a skimpy little red thing, scarlet high heels on her feet, flowery perfume making his head swim. He stopped breathing. His hands shook when Miranda laughed at him and led him inside. He smiled at the memory. No one had made him feel that way since-

No. Don't go there.

He closed his eyes and willed the memory away, took a few deep breaths, and pictured an empty black void in his mind, deep in the shadows where the demons live, where no light ever shines. The emptiness swelled and stretched and cast aside the pain of loss and regret. In a moment, he was warm, and quiet, and in control again.

A hand touched his face and he jumped.

"Are you all right, Caleb?"

"Yeah, sorry. Think I might have dozed off. You startled me."

Miranda cupped his chin in her hand and ran a thumb over the mess of scars on his left cheek. "At least you didn't come up swinging. I heard Thompson does that sometimes."

Hicks nodded. "That he does. Caught me on the temple one time. Damn near knocked me out."

"Really?"

"Yep."

"You weren't mad at him?"

He shrugged. "Five second rule. He's a big guy, strong as hell, seen a lot of combat. I shouldn't have been standing so close."

"That's terrible."

"It's the world we live in."

The hand fell away. "Come on. Enough sad talk. How about you buy a girl a drink?"

Hicks stood up and kissed her on the cheek. "Sounds good to me."

`

*****

The good thing about the enlisted club at Fort McCray was they accepted federal credits, the currency by which soldiers were paid.

The bad thing about the enlisted club was it was full of grunts.

They had taken a booth in the back, out of sight of the bar. Nevertheless, people still kept finding excuses to wander close to their table and stare. Hicks was not quick to anger, but the attention was beginning to wear on his nerves. When soldiers wandered too close, he shot them a look that informed them in no uncertain terms they were not welcome. A few weeks ago, it would not have done any good. But now, in the wake of what Miranda had termed The Wilson Incident, Hicks had a reputation among the men of Echo Company.

"We are not going to have another Wilson Incident, Caleb," Miranda said, as if reading his mind.

He looked down and spun his glass, remembering.

*****

Private Randall Wilson was a giant, standing six-foot-ten and just shy of three hundred solid pounds. Hicks knew his story the same as everyone in Echo Company. He had played inside linebacker for Alabama, and after a stellar, record-setting junior year, was expected to go early in the draft.

Then the Outbreak happened.

He fled the University of Alabama when the National Guard showed up to evacuate the campus. The convoy he traveled with

34

made it all the way to Colorado, only losing a few dozen people along the way. Not long after arriving, with his only job prospects being to hunt salvage or join a federally run farming or construction corps, he opted to join the Army.

By then, Fort Bragg had been secured, and after basic training in Colorado, he and many other newly minted soldiers were flown to Bragg for advanced infantry training. Shortly thereafter, he had been assigned to Second Platoon of Echo Company.

While Hicks' platoon wintered in Hollow Rock, the rest of Echo Company had traveled to Kansas to assist with revenant extermination efforts. Due to Kansas' proximity to Colorado, its wealth of good farmland, and the overcrowding in Colorado Springs, the President had proposed a bill to help settlers relocate to the mostly abandoned state and begin growing crops to support the burgeoning population. The idea was met with great support and enthusiasm, but faced a serious problem.

The infected. Over two million of them.

So the President, facing the end of his term in office and concerned with his legacy, did the only thing he could. He called his generals and staff into a meeting, explained what he wanted, and told them to find a way to make it happen. A month later, they had a plan drawn up and were mobilizing troops and assets to carry it out.

At the beginning of the offensive—dubbed Operation Relentless Force—General Phillip Jacobs, head of Army Special Operations Command, wrote a brief, now-famous speech that he sent to all commanding officers at the company level. From there, every platoon CO in the Army read it to their soldiers in an effort to motivate them and mitigate their fears.

"I won't mince words," General Jacobs wrote. "You all have a tough job ahead of you. There are roughly 2.8 million infected in the state of Kansas, and only 100,000 brave men and women being sent to kill them. Which, when expressed in those terms, may seem like an insurmountable task. But I assure you, it is not. To prove this assertion, let us do the math. As I pointed out earlier, there are 100,000 troops being deployed. Therefore, in order to exterminate every infected in Kansas, each of you needs to rack up a body count of no more than 28. Put that way, it doesn't seem quite so difficult, now does it? So before you head out, I want you to check the magazine in your rifle and make sure you have at least 28 rounds in it. You should have several more magazines also loaded with at least 28 rounds on your person. If you don't, talk to your supply sergeant. Then grab your gear, lace up your boots, and go kick some ass. Your country is counting on you."

Despite the general's encouragement, it was a long, brutal winter marked by hardship, hunger, constant danger, and the loss of many comrades. The battles of Wichita and Topeka were especially bloody. But the Army and their accompanying volunteer militias got the job done, and thousands of settlers had applied for land grants.

After leaving the front and arriving at their new forward operating base (FOB) at Fort McCray, Second and Third Platoon had initially treated First Platoon with disdain. Their impression was that while the rest of the company had spent the winter half-frozen, half-starved, and up to their eyeballs in walkers, First Platoon had been fat and happy and snuggled next to a warm fire banging hot civilian chicks. First Platoon was quick to inform them that while they had not fought as many walkers, they had faced more than their share of trouble from insurgents and marauders, and had taken casualties.

Upon hearing the stories, most of the soldiers of Second and Third Platoon eventually accepted that First Platoon had not spent the winter in quite as much luxury as originally thought. And while Second and Third Platoon had killed thousands of walkers, they had run into very little trouble from the living. It only took a few encounters with marauders after the spring thaw for them to realize just how tough life had been for First Platoon. Consequently, for most of Echo Company, the subject had ceased to be grounds for argument.

Except for Private Randall Wilson.

For whatever reason, he never got over his animosity and tried to start trouble with First Platoon at every given opportunity. Eventually, Sergeant Isaac Cole finally grew tired of his mouth and invited him to disregard rank and settle the matter behind the mess hall. Wilson agreed, and promptly found himself on the wrong end of a very thorough, very one-sided beating. After the fight, under scrutiny from his squad mates over his fighting ability, Cole reluctantly admitted he had been a heavyweight Golden Gloves champion back in his teenage years. Hicks had the feeling it was a sore subject, and while curious as to why, he respected his friend enough not to ask.

Most people who witnessed the fight agreed it would be enough to shut Wilson's mouth.

They were wrong.

Wilson steered clear of Cole, but anyone else was fair game.

Including Hicks.

Hicks avoided trouble by simply staying out of Wilson's way when he could, and ignoring him when he couldn't. In most cases, all it took was a few stern words from Cole and Wilson backed off. There was one night, however, when Cole wasn't around and Hicks had brought Miranda to the enlisted club to hang out with some of the guys from Delta Squad.

It was supposed to be a quiet, fun evening of knocking back drinks, sharing old stories, and relaxing after a long, strenuous day. When it was Miranda's turn to buy a round, she kissed Hicks on the cheek and walked around the corner to the bar. Hicks didn't like the idea of her doing this by herself, but knew Miranda valued her independence and remained in his seat. A minute went by. Then two. Three.

Hicks knew she should have been back by then. So he stood up and walked over to the bar and saw Wilson standing with his back to him. Miranda's blonde head poked around his side as she tried to step around him, but Wilson cut her off. Hicks tapped the much bigger man on his shoulder.

"Fuck off, dipshit," Wilson said over his shoulder, barely sparing Hicks a glance.

"That's my girlfriend you're talking to. Step away. Now."

The former college football player turned, a joyfully vicious grin on his face. "Your girlfriend? No way. First Platoon is all fags. Go jerk off with your boyfriends over there."

Hicks set his feet. "I'm not going to tell you again."

Wilson reached out and seized Hicks by the front of his shirt, obviously not expecting trouble from the smaller man. But half a second later, Hicks was behind him, one hand on his wrist and the other on his shoulder, twisting Wilson's arm until it was barely an inch from ripping out of socket. He buckled the bigger man's knees and dropped him to the ground.

"You motherfucker-"

Wilson's voice cut off with a squeak as Hicks cranked up the pressure on his arm. "I'm done messing around with you. I've been putting up with your bullshit for weeks, and I'm sick of it. Now here's what's going to happen. I'm going to let you up, and you are going to do the smart thing and walk away. If you choose not to, I'm going to beat you within an inch of your life. Do I make myself clear?"

"Okay, okay. Jesus, man, I was just messing with you."

Hicks knew what was coming before he let go. He could feel the tension building in Wilson, waiting to be unleashed. The big man sprang up amazingly fast for someone his size and swung a backward elbow at Hicks' head. The young soldier ducked it easily, hooked a foot behind Wilson's ankles, and shoulder-checked him in the chest.

It would have been just as easy to rupture Wilson's testicles, stomp his knee in the wrong direction, or break his teeth with an upward elbow strike, but Hicks only wanted to teach him a lesson, not maim him for life. So when Wilson crashed to the ground, instead of stomping on his neck, he delivered a sharp kick to the big soldier's kidney. Wilson writhed in agony, a hissing cry erupting from his throat. While he was stunned,

Hicks grabbed him by the front of his shirt and started hitting him.

He knew punching someone in the face full-force was a good way to end up with a broken hand. But long training had toughened his knuckles, and he knew exactly how hard he could hit someone without risking more than a few bruises to himself. He let Wilson have six of them, then bashed the back of his head on the concrete floor hard enough to make his eyes roll up.

The room went silent.

Hicks let him lie groaning on the floor a few seconds, then grabbed the nearest drink and dumped it on his face. Wilson came back to himself, sputtering and coughing.

"Had enough, or do I need to bust you up some more?" Hicks asked.

Wilson said nothing. He simply struggled to his feet and began stumbling and weaving his way to the door.

"Hey," Hicks called.

Wilson stopped, blood dripping from his face.

"You're done talking shit to my platoon. I took it easy on you tonight. Next time, I won't be so nice."

After that night, First Platoon had no further trouble from Private Randall Wilson. Or anyone else, for that matter.

In the wake of the incident, Hicks fully expected to find himself standing at attention in front of his company commander, Captain Harlow. Fighting was grounds for an Article 15, which could result in reduction of rank, forfeiture of half a month's pay for up to two months, and 45 days restriction and extra duty. But days went by and nothing happened. Finally, a week after the incident, Lieutenant Jonas approached him just after dismissing the platoon for the evening.

"Specialist Hicks, a word with you," he said quietly. Staff Sergeant Thompson looked on but said nothing.

"Yes sir." Hicks dropped his equipment and followed his lieutenant.

"I heard about what happened," Jonas said when they were out of earshot of the rest of the platoon.

Hicks nodded. "Yes sir."

"I'll tell you I'm not happy about it. I know Wilson is a royal pain in the ass, but you are well aware the rules, Specialist."

"Yes sir."

"I talked to Lieutenant Chapman. He's willing to let the matter slide, but there are to be no more altercations between the two of you. Any further incidents will be punished harshly. And just so you know, Wilson is getting the same speech from his CO you're getting right now. The message to both of you is that these hostilities are to cease and fucking desist. Do I make myself clear?"

"Crystal, sir."

Lieutenant Jonas straightened. "You're a good soldier, Hicks, and that's why I'm cutting you some slack this time. But in the future, I expect better from you. Disappoint me at your very great peril. Understood?"

"Yes sir."

"Now I need you to answer me a question."

"Sir?"

"How in the hell did you beat that big son of a bitch? I mean, the thing with Cole doesn't surprise me. He's huge. But Wilson must outweigh you by at least eighty pounds and none of it fat."

Hicks shrugged. "If you want, I can show you sometime. The techniques are simple. Wilson's problem is he relies too much on strength. All things being equal, in most cases, the bigger guy is gonna win. But if one fighter has better technique, and he's big and strong enough not to be overwhelmed, it's possible to beat the bigger guy. Wilson's big, but I'm not so small myself, and I know how to fight. He doesn't."

Jonas gave him a long, measuring look. "You know, Specialist, I get the feeling there's a hell of a lot more to you than meets the eye."

Hicks looked away and said nothing.

*****

"Earth to Caleb," Miranda said, tapping a finger against the back of his hand.

He looked up. "Sorry."

"You went away for a minute there."

"Yeah. I do that sometimes."

"I noticed. Where did you go?"

He shook his head. "Nowhere good."

"Tell me about it."

"I'd rather not."

"You were thinking about the fight with Wilson."

Hicks said nothing.

"I was afraid for you. He was enormous. I thought he would snap you like a twig."

"He's an idiot. All brute strength. Doesn't know the first thing about fighting. If he had, I might have been in trouble."

"When I saw what you did to him I was surprised, and kind of turned on."

Hicks raised an eyebrow. "Really?"

Miranda smiled. "Then I got to thinking, where did he learn how to do that?"

Hicks lowered his eyes again, suddenly finding the rippling surface of his drink interesting.

"Don't do that," Miranda said.

"What?"

"Shut me out."

"I'm not shutting you out."

"I asked a question. Are you going to answer it?"

Hicks spun his glass and sighed. "What difference does it make, Miranda? Can't we just be who we are now and leave it at that?"

"The other day when we were walking along the wall," she said, "I looked at you in the afternoon light, and the sun cut through your eyes from the side, and they looked like stained glass floating in water, and I loved you so much I thought my heart would burst. Then you smiled at me with your mysterious little smile, and leaned over and kissed me, and that love rose through me like a fire and burned me up inside, and I wished in that moment I had all the world to give you. If I could have, I would have reached up and given you the sun, and the moon, and the stars, and heaven, and Earth, and everything in between. Then we walked again, and I held your hand, and I thought about your hands, how big and strong and gentle they are, how your lightest touch can send me trembling like a schoolgirl with her first crush, and how I watched you use those same hands to beat a three-hundred pound ex-football player senseless. I realized, then, that I want to know you. Not just who you are now, but all of you, and everything you were before. I'm in love with this handsome, quiet, sincere man who treats me with so much kindness, and dignity, and gentleness, and love, and he's the most dangerous man I know."

Hicks remained silent.

Miranda reached out and took his hand away from the glass. "What's going on in there, Caleb? How are things supposed to work between us if you won't open up?"

Hicks pulled his hand away, suddenly angry. "Do I ask you about your life before the Outbreak? Do I grill you about your time with the Free Legion?"

He regretted it even as he said it. Miranda's expression grew brittle, sapphire eyes shimmering against her porcelain face. Her hands trembled as she clasped them together in her lap and dropped her gaze. "No," she whispered.

"I'm sorry, M. I shouldn't have said that."

"You're right. I have no right to pry."

Hicks closed his eyes, rested his elbows on the table, and put his head in his hands, frustrated.

On one hand, he was in the right. Since the Outbreak, it was an unspoken rule you didn't talk about life pre-Outbreak. You didn't ask people what they did, or if they had families, or who they lost. If someone wanted to volunteer that information, that was fine, but it was impolite in the extreme to ask. The kind of thing that could easily start a fight. It reminded Hicks of how prison inmates weren't supposed to ask each other what they were in for, or how war veterans hated talking about the war. He thought about the three million or so Americans who survived the Outbreak and how most of them suffered from PTSD in one form or another. An entire nation of prisoners and war veterans and victims.

A nation in mourning.

On the other hand, Miranda had just spoken one of the most heartfelt declarations of love he had ever heard, and he had thanked her with a proverbial slap in the face.

I am a son of a bitch, he thought.

"Miranda, I didn't mean that. You have every right to ask. I just … I don't know if I'm ready to talk about it yet."

"You're wrong, Caleb. I didn't have the right to ask. Because if you asked me about my family, or how I survived the Outbreak, or what the Legion did to me, I'd tell you it's none of your damn business. It was selfish of me to pry. Hypocritical. How can I expect you to talk about your past if I'm not willing open up about mine?"

"Give me your hand, M."

She did.

"Maybe someday we'll be healed enough to talk about our past. Maybe it'll help, maybe it won't. I don't know. What I do know is we're both here now, we're alive, and that's all that matters. Everything else is just picking up the pieces."

Miranda looked up with a sad half-smile, and Hicks felt a vise clamp around his heart. "You're right," she said. "Let's both say we're sorry and leave it at that."

"Agreed."

They finished their drinks in silence.

FOUR

They made love that night.

It was not as it usually was, with laughing, and caresses, and kissing, and long, languid movement of body against body. They went to bed in their nightclothes. Hicks lay on his back with his hands behind his head, a cool spring breeze blowing through the open window. Miranda lay beside him with her back turned, curled in upon herself, silent.

Then, without preamble, she rolled over and leaned over Hicks' face and kissed him urgently, one hand disappearing beneath his waistband. Hicks breathed in sharply against Miranda's mouth and felt his body respond. Hot tears dripped against his cheek, prompting him to gently grip her slender arms and push her away.

"What's wrong?"

"Shut up," she said, and twisted loose from his hands. Her shirt came off, tossed carelessly into a corner, and she began tugging at Hicks' shorts. He raised his hips so she could pull them off, then had to bite down on a moan as he felt the warmth of her mouth around him. He said no more until she climbed on top, and then it was all grunts and hard breathing and Miranda's insistent *hunnh, hunnh, hunnh, hunnh.*

And then it was over.

She stayed on top of him for a while, face buried in the hollow of his shoulder, saying nothing. With one hand, Hicks stroked her back with his fingertips, tracing the hollow between muscles and spine. With his other hand, he ran his fingers through her long hair, sweeping it back from her face. Finally, she sat up, kissed him briefly, and went to the bathroom. There was the sound of water running.

Hicks thought about the tower on the other side of town, and how nice it was to have running water. A moment later, Miranda emerged and crossed the room naked in the moonlight. She knelt next to Hicks with a damp cloth and began cleaning him up. He lay still, staring at her silhouette against the window.

"It's never like you see it in the movies," she said. "It's messy."

"In more ways than one."

Miranda made a low sound that might have been a laugh. "Very true."

Finished, she tossed the soiled cloth into the laundry bin and retrieved her shirt, then lay down beside Hicks. He offered to lift the covers for her, but she said it was too warm. Her arms went around his chest and they lay quietly together in the slowly cooling night.

"What was all that about?" he asked.

"I'm not sure if I even know."

"If you figure it out…"

"If I figure it out."

"Goodnight, M."

"Goodnight, Caleb."

*****

Hicks reported for duty the next day, which was a Saturday, well before sunrise.

First thing in the morning was PT, led by Staff Sergeant Kelly. Normally it would have been led by Sgt. Ashman, but he and Lt. Jonas had been called to company HQ at Fort McCray. There was much speculation as to why, with opinions ranging from suspicion of wrongdoing to rumors of a forthcoming offensive against the Midwest Alliance.

Hicks suspected the reason was far more innocuous.

Ashman was a damned good sergeant, easily the best in Echo Company. He had served in the Army for over fifteen years, had a bachelor's degree in history—earned via online courses prior to the Outbreak—and his service record was spotless. Hicks suspected Ashman was being offered a commission, and said as much to Derrick Holland.

"You think?" the diminutive soldier asked, brow furrowed in thought.

"It makes sense, doesn't it?" Hicks replied as they dropped to the ground at Sgt. Kelly's command and began doing pushups. "Fifteen years in, pre-Outbreak combat experience, college degree, exemplary record. I heard there's more officer billets out there than qualified officers to fill them. We lost a lot of people during Relentless Force. Seems pretty obvious to me."

Holland looked over and grinned. Hicks knew what was coming next.

After PT, Kelly ordered the platoon to clean up and get ready for patrol. As they bathed in the field showers, Holland began taking bets on why Lt. Jonas and Sgt. Ashman had been called away. The prevailing sentiment was that one or both of them were in some kind of trouble, until Holland posited the theory that Ashman was getting a promotion. The idea caught on quickly with no one willing to bet against it. Not to be deterred, Holland started taking bets on whether or not Ashman would accept the commission. That got people wagering.

Hicks listened, but remained silent. He was not a betting man.

After patrol and chow, Jonas and Ashman returned. The lieutenant, never being one to mince words or keep his men in suspense, called for everyone's attention.

"I'm sure you're all wondering why Sergeant Ashman and I were called away this morning," he said. "If you were thinking we're in some kind of trouble, the answer is no."

He waited for the inevitable round of chuckling and low comments to subside, a small smile on his face, then said, "Thankfully, the reason is a much happier one. Master Sergeant Ashman," he nodded his head toward the platoon sergeant, who stood nervously, hands clasped behind his back, "has just accepted a field commission to the rank of second lieutenant."

If he was expecting a round of applause, he was to be disappointed. Instead, he got a mournful chorus of *WHAT?* and *Come on, man!* and *Dude, you can't leave the platoon!* Jonas forestalled their complaints with an upraised hand.

"All right, all right, that's enough. Listen, I'm not any happier to see him go than you are. But the Army needs capable, proven leaders, and Sergeant Ashman here is one of the best. Besides, you've all been in long enough to know the only constant in the Army is change. People get moved around, shuffled around, promoted, assigned to other units, all kinds of shit. It happens. Sergeant Ashman has been an invaluable asset to Echo Company for the last two years, and his leadership and dedication to duty have been exemplary. But now his talents are needed elsewhere, and it's time for him to move on. Stay in the Army long enough, and it'll happen to you too. Except Holland. He'll be stuck in First Platoon for the rest of his life."

Another round of laughter. Holland grinned. "I love you too, sir."

Jonas tried to scowl, but didn't do a very good job of it. "Okay, enough jack-assing around. Sgt. Kelly, the platoon is yours for the rest of the day. I expect to see every one of you at the enlisted club at nineteen-hundred hours. First round is on me."

That got a cheer.

*****

Hicks hung around until 2200, figuring three hours and four drinks was a sufficient celebration for Echo Company's soon-to-be-promoted master sergeant. Before leaving, he took a moment to shake Ashman's hand and inform him the platoon wouldn't be the same without him. The big man accepted the compliment and leaned close so only Hicks could hear him.

"Jonas and I put in a good word for you with Captain Harlow," he said. "You're a hell of a soldier; one of the best I've ever seen." He gave a conspiratorial wink. "Don't expect to be a specialist for much longer."

Hicks said his goodbyes and left.

He thought about what Ashman said as he walked along the wooded stretch of gravel between Hollow Rock and Fort McCray. His first consideration was a promotion to sergeant would put him in charge of his fire team. Up until then, Holland was the senior specialist and was officially in charge, but both he and Private Fuller deferred to Hicks' judgment in most things. Taking the stripes would just make it official. It would also mean a significant pay raise, albeit in federal credits. Still, any raise was a good one. With the new PX being constructed at Fort McCray, he might be able to buy things he could trade in town.

His thoughts turned to a storage facility on the south side Hollow Rock, recently acquired by G&R Transport and Salvage. Within this facility was an eight-by-ten storage unit more than halfway full of salvage Hicks had accumulated through months of contract work for G&R as well as the spoils of war taken from various insurgent and marauder groups. In terms of federal credits, it was worth five times as much as a sergeant made in a year—enough to buy passage for him and Miranda to Colorado Springs. He would even have enough left over to buy one of the newly constructed revenant-proof homes in the nice part of town, away from the refugee districts.

He imagined going back to living in relative comfort and safety, not constantly worried about the next walker attack. A man with his talents would have no trouble finding work in the Springs. Government jobs were no longer the only opportunities. Merchants of all stripes bartered generously for soldiers with combat experience willing to work as caravan guards. Enough so a man only had to work three or four months a year to earn a comfortable living. It was not without its dangers, but it was no worse than the Army. And he had done pretty well in the Army.

He rounded a corner into the field surrounding Hollow Rock's outer wall, raised a hand, and waved toward the watch captain in his tower. A cowboy hat silhouetted against the full moon told him it was Mike Stall, owner and proprietor of Delta Squad's favorite drinking hole, Stall's Tavern. Mike acknowledged him with a wave, climbed down the steps, and slid back the panel of the check-in window.

"Howdy Caleb," the old cowboy said, one half of his bushy mustache tilted upward. "You're out late tonight. What's the occasion?"

"Celebrating with the platoon. Master Sergeant Ashman accepted a field commission today."

"Well how about that. Next time you see old tall and baldy, do me a favor and tell him I said congratulations."

"Will do."

"See any walkers on the way in?"

"Nope."

Hicks unslung his rifle and slid it under the bars across the window, then followed it with his Ka-bar combat dagger, his ammunition-laden MOLLE vest, and his Beretta M-9.

"They let you fellas carry sidearms now?" Mike asked.

Hicks nodded. "Yep. It used to be against regulation for most soldiers, but everybody was carrying them anyway, so the Army changed the regulations a few months ago. All soldiers are now permitted to carry sidearms, provided we choose one from an approved list and have it inspected by a qualified armorer."

"Well I'll be damned. Back in my day, you didn't usually see infantry grunts with sidearms."

"Evil times we live in."

"Ain't that the truth."

If it were up to Hicks, he would have only brought the Beretta. But Captain Harlow required any soldier traveling outside Fort McCray to carry a minimum loadout of an M-4 rifle and 120 rounds of ammunition. Normally, he would have also brought his spear, but its holster was lashed to his assault pack and he didn't feel like lugging the extra weight all the way to town. If he ran into any trouble he couldn't handle with the carbine and the pistol, he was probably a dead man anyway.

After checking in his weapons, he went through the required physical examination everyone entering the gate had to undergo, then dressed, retrieved his gear, and set off for Miranda's place. He crossed paths with a few people he knew along the way and nodded to them, but made no attempt at conversation. Finally, he arrived at Miranda's door and stood still, hesitating. He very much wanted to see her, but it was late in the evening and he was worried she might have already gone to bed. The windows were absent their usual warm yellow glow, and there were no sounds coming from inside. He had just made the decision to head back to base when he heard footsteps approach and the front door opened.

"Hey there," Miranda said, standing in her nightclothes. Her hair was loose, tousled, and falling down her shoulders. Hicks wanted to reach out and touch it.

"Hey yourself."

"Where've you been? I'd just about given up on seeing you tonight." There was an edge in her voice when she said it, a certain strain, the slightly clipped tones of someone who is trying to appear unconcerned but not quite pulling it off.

"Sorry about that," he said. "Ashman got a promotion. The whole platoon went out to celebrate."

"Oh. I was starting to think that after last night…"

Hicks shook his head. "Absolutely not. You're not getting rid of me that easy."

Miranda smiled and visibly relaxed. "In that case, come on in."

She held the door open so he could follow her inside. Hicks hung his gear on a set of hooks by the door while she lit a pair of candles in the small living room. With the room lighted, she took a seat on the couch and curled her legs beneath her. Hicks stared at the smooth shapeliness of her legs, and wondered how much time and effort she spent shaving them with the straight razor he had bought her. Sometimes he would visit her in the evening and she would have little squares of t-shirt fabric stuck to places where she had nicked herself.

"How was your day?" Miranda asked.

Hicks shrugged. "The usual."

"Kill any walkers? Capture any dangerous criminal types?"

"Nope. It was quiet for a change."

She picked up a glass of water from the table beside her and sipped it. "Are you going out with Eric's crew tomorrow?"

"Didn't know he was going out."

"He didn't send a runner?"

"Not that I know of," he said and then paused, a memory shaking loose. "You know, now that you mention it, I remember Thompson saying something about a salvage run last week."

"That makes sense," Miranda said. "He scheduled it a couple of weeks ago. It's getting harder and harder to reserve the transports, especially with all the work going on in the fields."

Hicks thought a moment longer and remembered Thompson gathering the squad together just before evening chow and telling them to keep their schedules clear for next Sunday. Eric Riordan had reserved one of Hollow Rock's large multi-fuel transport vehicles, and, barring incident, they would be heading out with Sanchez's squad from the Ninth TVM on a salvage-hunting expedition. He remembered being distracted at the moment, his mind replaying memories of-

No. Not now.

"I guess it slipped my mind," he said as he walked into the kitchenette.

From the corner of his eye, he saw Miranda tilt her head quizzically as he poured himself a drink. He didn't usually drink this late at night, but if he was going to tell her what he had to say, a little liquid courage was in order. He put the bottle back in the cupboard and sat down on the couch.

"Are you all right, Caleb?" Miranda asked. "You seem … distant."

He gave a weak smile and sipped his drink. It was simple grain alcohol from Mike Stall's distillery, devoid of color and taste, but it went down smoothly and the burn felt warm and comforting. He remembered a time when feeling that burn was the only thing he cared about, regardless of what he had to consume to produce it.

"You said last night you wanted to know more about me."

She was quiet for a long moment, eyes luminous in the golden light. She nodded slowly.

"It's a long story. I don't think I can tell it all in one night."

Her hand reached out for him. "Caleb, you don't have to tell me anything. I'm fine with you just the way you are. You were right about what you said last night. There's no need for either of us to go digging up the past. We're here now, we love each other, and we have our own little light in the darkness. That's all that matters."

Hicks looked down and stared at Miranda's fingers interlaced with his own. "You might not like what you're about to hear."

"I meant what I just said."

He kissed the back of her hand. "It's important. I want you to hear it."

Her eyes softened. "All right then."

Hicks tossed back his drink, set it on the table, and relaxed into the couch cushions. Outside, crickets chirped and night birds sang in the dark spring evening.

FIVE

Three years ago,

Houston Metro Area, Texas

I should start with my father. He was the lynchpin in everything.

We traveled a lot when I was little. I remember that. Dad seemed sad most of the time, especially when I asked him about Mom. He could only ever talk about her for a few minutes at a time, and then his hands would tremble, his voice would crack, and he would start shaking like a leaf. When that happened, I always hugged him and stopped asking questions.

He told me she was beautiful. That I had her blue eyes and light brown hair, and I looked so much like her. He said I would grow up to be tall and lean like she was. He told me there were complications the day I was born. Something went wrong and she bled too much. I know she got to hold me before it was over with.

I still have the picture.

Dad was a quiet man, so I guess I come by that honestly. He was medium height, medium build, dark hair and eyes. His skin was light brown even in winter—Italian blood on his mother's side. I remember watching him work outside with his shirt off and the way his scars gleamed dully in the afternoon light.

We stayed in motels and the occasional rented trailer. Dad never stayed in one town for very long because he liked being on the road. Even as a small boy, I had the distinct impression he was running from something. People tell me I was too young to remember that part of my life, but they're wrong. I remember scenes from it, distant and hazy, like looking through a dirty window.

Close to my fifth birthday, Dad knew things were going to have to change. I was due to start kindergarten in the fall. We were living in a rented double-wide somewhere outside of Houston at the time. There was a thin strip of paved road bisecting the two sides of the trailer park lined with mailboxes and old beer cans. Lauren lived directly across from us.

She was divorced, her ex-husband was a lawyer, and she lived on money from the divorce settlement and what she made waitressing nights at the diner down the highway. Her car was a little white Toyota. She was pretty and slender with auburn hair and light hazel eyes. I could tell Dad liked her.

Dad got a job at a service station not far from the trailer park. Changing oil, rotating tires, replacing air filters, that sort of thing. It was daytime work. Lauren offered to sit for me while he was away. Dad tried to pay her, but she wouldn't let him.

Most days, I would and run around the trailer park with the other kids my age while Lauren kept an eye on me from underneath the shade tree in the back yard. She always called me in for lunch at 12:30 on the dot and made the best ham and cheese sandwiches.

We didn't talk much. I guess that's mostly my fault. I got the feeling she wanted to talk, but couldn't think of anything to say. I have never, nor will I ever, understand why so many people feel the need to occupy every spare moment of company with a fellow human being with mindless chatter. It is my studied opinion that the best people in the world are the ones who appreciate a good companionable silence.

Anyway.

It was Dad who made the first move, at my prompting. You see, most days he would come home and ask if I behaved, and Lauren would say yes, and that he was lucky to have such a sweet, precocious little boy. Dad would thank her for watching me, and there would be an awkward moment, and Lauren would smile and say she had to get ready for work. On the days she didn't work, she just said goodbye and walked out the door. Then dad would get a strange look on his face and watch her walk across the little strip of asphalt until she disappeared into her trailer. Finally, one day, I got tired of it.

"Just tell her," I said, exasperated.

Dad jumped and rounded on me. "Tell her what?"

"That you like her, sillyhead."

His dark eyebrows came together and he sat down on the couch. "Is it that obvious?"

I rolled my eyes and went to my room to play.

It was a Friday. I remember that. Lauren had the day off. When Dad got home, they went through the usual ritual. At the part where they stood facing each other awkwardly, I leaned around the kitchen archway and shot my dad a piercing look.

"Well, I guess I better go," Lauren said, and started toward the door.

"Wait," Dad said, and reached for her arm. His fingers barely touched her elbow, but even from ten feet away I could hear the sharp intake of breath. "Would you like to stay for dinner? I'm making pasta."

She smiled, and I thought Dad might melt into the carpet. "Yes," she said. "I'd like that very much."

A week later, late at night when they thought I was asleep and the moans and gasps and creaking of bedsprings subsided, was the first time I ever heard my father laugh. I lay awake with the moonlight slanting in through the window and smiled.

Her lease was up at the end of that month. Dad got rid of our ratty old furniture so we could move hers in. At age five, I learned one of the important truths of life.

A good woman can make any place feel like home.

*****

"Joe, he has to start school in the fall," Lauren said, hands on her hips as she stood with feet firmly planted on the kitchen floor.

"I know."

"Have you even gone and looked at the schools around here?"

A moment's hesitation. "No."

Lauren stomped away and loudly clanged pots and pans around in the kitchen. I gave my dad a sympathetic look and crossed the room to sit beside him. He smiled down at me, put his hand against the side of my head, and pulled me close to his chest. I hugged him back.

"That is so irresponsible of you, Joseph Hicks. I thought you were a better man than that."

Dad looked miserable. Lauren stomped into the room and pointed at him with an accusing finger.

"You can't just treat him like a damn pet, Joe. He needs a proper education. I can't believe you-"

"Hey!" I shouted.

Lauren stopped, eyes wide. I stood up and faced her, fists balled at my hips. "That's my dad you're talking to."

There was a long pause. I felt Dad's hand on my shoulder. "Caleb, calm down son."

I glared at Lauren a moment longer, then sat down. "Listen," Dad said. "The schools around here are no good. You know that."

"How do you know if you haven't even looked at them?"

"I have ears, Lauren. I hear people talk."

She let out a sigh and sat next to me on the couch. "So what do you want to do?"

Dad's hand went down to my shoulder and gave a gentle squeeze. "I was thinking we could home school him."

Lauren looked skeptical. "Do you really think that's a good idea?"

"I think it's better than sending him to one of the lowest ranked school districts in Texas," he said flatly.

"Well … I guess we can look into it."

"That's all I ask."

Lauren stood up and started toward the kitchen. "I heard the phone ring earlier while I was outside," she said over her shoulder. "Who was it?"

"An old Army buddy of mine."

"What did you two talk about?"

"Me finding a better job. He told me he knows a guy who works at some private combat training outfit not far from here. Black Wolf Tactical, or something like that. Said they're hiring."

"What kind of work would it be?"

"According to their website, they teach marksmanship and survival skills to civilians. They also work with law enforcement and a few federal agencies. Weekend warrior kind of stuff."

"Sounds right up your alley."

"Yeah, I guess."

Dad's eyes strayed to a section of wall on the other side of the room. There were several pictures of him with other soldiers, a framed patch emblazoned with the emblem of the 10th Special Forces Regiment, and at the bottom was a picture of him and three other men wearing green face paint and holding M-4s. They were standing on the bank of a river, a hazy gray sky and jungle greenery behind them. It would not be until I was twelve years old before my father finally told me what was so special about that picture, why he kept it apart from all the others. They were friends of his, two of whom later died in combat, from a unit that did not officially exist.

Delta Force.

"Well that's good news," Lauren said. "Are you going to call them?"

"My friend will. He's going to try to get me an interview."

"When do you think you'll hear back from him?"

"Probably in the next day or two."

"Would it be more money than you're making now, do you think?"

Dad chuckled. "Yeah. Yeah it would be."

*****

Four days later, Dad left for the interview in a suit he bought at the Salvation Army with a big black duffel bag in his hand. When he came home three hours later, the suit was on a hanger, the duffel bag was half empty, and he was in combat fatigues. His hair was damp with sweat, his face crusted with dust and dirt, and he was smiling.

"Good lord, Joe," Lauren said at the sight of him. "What did they do to you?"

He dropped the duffel bag. "Ah, nothing much. Just put me through my paces. Ed warned me they were going to do that."

"You look like you just dug a ditch."

The old man laughed. "Lauren, BWT is a combat training facility. They don't just hire bums off the street. You have to prove you have the goods. Run the courses, shoot holes in cardboard bad guys, that sort of thing."

"Was it dangerous?"

"Nothing I couldn't handle."

She dampened a towel in the kitchen sink and handed it to him. Dad started wiping the dirt off his face. "Do you think you got the job?"

The smile widened. "I start on Monday."

"That's great! How much did they offer you?"

He told her. Her jaw dropped. "Are you kidding me?"

"Nope."

Despite the sweat and dirt, Lauren jumped into his arms.

*****

The first change was dad got a new truck. The dealership gave him five-hundred bucks for his rusty, beat up old Sierra and sold him a shiny new Dodge Ram. The next change was we moved out of that shitty trailer park and into a proper house. In late August, in an outdoor ceremony on a hill surrounded by elms and maples, Dad and Lauren got married in the sunshine. He let me be the best man.

That fall, I began my education. And what an education it was.

SIX

One of the perks of working for Black Wolf Tactical (BWT) was Dad got the run of the training facilities at no charge. I would not say he abused the privilege, but he sure as hell used it. Especially as pertained to my training.

On a typical day, I was up at 0500, then a workout (or PT as Dad called it), then breakfast, then school. School was me and Lauren at the kitchen table from 0830 to 1400. Afterward, I had a few hours to run around the neighborhood and play until 1700, at which time Lauren drove me to Dad's work.

By then, the students were done for the day, having driven back to their hotels, or for those with the big bucks, staying in one of the luxurious onsite rooms provided by BWT. Lauren would drop me off, and I would wait on the bench in front of the main office for Dad to finish shooting the breeze with his clients, and when he got free, he would look my way and motion me over.

He started with the basics. Unarmed combat, land navigation, how to read a map, how to use a compass, rapelling, traversing rope ladders and bridges, the obstacle course, first aid, CPR, and basic marksmanship. My favorite was rapelling. Dad used to joke he was going to bring me to work someday so I could shame the clients who were afraid to go over the edge.

"Bunch of grown men acting like scared kittens," he used to say, leaning on the rail at the summit of the rapelling tower. "Serve 'em right to get showed up by a little boy."

At first, it was just me and the old man. But over time, Dad made friends with his co-workers and trusted a few of them enough to help with my training. There were three of them: Mike, Tyrel, and Blake.

Mike Holden was an ex-Marine. Except you never called him an ex-Marine to his face because, according to him, there was no such thing as an ex-Marine. He was a big man, standing six-foot-two and tipping the scales at around two-fifty. Long arms and legs, the rangy type, bald on top, the sides and back of his head shaved down to a nub. He had a laugh you could hear from the next county over. I liked him immediately.

Tyrel Jennings was the only man I ever met who spoke less than my father. Ex-Navy SEAL, big bushy beard, long hair held back by an ever-present olive drab bandanna, and dark black eyes like little coals. He gave instructions in short, terse sentences and was fond of fist bumps and high fives. But only with me.

And then there was Blake Smith. About my dad's size, strongly built, Green Beret, never saw him without a smile on his face. Since Dad was a Green Beret himself, he and Blake hit it off quickly.

Something I always admired about Blake, beyond his general friendliness, was his dignity and sense of grace. He was the only black instructor at BWT, and he occasionally had to put up with offensive comments from ignorant clients and insensitive coworkers. But he never let it bother him. Said it was their problem, not his.

Of all my dad's friends, I would have to say Blake was my favorite. I miss him terribly.

But that's getting ahead of things.

Life went on this way for years, me spending a few hours every afternoon with Dad and his friends, and Lauren constantly finding social events to drag me to.

On Sundays it was church. I never cared much for church, and I don't think Dad did either. I have no problem with

Christianity, or religion in general. Jesus seemed like a genuinely nice guy, considering the central tenant of his teachings was for people to love one another. I don't see much of a problem with that philosophy—I even pray sometimes, in my darker moments. I just did not like dressing up in slacks, and a button-down shirt and tie, and sitting on a damn uncomfortable wooden bench, and being stifled and still for an hour and singing old hymns I didn't understand. Church always seemed to me like a bunch of people singing badly, and saying amen at the proper times, and listening to some paunchy old dunce tell them how to live.

I especially did not like the preacher. He was tall and broad, an ex-athlete gone to fat. His face jiggled and shook when he talked, and he had squinty little eyes that reminded me of a pig. He smelled of stale cigarettes, and cheap aftershave, and when he spoke he leaned in too close so you could smell the coffee on his breath. He made me uneasy.

The year I turned twelve, as the result of a nationwide sting operation by the FBI, he was arrested for possession of child pornography. He posted bond, drove home, locked himself in his bedroom, and blew his brains out with a shotgun. Justified my opinion of him, I suppose.

We stopped going to church after that.

Lauren tried to get me into sports, but I never cared much for them. In those days, I would much rather run BWT's close-quarters combat course than play baseball or soccer. Eventually, she gave up.

By the time I was thirteen, I could run the courses at BWT with sufficient precision and skill to qualify as an instructor. By fourteen, I was six feet tall and a hundred-eighty pounds, and the instructors at my dojo had me start training with the adults.

During the summers, I worked on a ranch not far from BWT. Feeding horses, mucking out stalls, that sort of thing. I developed an affinity for horses that persists to this day. There are few things I enjoy in life more than leaning forward in the saddle, hands loose on the reins, and letting the magnificent creature beneath me stretch out its stride, hurtling the both of us full tilt across open plain. Nothing else like it.

As I got older, my training increased in difficulty and intensity. I learned skills very few people ever do, and some I'm reasonably certain were illegal.

From the ages of twelve to sixteen, Mike Holden taught me the art of the sniper. How to break in a ghillie suit, how to camouflage it, to pick hides, to use my scope as a rangefinder, to compensate for drop and windage, to work the lever on a bolt-action rifle without coming off my point of aim, to use night vision and infrared, to move silently and slowly through dense foliage, to stalk someone without being seen. Most U.S. military snipers' initial training is between eight to twelve weeks, depending on their branch of service and what year they went through it.

Mine lasted four years.

Then there's Tyrel. The man who taught me how to pick locks, gave me my first set of picks, taught me how to hotwire old cars and trucks and construction equipment, the best ways to kill a man with a knife and keep it quiet, how to swim properly, how to shoot a pistol accurately with one hand while on the run—a skill which has saved my life many times—and how anything, absolutely anything, can be used as a weapon.

Dad and Blake handled the rest of my training: Patrolling, calling for fire (although I never got a chance to do it for real until after I joined the Army), how to use, break down, and clean a variety of weapons, combat tactics and marksmanship, booby traps, demolitions, survival and evasion, making bombs from household materials, vehicle searches, tradecraft (dead drops, brief encounters, pickups, load and unload signals, danger and safe signals, surveillance and counter-surveillance, etcetera, etcetera), dynamic room entry and clearing, urban combat, and, after I obtained a driver's license, an advanced driving course.

In summation, I was raised by a former Delta Force operator, a SEAL, a Force Recon Marine, and a Green Beret. These men had access to one of the most well equipped training facilities you will ever see outside the military special operations community. They all cared for me a great deal—Blake and Tyrel were unmarried and had no children of their own—and they took great pleasure in training me. Furthermore, I took to the military lifestyle like a fish to water. I loved it. I loved them.

And let's not forget Lauren. Any discussion of my upbringing would be incomplete without mentioning the love of literature she passed on to me.

When it came to schoolwork, I taught myself for the most part. The textbooks and assignments all seemed simple to me. I never understood why so many of the children I knew who went to public school found it so difficult. I aced exams with little trouble and wrote papers and essays quickly. Math was just a question of diligence and practice. I will not say I liked schoolwork as much as combat training, but I did not mind it either.

Beyond the standard required curriculum, Lauren had me read the classics: Dickens, Faulkner, Thoreau, Kipling, and Dostoyevsky, just to name a few. On my own, I devoured Bradbury, Asimov, Herbert, and Heinlein. I marveled at the prose of Steinbeck, Tolstoy, Salinger, and Shakespeare. The poetry of Yeats, Dickenson, and Frost roared through me like thunder over the mountains. At night, in the late, cricket-chirp hours when most people plant themselves on a couch and stare at a television, I sat cross-legged on my bed with lamplight glowing soft and yellow from my bedside table, book in hand, exploring the world as only an imaginative young boy can.

I followed Robert Jordan and his band of guerillas as they struggled with their mission and each other. I felt my heart beating with the earth as I lay on the ground, leg broken, and waited for the enemy officer to appear in my sights. I wondered what became of Pilar, Pablo, and Maria. Their side lost the war, after all.

Wang Lung made me like him, then hate him, then grudgingly respect him, and I felt sorry for him when he was an old man. I wept when, after knowing crippling poverty and starvation and war and surviving to become wealthy and prosperous, he told O-lan on her deathbed he would trade all he had gained to save her life.

I strode the kingdoms of Hyboria, sword in hand, dealing death to enemies, drinking deep of wine and women and life. Great was my mirth and great was my melancholy. And by my own hand, I became a king.

Through books, all this and more did I live and know.

When I was seventeen, after all the years of feeling the rifle buck against my shoulder, the pistol snapping in my hand, the rubber grip of training knives, the smell of cordite in cold morning air, the satisfying ping of a steel target in the distance, the echo of my father's .308 across the hills as the deer bolted, faltered, and fell, the power of horseflesh rearing beneath me, and the smiles and laughter and thousand little corrections from Dad, Lauren, Mike, Tyrel, and Blake, I finally had occasion to put my training to use.

The year I turned seventeen was the first time I killed a man.

SEVEN

The car was a 1998 Honda Accord.

Price: $2500.00. Odometer reading: 98,319.

I could not have cared less about the mileage. After five summers at the Lazy J Ranch, weekends mowing lawns around the neighborhood, and afternoons swapping bullet riddled paper targets at Black Wolf Tactical for five bucks an hour, it was mine. Any excuse to go for a ride was fine by me—a fact Lauren had no qualms about taking advantage of.

Caleb, could you run to the grocery store and pick up some milk?

Sure.

Would you mind taking this package to the post office for me?

Not a problem.

Your dad forgot his lunch. Could you take it to him, please?

Be glad to.

I don't think I ever said no. The day it happened, I wished I had. But not for me.

For Lauren.

It was early in the afternoon on a warm, pleasant Tuesday in April. She had sent me to the dry cleaners to pick up the dress she wore to her friend Nancy's baby shower. Mary Sue Lewellyn, who my stepmother liked not at all, had spilled a glass of pinot noir on her cream-colored Burberry London. Afterward, there followed the requisite gasp of surprise, a round of horrified apologies, graceful forgiving noises on Lauren's part, and her landing a real stinger when Mary Sue suggested she would buy a replacement.

"Oh no, honey," Lauren said, smiling sweetly. "I wouldn't want to put you out. Stan's tire shop went under last month, didn't it? Just save that money. I'm sure you need it more than I do."

So I took my time that day. I stopped at a gas station to fill up, even though the tank was only a little over half empty. I bought a Slim-Jim and ate it as I cruised down the mostly empty streets. The little Vietnamese lady who owned the dry cleaning business recognized me and we had a short, pleasant chat. I paid with the ten-dollar bill Lauren gave me, pocketed the change, then carefully hung her dress from a plastic hook above the back seat.

As I neared home, I had a strong feeling something wasn't right. The front door was shut, even though it was only seventy-five degrees that day. When the weather was cool enough, Lauren always opened every window in the house and held the doors open with wooden stops, leaving the screen doors latched to keep bugs out. She loved the scent of a warm spring breeze as it aired out the stuffiness left over from winter. I tried to remember if I had shut the front door out of habit when I left, and decided no, I had not.

So what was it doing closed?

Rather than slowing down, I kept going, circled the block, and parked on a street parallel to my house. After killing the engine, I hesitated for a moment, wondering if I was being paranoid.

There's no such thing as paranoid, my father's voice told me. *It never hurts to be extra careful. If something doesn't look right, it probably isn't.*

I could have credited the closed front door to an absentminded mistake on Lauren's part, but that did not fit her patterns. She was a meticulous, detail-oriented woman. She folded all the towels in the bathrooms exactly the same way, her car went through the carwash every Saturday morning, she never missed an appointment, the spices in the kitchen were stored in identical little tins with magnets on them, each one labeled in Lauren's neat, precise handwriting. Each pair of shoes had assigned parking on the closet rack, her CD collection was in alphabetical order, and she never left a room without turning off the lights. Why would someone like that open every window in the house and then shut the front door by mistake? Why would she walk by and leave it shut if it was not her habit to do so?

The answer was obvious: she wouldn't.

Something had to be wrong.

I didn't have a gun or a knife, not even the Gerber pocketknife I usually carried. I pondered my options for a moment, then popped the trunk, lifted the thick piece of cardboard under the upholstery, and took the lug wrench from beneath the spare tire. A heavy, L-shaped hunk of steel about the length of my forearm.

Better than nothing.

I tightened my belt and slid the lug wrench into my waistband. Once I was satisfied it would not fall out, I got moving.

The thought occurred to me to knock on a neighbor's door and try to call Dad, but most people in the neighborhood were at school or work at that hour. And even if someone was home, how long would it take to get Dad on the line? What if he was at the range with a class? Even if I told whoever answered the phone it was an emergency, it would take a minimum of twenty minutes before Dad could get home.

Not fast enough.

So I hurried to the Taylors' house, whose backyard shared a border with ours along a tall wooden privacy fence. There was an entrance on my side of the street, latched, but easily defeated by inserting a thin twig between the slats and lifting. I shut the gate behind me, crouched low, and crept into the Taylors' yard hoping no one was home.

The backyard was empty except for the Taylors' patio, a stainless steel grill, and a hammock off to my left. I stayed close to the edge of the fence and crouch-walked to the far side, watching the windows and straining my ears. There was no movement, but I thought I heard a thump in one of the upstairs rooms followed by a muffled shout.

The fence was over six feet tall, with sharp points atop the slats and 2x4 crossbeams between the support posts. I gripped the V between two slats, stepped up on a crossbeam, and leapt as high as I could. My feet cleared the fence as I did a 360 in mid-air and landed in a three-point stance. Looking up, I could see the inner part of the back door was open, but the screen section was latched shut.

Above me, I heard a whimper and the dull thud of flesh striking flesh.

The urge to run into the house was strong, but as it has many times since that day, my training took over. I knew it was stupid to run into a building of any kind when I didn't know what was waiting for me inside. So I drew the lug wrench from my belt and took position beside the back door. A quick peek around the corner revealed the kitchen was empty, so using flat end of the wrench, I cut a hole in the flimsy screen and carefully undid the latch.

Slowly, ever so slowly, I turned the handle, opened the door, and waited. There were a few more thumping sounds from upstairs, but nothing else.

I stepped inside, lug wrench raised over my shoulder, ready to swing or throw it in an instant. My shoes made almost no sound on the laminate floor as I crossed the kitchen and turned the corner to the living room. Just inside the front door, the foyer table was overturned, the lamp atop it broken on the ground, and several family pictures along the wall had been knocked askew. On the floor, a blood trail ran across the living room carpet and up the stairs.

Cold rage burned low in my stomach. I stepped back into the kitchen, closed my eyes, and breathed in through my nose, out through my mouth.

In through the nose, out through the mouth.

Think, dammit.

In through the nose, out through the mouth.

Assessment: There is an intruder in the house, possibly more than one. Assume they are armed. They have Lauren, and she is most likely injured. Secure the house, then immediately call for police and medical assistance.

Dad had stashed firearms in five different places throughout the house. I was guessing Lauren had been attacked and subdued before she could get to one. The closest was a pistol under the kitchen sink, a CZ-75 9mm automatic. I grabbed a bottle of olive oil from the counter, rubbed some of it into the cupboard hinges to keep them from squeaking, then opened the door just enough to reach inside. After a bit of feeling around, my fingers grazed the pistol's checkered grip. The holster had no retaining strap, just a thumb paddle. I pressed it and drew the weapon. After checking to make sure there was a round in the chamber, I thumbed the safety off and headed for the stairwell.

Ascending stairs is one of the worst tactical situations a person can face. Your enemy has the high ground and multiple angles of attack, whereas the person going up the stairs has a limited range of motion and no cover. The best way to handle it is to keep your weapon up and move quickly, covering as many vectors as you can.

The carpeted stairs were mercifully quiet. I kept my weight close to the wall to avoid making the steps creak. Once at the top, I checked my corners and crouch-walked toward my parents' bedroom. The door was shut, but from behind it, I could hear a low moan and a sound like fabric tearing. The rage in my gut soared to a crescendo.

I pressed my ear gently to the door and listened. More sounds of fabric ripping. My stepmother's voice, speech slurred, a plaintive tone.

The lug wrench was still poised over my left shoulder, my right hand holding the gun. There was no way to know how many intruders I was facing or how well they were armed. But what I did know was that Lauren was in there, she was hurt, and I was the only person in a position to do anything about it. Equal parts rage and fear coursed through me as I took a half step back, lunged forward, and slammed my foot just left of the door handle.

The door burst open hard enough to crack the drywall behind it. I stepped into the room and darted my eyes from one side to the other. My parents' bed was to the left, a dresser and Lauren's jewelry stand against the wall to my right. Lauren lay flat on the bed, gagged and bound with duct tape.

There were two intruders, Caucasian males, one young, maybe early twenties, the other in his mid to late forties. Both wore identical blue polo shirts and tan slacks with dark brown dress shoes—the kind of thing a door-to-door salesman might wear on a temperate spring day. One crouched to my right, rooting through Lauren's jewelry stand, while the other sat astride Lauren's hips, ripping away at her blouse. Pale pink fabric lay in tatters on the bed around them, one side of her bra torn away to reveal her small right breast. Both men looked up in almost comical surprise as I entered the room.

Without hesitation, I hurled the lug wrench in a straight overhand toss. By good fortune, the flat end hit the man astride Lauren full in the mouth, causing the lower half of his face to explode in a crimson burst of blood and broken teeth. He let out an inarticulate cry of agony and toppled backward off the bed.

The other man saw the gun and lunged.

It is hard to describe what happens to you in situations like that. The adrenaline rush, the taste of copper on the back of your tongue, the tunnel vision, the way the world goes gray around the edges, the sound of your heart hammering in your ears, the way everything happens in the course of seconds but there are so many details.

I once heard a commercial where a coach exhorted to his team how life was a game of inches. How the small distances— the space between a receivers hand and a football, how close a soccer ball rolls toward the goal line, whether a boxer's punch connects with his opponent's chin or empty air—these tiny gaps, or lack thereof, are what make the difference between victory and defeat.

In mortal combat, they make the difference between life and death.

The intruder crossed the space between us in less than a second, hands outstretched toward my gun. But as fast as his legs propelled him across the room, my trigger finger was faster.

The first shot went low, striking him in the abdomen. I'm not sure if he even felt it—he didn't make a sound—but by then he was halfway across the room. I raised my aim to avoid his grasping hands and fired again the instant before he hit me. He was shorter than me, but heavier, his weight enough to send both of us tumbling into the hallway. I had the presence of mind hook my instep under his thigh as we went down, and by rolling with the fall and thrusting with my arms and legs, I flipped his body up and over me. He landed flat on the floor, the air whooshing out of his lungs.

I twisted on the ground, brought my gun to bear, and fired twice into his chest at point blank range. In the fraction of a second it took me to fire, I realized I was wasting ammo. There was a neat nine-millimeter hole in his forehead. A pool of blood began to form beneath him, crimson liquid pouring from the back of his skull like water from a faucet. For a second or two, all I could do was stare in horrid fascination, and then I heard a curse and a thump from the bedroom.

Wake up! You're not out of danger.

Just as I rolled flat on my back to face the doorway, a gunshot rang out. I could see the other man kneeling on the ground with one hand over his ruined mouth, the other holding a snub-nosed revolver. His shot went wide, smashing into the drywall to my left and dusting my face with white powder.

With my legs pressed flat to the ground to avoid shooting them, I fired four times. The first three shots caught the intruder center of mass, the impacts causing him to jerk violently. The last shot went wide and perforated the wall behind him. His gun fell from nerveless fingers as he slumped over and coughed out a bright spray of blood. Wide, surprised eyes stared at me for an eternity of seconds, then went blank. His face slackened just before I heard his bowels let go.

Then there was silence.

I lay on the ground, eyes stinging from the drywall dust, my own harsh breath grating in my ears. The three white dots on the CZ's sights stayed lined up on the intruder's chest, my finger tight on the trigger. Slowly, I eased my index finger along the slide and stood up. The intruder's corpse shuddered a few times as I approached, but soon went still. To my left, I heard Lauren groan.

I ran to her side and looked her over. One eye was badly swollen, and there was a nasty split on her lower lip. But aside from a few scrapes and scratches where her blouse had been torn away, I couldn't find any other injuries.

My father kept a pocketknife in his bedside table, which I used to cut away Lauren's restraints. She was still only half conscious, so I tapped her on the cheek and said her name. Her eyes rolled, fluttered, then looked at me and began to focus. I pulled up a corner of the tape on her mouth and said, "Ready?"

She nodded, and I ripped it away. Her eyes watered from the pain. "Caleb, are you all right?"

"I'm fine, Lauren. Are you hurt?"

"My head…" One of her hands gingerly touched the swelling around her eye. I grabbed it and put the hand back down at her side.

"How bad is it?"

"One of them…hit me…"

Her eyes aren't tracking. Concussion. She needs an ambulance.

"Listen, Lauren. How many of them were there? Was it just the two, or are there more?"

"Just two, I think." Her voice was getting stronger.

"Okay, just stay here. Try not to move, okay? I'll be right back."

I did a quick sweep of the house and found no other intruders. Before going back upstairs, I called 911, explained the situation, and requested police and medical assistance.

"Are the intruders still in the house?" The dispatcher's voice was female, older sounding, but firm and confident.

"Yes ma'am. Two of them. They're both dead."

A pause. "Are you sure?"

"Yes ma'am. One of them took a shot to the head, and the other took three slugs to the heart. I checked them both for a pulse."

"Did either one of them have a pulse?"

"No ma'am."

"And you were the one who shot them?"

"Yes. I already told you that."

"Do you still have the weapon?"

"Yes. I'm going to unload it and put it on the coffee table in the living room."

"Okay, I'll let the responding officers know. Are there any other weapons in the house?"

I pinched the bridge of my nose. "Have you dispatched an ambulance yet?"

"Yes, I have. They're on the way. Can you stay on the line with me until they get there?"

"How long until they get here?"

"I'm not sure, honey. They're on the way, though. It shouldn't be long."

"I'm going upstairs and staying with my stepmom until they get here."

"That's fine, honey, just try not to move her, okay?"

I bit back an irritated retort; I probably had more first responder training than the paramedics answering my call. "Okay," I said. "I'll be careful."

I knelt next to the bed, held Lauren's hand, and kept her talking. Perhaps three minutes later I heard sirens coming down the street. I went outside, flagged them down, and then showed them where to find Lauren. I will never forget the looks on their faces when they saw the bullet-riddled corpses of the intruders.

"Jesus Christ, kid," one of them said, a big Hispanic guy. His nametag read Ortez. "You did all this?"

I nodded.

Ortez went to look over Lauren while his partner, a pretty blonde woman with brown eyes and strong, useful looking arms checked the corpses for signs of life. When she finished, she stepped in front of me and placed a gentle hand on my shoulder. Despite her outward calm, she positioned her feet like a fighter and there was a touch of wariness in her eyes.

"Can you wait downstairs for the police to get here, please?" she said. "Don't worry, we'll take good care of your mom."

I thought about correcting her that Lauren was my stepmother, but decided against it. I simply nodded and went outside to wait.

Sitting there on the front porch, I thought about that hole in the drywall next to my head, and remembered something my dad once told me about marksmanship and ballistics. I think I was maybe eight or nine at the time. We were eating kabobs at an outdoor picnic table at a bar-b-que place near downtown.

"Here's something you need to understand about shooting, son," he said as he slid the meat and vegetables off a kabob and pointed it at the sky. "Here's where you are when you're shooting." He pointed at the bottom of the kabob. "And here's the bullet." His finger touched the tip. "Any little movement on this side here at the bottom translates to a much larger movement here at the end." He pivoted the kabob from left to right like the striker on a metronome. Looking at it that way, I understood the concept. A fraction of an inch of movement at the bottom of the kabob became several inches of movement at the pointy end.

"See what I'm saying, son?" he asked.

"Yeah, I think so. If I move just a little bit when I'm shooting, it doesn't look like much, but the bullet is going to travel for hundreds of yards. That little movement of the barrel makes a big difference as to where the bullet ends up."

Dad smiled. "That's right."

The guy who shot at me as maybe ten feet away when he pulled the trigger. The bullet hit the wall about ten inches to my left, and to hit at that angle, it must have traveled over and across my face from the right. Judging by where it punctured the wall, I figured it missed me by no more than three inches. If the intruder had aimed the barrel just a bit lower, or had the presence of mind to make a follow up shot, I would be the one dead and not him. And God only knows what would have happened to Lauren.

As the sirens grew louder and my hands began to shake, I remembered that commercial again, the one with the coach giving a speech to his team. The old fellow had it right.

Life really is a game of inches.

EIGHT

Hollow Rock, Tennessee

A few minutes after midnight, Caleb stood up and returned to the kitchen for another drink. He felt Miranda's eyes on him as he poured it and leaned against the counter.

"The cops found their car a few blocks down," he said. "Said it was full of stolen property. Jewelry, mostly. Some old coins, cash, a few laptops, prescription drugs, that kind of stuff. Things they could fence easily and carry out in briefcases to avoid rousing suspicion."

Miranda shook her head sadly. "Clever. Devious, but clever."

Caleb nodded. "When they searched the bodies, they found a set of lock picks on the guy who shot at me. They'd been breaking into houses all day. Never hit more than one house on any block. Mine was the only one where someone was home."

Miranda's pale eyebrows pinched together. "If they were just petty thieves, why did they attack Lauren? Seems like a big jump from breaking and entering to sexual assault."

"From what the cops told me, they had done that kind of thing before. Departments in four different states were investigating similar crimes. With the DNA and fingerprints they got off the guys I shot, they were able to wrap up all but one of them."

"Jesus Christ."

"I doubt he had anything to do with it."

Caleb returned to the living room and sat down. Miranda scooted closer to him and rubbed a hand across his chest. "So what happened when your dad got home?"

"He wasn't very happy, as you can imagine. He made sure I was okay, then rode in the ambulance with Lauren. I met them at the hospital."

"Was she okay?"

"Yeah. Had a concussion, bumps and bruises. They kept her overnight, then released her the next morning. The real damage was emotional."

Miranda's face darkened. "I can imagine."

He looked down at her and remembered the night she was rescued, and what she and the other former sex slaves had looked like. Not all of them survived their injuries. Some had diseases, while others buckled under the pain and took their own lives. Of all of them, Miranda seemed to be making the best recovery.

Caleb tucked a strand of hair behind her ear. "Yeah. I guess you can."

"I'm tired, Caleb. I think I'll go to bed. You staying up for a while?"

He nodded. "Not sure I can sleep right now."

She kissed him softly. "Don't forget to set your alarm clock."

"I won't."

He watched her walk into the bedroom, silhouetted against the window, and thought how much she looked like another girl he had loved. She had been gone only a little over two years, but it felt like a lifetime.

He managed two more glasses of grain liquor before he passed out on the couch.

*****

Morning. Bright sunlight through the window.

The piercing rattle of Caleb's wind-up alarm clock ricocheted behind his eyes like a swarm of angry hornets. He checked the time—0700—and had a moment of panic thinking he was late for duty. Then he remembered it was Sunday, and he didn't have to be at the VFW hall until 0800.

With a groan, he stood up from the couch and stumbled into Miranda's bedroom. She lay on her side, pillow clutched to her chest, snoring softly. As quietly as he could, he peeled off his sweat-soaked uniform, folded it neatly, then stepped into the bathroom and closed the door. After brushing his teeth, he turned the shower knob and stepped into the narrow stall.

The water was surprisingly warm. Caleb guessed the bright sun shining on the water tower across town must have heated it. He relished in the balmy flow as he grabbed bar of soap and a washcloth and began scrubbing away old sweat and dead skin. Beyond the frosted glass of the shower stall, the bathroom door opened and Miranda's distorted, flesh-colored shape stepped in. Caleb listened to the sound of water running, her toothbrush going to work, and then she opened the door to the shower.

"Mind if I join you?" she asked.

Caleb took in the sight of her bare alabaster skin in the morning light, soft blonde hair spilling down delicate shoulders, amorous cheekbones, bottomless sapphire eyes, the mobile, graceful curve of sensuous mouth, heavy breasts, rigid stomach muscles, broad flare of womanly hips, strong, supple planes of muscular thighs. His heart pounded in his chest as he stepped back to allow her inside.

The shower was small, but Miranda was very flexible. When they stepped out a short while later, spent and smiling, Caleb decided it was a good start to the morning.

*****

The sun was well into the sky by 0900.

Caleb sat on the front porch of the Hollow Rock General Store, his back against an awning post, waiting patiently for the arrival of Delta Squad and Sanchez's militiamen. The store was open but had yet to see its first customer of the day. Miranda was inside updating the inventory logs, straightening merchandise on the shelves, and deciding what items to discount for the day.

While the two of them no longer made any effort to conceal their relationship, Miranda had made it clear he needed to respect her space when she was at work. Caleb knew she loved her job and took it seriously, so he kept a respectful distance while she was on the clock. There was an unavoidable desire to go inside and help her, but he knew he would only be a distraction. So he stayed outside, and sat, and waited.

Eric Riordan was the first to arrive. He had trimmed his blond beard since the last time Caleb had seen him and had put something in his longish hair to slick it back. From a distance, Caleb thought he looked a bit like the British actor Charlie Hunnam. The effect diminished as Eric drew closer and the crooked ridge in his nose—obtained during his time infiltrating the now-defunct Free Legion—became visible. Eric had once shown Caleb a picture of what he looked like before the Outbreak, and Caleb had a hard time reconciling the lean, weathered, hard-eyed man he knew against the gym-muscled, hair-gelled, dimple-cheeked pretty boy in the picture.

Eric stepped up on the porch and thumped Caleb on the shoulder, speaking in his North Carolina drawl. "You're awful early. Nothing better to do this mornin'?"

"Like what, wait for somebody to put me to work? Hell no. Sergeant Kelly had our passes ready to go when I got to the VFW Hall. Took off as soon as he signed me out."

"Any clue where the other guys are?"

"Sleeping, last I saw 'em."

Eric pursed his lips and nodded. "Figures. Miranda inside?"

"Yep."

"Need anything? Had breakfast yet?"

"I'm good."

"Cool. Be back in a bit."

The door shut behind Eric. Caleb heard muted voices as the R in G&R Transport and Salvage exchanged greetings with Miranda.

He knew the story of how Eric and Gabriel Garrett, Riordan's business partner and best friend, had rescued Miranda from the Free Legion. He also knew that while the two men accepted his relationship with Miranda, they were also ever watchful, and as fiercely protective of her as she was unswervingly loyal to them. Although he didn't need it, it was good motivation to treat her with the utmost kindness and respect. Riordan and Garrett were two men on whose bad side he had no desire to be.

At 0915, Sanchez and his crew arrived. They greeted Caleb with smiles and loud talking. He nodded silently in response, accepting handshakes when they were offered. Private First Class Anthony Vincenzo took a seat next to him.

"Nice morning, huh?" he said in his pronounced New York accent.

"Yep. Sure is." Caleb was silent a moment, then said, out of curiosity, "Say, Tony, what part of New York are you from?"

Vincenzo took a small bag of rare and valuable tobacco from his pocket, papers from another, and began rolling a cigarette. "Brooklyn. Why?"

Caleb shrugged. "Just wondering."

"You're from Texas, right?"

"Yep."

"What part?"

"Right outside of Houston. Small town."

"I been to Houston."

Caleb looked at him. "No shit?"

"No shit. Had an aunt lived down there, my mother's sister. Used to live in Poughkeepsie. Went down there for business and met some guy, worked for an oil company. Moved down to marry him. Ma took me and my sister to see her when we were teenagers."

"Huh. Small world. What'd you think of the place?"

"Tell you the truth, when Ma told me we were going, I was pissed. All I knew about Texas was shit I saw on TV. Nothing that appealed to a New Yorker, you know? But I was surprised when I got down there. It was nice. Cleaner than New York. Open. Felt like I'd been inside this box, and didn't know there was a world out there, and somebody opened the box and let me out. The first morning we were there we were staying at my aunt's place, and she lived in this nice little suburb, clean air, plenty of parking, and I woke up before everybody else and stepped out on her back patio and took a breath, and it was the cleanest breath I'd ever taken. Felt like I was breathing for the first time. Years later, I always wanted to go back. I love New York, don't get me wrong. But I always told myself I'd get back down there someday. Breathe that air again."

Caleb looked out across the distance of the town square, and time, and said, "Sorry to disappoint you, but there ain't much left of Houston, now."

Vincenzo lit his cigarette and inhaled. "I remember from the news. Fires were pretty bad down there, right?"

"Bad is an understatement. The sky was black and orange like a campfire at night. Ash fell from the sky like snow. The wind was hot and dry, like standing in front of the world's biggest blow dryer. You couldn't go outside without goggles and something tied around your nose and mouth. The fires drove the infected out into the countryside, thousands and thousands of them. We were lucky any of us managed to get out of there alive."

Caleb watched a robin bouncing around in the grass a few feet away, the images of that era of his life flashing before his mind's eye. More than a minute passed before he realized Vincenzo was staring at him.

"Sorry," Caleb said, glancing aside. "Got lost for a minute there."

Vincenzo patted him on the back. "Don't sweat it. Happens to me all the time."

The two soldiers shared a comfortable silence as they waited for the rest of Delta Squad to arrive. As minutes ticked by and Delta did not show up, Sanchez's squad of militiamen grew increasingly impatient. One of them asked Caleb where the hell his guys were, to which he responded with a condescending, "How the hell should I know?"

"They're your squad."

Caleb stood up and held out his arms. "You see a radio anywhere, dumbshit?"

The militiaman sullenly relented.

Eric came outside and looked around, one hand shielding his eyes from the sun. He looked at Sanchez. "No sign of them?"

The former professional boxer—once known to the sports media as the Pride of Hermosillo—shook his head. "*Nada, jefe.* Something's not right. They should have been here by now."

Moments later, the clomping of hooves sounded in the town square a few blocks down, preceding the appearance of a rider around the corner of town hall. The man in the saddle was Quentin Reid, an earnest young sheriff's deputy who, while off duty, utilized his family's brown Saddlebred mare to earn extra trade by working as a messenger. He had another horse in tow, one of Echo Company's quarter horses.

"Please tell me something good," Eric called out as the deputy approached. The young man shook his head.

"Delta Squad's been called to company HQ, along with the rest of their platoon. Lieutenant Jonas sent me here to round up Specialist Hicks."

Without a word, Caleb stood up, walked over to the quarter horse, and swung into the saddle. The creature accepted his weight with meek indifference. He guessed it at about seven years old, Kentucky bred, and by the sway in its back, had spent its years under the weight of countless heavy burdens. Whoever saddled the beast had done so sloppily, with no regard for the animal's comfort. Caleb rubbed its neck and inwardly vowed to track down the responsible party and correct this affront to the dignity of such a humble, affable mount.

As they turned their horses to leave, Eric called out to them. "Has First Platoon left yet?"

Deputy Reid looked over his shoulder. "No, not yet. They're waiting on Hicks."

Caleb met Riordan's eyes and knew what he was thinking. *Nosy bastard.* "Come on then," Caleb said. "I'll tell the Lieutenant you threatened to buy his gambling debts if I didn't bring you along."

Eric grinned savagely as he accepted Caleb's hand and climbed into the saddle behind him. "You know, that's not such a bad idea."

Caleb fought down a laugh as they took off in a clamor of iron-shod hooves on crumbling pavement.

NINE

Lieutenant Jonas was not surprised.

"You have a way of sticking your nose into things, don't you?" he asked Eric. The old soldier stood at the north gate, his platoon in ranks behind him waiting for the guards to let them out.

Caleb stood out of the saddle and stepped down, followed closely by Riordan as he walked over to his platoon CO. Jonas directed his disapproving gaze in Caleb's direction. "How'd he Shanghai you into this?"

Caleb stepped close and kept his voice low. "Probably best if I don't say it publicly, sir."

The lieutenant paled visibly. He was a good man and a fine soldier, but he had a weakness for games of chance. It was a character flaw he worked hard to conceal from those higher up in the chain of command. By his expression, Caleb could tell that was the first place his thoughts went.

"Very well, Specialist. Fall in with your squad."

Caleb walked a few steps behind his CO, then stopped to watch and listen. Lt. Jonas didn't notice, his attention turning to Deputy Reid. "Quentin, I don't suppose you'd mind running our horse back up to HQ?"

The young man shook his head. "Not at all. I'll leave a note with the disbursing clerk."

"Very well." Jonas shifted his attention to Eric. "Something I can do for you?"

"Going on a salvage run today. Thought I'd bring Delta Squad along. Standard fee."

Jonas shook his head. "Afraid not, Mr. Riordan. Word came down from General Kyle himself. We're to report to company HQ and await orders."

"What about the guys from the Ninth?"

"Them too. Lieutenant Cohen just sent a wagon for Sanchez's men a few minutes ago."

Eric put his hands on his hips and leaned closer. "Come on, you can spare one squad, can't you? I got the transport for the next two days, but I can't do a salvage run on my own."

The lieutenant shook his head again. "It's out of my hands. Orders are orders. Maybe you can hire a few guardsmen."

Caleb watched Eric stare at the ground for a moment, gears turning behind calculating eyes. "Okay," he said finally. "How about I tag along? You've hired me as a contractor before, scout work and such. Captain Harlow knows me. Just tell him I offered to help out."

"He's pretty tight about our budget. I can't afford to hire you right now."

"I'll waive my fee, then."

Jonas thought it over. "I don't suppose you're doing this out of the kindness of your heart?"

Eric shrugged, expression neutral. "Thomas Edison once said opportunity is missed by most people because it's dressed in overalls and looks like work."

The old soldier laughed. "All right then. Fall in with Delta, but keep a low profile."

"Will do." Eric gave Caleb a wink as he stepped past the lieutenant and walked with him toward his squad.

"Nicely done," Caleb said.

Eric suddenly grew serious. "Anything dangerous enough to require the attention of all of Echo Company and the Ninth TVM is something the people of Hollow Rock need to know about."

Caleb said nothing as the gate opened and they marched toward Fort McCray.

*****

As Master Sergeant Ashman called the platoon to a halt, Caleb thought about how well the day had started, and that he should not be surprised the fates had decided to balance the scales to the side of shitty.

On the gravel trail between Hollow Rock and Fort McCray, the path wound down around the back of a heavily wooded hill in defilade from the guards in the towers—meaning they couldn't see it even with field glasses. Worse, the depression between hills followed the natural contours of the land, making it the path of least resistance for someone on foot.

And the undead, generally speaking, always followed the path of least resistance.

Consequently, every man in First Platoon was on alert, fully aware that if they were going to run into walkers, this was the most likely place. And because Caleb's day had started out so well, he blamed himself for the bad luck his platoon had just encountered.

Delta Squad was close to the back of the formation, so Caleb's first indication of the trouble ahead was a not-so-distant chorus of moans and howls. No matter how many times he heard the mourning call of the undead, it still sent a chill down his spine. The men around him groaned in irritation.

"Great," Holland said. "Just fuckin' great. This is exactly what we need right now. More walkers."

"Shut up a minute." Thompson fluttered his hand impatiently at Holland, two fingers pressed against his radio earpiece. Finally, he took his hand from his ear. "Okay, there's a big horde up ahead, about three hundred strong, spread out over a few hundred meters in the saddle between this hill and the one leading up to Fort McCray. We're to fan out fifty meters ahead in standard crescent formation. Rifles only, no SAWs, no grenades."

"Man, shit." Cole slid his SAW around to his back and turned toward Caleb. "Mind helpin' me out?"

Caleb unlashed an M-4 carbine from Cole's pack and handed it to him. The big man checked the round in the chamber before switching off the safety.

Thompson watched the exchange quietly, then said, "We're to take position on the far right. Our squad will lead off and get the Rot pointed in our direction. Once we have them bunched, we'll form a shitpile at a forty meter standoff with Charlie Squad backing us up. Alpha and Bravo will circle ninety degrees from our line of fire and light 'em up from the left flank. If they start to move around the shitpile, Charlie will leapfrog us and box them in. No matter what, we are to hold position. Any questions?"

Caleb shook his head, along with the other men in his squad. None of what Thompson said was anything new. Every man in First Platoon had fought countless battles with the undead, and the tactics Thompson described were as familiar to them as the grips of their rifles.

"Hey Ethan, what about me?" Eric said, stepping around Cole.

Sgt. Thompson smiled at his old friend, reminding Caleb the two men had known each other since before Thompson joined the Army. "What are you packing?"

Eric slid his state-of-the-art rifle around on its sling and held it up for Thompson to see. "M-6. Law enforcement configuration, ACOG scope, suppressor ready." He patted the military grade suppressor on his MOLLE vest.

"Ammo?" Thompson asked.

"Two-ten in mags, another hundred boxed up in my pack."

"LT won't be able to reimburse you."

Eric shrugged. "I'll be all right."

Thompson nodded. "Fair enough. Fall in with Holland's fire team; we can always use another marksman. As for the rest of you, once we whittle 'em down to about a hundred or so, expect to move in with hand weapons. Now, last chance—any questions?"

The young staff sergeant was met with silence.

"All right. Move out."

Eric fell in behind Caleb as the squad moved into position. When they were halfway down the hill and forty meters from the trail, the horde below came into view. The ghouls noticed First Platoon, sent up a swarm of howls, and began scrambling up the embankment to reach them. In their desperation, they bounced off one another and crawled heedlessly over those who fell. There was no cohesion to the horde, just a mutual desire to sink their teeth into the walking fleshy things up the hill.

Caleb took his usual spot on the far left, unfolded his aiming stick, and balanced the foregrip of his M-4. Eric set up a few feet to his right, sitting down to fire from a seated position. The rest of the squad followed suit until they were a few feet apart, rifles aimed, ready to go to work.

"Standby a minute, fellas," Thompson called out. "The rest of the platoon is still getting into position."

Caleb relaxed, stood up straight, and took a few deep breaths. He remembered his earplugs and put them in, grateful it occurred to him before the shooting started. He turned his head and shouted at the other members of his squad to do the same. Cormier, Page, and Fuller cursed softly as they too realized they didn't have their ears in. Their standard issue M-4 rifles were accurate, reliable weapons, but extremely loud.

Down the slope, the horde drew slowly, inexorably closer. A couple of minutes passed before Thompson's voice cut the air.

"All are stations in position. Fire at will."

Caleb leaned over his rifle, picked a target, and centered his ACOG reticle. The walker in his sights was female, clothes long since disintegrated, gaping black wounds visible on her arms, legs, and torso from where other infected had torn into her before she died. Caleb felt a pang of pity for the person she had once been. Judging by her wounds, she had literally been eaten to death.

Hell of a bad way to go.

He let out a breath, squeezed the trigger, and felt the rifle's recoil. In his sights, a spray of black and red erupted behind the walker, painting the ghouls behind her with matted gore. Her body stiffened, gave a final shudder, and fell.

One down, about seven billion to go.

Despite the earplugs, the gunfire to his right was still very loud. He ignored the noise and kept firing, heartbeat steady, posture relaxed, leaning into his weapon, feet braced, a slight bend in the knees, the movements as familiar as breathing. It would have been easy to pick up the pace and drop walkers at double his current rate, but he didn't want to draw attention to himself. His father's words came back to him, always compelling despite the passage of years:

Never let anyone know what you can do, Caleb. People will try to make a tool out of you. Bend you to their will. If they can't win you over with charm, they'll find some leverage, some way to hurt you. They will try to own you. Believe me, son. I know.

In the early days after joining the Army, he had shown off a few times. Couldn't help himself. He had used his tracking and marksmanship skills to hunt game and supplement his platoon's meager rations with fresh meat. It had won him many friends, but had also attracted the attention of Lieutenant Jonas.

While standing watch one night, eyes searching the forest around him for walkers, ears straining for footsteps, he heard the old soldier approaching. The lieutenant was trying to be stealthy, but he was as loud as thunder compared to Caleb's father.

Caleb knew who it was by the tread, but because the night was pitch dark, he was expected to call out a challenge to anyone approaching the camp. When Jonas was close enough to hear him, he whispered, "Mockingbird."

Jonas answered with the appropriate pre-arranged response. "Fireball."

"Approach and be recognized."

Caleb kept his rifle at the low ready as his CO stepped into sight. "Nicely done. You've got good ears."

"Thank you, sir."

The lieutenant stopped beside him and peered out into the forest. "Everything quiet?"

"Yes sir."

"Any sign of walkers?"

"No sir."

Jonas was silent a moment, then said, "Mind if I ask you a personal question, Private Hicks?"

"Sir?"

"Where did you learn how to track and shoot?"

Never let anyone know what you can do, Caleb. "If you don't mind me asking, sir, why do you want to know?"

"You stalked a deer on foot today and brought it down with one shot from a 5.56. Any man can shoot like that is wasting himself as a regular infantry grunt. Might be we can find something else for you to do, if you're up to it."

Caleb looked down and shuffled his feet. "I don't know, sir. I feel like I still have a lot to learn."

The lieutenant nodded. "No pressure, son. Just thought I'd bring it up. Give you something to think about."

"Thank you, sir."

"Now you still haven't answered my question."

"Oh, right. My dad used to take me hunting a lot. Taught me how to recognize tracks, read terrain, find breaks in foliage, that sort of thing."

"Hm. Your old man must have been a hell of a hunter."

"Yes sir. He was."

Jonas hadn't bothered him about it since, but if Ashman's prediction of his forthcoming promotion was correct, Caleb figured it was only a matter of time.

Nothing I can do about it right now. Worry about it when it happens, not before.

Caleb kept firing until his magazine ran out, reloaded, and began firing again. Despite the toll his squad's rifles were taking, the bulk of the horde was still making progress up the hill. The walkers had bunched into a single mass, attracted by the cacophony of noise echoing above them—exactly what Delta Squad wanted them to do. The ones with fewer mechanical injuries outpaced their more tattered brethren, causing the horde to coalesce into the now-familiar teardrop shape. Caleb aimed his fire along their left flank, causing ripples in the horde where ghouls stepped over the bodies of their fellow undead. In his peripheral vision, he saw Thompson had stopped firing and was squinting into the eyepiece of a handheld rangefinder.

"All right," he shouted over the noise. "They reached standoff range. Start piling 'em up." He then said a few quick words into his radio, stashed the rangefinder on his vest, and began firing again.

The first step in forming a shitpile, as they termed a large mound of permanently dead ghouls, was to drop the ones closest to the center of the horde until they formed a stack. As the flanks slowly caught up, Holland and Thompson would maintain fire on the center while the rest of the squad shifted fire farther down the flanks. The result was a gradually building wall of dead bodies at a set distance that slowed the progress of the horde to a crawl. As the bodies piled up, the walkers would naturally try to go around it rather than over it, which served to spread out the line.

Just as it was getting to the point Caleb couldn't shoot fast enough to keep his section of the horde at standoff distance, he heard Alpha and Bravo squads open up to his left. A hail of bullets ripped into the horde from that side, preventing them from going around the rapidly building pile ahead of them. The slope of the hill compounded this difficulty, forcing the walkers to crawl up the middle. When their heads popped up over the pile, they were easy pickings.

The number of ghouls in Caleb's sights began to rapidly diminish, which was good because he could feel the heat of his barrel radiating through the rail shroud. The smell of spent cordite was strong in the air, stinging his nostrils. He found it oddly nostalgic.

Just as the chamber latched open on the last round in Caleb's magazine, Thompson gave the order to cease fire.

"Drop your packs, vests, and extra gear," he said. "Hand weapons only. If you have a sidearm, bring it, but don't use it unless absolutely necessary. If you do, maintain muzzle discipline at all times. And no fucking heroics; we fight as a team. If you get in trouble, call for help. Don your PPE now, don't wait until we get there. Understood?"

The squad gave a round of acknowledgements. Thompson wasn't telling them anything they didn't already know, but they all knew it made him feel better to say it.

"We're to move down the hill and attack on the right flank," Thompson went on. "Alpha will hit them on the left while Bravo circles around behind. Charlie will stay in reserve and take out any walkers who make it over the pile. Any questions?"

There were none.

"All right. Let's get it done."

Caleb dropped his pack to the ground, followed by his MOLLE vest and rifle. His Beretta was in a drop holster on his hip, which he kept. His scarf went around his mouth and nose, his combat goggles went over his eyes, the armored gloves went over his hands and forearms. After drawing his spear, he followed Thompson and the rest of his squad down the hill. Beside him, Eric hefted a Y-shaped stick and a rapier-like sword. "Mind if I tag along?" he asked.

"Not at all," Caleb replied. "I usually team up with Cole and Holland."

"Works for me. Where do you want me?"

"Let Cole take point and kill anything that approaches on his right. I'll move left with Holland."

"Sounds like a plan."

Cole turned to them and grinned. "And make sure you give me plenty of room to swing."

Eric eyed the massive bar mace in the gunner's thick hands. "I'll be sure to do that."

When they were in position, lined up along the horde's right flank roughly thirty meters away, Thompson held up a hand. "Hold position and wait for my order."

Caleb gripped his spear, hands tightening on the familiar texture of the hickory shaft. The handle was short, only three and a half feet long, tipped with a heavy ten-inch blade. The blade was triangular in shape with a narrow profile and a thick spine in the middle, making it perfect for ramming through nasal cavities and soft palates. Caleb remembered all the times his father had taken him hunting for wild pigs on horseback armed only with boar spears, and all the times they had sparred with rubber training spears. His father had always gotten the best of him until he was about fifteen and accidentally broke Caleb's spear in a sparring match. His father kept attacking anyway, loudly reminding him that in a real fight, his opponent wouldn't stop to let him carve a new one. To his surprise, he found he could handle the weapon much better with the shorter handle. That day marked the first time he ever beat his father in a training match.

A glint of sunlight flashed from his spear's point, reminding him of the gleam in his father's eye when he batted aside a thrust aimed at his chest, closed the distance, and pressed the rubber tip of his training weapon to his father's throat.

"Good," the old man had said, smiling. "Very good, son."

He smiled at the memory, feeling the familiar anticipation of hand-to-hand combat building in his gut. It was a good feeling, a release of worry and doubt, a strange sort of catharsis. In battle, Caleb could forget who he was, forget all he had lost, forget the pain and regret and worry for the future, and lose himself in the red mist of the melee.

"All squads are in position," Thompson said, pointing his rifle toward the horde. "Advance."

TEN

Caleb's team approached, Cole out front, the rest of the squad formed up and advancing on their right. Thompson brought up the rear, rifle in hand, the only one still armed with an M-4. As squad leader, it was Thompson's job to hang back, direct the fight, and use his carbine to assist anyone who got in trouble. The rest of the squad—Caleb included—had to engage the enemy with hand weapons. It was not an ideal way to fight the undead, but with the Army's resources stretched as thin as they were, conserving ammunition was critical.

He watched Cole wade into the press with his usual glee, bar mace moving in a steady figure-eight pattern, an infected skull crushed like a melon with every downswing. To Cole's right, Eric went to work with his Y-shaped stick and long, elegant sword. The sword had no edges, just a wickedly sharp tip. Eric dispatched walkers by holding the stick under his arm like a jouster's lance, catching a ghoul by the throat with its Y-shaped end, and stabbing it in the brain through the eye socket.

When Eric had first described his method to Caleb, he had doubted Eric's claims of how well it worked.

Then he had seen it in action.

Eric could kill walkers twice as fast as anyone Caleb had ever met, himself included. Lieutenant Jonas had even recorded Eric's tactics on a digital camera and sent it back to Central Command for review, recommending that the folks at

AARDCOM (Army Anti-Revenant Defense Command) find a way to adapt the method for use by regular infantry.

Caleb's thoughts were interrupted as a walker stumbled away from one of Cole's backswings, but did not go down. He stepped forward, spear cocked back at shoulder level in a two-handed grip, and thrust forward. The needle-sharp point crunched through the ghoul's nasal cavity and pierced its brain with such force that two inches of blade protruded from the back of its skull before Caleb yanked his weapon free.

Beside him, Holland's twin tomahawks flashed in the sunlight as he began frenetically attacking the ghouls coming at them from the left. A second-degree black belt in tae kwon do, Holland utilized hard kicks to knock walkers to the ground, then dispatched them with precise chops to the brain stem. When his kicks failed to knock a ghoul over, he moved in and slashed at their knees and ankle tendons, then backed off to let other walkers trip over them, making for easy kills.

Caleb stayed busy, utilizing front kicks to keep walkers at distance and thrusting his arms like twin pistons, every stab claiming another ghoul. The fight raged around him, the howls of the undead mixing with battle cries and grunts of effort from his fellow soldiers. One of the men in his squad shouted for help somewhere to his right, followed by the crack of Thompson's rifle.

A ghoul appeared in front of Caleb, mouth gaping, black tongue rolling in its putrid mouth. It moaned at him, the stench of its breath threatening to gag him through his scarf. Before he could bring his spear to bear, the corpse grabbed his shoulders and lunged at him. He caught it by the throat with one hand and pushed it away, its teeth snapping inches from his face.

Knowing his strength would not last long against the unnatural power of the ghoul, he thrust his spear into the ground next to him and drew his Beretta. After a quick glance to make sure no soldiers were in the line of fire, he pressed the barrel to its infected forehead and pulled the trigger. The pressure on his arms released immediately as the ghoul fell, but there were three more hot on its heels.

Caleb re-aimed his pistol and fired twice in rapid succession, dropping two of them. The falling ghouls tripped the third one on the way down, giving him time to holster his pistol and retrieve his spear.

"Hicks, you okay?" Thompson shouted.

"I'm good," Caleb said through clenched teeth as he rammed the blade of his spear upward through a walker's soft palate and then kicked it away. The fight continued a few more minutes before the press of walkers began to thin and he could see Alpha and Bravo squads fighting their way toward him. The walkers paid no heed to their impending doom, focused solely on the gnawing hunger driving them onward.

Caleb watched one of the last infected's eyes as he killed it. The mindless, enraged half-light burning within winked out of existence. He let it slide from his blade and stood panting, eyes searching for the next target, but saw only other soldiers in gore-spattered uniforms. All four squad leaders pressed fingers to their ears at the same time, receiving instructions from Sgt. Ashman.

Sergeant Kelly, the most senior squad leader, was the first to speak up. "All right, we got the all clear from Sergeant Ashman. Squad leaders, form your men up and rally back at the trail. We need to decon ASAP and get back on the road."

Caleb turned to his staff sergeant, along with the rest of the squad. "You heard him," Thompson said. "Let's go pick up our gear."

There was no cheering. The men removed their armored gloves, checked each other for bites, and walked wearily back to where they had left their belongings. From their backpacks, they removed green aerosol cans with DECON AGENT stenciled on the labels. It was one of the Army's many new innovations: a disinfectant spray that could kill just about anything. From what Caleb understood, it was essentially just a more caustic version of Lysol. While no one fully understood how the Reanimation Bacteriophage worked, it was well known that outside its host, the Phage was as vulnerable to disinfectants as any other pathogen.

The men sprayed each other down, taking care to scrape off dead tissue and soak any area of cloth that had come into contact with infected flesh or blood. When all squads were finished, and the squad leaders had reported in, Ashman gave the order to march.

"Nothing like a workout first thing in the morning, eh?" Eric said, nudging Caleb in the arm as they trudged along the path.

Caleb thought about the last ghoul he killed, and the way it seemed almost relieved as it died, and shook his head.

He was silent for the rest of the march.

*****

The situation at Fort McCray, as per usual, followed the ages-old pattern of activity known to every army since the dawn of warfare.

Hurry up and wait.

While Caleb and the rest of his platoon awaited orders in the mess hall, Eric stayed busy. His first order of business was to corral a radioman and bribe him into sending a message to the sheriff's office. It was a coded message, the cypher of which only he and a few other people in Hollow Rock knew. The gist of the message was that something big was going down with Echo Company, and Mayor Stone needed to contact Captain Harlow at her earliest opportunity.

Next, he waited in the shade of an oak tree outside the headquarters building where he could be easily found. Less than ten minutes later, an earnest young MP approached him and politely asked if he would accompany him to Captain Harlow's office.

The best way Eric could describe Captain Harlow would be to say he was medium. Medium height, medium build, voice a solemn tenor, black hair carefully trimmed and combed to the side, uniform immaculate, shoe shine impeccable, as neatly put together as anyone Eric had ever met.

He had a hard time picturing Captain Harlow in combat attire, rifle in hand, leading men into battle. He would have looked more at home in a suit and tie selling tax-free municipals to Florida retirees. But upon closer inspection, Eric detected a certain firmness to the set of his jaw, a clarity in the chilly gray eyes, a surprising strength in the proffered handshake, his movements brisk and efficient, his demeanor possessed of an air of assured authority that belied of his youthful appearance.

"It's good to see you again Mr. Riordan," Harlow said. "Please, have a seat."

"Thank you, Captain." Eric sat in one of two folding chairs in front of Harlow's plain metal desk.

"Mayor Stone contacted my staff a short while ago. It seems she's concerned as to why I've called First Platoon to headquarters."

Eric nodded. "And the Ninth TVM."

"I'm sure the mayor understands why I can't contact her by radio. Operational security. I'll need to speak with her in person."

"Of course. In the mayor's message, did she appoint a representative in her absence?"

Eric detected a slight narrowing of Harlow's eyes. "Yes. That would be you."

"I thought as much. So, would you mind telling me exactly what's going on?"

"You have to understand, Mr. Riordan, the nature of that information is very sensitive."

"I understand completely."

"Then you understand I can't divulge information about ongoing operations to civilians simply because they drop by and ask me to."

Eric sat forward in his seat, not caring for Harlow's tone. "You do realize you're talking to the guy who infiltrated the Free Legion, right?"

"Yes, I am aware of that. And I certainly appreciate everything you've done for your country, but-"

"And you do realize that General Phillip Jacobs, head of Army Special Operations Command, is a good friend of mine, right?"

Harlow stared, but said nothing.

"Furthermore, the treaty between the free community of Hollow Rock and Central Command stipulates that the mayor's office is to be briefed on any military operations which might affect the safety of the community's citizenry. Were you aware of that?"

A few seconds ticked by. "I'm afraid I haven't read the treaty yet, Mr. Riordan."

"Well, you should. It's a bit dry, but once you get past the boilerplate there's some important information there."

Harlow steepled his fingers under his chin. "Tell me, Mr. Riordan. What did you do before the Outbreak? I'm guessing … lawyer."

"Financial analyst, actually. Now let me ask you a question, Captain. Is there a possibility these ongoing operations you referred to could adversely affect the people of Hollow Rock in any way?"

A muscle in Harlow's jaw twitched a few times before he answered. "Yes. That is a possibility. Which is exactly why we have to keep a tight lid on what's going on."

Eric sat back in his seat. "I'm listening."

Harlow let out a slow breath and placed his hands flat on the desk. Eric had the distinct impression the young captain would have liked nothing better at that moment than to gut him with a rusty machete. When he spoke, his tone was frosty.

"You understand any information I share with you is classified, and is to be shared only with Mayor Stone, correct?"

"Of course."

"And you are aware of the penalties for leaking this information, correct?"

"Correct. And I am duly intimidated. Now can we get on with it?"

Harlow scowled. "I'm sure you've kept up to date on the trouble we've been having with the Midwest Alliance."

Eric nodded. "Allow me to summarize: What was once a loose affiliation of independent city states came together nearly a year ago under a centralized government and declared their independence from the Union. While the federal government has not officially recognized their independence, they haven't attempted to bring them to heel either. In the interim, the Alliance has been fighting a shadow war against the Union and its interests, including but not limited to supplying arms and personnel to anti-Union militant groups. There is also evidence to suggest the Alliance is in cahoots with the Republic of California, which is really just a puppet government under the control of foreign forces who have invaded and subdued a large section of Northern California, Oregon, and Washington. Did I touch on all the major points, Captain?"

"Yes, you did. Are you also aware of the problems we've been having with marauders harassing border communities in Kentucky and Kansas?"

"I've heard a rumor or two. Some people think the Alliance is behind it."

Harlow nodded. "A few months ago, a special operations task group was deployed to the border to assess the severity of the problem and determine if the Alliance was indeed involved. Long story short, the answer is yes, although we can't prove it beyond plausible deniability on the Alliance's part. However, the problem is much worse than we thought."

"How so?"

"What they're doing goes far beyond simple harassment. It's a land grab. They're trying to get the people living in these border communities to flee south and abandon their territory."

"And how are they doing that?"

"I'll give you an example. What used to be the town of Kevil, Kentucky is now known as Fort Carter. Like many towns that survived the Outbreak, it's population has grown significantly in recent years as survivors from nearby areas have filtered in. Fort Carter is surrounded by fertile farmland, grows enough crops to feed its population and then some, and until recently, the town's principle export was livestock. Goats and chickens, mostly."

"So what happened?"

"These so-called marauders happened. They showed up with a horde of about two-thousand revenants and unleashed them on the town. While the town's defenders were busy trying to keep the undead from beating down their walls, the marauders went to work on the fields and livestock. They didn't destroy everything, but the damage was pretty severe. Fort Carter will need federal assistance to make it through the winter this year. And that's just one example; this is happening to towns all along the border."

"Jesus. I didn't realize it was that bad."

"No one did. Not until the task group got there."

"And now that the Army knows, you have to do something about it."

"Exactly."

"And unless I miss my guess, Fort McCray is the nearest FOB to the border."

"That we are."

Eric was quiet a few moments, fingers drumming on his knee. "This is all very interesting, Captain, but what threat do these marauder groups pose to Hollow Rock? They'd be crazy to attack here."

106

"One would think. But according to our intelligence sources, that's exactly what they intend to do."

Eric let out a low whistle. "The Alliance's leadership isn't completely stupid, Captain. I guarantee you they have people watching this place. They know we have tanks, and helicopters, and heavy artillery, and hundreds of troops."

"I concur."

"So how do they expect to win against all that without starting a war?"

Captain Harlow held out his hands, palms up. "That, Mr. Riordan, is the million dollar question."

ELEVEN

Caleb sat on the concrete floor of the drill hall—a massive pre-fab metal building resembling a small airplane hangar—and listened to the briefing.

An hour after hustling to Fort McCray and being told to wait in the mess hall, Lieutenant Jonas returned from headquarters and ordered them to leave their gear behind and follow him to the drill hall. There, they were ordered to have a seat on the floor and wait for Captain Harlow to arrive. Second and Third Platoons showed up shortly thereafter, followed closely by the Ninth TVM. The sound of a generator roaring to life and the lights coming on overhead preceded the captain's arrival by five minutes.

The captain greeted his company, then nodded to a sergeant who turned on a projector connected to a laptop. As he often did, Captain Harlow spent an hour droning on about a plan that should have taken no more than five minutes to convey.

In short, First Platoon was being deployed to the border to meet up with special operations forces, designated Task Force Falcon, already in the area. Half of Third Platoon, which was essentially an ad-hoc detachment of tank and helicopter crews, pilots, artillerymen, and mechanics, would go along as support, as well as a few scouts from the Ninth TVM. The other half of Third Platoon, all of Second Platoon, and the remainder of the Ninth TVM would stay behind to defend Hollow Rock.

While his company commander's briefing method was repetitive and overly detailed, Caleb had to admit it was effective. By the time it was over, every soldier in the room had a clear idea of what lay ahead of them, and what role they were to play. When he was finished, Captain Harlow instructed those troops bound for the border to be ready to deploy in forty eight hours, and then turned them over to their platoon leaders. Lieutenant Jonas held a quick meeting with his squad leaders and instructed them to get their men ready to move out. As they were leaving, Caleb spotted Eric approaching and motioned him over.

"Learn anything?" Caleb asked, keeping his voice low.

"Yeah, lots. But you heard most of it in the ops briefing. The rest I can't talk about."

Caleb raised an eyebrow. Eric leaned in close. "Look, there's some serious shit headed our way. All right? Keep your eyes open and your ear to the ground."

"I always do," Caleb said. Eric clapped him on the arm as Sgt. Ashman gave the order to march.

As First Platoon exited the gate, Caleb looked back to see Eric staring after them.

*****

"You're squared away, Hicks," Thompson said. "See you Tuesday morning."

"Thanks."

As he stowed his spare gear in his footlocker, he noticed Thompson staring at him. "Hey," he said. "Everything all right with you? You've been more quiet than usual lately."

Caleb did not pause in his work. "I'm fine."

"Listen, man, I'm not talking to you as your squad leader right now. I'm talking to you as your friend. What's going on with you?"

Caleb looked Thompson in the eye, measuring. Finally, he looked away and said, "Personal things."

"Miranda?"

Caleb nodded.

"Everything okay between you two?"

"Yeah, we're fine. It's me that's the problem."

Thompson stepped closer. "Catch up with me when I'm off duty. I'll buy you a drink. We'll talk about it."

"Nothing to talk about, really. Just letting her weigh the baggage."

The staff sergeant smiled. "Sounds like things are getting serious."

Caleb shrugged silently and left the barracks.

*****

"So how long do you think you'll be gone?" Miranda asked. She and Caleb were sitting on her couch with the last fading light of the afternoon slanting in through curtained windows.

"No telling. Could be a couple of weeks, could be more than a month."

Miranda chewed her lip, absorbing the news. "You've been on missions like this one before, right?"

"Yep. Lots of them."

"You don't sound worried."

"That's because I'm not."

Miranda smiled and ran a hand down his left cheek, fingers tracing over the splatter of scar tissue there. "You're not invincible, you know."

"I know."

"Then you should be at least a little scared."

"I'll save it for when the shooting starts. A healthy measure of fear keeps you sharp; worrying just makes you tired and sloppy. Burns up energy. That's how people get killed. They lose focus."

Miranda stared at him with irritation and affection, then slid closer to lay her head on the hollow of his shoulder. "When do you leave?"

"Tuesday morning. 0900."

"Do you have to report for duty tomorrow?"

He shook his head. "Not until Tuesday morning. Got all my stuff ready earlier. All I have to do is grab it and go."

She smiled and kissed him on the side of the neck. "So we get to spend the day together?"

"Yep. What do you want to do?"

Miranda sat up on her knees and began unbuttoning her shirt. "I can think of a few things."

Caleb grinned and pulled her onto his lap.

*****

Later, after the sun set and they had enjoyed a shower together, Miranda lit a few candles in her bedroom and she and Caleb lay entwined in the soft light, their faces almost touching. "So you left off with the men who attacked Lauren," she said.

Caleb waited a few heartbeats to answer. "Yeah."

"What happened next?"

He pushed a lock of blonde hair behind Miranda's ear and let out a heavy sigh. "Had to come up sooner or later, didn't it?"

"It's all right if you don't want to talk about it."

"No. It needs to be said. Full disclosure and all that."

"Okay."

"I'll warn you again: you might not like what you're going to hear."

Miranda kissed his lips and then the tip of his nose. "I'll take my chances."

TWELVE

Houston Metro Area, Texas

Lauren was never the same again after the attack. The next year was a bad one for us all.

She lost weight. She had nightmares. The lines of her face deepened, and dark rings took up permanent residence under her eyes. Little sounds made her jumpy. She got a conceal and carry license and wouldn't leave the house unarmed. Dad tried to convince her to start seeing a therapist, but she was having none of it. She insisted she was fine, though it was plain for anyone to see she wasn't. There were cracks in her foundation.

Then came the Outbreak.

I remember exactly where I was that day. I had just turned eighteen and had finished school a few months early. We were out on the patio eating a steak dinner to celebrate when my dad's cell phone rang. He picked it up, checked who was calling, and answered.

"What's up, Blake?"

I watched his face grow confused, then disbelieving, then tight with strain. "How bad is it?" he asked.

That got Lauren's attention. We sat still, the two of us, watching him intently.

"Okay. I'll do that. No, not yet. If it comes to that, we'll communicate via radio. All right, see you soon." Dad hung up and sat quietly, staring into nowhere.

"What is it?" Lauren asked, eyes worried.

"Trouble in Atlanta," Dad said and stood up. "Come on, let's see what's going on."

Lauren and I shared a confused glance, then got up and followed him inside. Dad turned the television on to CNN and increased the volume. By then, the first of many, many hordes had already overrun the initial police barricades and begun to spread throughout the city. Fires raged, riots broke out, people looted stores, neighbors turned on each other, violence grew rampant. The city looked like a war zone. The three of us sat on the couch in shocked disbelief, our dinner sitting forgotten on the picnic table outside. An hour or so after turning on the TV, we watched three ghouls drag a reporter to the ground and begin ripping him apart. As the cameraman fled, the news feed abruptly cut away.

Lauren made a small choking sound and ran for the bathroom. I looked over at my father, a cold feeling spreading through my hands and face, and said, "Dad, what the hell are those things? They can't be people."

The old man said nothing for a long time. Finally, he stood up and walked over to the window. "I heard rumors from other operators, but I didn't think they were true."

"What rumors? What are you talking about?"

He put his hands on his hips and looked down. "About some kind of disease that turns people into … those things you saw. Other operators, guys who did missions in North Korea and China talked about it-" Dad looked up suddenly, realizing what he was saying. He never talked about his time in Delta Force, not even to Lauren and me.

"Caleb, son, we might be in trouble here."

"What do you know, Joseph?"

Dad and I turned to see Lauren standing in the hallway. We hadn't realized she was standing there. Her arm trembled as she pointed at the television. "Joseph Hicks, if you know something about what's going on in Atlanta, you tell us right now."

Dad shook his head. "Lauren, you know I can't talk about that stuff. I signed a con-"

"I don't give a shit about your confidentiality agreement!" Lauren advanced on Dad, hands balled into fists, veins standing out on her forearms. "If you know something, you tell us now!"

"Okay, okay," Dad said, hands upraised. "Calm down, honey. Listen, just sit down, all right? Come on." Moving slowly, he put a gentle hand on her arm and carefully guided her back to the couch.

It wasn't the first time since the attack that she had blown up under stress. Dad and I knew the best way to handle it was to give her time to calm down, but I didn't think it would work in this case. She practically hummed with tension.

When we were all seated, Dad kept his voice low. "Look, all I know is rumors. Okay? Stuff I heard in bars over too many drinks. The first time I heard about it, this guy I knew from another unit and I were talking, and he got drunk, and he told me the North Korean's had some kind of virus or something that turns people into cannibals. Said it … messes up their brains somehow. They can't move very fast, but they don't feel pain either. The only way to drop them is to shoot them in the head. He said …" Dad stopped and put a hand over his mouth.

"What, Joe?" Lauren asked. "What did he say?"

"This is going to sound crazy."

Lauren's voice rose. "What did he say, Joe?"

"He said they're dead." Dad looked Lauren in the eye. "He said they're walking dead people."

If not for the television and the low drone of household appliances, you could have heard a pin drop.

"Joe," Lauren said, "that's not possible."

Dad held out his hands. "Look, I didn't believe him either. Later on, I heard the same thing from other people and I still didn't believe it. I passed it off as superstition, or people seeing something that wasn't there. There had to be some other explanation. Those guys were soldiers, after all, not scientists. But after what I've seen today ..."

"Is it contagious?" I asked.

He turned to look at me. "From what I've heard, yeah."

"Oh God, is it airborne?" Lauren asked.

Dad held out his hands. "Look, at this point, you know as much as I do. For now, let's just stay calm and keep an eye on things. I'm sure the government will get it all sorted out."

It comforted me, then, to hear him say that. But in retrospect, we should have followed our instincts.

We should have run for our lives.

Instead, for the next few days, we huddled together around the television and watched the end of the world unfold.

*****

Hope is a powerful force.

The best thing about hope is it is tenacious. It does not die easily. And like every emotion, it has it's dark counterpart. To love, hate. To joy, sorrow. To confidence, fear.

To hope, despair.

The bad thing about hope is it can get in the way of another, more important emotion: acceptance. And acceptance, important and helpful at it is, also has its counterpoint.

Denial.

We held out hope in those early days. Hope that the government would find a cure, that the military would find a way to defeat the undead (and by then we knew that was what they were). We kept faith that someone, somewhere, would figure out a solution. But by the time the Outbreak crossed the Mississippi River, it was no longer hope.

We were in full-blown denial.

Eleven days after the Outbreak started, I woke up to an angry orange sky out my bedroom window. Not the soft yellow of a spring morning, or the gray of a rainy day, or even the clear blue of a cloudless sky.

No.

Orange. Dark orange, like some great torch had suffused the surface of the sky. I got out of bed, dressed quickly, and went to wake up my father.

"Hey Dad, you need to see this," I said, shaking his shoulder. He awoke in an instant, the glaze of sleep clearing rapidly from his eyes.

"What is it, son?" he asked. Beside him, Lauren stirred and began to sit up.

I pointed. "Look out the window."

His eyes shifted and grew wide. "Mother of God."

Lauren's hand went to her mouth. "What …"

Dad threw off the covers, shrugged into a shirt, and started toward the front door with me and Lauren following close behind. I kept my hand on his shoulder as he opened the door like we were about to execute a room entry. Dad hesitated for a moment and looked back at me.

"Caleb, take a deep breath, son."

I did, and let my hand drop.

"Stay calm." His eyes tracked back and forth between Lauren and me. "Whatever is happening, we'll handle it together, okay?"

I nodded. "Okay."

Behind me, Lauren was silent, but I could feel her fingers gripping the back of my shirt.

I was a head taller than my father by then, so I could see over his shoulder as he opened the door. According to the clock in the living room, it was just after eight in the morning. But judging from the darkness outside, I would have thought the hour no earlier than five or six. A malignant haze hung over the neighborhood, painting houses in shades of amber and black. Everywhere I looked something drifted down like snow, covering lawns, streets, and cars with a thin sheen of gray.

"Is that … ash?" I asked.

Dad said nothing. He pushed out the door and strode into the front yard, one palm turned upward. He stared at it for a few moments, then rubbed his fingers together. Looking around, I could see a few of our neighbors standing in their yards doing the same thing, faces locked in dumbfounded fear.

"It's ash." Dad said. "Come on."

I followed him to the end of the street and around the corner. Our house faced south, away from nearby Houston. There was a hill at the end of the street where we could see the city's skyline to the east. The three of us climbed it, Dad leading the way. When we reached the summit, we stopped cold.

At the edge of the horizon, Houston was in flames.

Great black pillars of smoke streaked upward, staining the clouds above. The city skyline was invisible, obscured by the choking haze. Undulating silvery streaks extended along the highways where people were fleeing the city. The sounds of explosions and gunfire popped and echoed across the distance. I stood transfixed, unable to speak or even think, Lauren's hand clutched in my own.

My father chose that moment to utter the most profound understatement in human history. "This is bad."

I couldn't help it. I let out a bark of hysterical laughter. "Oh, really? You think?"

Dad turned and glared at me. It was on his lips to say something harsh, but whatever he saw on my face stopped him. His dark eyes softened and he laid a hand on my shoulder. "Come on, son. Let's go home. We have things to do."

*****

If there was one thing my father believed in, it was preparedness.

He and I stood in front of a workbench in the garage. In front of us lay a collection of pistols and rifles, boxes of ammunition, spare magazines, tactical gear, and freeze-dried emergency rations.

"We'll take a rifle, a pistol, and a backup piece each," Dad said. "No point in bringing anything else. It'll just be extra weight."

"We should bring the hunting rifle and the .22s," I replied. "Useful. Ammo's easy to find."

Dad thought it over for a moment, then nodded. "Agreed."

I scanned the collection of pistols, shotguns, and carbines, and wondered what to do with the ones we weren't bringing along. My father glanced at me, and I could tell he was thinking the same thing.

"We'll give them away," he said. "No sense in letting them go to waste. Things are going to get bad pretty soon. People will need a way to defend themselves."

I let out a breath. "Yeah. Okay."

"When we leave, I'll open the garage door, put a note on them. Let folks take what they need."

"Sure."

"You all right, son?"

I shook my head. "No, Dad. I'm pretty fucking far from all right."

For once, he did not reprimand the use of profanity. Behind us, the door opened.

"Gary's on the phone," Lauren said.

We turned toward her at the same time. Her jaw was tense, the veins in her neck pronounced. Over the last few days, the tension in her had grown to a fever pitch. There was a jitteriness in her eyes, like she was afraid to look at any one thing for too long. A sharp pang of worry lanced through my stomach as I looked at her, and I wished I could think of something to say to calm her down. But I knew nothing would make any difference just then.

I followed Dad inside as he went into the kitchen and picked up the satellite phone. All of the instructors at BWT had been issued one in case of emergency. At that point, both landline and cell phone communication had shut down.

"Hello? Gary?" he said.

Gary was Dad's boss and the owner of Black Wolf Tactical. He lived in Oklahoma and trusted his employees to manage his many businesses, so I saw him only rarely. He was a big man, well over six feet tall, balding, fantastically obese, and always in possession of some silicone-breasted, botoxed, bleach-blonde trophy a couple of decades younger than he. But for all that, he had always treated my father and the other instructors at BWT with respect. His booming bass buzzed through the phone loud enough I could hear it from three feet away.

"Joe, how you holding up down there?" he said.

Dad scraped a hand across his beard stubble. "If I'm honest, Gary, not too good. Houston is gone."

There was a long silence. "Listen, Joe. I've already called most of the other fellas. I want you all to go to BWT and take whatever you need, then get the hell out of there."

"You heard anything from your contacts on the east coast?" Dad replied.

"No, Joe. That whole part of the country has gone dark. Listen, friend. Do what I said. Get your family, take what you need, and get the hell out of East Texas. The Army won't be able to stop those *things* from overrunning the place. Head for Colorado. That's your best bet."

"What about you, Gary?"

"Don't worry about me. I have my own plans. Just do what I said."

Dad ground his teeth, his grip tight around the phone. "Gary?"

"Yes, Joe."

"Thank you."

"You're welcome. Good luck, my friend. God be with you."

"Yeah," Dad said bitterly. "Same to you."

He hung up, then looked to Lauren and me. "Come on," he said. "We're leaving."

THIRTEEN

We were the last to arrive.

Dad took back roads on the drive over. We saw only a few other cars along the way, all laden down with as much cargo as they could carry, wide-eyed drivers clutching steering wheels with strained white knuckles and driving faster than was safe for conditions. I wondered how many of them we would pass wrecked on the side of the road.

What few houses we passed looked abandoned, some of their front doors hanging open as a result of their former residents' haste to escape the approaching blaze. The sky above grew steadily darker while the choke of falling ash became thicker and thicker. When we finally arrived at BWT, Blake, Tyrel, and Mike's vehicles were in the main office parking lot.

"Leave the rifles," Dad said. "Pistols only for now."

Reluctantly, I laid my carbine aside. The three of us piled out of Dad's truck and went to the front door to find it unlocked. Dad put a hand on his pistol, pushed the door open, and leaned inside. It was dark in the foyer, but I detected a faint illumination deeper within.

"Blake? Mike? Tyrel? It's Joe. Anybody in there?"

A muffled voice shouted back. "Yeah, just a sec." A moment later Mike appeared around the corner. "The others are in the armory. Come on."

I followed Dad inside as he proceeded down the hall past the empty receptionist's desk. He took a small LED flashlight from his tactical vest and shined it ahead of us. The light at the end of the hall grew steadily brighter until we turned the corner and saw shadows of people moving around in the armory.

"What's the story?" Dad asked as we drew near.

Mike put down the box he was moving and pointed at the rows of metal shelving. "Sorting through it all. Prioritizing."

"Beans, bullets, and bandages?"

"Pretty much."

Stepping further inside and looking to my left, I saw Blake and Tyrel sorting through the ammo stacks. To my left, I saw Mike's daughter, Sophia.

For a moment, I stopped breathing.

Sophia was my age, a senior in high school, and the star of her school's soccer team. Tall, trim, and fit, she had straight blonde hair down to her shoulders, chestnut brown eyes, and was as pretty as a spring morning.

Mike rarely brought his daughter around BWT, as she had no interest whatsoever in what he did for a living so long as he handled the car payment and insurance on her brand new Infinity G-35. I had known her for years, the two of us attending the same barbeques and holiday events and such, and she had always been distantly, indifferently polite. I guess when a girl has a veritable legion of testosterone-fueled teenage boys lusting after her, it is hard to be impressed by a gangly, taciturn home-schooled kid.

Our eyes met across the dim gray room, and I felt a lance of pain in my chest. She looked haunted, her face red and puffy from crying, the thin coating of ash on her cheeks smeared from wiping at tears. She had tied her hair back in a loose knot, but a few errant strands hung loosely over her face. She sat alone on top of a wooden crate looking heartbreakingly delicate and vulnerable. Out of protective instinct, without thinking, I walked over to her.

123

"Sophia, are you okay?"

She looked up in mild surprise; I think it was the most I had ever spoken to her. Not that I had never wanted to, mind you. But when she was around, I always found it difficult to form coherent sentences.

"I'm all right, I guess," she said. "All things considered." Her voice was thick with the stuffiness that comes from crying. She crossed her arms and seemed to shrink without moving.

"Is your mother okay?" I asked gently, looking around. "I don't see her anywhere."

"She's in Oregon, visiting my grandparents," Sophia replied. "She wanted to come back when things … you know. Dad told her to stay put."

"Probably wise," I said. Then, realizing I had nothing else to say, I gave Sophia a short nod and stepped back. "Let me know if you need anything."

She looked me over candidly, gaze lingering on my weapons, fatigues, and tactical gear. Her eyes were pools of shadow in the bluish light. "Thanks," she said.

I walked away before things could get awkward.

Across the room, I saw Dad, Blake, Mike, and Tyrel standing in a cluster with Lauren hovering nearby. Lauren's face looked gaunt, the strain in her eyes matching the tenseness of her posture. It didn't take a great deal of perceptiveness to tell she was close to the brink. I had a second or two to worry for her before I came within earshot of the conversation.

"Has anyone given thought to where the hell we should go?" my father asked. "Just heading west until we run out of west doesn't seem like the best idea. Everybody and their brother will be doing the same thing."

No one said anything for a moment, then Tyrel spoke up. "I think we should follow Gary's advice and head for Colorado."

Everyone looked at the former SEAL. When he said nothing else, dad asked, "Why is that?"

"I'm from there," he answered. "I know places we can go."

Dad crossed his arms. "Can you elaborate on that, Tyrel? What kinds of places? Where?"

Tyrel breathed a sigh through his nose. "I think maybe we should talk about it on the way, Joe. Those fires coming our way ain't gonna slow down while we chit-chat."

Dad nodded, then looked at Mike. "What about you? You coming with us or striking out for Oregon?"

Mike pondered a few moments, then said, "I'll stick with you until we find someplace safe for Sophia. Then I'll head for Oregon. When we do find a safe place, can I trust you to look after my daughter for me?"

Dad didn't hesitate. "Absolutely."

Mike gripped his shoulder and looked him in the eye. "Okay, then. Let's go."

*****

Because Black Wolf Tactical was sufficiently in compliance with the National Firearms Act to possess automatic weapons—and because people were willing to pay significant sums of money to fire them—the facility had a number to choose from. Mostly small arms, but a few SAWs and M-240s as well.

Then there were the Humvees.

Three of them, although we only planned to bring along two: one to lead the convoy and another to bring up the rear. Blake and my father mounted M-240s to both Humvees' roof turrets and divided the supplies and ammo between all five vehicles. Mike volunteered to take point in the lead Humvee, my father in his truck behind him. Lauren and Sophia would be in Mike's four-wheel-drive Tundra, Blake and I behind them in his Jeep, with Tyrel bringing up the rear in the second Humvee.

As we were loading the supplies, it occurred to me if a casual observer saw us dressed in our modern tactical gear, they might mistake us for a military escort. Which posed the risk someone might flag us down for help, and possibly respond badly if we didn't stop. There was also the risk a real military convoy might mistake us for deserters. I mentioned this to my father, but he just shook his head and said there was nothing for it. It was a risk we had to take.

Once we had everything ready to go, Blake tossed me the keys to his Jeep. "You drive," he said. "I'll navigate."

For once, he wasn't smiling.

We got seated and belted in, engine idling, wipers fighting a losing battle against the falling ash. The orange haze in the distance grew steadily brighter. Blake turned on the overhead light, plugged his handheld radio into a dashboard power outlet, and consulted his trucker's atlas.

"All stations, looks like we can stick to the back roads and parallel the highways all the way to I-35. From there, we'll have to find a safe place to get across. Any ideas? Over."

Mike cut in. "You see Five Mile Dam Park on your map? It's between Kyle and San Marcos. Over."

Blake's finger traced the map where indicated. "Yeah, I see it. Over."

"Take us that way. I know a service road overpass hardly anyone uses. Should get us across no problem. Over."

"Sounds good to me. Head for 1094 West until it turns in to Bastrop Road, then hang a left. Will advise from there. Over."

"Roger. Out."

Blake shot me a level stare. "Remember, Caleb. No matter what happens, Do. Not. Stop. If we get hit, keep going. If a vehicle gets in trouble, we can always regroup and double back if there's still a chance to help them. Understood?"

I swallowed and nodded.

"If we run into any problems, let your father and me do the talking. If diplomacy fails, remember your training and don't hesitate. And always, always follow our lead. Okay?"

I nodded again.

Blake put a hand on my shoulder. "You okay, man?"

"No, Blake. I'm not."

He smiled then, sharp white teeth bright against his dark skin. "That's good, kid. I'd be worried if you were."

Mike's hand came out the window and made a circling motion as he began to drive out of the parking lot.

The rest of us followed.

FOURTEEN

Humvee's are good for many things, but speed is not one of them.

Their top speed is just over seventy MPH on a good day, but as laden as ours were with ammunition and supplies, the best we could hope for was a little over sixty. This did not fly well with what few cars we encountered on the way to I-35, whose drivers proceeded to swerve around us at breakneck speed, horns blaring.

I saw only one car crashed by the side of the road, but it was a doozy. The driver had misjudged a curve and skidded off the shoulder to plow headlong into an unyielding stand of trees. The front end of the little sedan was completely smashed in, the cargo formerly on the roof scattered like tornado wreckage in the woods ahead.

Amidst the ruin, I saw the driver. He—or she, I couldn't tell—should have worn a seatbelt.

If I had wanted to, I could have looked inside the little sedan's windows as we passed, but I didn't dare. If there had been children in there, I'm not sure how I would have reacted. The sight of the driver had me breathing heavily and choking down bile as it was.

Focus on the road, I thought. *Just stay focused.*

Despite the road conditions, we managed to outrun the raging fires to the east, if only by a slim margin. The billowing ash waned in intensity, but the sky grew inexorably darker as the afternoon wore on. Toward nightfall, the gray-shrouded road became almost indistinguishable from the tainted, wind-blown air. Visibility dropped to about twenty meters, forcing us to slow to a crawl. When we finally reached the service road near Five Mile Dam Park, Dad got on the radio and called the group to a halt.

"We need to scout the way ahead before we try to cross," he said. "Blake, how far to the overpass? Over."

Blake referenced his map under the pasty yellow dome light, and said, "About two-hundred meters, little less. Over."

"I got this," Tyrel cut in. "Blake, you're with me. Caleb, come take the wheel and keep an eye on our six. Over."

Dad started to raise an argument, but cut off with a curse when Tyrel went sprinting by. Blake grabbed his carbine before jumping out and following him. As they ran, both men donned goggles and tied a scarf around their mouths to shield their eyes and airways from the suffocating fume. I did the same, then picked up my rifle and ran back to the rear Humvee.

Once outside the air-conditioned cab of Blake's tricked-out Jeep, the heat enveloped me like an ocean wave. The ambient temperature was well in excess of a hundred degrees, while the wind blowing in my face felt like standing in front of the world's biggest blow dryer. Despite the scarf around my face, the air was harsh and difficult to breath, permeated with heavy smoke. Even a respirator would have been hard-pressed to scrub it clean. By the end of the short run from the Jeep to the Humvee, my throat was raw and my lungs felt hot. I worried for Blake and Tyrel, who had farther to go and were no better protected.

A wave of coolness washed over me as I leapt inside and slammed the door. Although military Humvees do not normally have air conditioning, ours had been modified for the comfort of

BWT's clients. It was a welcome respite from the suffocating heat.

Several anxious minutes ticked by as we waited for word from Blake and Tyrel. I focused on the mirrors on both sides, looking back and forth between them every few seconds, searching for approaching headlights. The wind howled outside my windows, jostling and tugging at the Humvee, wearing my nerves thinner and thinner. Just as I was about to grab a respirator and go look for Blake and Tyrel, the radio on the dash crackled.

"The way is clear," said Blake, voice rough and strained. "Drive to the bridge; it'll be faster if you come pick us up. Over."

"Roger," Dad said. "On our way. Lauren, can you put Sophia on the radio? Over."

There was a moment of silence, then Sophia's nervous voice came on. "Yeah?"

"Sophia, honey, I need you to drive your dad's truck. Do you think you can do that for me? Over."

"Yeah, I think so." A pause, then, "Um … over."

"Have you ever driven it before? Over."

"No. He won't let me."

Dad waited for an 'over' that wasn't coming, then said, "It's an automatic, so it's just like driving a car. Be careful with the brakes, though. They'll have a little more travel than what you're used to. Over."

"Okay."

"Lauren, can you hear me? Over."

A pause. "Yes, over."

"Give Sophia one of the radios in the back seat and show her how it works. Also, make sure you wear goggles and cover your mouth before you head for the Jeep. Move as fast as you can and don't stop for anything, you hear? Over."

"I'll do that. Out."

A few seconds later, Lauren stepped down from Mike's truck and sprinted for the Jeep. I could tell by her body language she was having the same shocked reaction I had to the stifling heat and nigh-unbreathable air. In seconds, she was in the safety of the cab.

"All stations sound off if you're ready to move. Over."

Mike answered first, then Sophia, Lauren, and finally me. "Ready to go," I said. "Over."

Static. "Let's move out."

We followed Mike at a stately twenty miles an hour until the slope of the overpass loomed into view. Up to that point, thick forest had lined both sides of the road, brittle and dry from a lack of rain that year. But as we emerged onto the bridge, the trees fell away to reveal a storm of swirling cinders and dust borne along by great heaving gusts. The sky above was nearly black, only a thin, bloody crease on the horizon as evidence the sun still existed. Our headlights burned a short distance ahead, barely penetrating the gloom. As we crossed the bridge, I noticed a sickly ochre lambency struggling upward only to be swallowed by the stygian maelstrom above. The blare of thousands of horns reached my ears, followed by a thunderous cacophony of screams. For one terrifying moment, I wondered if I had died and was driving a Humvee through the gates of Hell. Then I realized what I was hearing was not the fiery gates of damnation, but the sounds of chaos on the highway below.

Brake lights cut the darkness ahead of me, forcing me to stop. A few seconds later, I saw Tyrel running toward my vehicle. "Fuckin' shit," he said, coughing as he climbed in and shut the door. "It's Dante's goddamn Inferno out there."

"I noticed."

He craned his neck to the side, trying to get a better look out the front windshield. "The hell is Joe doing?"

I leaned over but couldn't see anything. "Dunno."

"He say anything over the radio? I don't have a handheld."

"No."

Tyrel rooted around in the back and dug out a respirator and a couple of filters. BWT had always kept a ready supply of the masks on hand because of some OSHA regulation or another. Dad figured it would be wise to bring them along, considering we had a forest fire half the size of Vermont bearing down on us.

"Wait here," Tyrel said, his voice muffled by the respirator over his face. "I'll be right back." He jumped out and sprinted for the front of the convoy.

Like hell I will.

I let him get about ten steps away, then donned a respirator of my own, grabbed my rifle, and followed. Before I had gone five feet, a thought occurred to me and I stepped back into the Humvee long enough to locate a little black case I had grabbed from a shelf in BWT's armory. Inside was a night-vision rifle scope—just the thing to overcome the poor visibility caused by the firestorm. After affixing it to my rifle, I sprinted to the front of the column. Dad, Mike, Blake, and Tyrel were all standing on the narrow strip of concrete shoulder lining the side of the overpass. Mike stared down at the road below through a pair of NVGs, then handed them to my father. As I drew near, Tyrel saw me coming and gave me a hard stare. I stared back.

"I'm not a kid anymore, Ty."

He glared a moment longer, then went back to looking at the highway. Just as I was about to raise my rifle and peer through the NV scope, Dad reached over and laid a hand on the rail.

"Son, before you do that …"

"What?"

"It's bad down there, son. Real bad. And I've seen some things."

My father's expression gave me pause. I did not know much about his past, but I had done a lot of reading about the Green

132

Berets and Delta Force growing up, and if what he had faced was anything like what I read about, then him saying he had 'seen some things' was one hell of an understatement. I looked down at the pavement for a moment, watching swirls of grayish powder wind around my feet like a sea of ghosts, and made a decision.

"Whatever's happening down there," I said, "it's happening everywhere. Remember that rule you're always telling me to remember, the one from The Art of War?"

Dad nodded, a sad smile in his eyes. "Know your enemy."

I spoke softly. "Whatever is down there, Dad, that's our enemy. And if I'm going to survive this, if any of us are going to survive, we need to know what we're up against."

Dad's gaze stayed down, but he took his hand off my rifle. "Okay, son. Just remember what I told you—it's bad."

Slowly, reluctantly, I brought up the scope. At first, the magnification was set too high and I couldn't see much of anything. So I adjusted it down to 2x and looked again.

And it was a scene straight out of Hell.

Before the news feeds gave way to snowy screens and emergency advisory notices, reports came in on every network that the undead were following the highways and attacking anyone they could get their hands on. Drivers were being advised to use side roads to flee major cities, and if trapped on the highway, to abandon their vehicles and seek safety on foot. All during that time, I thought I understood the horror those people trapped on the interstates must have felt. The horns, the flaring tempers, the shouted obscenities, the fights, the helicopters overhead blaring warnings on loudspeakers, the crack and pop of gunfire, the growing crescendo of terrified cries as a hungry tsunami of the dead arrived, the fires in the distance, the acrid burn of gasoline smoke, the gut churning imminence of lethal danger they didn't understand or know how to combat. And worse, there was the knowledge that every person the undead killed did not stay dead, but rose to take their place among the exponentially multiplying army of ghouls.

I thought I knew what to expect.

I had seen it on television, after all. But there is a problem inherent with viewing violence through a pixelated screen—it is at arm's length. You watch it all from a good safe distance, affected emotionally but not viscerally. Television had everyone—including me—so used to the unreality of sit-coms and superhero shows and singing competitions and the careful editing endemic of scripted pseudo-reality TV that the sense of disconnect applied even when we knew what we were seeing was real. And in my boyish overconfidence, I thought I had looked upon the horror in all its terrible majesty and prepared myself to face it in person. I thought I could handle it.

But I learned something on that hellish afternoon when the flames roared high, and the smoke choked the air, and the sky turned black, and a great empty maw of nothingness swallowed the sun. When I saw people being torn apart, eaten alive, screaming for help. When I saw a panicked mother abandon her child, and watched that child disappear beneath a swarm of hungry infected, her piercing screams tearing at my heart and my sanity. When I saw the limp body of a toddler and his father lying side by side, ghouls burying bloody faces in their guts, snapping at the entrails in their teeth, sucking them down like errant pasta noodles. When I saw a man in a suit and tie standing on top of his car firing a pistol at the ghouls who crawled up the hood and trunk, not killing them fast enough to stop their advance.

He emptied a mag, reloaded, and counted down from fifteen in a grim, strident voice. When he got to one, he squeezed his eyes shut, put the gun to his temple, and pulled the trigger. He left a wide, bloody smear on the roof of his Mercedes as the undead dragged him to the ground.

I learned something that day, all right.

Television doesn't prepare you for shit.

FIFTEEN

Near San Marcos, Texas

When I had seen enough, I quietly handed my rifle to my father, took a few steps away, and was violently sick. When the dry heaves subsided enough so I could stand again, I felt my Dad's hand on my shoulder.

"You all right, son?"

"Do I look all right?" I snapped, shrugging him off and snatching my carbine out of his hand. "And why does everyone keep asking me that? I think the answer should be pretty fucking obvious at this point."

My father's palm cracked across the side of my head so loud the others heard it and snapped their heads to look. I stumbled back, stars dancing across my vision. Dad had hit me plenty of times in training, but never in anger, and never full-force. Oddly, I didn't mind. The pain and stun of it was a welcome distraction from the hellish scenes burning themselves into my memory. When the cobwebs cleared, I looked at my father, expecting to find him angry. Instead, he simply looked worried.

"Sorry about that," he said. "Your breathing was rapid and your pupils were dilated. Your hand shook when you took your rifle from me. Did you even notice?"

"No, I didn't."

"You were showing signs of panic, Caleb. You can't go into shock or hysterics. Not now. Not until we get to safety."

I rubbed my head where he had struck me, the hot skin raising into welts under my close-cropped hair. "Okay. Sorry, Dad."

His hand squeezed my arm. "You got your head screwed on straight now?"

I nodded, forcing the images of the carnage on the interstate to the back of my mind. "Yeah. I think so."

Dad watched me for a second, then grunted in satisfaction. He turned to the others. "We've seen enough. It's time to get moving."

The other men muttered agreements and dispersed to their vehicles. I turned to head for the rear Humvee, but Dad grabbed my elbow. "Wait," he said. "I want you to take over for Sophia. You're close to her age, so she'll probably listen to you better than the rest of us. I want you to look after her, all right?"

My heart sped up at the thought. I swallowed dryly and nodded. "Okay. I can do that."

Dad took a step closer, whispering. "I know you like her, Caleb. It's natural; she's a pretty girl. But you need to clear that shit out of your head right now, understand? We're in survival mode. Act like it."

Survival mode. That I can do. "Yes sir."

He patted me on the arm, hesitated a moment, and then pulled me into a tight hug. I hugged him back, squeezing hard.

"I love you, son," he said, his voice thick with emotion.

I had to blink a few times and clear my throat before I could speak. "I love you too, Dad."

"We're going to get through this. We'll do it together, just like we always have."

For a moment, I wondered who he was trying to convince. Pushing the thought aside, I said, "Damn right we will."

Dad stepped back, and although I could not see his mouth under the respirator, I could see his eyes. He was not smiling. "Let's get the hell out of here."

*****

Sophia gratefully surrendered the wheel.

I tried unsuccessfully not to stare at her ass while she scrambled over the center console and plopped down in the passenger's seat.

"I can't see shit out there," she said, looking at me as we drove away from the overpass. "How can you drive in this?"

"Your dad is wearing NVGs in the lead Humvee," I replied. "He can see the way ahead. I'm just following tail lights."

We were silent for a few miles as we headed south, bypassing San Marcos and eventually merging onto Highway 12. The wind-blown dust and ash gradually lessened the farther west we drove, but nightfall prevented an improvement in visibility.

Sophia sat curled in her seat next to me, knees under her chin, chewing nervously at her fingernails. I thought about asking her to put her seatbelt on, but being that we were driving less than twenty miles an hour, I didn't figure it would make much of a difference. Under other circumstances, I would have had a hard time not staring at her eyes, or hair, or the graceful curvature of her legs. But right then, just staying on the road and maintaining visual on the lights ahead of me consumed all my concentration. Nevertheless, from the corner of me eye, I noticed Sophia shooting curious glances at me as she shifted and fidgeted in her seat, broadcasting a sense of growing agitation.

"Do you have any idea where we're going?" she asked finally.

I thought for a moment, eyes narrowed. "You know what? That's a damn good question."

Our radio was in a cup holder in the center console. I picked it up and keyed the mike. "Blake, this is Caleb. Got a question for you. Over."

Static. "Roger. Go ahead."

"Where the hell are we going? Over."

It took him nearly a full minute to respond. "Well, we have a few options …"

"We're going to Canyon Lake," Dad interrupted. "An old friend of mine owns a cabin there. He gave me a key years ago, told me to use it whenever I wanted. We'll be safe there for a while."

Mike keyed in. "What about the fires? What if they catch up to us?"

Dad said, "Dale owns a cabin cruiser big enough to fit all of us. If need be, we can take it out on the lake and wait the fire out. I doubt it'll be a problem, though. There's not much to burn around this place; it's mostly sand and rocks. A few trees, but none too close to the cabin. We should be all right."

Blake spoke up. "Any objections?"

No one responded.

"All right then," he said. "Canyon Lake it is."

*****

We followed Highway 12 northwest until we came to a side road marked as Cascade Trail and took it south until it terminated at a narrow two-lane labeled Hugo Road. From there, Mike spotted a dirt two-track headed southwest, which later gave way to an open patch of bare field that ended near a small pond. Dad said we should stop and rest a few minutes, and asked Blake to find a route to the lake that avoided the main

138

highways. We could see the lights of the cars on those roadways in the distance, and it did not look as if anything was moving.

"If we go off road for about a mile eastward," Blake said over the radio, "we can pick up Estrellita Ranch Road. That'll take us to the access roads around the lake. Joe, where's this cabin we're looking for? Over."

"Look for Colleen Drive," Dad replied. "It's on the point of the first peninsula south of Comal Park."

Sophia and I waited, exchanging a quick glance in the darkness. The moon was full that night, but the soot-filled sky allowed only a fraction of silvery blue to sift down and light upon her face. I could see the curve of her cheek and a faint glimmer of red where the tail lights of my father's truck floated in her eyes.

"What?" she asked.

I realized I had been staring, blinked, and looked away. "Sorry."

"Don't be." She shifted and stared out the window, arms crossed over her knees. "Guys stare at me all the time. It's like when a boy sees a pretty face his brain falls out of his ass."

I felt my face burn, embarrassment rousing my temper. "I said I was sorry, Sophia. You're beautiful. I'm human. Sue me."

"Just don't get any ideas. You try anything, and my dad will break your neck."

I snorted. "Don't flatter yourself."

Even in the gloom, I could see the anger on her face. She started to say something else, but the radio interrupted her.

"Okay, got it." Blake said. "Route is plotted. Mike, please tell me you have a compass up there."

The big Marine keyed his radio. "Who you talkin' to? Just give me a bearing."

Blake did, and we were off. Sophia stewed in anger next to me, eyes focused out her window steadfastly refusing to look in my direction. That was fine by me. She may have been pretty, but I did not appreciate her implying I might try to do something against her will. The fact she would even think me capable of something like that knocked her down several notches in my book. Furthermore, I was willing to bet I had a better relationship with her father than she did, and Mike knew damned well I would never lay a hand on a girl without her permission. For her to threaten me with his wrath, a man I loved almost as much as my own father, rankled even worse than her accusation of being a pervert. We did not speak to each other for the rest of the ride to the lake.

At just after 2300, our little convoy turned onto Colleen Drive and rolled through the dark, silent neighborhood to Dale's cabin. Dale Forester was one of Dad's old army buddies, a man he had gone through basic training and AIT with. They had served in the same infantry unit before Dad moved on to Special Forces, and they had stayed in touch over the years, getting together at least once a summer to start drinking too early in the morning and feign interest in catching fish. Dad always brought me along, claiming it would give me a better appreciation of nature. This was a lie. He just wanted someone to fetch his beer and drive the boat when he and Dale got too drunk.

As we approached Dale's place, I searched the neighborhood around us for signs of habitation. At that time of year, there should have been at least a few people vacationing in their lake homes, not to mention retirees who lived in the area year round. But only a few driveways had cars in them, and there was nary a light to be seen. This struck me as odd until I noticed that even the streetlights were out.

Grid must be down. Good thing Dale has a generator.

At a word from my father, all the cars cut their headlights. Mike and Tyrel switched to the Humvees' blackout lights, making them practically invisible in the darkness but still allowing them to navigate easily with NVGs.

At Dad's direction, Mike pulled into the appropriate driveway and drove around to the other side of the house, out of sight of the road. The rest of us followed suit, lining up and parking near the shore of the lake. The property's sizable backyard sloped down a hill to the shoreline, not too steep, but enough to keep us hidden from the casual observer. If someone wandered into the yard, however, they would have no trouble spotting the five vehicles.

The cabin cruiser sat atop its large trailer in the backyard looking like a white beached whale. Since Canyon Lake did not allow private docks, Dad would have to drive it north to Comal Park to launch it. From there, it would be a short transit to anchor out away from the property. A dinghy near the shore would allow us to travel back and forth.

Once parked, I climbed out of the truck and had a lengthy stretch. It had been a long, grueling day, and I was exhausted. I wanted nothing more than to collapse into one of the guest beds in Dale's cabin and pass out for twelve hours. But there were things to do before I could allow myself the luxury of sleep.

"All right," Dad said, motioning everyone to gather round. "First things first: Caleb, you're on refueling detail. When you finish, reposition the cars so we can get out of here quickly if need be. Got it?"

I gave a thumbs-up. "Got it."

He turned to Blake and Tyrel. "Y'all mind helping me launch the boat?"

Tyrel grunted assent. Blake stifled a yawn and said, "Not at all."

"Mike," Dad said, "how about you fire up one of the emergency radios and see what you can pick up?"

The big man nodded tiredly. "Will do."

Dad dug his keys out of his pocket, found the one that unlocked the cabin, and held the keychain out to Lauren. "You and Sophia go inside and get some rest. We'll be along shortly."

Lauren accepted the keys, then stepped in and leaned her face against Dad's chest. "Don't be too long, okay?" she said, arms tight around him.

"I won't. I promise."

She kissed him, then walked over to me and stood on tiptoe to give me a peck on the cheek. "You be careful too, you hear?"

I nodded. "Yes ma'am."

She hugged me around the waist, her arms too thin and her shoulder blades too sharp under my hands. The hard knot of worry plaguing me since her attack had begun aching anew. It might have been my imagination, but I could swear I felt her trembling against me. I gave her a kiss on the top of her head.

"It's gonna be okay, Lauren," I said. "Dad and I will take care of you."

She looked up and gave me a weak smile. "Thank you, Caleb."

I watched her walk toward the cabin, motioning to Sophia to come with her. Sophia took a moment to shoot me a baleful glance, daring me to look away. I kept my face blank, showing nothing. When a few seconds passed and she didn't get the reaction she wanted, she rolled her eyes and stomped along behind Lauren. Mike watched the exchange and waited until Sophia was inside before walking over to me.

"Mind telling me what that was all about?" he whispered.

I looked him in the eye. "She's pretty, Mike. I got caught looking. She took offense and told me not to get any funny ideas or she'd have you break my neck."

Mike closed his eyes and rubbed at his forehead. "And what did you say to that?"

"I told her not to flatter herself."

At that point, I fully expected some kind of indignant reaction from Mike, even going so far as to brace my feet in case I had to elude his grasp. But instead, I watched his shoulders hitch as he fought down a chuckle. "You really said that to her?"

"I'm sorry, Mike. She insulted me for doing nothing worse than telling her she was beautiful. I was angry. I wasn't thinking."

He gave me a conciliatory pat on the shoulder. "And you think she's pissed at you, now, right?"

"Isn't she?"

"You don't know much about girls, do you, boy?"

Now I was confused. "What's that supposed to mean?"

This time, there was no attempt to hide the laugh. "You'll figure it out soon enough, kid. In the meantime, do what your dad says and go gas up the cars."

He grabbed an emergency radio out of his truck and then disappeared into the cabin. I stared after him, brow knitted.

What the hell is he talking about?

SIXTEEN

Canyon Lake, Texas

Dale's cabin had an open floor plan on the ground level, a two-car garage, a basement, and three bedrooms upstairs. Walking in the front door, the living room was to my right and the kitchen was to my left. An island with a countertop made of the same material as cutting boards separated the two rooms, complete with a few stools positioned under the overhang on the living room side.

Mike sat at the table, head low, thick fingers adjusting the tuner on the emergency radio. Lauren and Sophia had already gone upstairs, leaving the big Marine and me alone downstairs. I pulled up a seat next to Mike and kept quiet, listening. After a minute or two, Mike shook his head in frustration and turned off the radio.

"Anything new?" I asked.

"Not much. Most everything within fifty miles west of the Mississippi has been evacuated, but we already knew that. California is a clusterfuck, riots everywhere. Wildfires spreading from East Texas west to Baja and north to Colorado and Kansas. Been a dry year. Bad time for fires to break out."

"I heard something about Canada."

"The Canadian government closed the border. Nobody allowed in or out."

I digested that for a moment. "Anything about … you know. The infected."

Mike turned and looked at me in the gloom, exhaustion etched in the lines of his face. "Yeah. Looks like those guys your dad knew were right. There's only one way to kill 'em."

"How's that?"

Mike switched the radio back on, turned the dial a few times, and pushed it over to me. "Listen," he said.

I held my ear down close to the speaker. "…not to be treated as living people. Repeat, those infected with the revenant virus are not to be treated as living people. Once an infected person reaches the reanimation stage of infection, they will exhibit psychotic, cannibalistic behavior, and will attack anyone who comes into contact with them, including friends and family. If a member of your family becomes infected, report them to the authorities immediately. If there are no authorities available, be advised the only way to stop an infected person past the reanimation stage from attacking is to destroy their brain or sever their brain stem. Anyone bitten by an infected person will also become infected. Do not attempt to physically restrain or subdue an infected person, as this may result in bites, which will cause further spread of the contagion. This is a joint safety advisory from the Department of Defense, Federal Emergency Management Agency, and the Centers for Disease Control. Be advised, infected persons are not to be treated as living people. Repeat, those infected with the revenant virus are not to be treated-"

The transmission stopped abruptly as Mike turned it off. "Long story short," he said, "shoot 'em in the fuckin' head."

I tried unsuccessfully to repress a shudder. "This can't be real, Mike," I said. "Dead people don't come back to life."

"Listen, son," he said. "We don't know what the hell is going on with these people. Even the government hasn't figured it out yet. Maybe they're dead people, maybe they're not. Who knows? Bottom line is this: they're dangerous, and if you see one, don't hesitate to put a bullet in its head. Got it?"

I nodded quietly. Mike gave my shoulder a squeeze before standing up and stretching. "You been here before, right?"

"Yeah, 'bout every year. Why?"

"Dale keep any hooch around this place?"

I pointed to the cupboard above the stove. "Couple bottles up there. Bourbon, I think."

Mike walked over, opened the cabinet, and after a moment's consideration, took down a bottle of Buffalo Trace. "Sorry, Dale," he muttered. "Pay you back if I live."

"Glasses are over there," I said, pointing. Mike selected two tumblers, sat down next to me, and poured a couple of fingers in each glass. He pushed one in front of me.

"Drink it," he said.

I hesitated, frowning.

"What's the matter? Never had a drink before?"

"Couple times. Didn't care for it."

"What'd you have?"

"Vodka, once. Beer another time."

Mike made a disgusted noise. "Vodka is for sorority girls and beer is for pussies. Whiskey is a man's drink. Give it a try."

I picked up the glass and sniffed at it. "God, this shit smells like turpentine."

Mike laughed, his deep voice rattling in his chest. "Just don't gulp it. Little sips." He held out his glass.

I clinked mine against it, then allowed a little of the amber liquid past my lips. The flavor was surprisingly sweet, at least until I swallowed it. Then a golden burn started in the back of my throat and tore its way up through my nose and eyes. Mike chuckled as I snorted and coughed.

146

"Fuck," I sputtered. "It burns."

"That's how you know it's working." Mike tossed his drink back in a single gulp, then breathed deeply through his nose. Even though the room was dark, I could see his eyes water. A waft of alcohol-scented air blew toward me as he breathed out.

"Mmm. That's good stuff." He poured another drink.

We sat there for a while, the two of us, him putting his booze away in heavy gulps and me nursing my tumbler until it was empty. By the time I had finished, the burn didn't bother me so bad anymore and I found I actually liked the flavor. A slow, steady buzz relaxed the tension in my shoulders and back, making my eyelids droopy with weariness.

"Have another?" Mike asked, holding up the half-empty bottle.

"No, I'm good. Think I'll go lay down now."

"Okay. Get some sleep, kid. Gonna be a long day tomorrow."

I nodded as I trudged toward the stairs.

One of the guest bedrooms had a set of bunk beds on one side of the room and a single bed on the other. I doubted any of the others would want the top bunk, so I headed that way. Just beyond the doorway, I heard the sound of gentle snoring and stopped. Looking down to my right, I saw Sophia curled under the blanket in the single bed, eyes closed, mouth partially open. The sneering expression of contempt from earlier was gone, replace by the smooth, guileless innocence of sleep. It was an effort of will not to step closer and run a finger along the soft line of her cheek. I resisted, though, and took off my boots before climbing into the top bunk. It occurred to me Sophia might be angry I chose to sleep in the same room as her, but right then, I was too exhausted to care.

I managed to lever myself into the middle of the bed before the waves took me under.

*****

One of the perks of Dale's cabin was both the water heater and the stove ran off a rather large propane tank. According to an invoice on the table in the foyer, the propane supplier had been out less than two weeks ago to fill it up. As Tyrel and I made breakfast for the group, I thought longingly of the hot shower I planned to take that afternoon.

Another interesting development was Sophia's markedly increased appetite. The few other times I had broken bread with her she had eaten like a very small rabbit with severe food allergies. The next morning, however, she filled her bowl with two heaping scoops of rice and beans, grabbed a handful of tortillas, and carried her food into the living room where she plopped down on the sofa and ate alone, sullen gaze directed at the television's blank screen.

The rest of us were equally ravenous, each one sitting at either the island or the dining room table and scarfing our breakfast wordlessly. We had discovered earlier, to our pleasant surprise, the cabin still had running water. When I asked how that was possible without electricity, Blake solved the mystery. "Gravity fed," he remarked. "Gotta be a water tower nearby. Better enjoy it while we can; that tower runs empty, we're drinking lake water."

I decided to move up my timetable on the shower.

Lauren and I washed and dried the dishes after breakfast, both of us preoccupied with our own thoughts. Everyone else looked equally worried, eyes distant and puffy around the edges, hands clasped on tabletops or fidgeting absently. I got the feeling we were all waiting for someone to speak up, but no one was quite willing to be the first to do it. Finally, Dad stood up, leaned against the kitchen counter where everyone could see him, and cleared his throat.

"First thing we need to do is gather supplies," he said. I watched Blake and Tyrel nod silently while Mike merely grunted.

"From where?" Sophia asked. It was the first thing she had said all morning.

"The other houses around here," Dad replied. "The empty ones, anyway. We also need to see who our neighbors are, figure out if they're friendly or not."

"You sure that's a good idea?" Tyrel asked. "I mean, not to sound too callous, but we got enough mouths to feed as it is. Not to mention the natives might not take too kindly to us pilfering from their neighbors. Especially as they might be having the same notion."

Dad's eyes drifted to me and hardened. "Then we go armed and make it clear we're not to be fucked with."

"Joe," Lauren said.

"What?"

"We can't just go around stealing from people."

"Like hell we can't."

"Are you listening to yourself?" Lauren said. "You're talking about robbing people. That's insane. What the hell has gotten into you?"

Dad heaved a long sigh and shook his head. "Lauren, I don't think you've quite grasped the gravity of the situation."

Lauren stiffened with anger. "What's that supposed to mean?"

Dad pointed a finger at the dark orange glow pressing through a curtained window in the living room. "You see that out there? You know why it still looks like that? Because those fires we escaped yesterday are still burning, that's why. And they're not going to stop any time soon."

"The government will get everything under control, it's just a matter of-"

"No, Lauren," Dad said sadly. "They won't. We're already past the point of no return."

My stepmother's lips began to tremble. "Don't say that, Joe. You don't know that."

"Lauren," Blake cut in, "open your eyes. The eastern seaboard is gone. Do you understand that? Everything east of the Mississippi—New York, DC, Boston, all of it. Gone. No one knows where the President is. More than half of Congress and the Senate are presumed dead. Martial law has been declared nationwide, not that it's gonna do a damn bit of good. State and local governments are collapsing everywhere. What's left of the military is in full retreat, headed for Colorado Springs. We're on our own, Lauren. No one is coming to help us."

The room went still as Lauren stared at Blake, her face slowly crumbling. She had heard the same newscasts and radio announcements we had, but evidently had not absorbed the full consequence of their meaning. Like many people in the early days of the Outbreak, she simply could not wrap her head around the fact that the rule of law had broken down and it was not coming back. After a harsh stretch of silence, Lauren's shoulders began to shake and she let out a dry, choking sob.

"Honey …" Dad moved toward her, hands outstretched. Lauren slapped them away.

"DON'T TOUCH ME!" she screamed, and fled up the stairs.

I stared in shock. I had seen Lauren upset before, but never anything like that. It rattled me. I began to follow her up the stairs, but as my foot touched the first step, my dad's voice cut the air like a whip.

"Don't, Caleb."

"But Dad-"

"Trust me, son. Let her be for now. She needs some time alone."

A door slammed upstairs. "Are you sure?" I said. "I think I should try to talk to her."

Dad approached and gently led me back to my chair. "Like I said, just leave her be for a while. I'll go talk to her in a little bit."

"Okay," I muttered, not convinced.

"Mike, you stay here with the girls," Dad said. "Blake, you're with me; we'll take my truck. Tyrel, you and Caleb take Mike's Tundra. First things first, let's try to make contact with the other people in the area. I don't think there will be many of them, but we need to know their disposition regardless. ROE is best judgment, but try not to start a fight if you can avoid it. Questions?"

We all shook our heads.

"Tyrel, you and Blake know what to do. Caleb, follow Tyrel's lead and do exactly as he says. Clear?"

"Yes sir."

"Good. Let's get moving."

SEVENTEEN

Hollow Rock, Tennessee

At almost two o'clock in the morning, Miranda finally spoke up.

"Why Tyrel?" she asked.

"Huh?" Caleb replied.

"Why did your father pair you up with Tyrel? Seems to me he should have asked Mike along and left you to look after Sophia and your stepmother."

Caleb shrugged. "Objectivity."

"What do you mean?"

"Dad knew nobody would fight harder to protect Sophia— and by default, Lauren—than Mike. And if we paired up, he would spend more time worrying about me than focusing on what he was doing. That's the kind of thing that could get both of us killed. Besides, he knew I could handle myself, and I was in good hands with Tyrel."

Miranda traced her fingernails down the ridges of Caleb's abdomen, raising goosebumps on his skin. "Seems awfully … impersonal."

"Dad was a pragmatist," Caleb said defensively. "He knew how to take his emotions out of the equation and think clearly. It was the right call."

"I don't know if I could have done that."

"You don't have the training my father had."

"What about you?" Miranda asked, raising up on one elbow and looking Caleb in the eye. For once, despite the fact she wasn't wearing any clothes, he wasn't distracted by the view. "Would you have made the same decision in his place?"

It struck Caleb he had never asked himself that question. "I don't know, honestly."

Miranda leaned down and kissed his forehead. "I want to hear the rest, but I'm having trouble keeping my eyes open."

"I'm pretty tired too. I'll tell you the rest tomorrow. What I have time for, anyway."

Miranda snuggled her head in the hollow of his shoulder and breathed deeply. "I'll hold you to that."

Minutes later, Miranda's breathing slowed and she became heavy against his side. For Caleb, sleep was much longer in coming.

*****

After breakfast, seated at the little table between the kitchenette and living room amidst the trailer's 1970s era decor, Caleb asked Miranda what she wanted to do with their day together.

"If it's all the same to you," she said, "I'd just as soon stay home."

"Fine by me," Caleb replied.

One of the many things Caleb acquired during his travels with the Army was a portable solar charger, weighing less than two pounds, which could be rolled up for easy storage. It didn't generate a tremendous amount of electricity—12 volts was its max—but it was enough to charge the batteries on small devices, laptops, and tablets.

Things like iPads and smartphones, once more or less considered minor luxury items, were now one of the cheapest things a person could buy. During the Outbreak, after the grid went down, most people left their electronic devices behind. Consequently, a quick search of any abandoned home or residential neighborhood yielded a plentitude of the once-treasured items. Caleb had a sizable collection in his storage unit on the other side of town.

After he and Miranda finished eating and all the dishes were cleaned and put away, they sat together on the couch, perched an iPad on the coffee table, and watched a few episodes of *The Sopranos*. Caleb had never cared much for television, but found he didn't mind it with the warmth of Miranda next to him.

Four episodes in, Caleb declared he was hungry and went outside to start a cookfire. Miranda connected the iPad to the charger and followed him to the backyard where there was a small patio table situated beneath the shade of several tall trees. Miranda sat in a chair next to the table, feet outstretched, watching Caleb as he mixed flour with water, eggs, and dried meat while heating a non-stick skillet over a small fire.

"Be nice when Jutaro finishes repairing the grid on this side of town," Miranda said. "I'd dearly love to cook indoors again."

"It's not so bad, cooking outside," Caleb said. "Least not when the weather's nice."

They spoke no more until Caleb brought a stack of soft flatbread and beans to the table. Miranda made small talk about a few goings on around town, but Caleb only half listened. He found his thoughts wandering as he ate, long-repressed memories scuttling across his mind on needle-sharp legs. It wasn't until he finished eating that he realized Miranda had stopped talking and had been watching him thoughtfully the last few minutes.

"Sorry," Caleb said.

Miranda's mouth turned up at one corner. "Where you been, soldier?"

"Outbreak. Stayed away a long time, but it looks like I'm back for a visit."

Soft fingers settled over his knuckles. "Tell me."

"You don't mind? I mean, it's a nice day and all, and I'm leaving tomorrow."

"Caleb, there's nowhere else I would rather be, and no one else I would rather be with. Now come on, out with it."

A single nod. "All right, then."

*****

Canyon Lake, Texas

The plan had been to begin searching right away, but after walking outside and seeing the opposite side of the lake, we all stopped and stared in mute shock. Being the first one to recover, I offered to grab the big eyes from one of the Humvees and survey the area before we headed out. Dad nodded absently and waved a hand toward the vehicles, his eyes never leaving the smoke in the distance.

Canyon Lake was, at one time, a popular destination for people from San Antonio, Austin, Houston, and just about every town in between. It had everything you could want: resorts, boating, fishing, watersports, swimming, sandy beaches, golf, small family amusement parks, even helicopter tours. Any other summer, the place would have been crawling with tourists. The roadways would have been clogged with vehicles, parking on the lakefront would have been a nightmare, and boats and jet-skis would have crisscrossed the water in teeming, booze-fueled multitudes.

But by the next morning, Canyon Lake was abandoned.

The massive fires that chased us all the way from Houston reached the eastern side of the lake and spared almost nothing. The Texas hill country for thousands of acres in every direction had become a blasted hellscape. Where once had grown lush, verdant greenery, trees now stood naked and blackened over scorched sand and incinerated brush. The once-blue lake was now a sullen, metallic gray from the tons of ash fallen into it. Thousands of fish of too weak a constitution to survive the water's increased acidity floated belly up, staining the air with the pungent odor of rot. The cabin cruiser Dad and the others had anchored out last night had gone from white to the color of a cloudy winter sky.

Standing on the roof of Dale's cabin and scanning the shore with a pair of sixty-power binoculars, I saw only a dozen or so structures still standing to the east. The long rows of buildings past the shoreline—houses, condominiums, vacation rentals, resorts, country clubs, mini-golf, parks, all of it—had been reduced to piles of smoldering ash. The entire peninsula of Canyon Park was a burned-out ruin, only a few soot-covered brick and cinder-block walls remaining as mute testimony to the lake's former prosperity. The scene reminded me of old videos of Hiroshima after the bomb.

The north side of the lake didn't fare much better; the fire leapt the Guadalupe River and kept right on trucking. Somehow, though, it missed the tips of a few peninsulas on the northwestern side of the lake. I studied them, but saw no signs of life.

The western shore was mostly gone except for a thin strip of shoreline north of us just below Comal Park Road. Only two houses had cars in their driveways, less than a quarter-mile apart.

I shifted focus westward, trying to find Canyon Lake Golf Club and Biscuit Hill Bed and Breakfast, both places I had visited before with my father. The golf club and accompanying fairways may as well have never existed, and the bed and breakfast was nowhere to be found. As near as I could tell, the

156

fire had crept as close as Bridget Drive on the southern part of the peninsula, but then, by some miracle, stalled out. The fact the fire had gotten so close and we had all slept right through it gave me a case of the shivers.

On the peninsula immediately south of us, it appeared the same thing had happened to the lower half of Village View Drive. Although a good number of houses remained, I saw no more activity there than I had seen to the north. Other than those few untouched areas, not much of anything was still standing for as far as I could see.

I climbed down and gave the others my report. Dad nodded gravely and gestured back and forth between himself and Blake. "We'll check the peninsula to the north, see if there are any survivors. Tyrel, you and Caleb search this neighborhood, then head south and see what you can find."

Tyrel gave a thumbs-up. "Roger that."

"No matter what," Dad said, "we meet back here before sundown. Agreed?"

He got a round of acknowledgments. We dispersed to our vehicles.

Later that day, Dad and Blake told us how they made contact with three people in the section they searched, two of them an elderly couple in their eighties: Bob and Maureen Kennedy. According to Blake, they were happy to see friendly faces, but didn't seem terribly bothered by what was going on.

"It's a shame about those fires," Bob said. "Last week or so, damn near everyone lives around here took off like scalded dogs. Even the tourists lit out. Can't say as I blame 'em, though. Maureen and I were up all night watchin' the fires, hopin' they'd miss us. Was a little while there I thought we's gonna have to go out on the boat. But we got through it all right, thank the good Lord."

"Are you two going to be okay out here?" Blake asked. "Do you have enough food, water?"

157

"Well, as far as food goes, we both love to fish," the old man said, "and I don't mind saying we're pretty damn good at it. What you see floatin' out there ain't the tip of the iceberg. This lake's got more fish than a beach got sand. Not to mention we got a vegetable garden here in the backyard and plenty o' mason jars for cannin'. As for drinkin' water, we can always filter and boil what we need from the lake. The folks at the dam fixed it so the river can flow just fine before they left. We ought to be all right until the government can get things settled down."

Dad and Blake exchanged a glance at that, but didn't argue with the old man. Instead, they gave the couple a flare and told them to send up a signal if they needed help. Bob accepted it with a smile and said they would be sure to do that.

The man living down the street from them was a different sort entirely. Blake caught sight of him through a window moving around in his house, but he refused to answer his door. Dad used the loudspeaker connected to the CB radio in his truck to announce who he and Blake were, and that while they meant the man no harm, they intended to search the surrounding houses for supplies. At that point, an upstairs window opened and the man shouted down to them.

"What gives you the right to do that?"

Dad said, "You see any cops around here, fella?"

The man came closer to the window. He was in his late forties, bald, shaved head, several days' growth of beard on his face, pale and haggard, fleshy cheeks shot through with veins under sunken eyes. "That don't make it right."

"You're welcome to come with us," Dad said. "Load as much as you can carry and bring it back with you."

The man thought about it for a few seconds, then said, "How about you just leave the houses on this block alone? There's plenty of others to root through, and a housing development not three miles from here. If it ain't burned down, it's probably just as empty as this place."

Dad looked at Blake, who shrugged. "Don't see why not."

"Okay," Dad said. "You got a deal. I'm going to leave a flare on your porch. You run into trouble, pop it. One of us will see you, and we'll help if we can."

The man nodded. "Fair enough."

He was about to shut the window when Dad spoke up again. "Hey, you got a name?"

"Phil Cary. Nice to meet you." With that, he shut the window. Dad and Blake took it as their cue to leave.

Tyrel and I located two other holdouts, the first one only six houses down from us. He must have seen us pass by the night before because he was standing in his yard with a civilian model M-4 slung around his neck as if to make a statement. He kept his weapon low as the two of us rolled closer, but Tyrel wasn't taking any chances. He drew his pistol and held it across his lap, out of sight, barrel pointed so he could shoot the man through the door if need be.

"Morning," Tyrel greeted him.

The man inclined his head. He was tall, maybe six foot four, lean, strongly put together, graying brown hair in a tight crew cut, clean-shaven, dressed in a simple t-shirt, jeans, and sensible work boots. His alert gaze and erect posture said either ex-military or law enforcement.

"Good morning," the man replied. He took in Tyrel's dark beard and longish hair tied back under a headscarf, expression saying *not impressed*.

"Tyrel Jennings. This here's Caleb Hicks."

I leaned forward so the man could see me better and waved. He nodded to me, then shifted his attention back to Tyrel. "Name's Lance Morton. Saw you folks come in last night. Some trucks, a jeep, couple of Humvees."

Tyrel nodded. "Yep. That was us."

"What are you doing here?"

"Friend of ours knows a guy owns a cabin up here. Had a key. Figured it would be a good place to hole up for a while."

159

"What's the guy's name owns the cabin?"

"Dale Forester."

Morton seemed to relax a bit. "I know Dale. Good fella. What's his friend's name?"

"Joe Hicks."

"You don't say. Dale mentioned him a few times." Morton stepped closer to get a better look at me. "Say, you Joe Hicks' son? I seem to recognize you."

"Yes sir," I said. "We come down about once a year or so, go fishing."

"I've seen the two of you around before. Don't believe we've met."

Now that I thought about it, Morton did look vaguely familiar. "I think I might have seen you at the bait shop a time or two," I said.

"I remember that. Your father around?"

"Farther north up the lake," Tyrel said. "He'll be back sometime this afternoon.

"Where are you two headed?"

"Recon. Getting ready to round up supplies." Tyrel said it casually, as if it were the most natural thing in the world. I was worried Morton might take umbrage, but he surprised me by simply nodding.

"Figured. Was thinking about doing the same thing myself."

"You're more than welcome to come with us."

Morton shook his head. "I'm just fine on my own. If we happen to show up at the same place, should I expect trouble?"

There was no challenge in his voice, but I could feel the tension in Tyrel as he replied. "We're open to negotiation, no need to fight over things. With all these houses, seems there'll be plenty to go around."

"Agreed," Morton said. "Guess I'll be seeing you."

160

Tyrel nodded once. "Take care. Come see us sometime."

"I might do that."

We spent most of the rest of the day searching what remained of the peninsula south of us. By four in the afternoon, we had almost given up on finding anyone else alive. As we were just about to leave the last neighborhood on our part of the map, I spotted a curtain moving in an upstairs window of a house on a flat portion of the lakefront. We had tried the house before—there was a BMW sedan in the front yard—but no one answered. I pointed it out to Tyrel.

"Think we ought to try that one again?"

"Probably best to. Pull on up."

I parked the truck in the driveway and got out. Tyrel motioned me to stay put and approached the front door. He knocked several times, calling out that we had seen someone in there and just wanted to talk. Several minutes passed with no response.

"Listen," he said, irritation in his voice. "If we meant you any harm, we could have busted down the door by now. Can you just come talk to us for a minute, please?"

More time passed. Finally, Tyrel threw up his hands. "Fuck it. Can't say we didn't try."

As he was walking back to the truck, I heard the latch click on the front door and a squeak as someone pulled it open a few inches.

"Hello?"

The voice was soft, definitely female. Tyrel turned around slowly, hands upraised in a non-threatening gesture. "Hi there," he said. "Name's Tyrel. The kid over there is Caleb. We're new around here."

The door opened a little further, and I saw a slender, unmistakably feminine silhouette in the doorway. It was too dark inside the house to make out any of her features. "I'm Lola," she said. "Lola Torrance."

"Pleased to meet you, Lola Torrance," Tyrel said, putting his hands down.

Lola stepped out the rest of the way. She was petite, maybe five foot two, brown hair, glasses, early thirties, not especially pretty, but not unattractive either. She kept one hand out of sight behind the door. It probably says something about my upbringing that I could tell by the angle of her arm and the set of her shoulder she was holding a gun.

"You said you wanted to talk. So talk."

By Tyrel's body language, he also knew she was armed. Honestly, I couldn't say I blamed her. I would have done the same thing.

"We got in yesterday," Tyrel said. "We're planning to gather supplies from the empty houses in the neighborhood. Figured we'd offer you a chance to come along, take what you need."

Silence stretched for several seconds. "That's stealing," Lola said.

"No ma'am, it's harvesting. Things back east are pretty bad. Houston's gone. I doubt anyone is coming back here any time soon. No sense in letting perfectly good supplies go to waste. Seeing as you were here first, we figured you got a right to your share, but you should start gathering it pretty soon. No telling who might come through here looking for food."

Lola hesitated. I had a feeling none of what Tyrel said had occurred to her.

Peering closer, I noticed she looked exhausted. Not just road weary and sleepy like my group, but the kind of tired where your cheeks hollow out and your clothes hang loose from your bones. She obviously had not been sleeping or eating very much for a long time. As she stood watching us, her eyes clouded over with warring thoughts, apprehension written plainly on her face. Finally, she seemed to come to a decision.

"I'm going to step outside," she said. "Just so you know, I'm armed."

"I know," Tyrel said.

This gave her a moment's pause. Gingerly, she stepped out on the porch, a massive .44 magnum revolver in her hand. I almost laughed—that much gun would have broken her wrist if she had tried to shoot it.

"Do either of you have any medical training?" she asked.

Tyrel and I exchanged a glance. "We both have extensive first responder training, ma'am. Is someone injured inside?"

She nodded, her shoulders beginning to shake. When she spoke, her voice came out in a tremulous whisper. "My husband, there's something wrong with him. He's ... not right."

Tyrel stepped slowly closer. "Ma'am, we'd be glad to help, but I'm going to have to ask you to put the gun down first, okay?"

She looked at him with eyes like a hunted thing. Her hand slowly came up, offering Tyrel the gun. He plucked it gently from her grip, unloaded it, stuffed the cartridges in his pocket, and held a hand toward the house.

"Lead the way, please."

We followed her inside.

EIGHTEEN

The house must have been nice, once.

Tasteful decorations on the walls and over the fireplace, Monet and Rembrandt prints, plush expensive-looking furniture, rich cherry and rosewood coffee table and bookshelves, hardwood floors, gorgeously intricate rugs in burgundy and black, and a collection of vases that probably cost more than both the Humvees back at the cabin. People who lived on the lake were not known for being impoverished.

The house had an empty, lost feeling about it. Our feet scraped and echoed a little too loudly on the floor, the rustle of our clothes grating and garish as we entered the foyer. Empty wine bottles occupied nearly every tabletop, the redolent scent of sour grapes heavy in the air. Dust covered everything, even Lola's clothes. It looked like she had not changed them in a while. Despite the lush décor, I felt like a sane person walking into a rundown asylum.

"Perry, my husband, he's in the basement," Lola said. "I can't … I can't go back there."

"Why not?" Tyrel asked. "What's wrong with him?"

She shook her head, arms crossed tightly under her chest. "I don't know. He went to Houston last week, said he was going to find his parents and bring them back here."

"Did he?" I asked.

"No. He came back alone. Said he couldn't get to them, there was too much rioting. There was a bandage on his arm, bleeding through. I tried to get him to change it, but he acted funny about it. Wouldn't let me touch it."

"Anything else wrong with him?" Tyrel asked.

"He was upset about his parents, but otherwise, he seemed fine. Then a few hours later, he started feeling sick."

"What were his symptoms?"

"Fever, nausea, diarrhea, vomiting, runny nose, coughing. Like he all of a sudden came down with a bad case of the flu. Started shaking really bad and talking funny, kind of delirious. I wanted to drive him to the hospital, but he said that was a bad idea. Said the hospitals were overrun with those *things*."

As Lola talked, a low sinking feeling began to weigh in my stomach. I remembered the newscasts and the emergency bulletins about the infected, and what to do if someone was bitten by one of them. Tyrel and I looked at each other, and I could tell he was thinking the same thing.

"Ma'am," Tyrel said. "did your husband happen to mention how he got the wound on his arm?"

"No. I asked him, but he told me not to worry about it. Said it was nothing."

"Mrs. Torrance-"

"Lola," she interrupted. "Please, just call me Lola. Not ma'am or Mrs. Torrance. It makes me feel like an old woman."

Tyrel held up a hand in apology. "All right then, Lola. Can you tell me how your husband ended up in the basement?"

Her bottom lip began to tremble. "He sealed himself down there, said he had to do it before it was too late. Went out back and got some old boards and a hammer and nails from the tool shed. I heard him hammering, putting planks over the door. He told me where to find his gun."

At that point, she put her hands over her face, slumped to the floor, and began wailing like a child with a skinned knee. Tyrel hesitated a moment, then knelt beside her and put an arm around her shoulders. For a while, he whispered gently to her, trying to calm her down. Pity and more than a little embarrassment drove me from the room.

In the kitchen, a few steps past the doorway, I heard a sound that had not been audible from the living room. It was coming from a door on the opposite side of the kitchen next to what I assumed was the entrance to the garage. I stepped closer, straining my ears.

Thump-scraaaape. Thump-scraaaape.

"Hello?" I said, voice pitched low. When I spoke, the noise stopped abruptly.

"Hello? Mr. Torrance?" A little louder this time.

A low moan came from behind the door, making the hair on my neck stand on end. It reminded me of a sound my father once made in his sleep in the grip of a nightmare. I had been very young then, but the plaintive, agonized, un-self-conscious raggedness of it never left me.

My instincts told me to back away, but instead, I raised a hand and knocked gently. "Mr. Torrance, can you hear me?"

There was a moment of silence, then a tremendous *THUMP* that rattled the door on its hinges and sent shockwaves along the kitchen wall. Dishes rattled in a cupboard somewhere to my right. I stepped quickly back in surprise, my right heel catching the corner of a chair leg. I tried to catch my balance but wasn't fast enough and sat down hard on the ceramic tile floor. At some point, my right hand drew my pistol and leveled it at the door, but I don't remember consciously doing so. A second or two after the *THUMP*, I heard the same wailing sound as before, but louder now, anguished, enraged, and unmistakably predatory. The noise continued in ululating waves, punctuated by continued crashes against the door. *THUMP ... THUMP ... THUMP ...*

Footsteps sounded to my right. I looked over to see Tyrel standing in the doorway, rifle leveled, finger not yet on the trigger. "The fuck was that?"

I kept my aim steady on the basement door as I stood up. "I'm guessing it's Mr. Torrance."

Tyrel approached slowly, eyes wide, but not in fear. His gaze was swift and calculating, absorbing and processing information for split-second decisions. His gait was even and steady, hands firm on his carbine, the barrel steady as a rock as he walked. I had a strange moment of pity for the people he had faced in combat, or at least their families. I doubted the combatants themselves were still among the living.

Lola followed close behind him, one hand on his broad back to steady herself, cheeks streaked with tears, the skin of her face pale and sickly looking. I did not think it was a good idea for her to be in the kitchen with us, but then again, it was her house.

"What do you want to do?" I asked.

Tyrel took a couple of deep breaths, watching the door. The thumping was loud, but the door seemed to be withstanding it. He lowered his carbine and stood up straight.

"Doesn't look like he's going anywhere. Lola, is there another entrance to the basement?"

"There's a storm access on the other side of the house, but we keep it locked."

"Do you have a key?"

She walked over to a decorative set of key hooks on the wall beside the back door and came back with two keys on an aluminum ring. She held them out to Tyrel, then stopped and pulled her hand close to her chest. "What are you going to do?" she asked.

"Take a look at your husband and see if there's anything I can do for him."

"Do you think you can?" The desperate hope in her voice made my chest tighten.

"I don't know," Tyrel said. "But I can try." He held out a hand for the keys. Lola hesitated before handing them over.

"You might want to stay in the house until this is over, Lola."

She nodded and shuffled back to the living room. When she was gone, Tyrel turned to me and jerked his head toward the back door. "Come on."

The backyard was spacious, boasting a large brick patio, top-of-the-line grill, outdoor fireplace, wooden terrace strung with party lights, and a pool and a hot tub to my left. Both had a thin layer of algae across the surface along with several weeks' worth of leaves and enough ashes to color the water gray. The lawn had been left untended and un-watered, the longish grass brown and yellow interspersed with a few surviving islands of green. There was a sprinkler system, but it looked like no one had turned it on in a while. Without water, the lawn had dried and withered in the baking Texas sun. The dying lawn led down to a narrow strip of sandy beach as wide as the property, with the carefully crafted lines of something manmade. Soft waves lapped lazily at the rocks along the edge of the shore.

"Over there," Tyrel said.

I looked where he pointed and saw slanted wooden shutters butting up against the exposed portion of the house's foundation. It looked like a tornado shelter only smaller, barely enough for one person to fit through.

"Too narrow for stairs," I said. "Must have a ladder."

"Probably right." Tyrel walked over and inserted the key in the padlock holding the shutters closed. A quick twist, and he set the lock aside.

"You ready?" he asked.

I took position beside him and aimed my pistol down at the center of the entrance. "Ready."

He tossed the shutters open and stepped back, hand going to his pistol. I peered down, but couldn't see more than a few feet.

The entrance led straight down, lined on two sides with painted white cinder blocks. I reasoned we must have been standing at the corner of the basement. There was a ladder leading down, but I could only see the top four or five rungs.

From my vest, I produced a tactical light, pressed the switch, and shined the light downward. Other than dust motes and a few dead bugs, I didn't see anything. All was quiet for a few moments.

Then the shuffling began.

"You hear that?" I asked Tyrel.

"Yeah. I think he's coming our way."

We waited, feet braced, weapons aimed. The shuffling increased in volume until the top of a man's head came into view. He was tall, about my height, dark hair, a bald spot beginning to form in the back. He did not walk with the smooth rolling stride of a healthy, able-bodied person. It was not the carefully coordinated series of controlled falls that normally comprise human locomotion. His feet dragged, as if he had to keep them in contact with the floor or he would fall over. His head bobbed back in forth in jerky, unsteady movements, arms stiff at his sides, hands clasping and unclasping.

"Mr. Torrance?" I said.

His head snapped up, and for a moment, I couldn't breathe.

"Jesus, Mary and Joseph," Tyrel whispered.

His face was gray. Not pale like he hadn't had enough sun, or the light pallor of someone who is very ill, but a different color entirely. It was the gray of hurricane clouds over the Gulf of Mexico, the color of the ashes that settled on my car the day my family and I fled our home, the leaden pewter shade of oil refinery smoke arcing toward the sky. I had never seen that particular tone on a human being before, but I knew instantly what it meant. It was as though some dim, forgotten part of me remembered that color, the same as it knew to fear the night and find comfort in the brightness of the sun. If not for Tyrel standing next to me that day, I might well have turned and fled. As it was, I shifted my aim, finger tight over the trigger.

"Tyrel, wh-"

Whatever I was going to say died on my lips when the thing that was once Perry Torrance let out a shrieking, hungry wail. It was loud enough I felt it rattling in my chest. The dead man's voice went ragged as he cried out, the vocal cords in his neck rupturing from the force of the scream. No living person could ever have made a sound like that unless they were in the grip of indescribable agony. It was primal, animal, but at the same time, all too human.

Fear coursed up my spine and made my bowels clench. The urge to shoot the thing squarely between the eyes was almost overwhelming, a physical force that made my face burn and my hands tremble. I watched in horror as the man-thing slammed against the wall hard enough to dislodge a tooth. It showed no sign of pain as it scraped and clawed at the wall, desperately trying to reach us. Tyrel reached out and laid a steadying hand on my shoulder.

"Easy now, son." His calm voice cut through the panic like balm on a fresh burn. The heat in my face cooled, followed by a loosening of the tension in my arms. I took a deep breath and let it out slowly, shakily. The thing in the basement—I couldn't think of it as a person—continued to howl and scratch futilely at the wall.

"I didn't really believe it until now," Tyrel said.

"What?"

He pointed. "*That*, is not a living person. No fucking way."

"You think he's dead? Like, really dead?"

"Look at him, Caleb. You ever seen anything like that?"

I shook my head. "No. But he's up and moving, Tyrel. He couldn't do that if he were really dead."

The former SEAL holstered his pistol. "I know a way we can find out."

*****

Two lessons I learned that day:

Lesson the first: The infected are terrifyingly strong.

Lesson the second: Subduing one without breaking every bone in its body is damned near impossible.

But we managed it, sort of. The first thing we did was search the Torrance's garage until we found an old canvas duffel bag, a tennis ball, some duct tape, and a couple of bungee cords.

We duct taped a couple of trimmed saplings to the duffel bag and used it to cover Perry Torrance's head, figuring it would make it harder for him to fight us. But after forcing him backward from the ladder and descending so we were on the same level with him, he seemed to have no trouble locating us despite the fact he couldn't see us.

Next, we hit him with a classic schoolyard tackle, me hitting high and Tyrel hitting low. We managed to get him down, but the strength of the thing was enormous.

For a long time afterward, I thought the Reanimation Bacteriophage did something to human muscle to make it superhumanly strong. Later, I learned it did not. It simply eliminated the pain response, making it possible for ghouls to use a hundred percent of their strength at all times, something no living human could have done in absentia of psychotropic drugs. The human body is far stronger than people think it is, we just never realize that full potential because doing so damages tissues and muscle fibers, which causes pain, which causes us to back off. The undead do not have that problem.

I pinned Torrance to the ground by sitting on his chest and holding my rifle across his throat. One of the fundamental rules of body mechanics is if you control the head, you control the body. I managed to hold him down long enough for Tyrel to tape his ankles and knees together, but it was a near thing.

In the process, while desperately trying to keep him from sitting up, I heard the crunch of Torrance's hyoid bone giving way. I cursed, but kept my grip on the rifle. I kept expecting to hear him choking and gagging, but the only difference was his moans now came out in a disjointed rattle instead of the previous mewling. In that moment, it finally began to sink in that this man might be really, truly dead. And still moving around.

With this realization came an odd, inexplicable rage. I pressed down harder with the rifle, teeth bared, wanting nothing more in the world than to kill the thing underneath me. The sound of harsh, labored grunting came to my ears, and after a moment of dimly wondering where it was coming from, I realized it was me.

"Caleb," Tyrel said.

I spoke through clenched teeth. "What?"

"Ease down, kid. Just hold him, don't rip his head off."

I relaxed, forcing myself to breath normally. "Sorry."

Once Torrance's legs were secured, we rolled him over and forced his hands behind his back. His right shoulder popped out of socket in the process, but again, the stricken man gave no indication of discomfort.

"That is just fuckin' weird," Tyrel said as we stood up and took a few steps away.

"No shit. What now?"

Tyrel picked up the tennis ball where he had dropped it, cut a hole in two sides, and threaded a bungee cord through it so it made a makeshift ball gag. "Now comes the fun part."

I held Torrance's head as still as I could while Tyrel applied the gag. He poised the ball over the man's mouth and waited for him to open it between gnashings. When the time was right, he grasped the gag by two ends of the bungee cord and forced the tennis ball into Torrance's biting mouth. A few quick motions later, and he had secured it in place by looping the bungee cords around the head and tying them off, then double securing it with duct tape.

"Okay," Tyrel said. "Let's see if he has a pulse."

I did my best to hold Torrance still while Tyrel laid two fingers on the left side of his neck, and then the right. He repeated the process two more times, eyes closed in concentration. Finally, he sat back with a sigh.

"Anything?"

"Nothing. No pulse."

"How the hell is that possible, Ty? Look at him."

We stood up and backed away, watching the thing that was once a man thrash around, its head smacking with wet hollow thuds on the concrete floor. "I don't know," Tyrel said, voice shaken. "That's the damnedest thing I've ever seen, and I've seen some shit."

"What should we do with him?"

Tyrel mopped sweat from his forehead with a sleeve. "I guess we let Lola decide that. He's her husband, after all."

"Used to be, anyway," I said.

Tyrel glanced at me but said nothing.

NINETEEN

"I don't know what to do," Lola said.

Tyrel rubbed a hand across his beard. "Well, it's not something I can decide for you."

She stood with us in the basement staring at her husband under the harsh glare of my tac-light. Perry Torrance's milky white eyes bulged from their sockets in impotent rage, his mouth working incessantly at the tennis ball. At some point during his struggles, he had dislocated the other shoulder so that both arms now hung limply from their sockets.

"Lola," I said, "did you catch any of the news or radio reports before the grid went down?"

She looked at me with red-rimmed eyes. "Yes."

"Then you heard what the government was saying about the infected?"

"You think that's what happened to him?"

I thought, *I think it's pretty fucking obvious, lady*. But my mouth said, "I believe so. There's no other explanation."

"We checked his vitals," Tyrel added. "He has no pulse, no respiration other than when he breathes in to make that damned moan. I cut a vein to see if anything came out. His blood is like sludge, partially coagulated. You only see that in corpses, Lola. I think it's safe to say he's dead."

Her voice rose. "Then how is he still moving around like that?"

"I don't know," Tyrel replied evenly. "Even the government's best scientists can't seem to figure that part out. But he's dead, Lola. There's no doubt about it. Whatever that thing is over there," he pointed, "it's not your husband anymore."

She turned away from us and walked to a far corner of the basement. Minutes passed while Tyrel and I waited, shuffling awkwardly, unsure what we should do. Finally, she heaved a breath and faced us. "The news reports said to sever their brain stem or …"

"Destroy the brain," Tyrel finished.

"Right."

"I'm going to go inside and have a glass of wine," Lola said. "In fact, I think I'll have several. We have a collection, over a hundred bottles, some of them rare vintages. Perry loved wine, said it was an investment. That we'd leave them to our kids someday."

Her voice choked on the last sentence, hand coming up to her mouth, tears spilling over her knuckles. She looked imploringly at Tyrel. "I think I'll stay in the house until tomorrow morning," she said.

Tyrel nodded. "He'll be gone by then. We'll clean up when we're done."

"Thank you. When I first saw the two of you I thought you were here to … you know."

"We're not like that, Lola. We're not that kind of people."

"I know that, now. Will I see you in the morning?"

"Of course."

"Until then."

She climbed the ladder and left without another word. Tyrel drew his knife and started walking toward Perry Torrance. As he reached down to roll him over on his stomach, a thought occurred to me.

"Wait," I said.

"What?"

"Have the others seen one of these things yet?"

Tyrel's eyes glimmered in the dark. "No. But they should."

"Maybe we wait a while, let Lola get a few glasses in. Take care of things later, after she's asleep."

"Take the truck," Tyrel said. "I'll wait here."

"On it."

The air was cool, the afternoon sun low in the sky when I climbed out of the basement. A breeze picked up from the south, drying the sweat on my face and hands. I stood for a moment, eyes closed, mind empty until the breeze died down.

The truck was where we left it. I drove slowly through the empty streets watching brown grass, empty houses, and the leftover ashes from distant fires passing by on either side. I kept the truck pointed in the middle of the road, straddling the lanes for no better reason than I could. It was not as if I had to share the road with anyone.

Dad and Blake had already returned to Dale's cabin. They radioed me coming in, and I told them I was on my way, but I was alone. No, Tyrel is fine. We found a couple of survivors and one infected. I'll explain when I get there.

So I did.

They all went to the Torrance's lake house. Sophia did not want to, but Mike deemed it necessary she see an infected for herself. I told him to make sure she stayed no less than ten feet away. For a second there, he seemed to think I was joking. Then he caught something in my expression and clamped his mouth shut on whatever he was about to say.

They were gone for the better part of two hours. I later learned they spent some time examining Perry Torrance's reanimated corpse, tried to kill it a few different ways, and finally settled on slipping a knife into the base of its skull. Afterward, they drove the body a few blocks away, wrapped it in a tarp, and buried it deep in an abandoned back yard.

I spent that time sitting on the front porch watching the sun slide down the horizon on the western side of the continent. Clouds in the distance blazed orange, then purple-blue, then burnt scarlet, dark as blood over the corona of our nearest star. Birds took flight and bats emerged from hiding under a neon sky as I drank Dale's bourbon and wondered what the sunset looked like in California.

*****

I was in bed by the time they came back.

From the chatter I heard downstairs, Lola Torrance was falling down drunk when they returned to her house after burying her late husband. Tyrel decided she should not be alone in that condition and stayed behind to keep an eye on her. Having dealt with the drunken shenanigans of my father and Dale Forrester enough times, I did not envy him the task.

Mike volunteered to take the first watch, Blake the second, Dad the last before dawn. Blake suggested waking me up to shorten the watches, but Dad vetoed him.

"The kid's been through enough today," he said. "Let him rest."

That settled, they dispersed. I stayed still and quiet as Sophia entered the room and eased the door shut. It was night outside, but moonlight through the thin curtains gave enough illumination to see her silhouette in the dark. She sat on the bed a few minutes, saying nothing, head in her hands, legs folded beneath her. Then she stood up, took off her shirt and bra, and changed into a pair of tight mesh shorts and a clingy white tank top. I'm not proud of it, but I couldn't resist the temptation to watch.

She kept her back to me, the only part visible her left side, the moonlight painting her tan skin a pale bluish-silver. I studied the sweep of her torso and flare of hip as she raised her arms to untie her hair and let it fall down her shoulders in a deliciously tousled platinum cascade. The urge to reach out and run my fingers through it was strong, but I remained still.

It was too hot for blankets, so she covered up with a thin sheet and lay on her side, pale light outlining the valley descending her side and sweeping up over her hips. I stared and wondered how well my arm would fit in that space.

"Caleb?" she said, startling me. I waited a three-count before answering, pushing as much grogginess as I could manage into my voice.

"Yeah?"

"That guy, Perry. He was dead. Like, really dead."

"I think so, yeah."

"But he was still moving."

"Just like they said on the news, Sophia."

"It's not the same, somebody telling you something and seeing it for yourself."

"No, it isn't."

"He wanted to kill us. I could see it in his eyes."

"I saw the same thing."

"What does it mean, do you think? Dead people walking. I heard a lot of people saying it was God's judgment, the end of times, all that shit. Is it the end of the world? Like, for real, no fucking around, we're all gonna die, end of the world?"

"I don't know, Sophia. I don't think anyone does."

"So what do we do?"

"The same thing we're doing now." I rolled over so my back was to her, letting her know the conversation was over.

"We stay alive."

*****

Time passed.

Lola moved into a house down the street, saying she couldn't stand to stay in the place where her husband died. Tyrel helped her pack and drove her things to our part of the lake, helped her move in, gave her some food, a rifle, and spare ammunition. He visited her every day, sneaking off to see her whenever he could get away. If his attentions bothered her, she didn't complain to any of us about it.

Dad and Blake mapped out all the surrounding stores and housing developments. We spent most of our time scouting them, taking anything useful, and secreting it in various caches spread out around Canyon Lake. Pickings were sparse around the lake itself, but better in nearby areas the fire had missed. We gathered as much food and other supplies as we could, cleaned out Dale's garage, and packed it to the ceiling with non-perishables. The cabin had a den outfitted with old chairs and sofas and a massive coffee table meant to be a sitting room, a place of conversation, no TV. We tossed the furniture in the yard and filled the room with toilet paper, feminine hygiene products, soap, toothpaste, laundry detergent, and the entire contents of an abandoned drug store. The large supply of antibiotics, painkillers, and various other medicines seemed to grant everyone a measure of ease.

Everyone but me, that is.

Because Mike was Mike, and there was no stopping him from being Mike, he relieved every house we found of their finest booze. Nobody complained.

We saw Lance Morton a few times and gave him some antibiotics and pain medicine. He was polite, but kept his distance. A loner, that one. Dad gave him a flare, same as the other survivors around the lake, and since he lived so close, a radio as well.

"Stop by in the mornings and we'll give you fresh batteries." Dad told him.

"Where you getting the juice?" Lance asked.

"Solar panels on the cabin, on the south side, facing the back yard."

"Oh. Never seen 'em."

"You run into any trouble," Dad said, "or see any coming down the road, give us a heads up. We'll do the same for you."

"Fair enough."

Against my wishes, Dad and Mike insisted Sophia and I work together, ostensibly to thaw the ice between us. It was a mute partnership that first week, both of us throwing ourselves into work to avoid dwelling on our situation.

It went well for a while. Sophia turned out to be a more perceptive creature than I had given her credit for. She left me alone for the most part, limiting the conversation to no more than what was necessary. The hostility she had displayed when we fled Houston largely dried up, replaced by a somber, unassuming acceptance. We rode together in silence, worked mostly in silence, and when we ate meals together away from the cabin, she didn't try to engage me in conversation. But I caught her watching me sometimes when she thought I couldn't see. If I had to pin a label on what I saw on her face, I would call it curiosity.

Outwardly, I suppose I put up a convincing enough front everyone thought I was holding it together. But the truth was, between helping out with the night watch rotation, inventorying and organizing supplies, doing everyone's scut work because they were too busy or too lazy to do it themselves, and trying to play peacekeeper between my father and stepmother as the tension between them intensified, I felt stretched to my limit.

So two weeks after arriving at Canyon Lake, when Dad and the other men announced they wanted me to stay behind with Lauren and Sophia while they headed to the outskirts of San Antonio, I was less than pleased.

180

"We should have seen other refugees by now," Dad said, interrupting my protests mid-sentence. "It's not like Canyon Lake wasn't popular. Everybody and their brother knew about this place. Whatever is keeping them away, it's something we need to know about."

"Not to mention we're low on gasoline and diesel," Blake added.

Dad nodded his way. "That too. Caleb, I need you to look after the girls while we're gone. Keep your eyes peeled for strangers. Lance Morton knows where we're going. He's got a radio with a fresh battery. You run into any trouble, call him."

"You sure that's a good idea?" I asked.

"He seems like a solid guy. If we were going to have any trouble out of him, I think it would have happened already. That said, don't trust him any more than you have to."

"I won't. Listen, are you sure about this, Dad? Maybe I should go with you. Maybe leave one of the other guys behind."

He shook his head. "Another time, when I'm a little surer of things. God only knows what we're going to find out there." He gestured to my three oldest and best friends. "You've known these guys most of your life. You think you know what they're capable of, but you don't know the half of it. Something like this, I need the best I can get. You're well trained, son, but you don't have their experience. So they go and you stay and that's the end of it. Understood?"

I wanted to argue, but he had that tone of voice which brooked no dissent. I knew better than to push, so I said, "Be careful out there, old man."

He smiled then, and I realized I had not seen him smile since we arrived at the cabin. "Old man my ass. I'll run circles around you, kid."

"On a fast horse, maybe."

He punched me in the arm. "Keep your head on a swivel. We'll be back soon."

They rolled away in the Humvees, a plume of dust marking their trail. I started to think about Perry Torrance, and how many more infected just like him were out there, and the population of San Antonio, and the fires we had all nervously watched to the south, the orange glow in the night sky, the crack of distant gunfire like a miles long string of ladyfingers, and knew I had to do something to clear my head or I would jump in Blake's Jeep and follow that plume at a good safe distance until I caught up to them too far away to send me back.

So I suited up in my tactical gear, cleaned my carbine and pistol, and went on patrol around the neighborhood. Every ten minutes my watch beeped and I called the cabin to make sure everything was okay. Lauren answered each time with a simple, "We're good."

If anything had been wrong, or if she were under duress, the answer would have been "A-okay." That was the signal to hurry my ass home and be prepared to do violence.

I finished my sweep, exchanged a few polite words with Lance, and was on my way home when a *crack* and a *pop* caught my attention.

"The hell …"

It didn't sound like a gunshot. I looked in the direction of the sound and saw a bright red flare light up the sky to the north, right over Bob and Maureen's house.

I broke into a sprint.

Lauren and Sophia were standing outside when I arrived. "Lauren, get your gun," I said as I went into the kitchen looking for the keys to Blake's Jeep. "You too Sophia."

"What's going on?" Lauren asked. "Was that Bob and Maureen?"

"I think so. I'm gonna go check it out."

Sophia emerged from her bedroom clutching an M-4. Her father had spent an hour each day over the last week teaching her how to use it. She had never shown much interest in firearms until now, but was quickly gaining proficiency. "Do you want me to go with you?" she asked.

I was so surprised by the question I couldn't answer for a moment. "Uh ... no, that's all right. Stay here with Lauren. Lock the doors, stay away from the windows, and don't open the door for anyone but me. If someone starts poking around, call me on the radio. If someone tries to break in, shoot them."

Sophia nodded, eyes hardening. "All right."

"Wait," Lauren broke in, "you can't go alone, Caleb."

"I don't plan to. I'll stop by Lance's place, see if he can help."

"And if he doesn't?"

I snatched up a first aid kit, a canteen of water, and started for the door. "I'll improvise."

TWENTY

Evidently, Lance had seen the flare as well. He stood in his yard, armed and outfitted with a pistol, rifle, and MOLLE vest, waiting.

As he approached, I got a look at his sidearm. It rode in a quick draw holster, and had been so thoroughly customized I could not figure out what model it was other than it looked like a nine-millimeter. The barrel was long, fitted with a muzzle brake, the trigger and hammer were chrome whereas the rest of the gun was black, and had a reflex sight perched atop a rail. The only place I had ever seen weapons like that were at shooting competitions, the kind where people competed for serious money and wore polyester t-shirts with sponsors' trademarks on them.

He saw me coming and approached. I leaned over to the Jeep's open window and said, "I'm gonna go check on Bob and Maureen."

"I'll go with you."

I opened the door and he climbed in. Neither of us spoke as I sped north around the perimeter of the lake, only slowing down when the Kennedys' house rose into view.

"Take a left at this alley," Lance said. "We'll circle the block and approach from the back."

"Sounds good." I turned onto the street he indicated, then took another right a couple of blocks later. When we were four houses down from Bob and Maureen's place, Lance pointed at a wide expanse of yard between two houses. "Stop here."

I did, approving of the location. We were around a bend in the street, the top of the Kennedys' house just visible over their neighbors' roofs. From where we were, no one in the immediate vicinity of the Kennedys' property could spot us, allowing us to move in unseen.

After I parked, Lance hopped out and beckoned me after him. "I'll take point," he said. "Follow my lead."

Lance knew the neighborhood better than I did, so I figured it best to defer to his wisdom. We leap-frogged from house to house, one of us covering the other as he moved, until we stood in the back yard of the home immediately behind the Kennedys' place. I kept my back close to the wall as Lance crept to the corner and looked around.

"Shit," he whispered.

"What?"

He rounded on me, a finger pressed over his lips. *Quiet*, he mouthed, then beckoned me forward. He stepped behind me and pointed ahead. I raised my rifle and pied out the corner, exposing as little of my profile as I could. The Kennedys' back yard was empty, but past the front corner on the north side I saw a knot of about ten people walking slowly toward the front porch. There was a brief moment where I felt a thrill of excitement at the prospect of contacting other survivors.

Then I noticed how they moved.

It reminded me of Perry Torrance: the shuffling, lumbering gait, the stiff posture, the jerky, birdlike movements of the head, the tattered clothes, the mottled gray skin, the white-glazed eyes. From the front of the house, I heard moaning, beginning with just one, then spreading to the others like a contagion. In seconds, dozens of voices rose like a hellish chorus, pounding at my eardrums. I stood on shaky legs, the coldness in my stomach making me feel like I was falling down a mineshaft. Nervously, I turned to Lance.

Infected, I mouthed.

He leaned close. "Are you sure?"

"Gotta be," I whispered. "They're just like that Torrance guy. My Dad told you about him, right?"

He nodded. "Wasn't sure if I believed him."

"Believe it. They're real."

He stared at the shamblers, indecisive. "What do you think we should do?"

It was the first time in my life I can remember someone older than me asking for my advice. "If the Kennedys are in trouble, we have to help them."

Lance nodded. "How do you want to do it?"

I thought for a moment, weighing what I knew against how I had been trained. "Those things are not like normal people. They won't be armed, so we don't have to worry about weapons. But they're vicious, Lance. And they're strong as hell. If one gets ahold of you, it'll kill you. The only way to kill them is to destroy the brain, so don't waste bullets shooting center of mass. Go for headshots."

"Are you sure?"

"Positive." I wasn't, but it was all I had to go on at the moment. If it didn't work, we could always retreat and come up with something else.

I checked my rifle: round in the chamber, safety off, covers flipped up on the optics. Same deal for my pistol, minus the optics. Lance followed suit.

"You ready?" I asked.

He nodded. "Two-man skirmish line. You take left, I'll take right."

"All right. On three." I counted down, and then we moved.

We got halfway to the Kennedys' yard before the infected saw us. There were six of them in my line of sight around the corner of the house. I swung a few feet to the left to give Lance a better shot. He made the adjustment without even glancing in my direction.

The walking corpses looked confused for a moment. They swung their heads toward the house, then toward us, then toward the house again in unison. Under other circumstances, it might have been comical. It quickly became un-funny when they focused their ravenous gazes on the two of us and belted out ragged, throat-rending screams.

I stopped, peered through the Aimpoint scope, and centered the glowing red dot on the nose of a smallish round man who had been in his fifties or sixties when he died. Most of the meat on his chest, left arm, and upper left thigh had been eaten away, causing him to shuffle along with a limp. I let out half a breath, held it, and squeezed the trigger. The carbine bucked a little— an M-4 does not have very much recoil—and a fine red mist erupted from the back of the dead man's head.

He stiffened, shuddered in place for a few seconds, then collapsed. *Well, at least I know* that *works.*

Lance spared me a glance, then sighted down his rifle and fired a double-tap at a walking dead woman behind the man I had just shot. Rather than shudder first, she simply went limp and slumped to the ground.

Lance and I lowered our guns and looked at each other. "It worked," he said, surprise in his voice.

"Told you so." I returned my attention to the dead.

We advanced slowly, picking our shots. I missed a couple of times, but scored kills on the follow up. Although we dropped them quickly, we soon found ourselves backing up as more and more undead packed the space between the Kennedys' house and the house to our left. When it was clear we couldn't kill them fast enough to keep moving forward, we turned tail and ran about twenty yards.

It was a good thing we did because the undead on the other side of the house had circled the screened-in porch and almost had us surrounded. If I had been on my own, I'm not sure if I would have made it out of there alive. But when Lance saw the situation we were in, he slung his carbine, drew his pistol, walked within ten feet of the undead, and fired eight rounds quicker than you can count it out loud.

Pop-pop-pop-pop-pop-pop-pop-pop.

Eight undead fell, newly-carved tunnels in their skulls. For a second, all I could do was stare.

"Holy shit," I said.

Lance smiled, holstered his pistol, and waved a hand at the opening he created. "Shall we?"

We ran until we had established sufficient breathing room. "Hey," I said, tapping Lance on the shoulder. "You see that?"

I pointed up the street and two houses over. There was a two-story colonial with a second floor deck accessed by an outdoor stairway. "Might be easier if we take the high ground."

"Good thinking," Lance said, and started toward the house at a jog. Once there, we clambered up the stairs and took a moment to assess the situation.

There were far more undead than I originally thought. We had killed more than twenty of them, but three times that many slowly converged on our position, watching us as they came, outstretched hands curled into grasping claws, moans filling the air.

"We don't have much time," I said. Lance nodded grimly. After taking a moment to kick away the balcony's flimsy wooden rail, we assumed seated firing positions and started shooting.

It was harder than anticipated. All my life, I had trained to shoot center of mass; headshots were something I did for fun, just to show off. Aside from the men who attacked Lauren, I had only ever shot at paper targets, never at ambulatory human bodies. If my optics had had magnification, it would have been easier. But they didn't, so I had to make due by firing more slowly than I normally would have. Lance seemed to be having a similar difficulty.

I quickly realized the undead moved faster than their shuffling steps let on. Their gait was slow, but constant, never stopping or slowing down. It reminded me of something Tyrel had once told me about a Navy cruiser he spent a few weeks on. The average cruising speed of the ship, depending on conditions, was usually around fifteen knots, or just over 17 MPH. Which may not seem very fast, especially considering the vast distances ships have to cross, but they travel at that speed *twenty-four hours a day*. As a result, they can cover a lot of miles in a relatively short amount of time. The effect was the same with the undead.

I had reloaded once and was ten rounds into my next magazine when the horde, now reduced by half, reached the bottom of the stairwell and began climbing toward the balcony.

"This isn't good," Lance said, getting to his feet. The undead not on the stairs were now beneath the overhang where we could not get a shot at them.

"They'll bottlenose on the steps," I said. "Ever read about the battle of Thermopylae?"

Lance used the stock of his rifle to bust out the window of the door leading inside the house, then unlocked it. "If it looks like we're going to be overrun, we'll head through the house, throw whatever we can in front of the door, and try to escape on the ground level."

I gave a single nod, then drew my pistol and knelt in front of the stairs. Lance took position beside me. "I'll kneecap a few of them," I said. "Try to slow them down. You take them out when they go down; I have a feeling they'll try to crawl their way up."

"Okay."

We let them get halfway up the steps so they were at point blank range before we started firing. Lance let off four quick shots that toppled an equal number of undead down the stairs.

For a few seconds, the tumbling bodies slowed the corpses behind them, but they quickly recovered and began marching upward again. I took careful aim and destroyed the kneecaps of four more, pitching them over face first on the steps. Lance's pistol cracked four more times, and they went still.

Now we had a pileup. The undead began clambering over the mass of bodies in front of them, but their lack of coordination made them clumsy. I let Lance empty his magazine, then began firing while he reloaded.

Slowly, one by one, we exterminated them all. When we ran out of ammo for our pistols, we switched back to our rifles. By the time we were done, the stairway groaned and popped beneath the weight of all the bodies.

"Let's get off this thing before it collapses," Lance said.

We went in through the back and made our way to ground level, exiting through the front door. I almost started back toward the Jeep, then realized I had gotten so caught up killing the undead I had forgotten about Bob and Maureen. The brief moment of confusion was lost on Lance, who stood still, staring at the mess we had made.

"How many of them are there?" he asked.

"Probably about eighty or so."

He frowned at me. "No, I mean all together. Like across the nation."

I wiped a hand across the back of my neck. "The news said the whole East Coast is overrun."

"More than half the country lives on the eastern seaboard," Lance said. "There must be millions. Tens of millions."

"Or hundreds," I said.

For the first time, I saw genuine worry in Lance's eyes. "I knew things were bad, but this …"

"Come on," I said. "Let's go check on the Kennedys."

TWENTY-ONE

I knew it was hopeless when I saw the front door.

To call it smashed in does not quite do the damage justice. Shattered and brutally cast aside would be more apt.

Broken glass, bloody footprints, and expended .22 shell casings littered the floor. The infected had broken through all three windows along the front of the house, ripped down the curtains, and knocked the furniture askew. It occurred to me the moaning had been so loud I had not heard the crack of Bob's gun. By the lack of bodies on the floor, I was guessing he was not aware of the headshot rule.

Looking upstairs, I saw red streaks along the walls and the blackened outlines of several pairs of bloody feet.

"Bob?" I shouted, standing at the base of the stairs. "Maureen? You all right?"

No answer.

I looked at Lance. He pointed upward and said, "I'll take point."

I let him go ahead of me, aiming my rifle at the vectors he couldn't cover. We climbed slowly until we reached the first landing where I heard a snuffling and snorting like pigs rooting in a trough. We exchanged another glance before walking the rest of the way up.

A trail of red prints like a macabre version of an old-fashioned dance mat led to the master bedroom. Lance held up a fist for me to stop, crept to the doorway, and quickly peeked inside. His gaze lingered in the room for less than a second, then he stepped back.

I looked at him and mouthed, *Well?*

He shook his head sadly and made a slashing motion across his throat.

My shoulders sagged as I cursed silently, feeling as if someone had let the air out of me. I had only spoken with the old couple a few times, but they had struck me as warm, genuine, kind people. A few days before, I had stopped by to check in on them and Bob gave me a nine-pound catfish he caught that morning in the Guadalupe River. My dad and I battered and fried it, and it was damned good eating. I resolved afterward to stop by again soon and give them a vacuum-sealed tub of coffee as a show of appreciation. But that wasn't going to happen, now. Not today, not tomorrow, not ever.

A warm, liquid darkness swelled at the back of my vision. The lights and colors in the hallway seemed to sharpen, growing in brightness and intensity. The grip of my rifle, once smooth, now felt impossibly rough, like low-grit sandpaper. Each individual *whump-thump* of my heart sang in my ears with biting clarity. I heard my teeth grind together, felt the muscles in my jaw tense, felt the air whistling in and out of my lungs.

"Excuse me," I said as I stepped around Lance, who saw my face and took a worried step backward.

I stopped in the doorway, staring. If I had known how enduringly the memory of that moment would burn itself into my mind, I would not have gazed upon that nightmare as long as I did. I would have closed one eye, sighted across the top of my carbine, and taken six quick shots. Then I would have stepped out of the room, walked back to the Jeep, driven back to the cabin, and gotten blackout drunk.

But I didn't know, then. So I looked.

There were four of them tearing at Bob, two more on Maureen. The old couple were almost unrecognizable, faces ripped apart, clothes rent asunder, blood splashed on walls and bed sheets and standing in puddles on the carpet. The undead had opened Bob up from chest to groin and pulled out his intestines, munching on them like plump sausages. A little girl who could have been no older than ten gnawed dutifully at the flesh of his left forearm. Maureen lay face down, the two creatures astride her ripping strips of skin and muscle from her back to reveal the red-soaked curvature of ribcage beneath. After a few seconds, one of the undead—a young woman, maybe early twenties—looked up and noticed me. Sunlight from the bay window threw off golden flashes from a diamond engagement ring on her left hand, the same hand clutching a ragged, half-chewed loop of Bob's small intestine.

Her white-gray eyes locked on me, lips curled back from bloody teeth, and she let out a rattling, gargling hiss. Blood droplets and a piece of half-swallowed gore expelled from her mouth and bounced on the floor in front of her as she began to rise.

"Not today, lady." I raised my carbine and fired twice. Lance cursed behind me as the narrow confines of the house amplified the reports to ear splitting volume. I took a moment to fish a pair of earplugs from my vest, put them in, and took aim again.

The sights seemed to line up of their own accord, red dot centering over the forehead of the nearest infected. A minor flex of my index finger spattered the king-sized bed with a coat of blood and brain matter. The other four began standing, mouths open, hands reaching. I aimed and fired until only one infected remained, a teenage boy, maybe only a year or two younger than I was at the time. I calmly removed the spent magazine, inserted a new one, and raised the weapon level with the creature's face. Its eyes never left mine as I pulled the trigger and watched it fall.

I looked down at Bob and Maureen, pity and anger burning the backs of my eyes. After all they had seen, all they had lived through, all the love they had shared, all the Christmases and

Thanksgivings and weekends, the children they raised, the grandchildren they doted on, after all the years they had spent working and saving to afford this house on the lake and retire in comfort, after all that *life*, this is where it ended—on the floor of this bedroom, dying screaming in the maw of mindless monstrosities.

Putting a bullet in each of their heads was, up to that point in my life, the hardest thing I ever had to do.

There was a bathroom down the hallway. I leaned over the toilet and heaved up everything I had eaten for lunch that day. When I finished, I rinsed my mouth with water from the sink, stepped outside, and found Lance waiting for me. His expression was carefully blank.

"We should head back. Your stepmother is probably worried."

"Yeah."

We left.

*****

Lauren and Sophia tried to talk to me, but I ignored them.

The bottle of Woodford Reserve was in the cupboard where I left it. Three fingers' worth went into a tumbler, which I carried outside and sat down in one of the Adirondack chairs near the lakeshore. I sat with my eyes closed, face turned up to the afternoon sun. I heard footsteps crunch behind me as Lauren followed me to my chair.

"Caleb, what are you doing?"

I took a sip of bourbon and said nothing. The burn was a comfort against the cold, slick knot rolling in my stomach. The tastes of honey, smoke, and charred wood competed for territory on my palate. I began to understand why Mike liked this stuff so much.

"What happened back there? I heard gunfire. Are Bob and Maureen all right?"

My eyes opened when a cloud drifted over the sun, its puffy shadow casting the lake in semi-darkness. A small group of ducks swam by, squawking at one another. What was the word for a group of ducks? Gaggle? No, that was geese.

"Caleb, look at me when I'm talking to you."

But geese are only a gaggle when they're on the ground, right? I was pretty sure once they took flight they were called a skein. Why they were called one thing on the ground and something else in the air, I had no idea. Probably some scientist's idea of a joke. It bothered me I could remember what a group of geese in flight was called, but not the correct term for a gathering of ducks.

"Do I need to have a talk with your father when he gets home?"

I tossed back the rest of the bourbon in one gulp and waited for the burn to fade before speaking. "You do whatever the hell you feel like doing, Lauren. Right now, it doesn't make a good goddamn to me."

Her shocked silence was a physical thing I could feel prickling at my back. "Young man, you do *not* talk to me like that."

I stood up, rounded on her, and threw the tumbler past her head. It whipped a lock of auburn hair backward before shattering against the cabin. "I AM NOT A FUCKING CHILD!"

She went still, eyes wide with fear. I stepped closer until our faces were less than a foot away. "Ever since we got to this cabin it's been nothing but 'Caleb do this, Caleb do that.' 'Go clean the guns, Caleb.' 'Go cook dinner, Caleb.' 'Tidy up the cabin, Caleb.' 'Clean up everybody else's mess, Caleb.' 'Try to keep your father and stepmother from tearing each other's throats out, Caleb.'"

I stepped closer, only inches away now. "I am telling you, Lauren, *no more*. I am sick of this shit. I am not your employee. I am not your slave. I am not at your beck and fucking call. I will not do all the goddamn dirty work around here while everyone else pisses their pants looking for excuses to stay out of your way. I refuse to walk on eggshells around you any longer. I'm tired of playing middleman between you and Dad because you're both too goddamn immature to just talk things out like adults are supposed to. And if I kill a shitload of infected, and have to see the mutilated corpses of two people who were alive just this morning, and I want to have a drink afterward, you are hereby informed that I am no longer under any obligation to explain myself to you, or to anyone else. I've done a man's goddamn work around here, and a man's goddamn fighting, and when those two men broke into our house and tried to rape you that time, I did a man's goddamn killing. So from now on, you will damned well treat me like a man, and I don't want to hear any more of this stupid wait-till-your-father-gets-home bullshit. You're done telling me what to do. You're done treating me like I'm fucking twelve. You're done taking me for granted and ordering me around like a goddamn butler. You and everyone else. Do I make myself clear?"

Lauren stood absolutely still, tears standing in her eyes. "Caleb ..."

"Yes or no question, Lauren."

She looked down, twin streaks coursing down her face leaving glistening trails across the borderland of black circles under her eyes. "Yes, Caleb. I'm ... I'm sorry."

"I don't want to hear your apologies."

"I know Caleb. But you have to understand, it's been hard. I don't know what to do, or what to think, or-"

"Do you honestly believe you're the only one having a hard time?"

She looked up, startled.

"Do you think you're the only one scared? The only one confused? Are you fucking blind? We're all scared, Lauren. The whole goddamn world is falling apart. There are walking, flesh-eating monsters out there. Lance and I just killed damn near a hundred of them not ten minutes ago. They tore Bob and Maureen apart like dogs on a side of beef."

Her hands went up to her mouth. "Oh my God ..."

"Yes, Lauren, that's right. Bob and Maureen are dead. Those things were still feeding on them when I found them. They tore them apart, Lauren. They ate them alive. Lance and I were lucky to get out of there in one piece."

"Hey, Caleb."

I looked up to see Lance standing on the back porch and hissed in frustration at the interruption. "What?"

"Stop shouting," he said.

I blinked at him. "I'm sorry, who fucking invited you to this conversation?"

His eyes hardened. "Calm the hell down and look behind you, kid."

"What?"

He pointed at the lakeshore to the north. "Look."

I turned and looked where he indicated. At first, I didn't see anything. Then I cupped my hands around my eyes to reduce the sun's glare and saw a rippling, undulating movement against the shore in the distance. I could make out no details; it looked like someone shaking a giant blanket in the wind.

"The hell ..."

Lance stepped down from the porch, stopped beside me, and handed me a small pair of binoculars. "Here."

I glanced at him, then brought the glasses up to my eyes. After turning the dial in the middle a time or two, the picture came into focus. It took a few seconds to realize what I was looking at, and then a plug popped free from my chest, and all the anger and frustration that had possessed me just a few short moments ago drained away. In its place, a coldness started in my hands and face and spread until it engulfed my limbs and froze my thoughts.

"Holy shit," I said shakily.

"My sentiments exactly."

Lauren came over to stand on my other side. "What is it?"

I handed her the binoculars, unable to speak. Much as I had done, her eyes narrowed in confusion for a moment, then all the color drained from her face.

"They're headed our way," Lance said.

My voice came out high and weak. "Do you think they heard me?"

Lance shrugged. "I'd say it's a possibility." He started walking away. "Come on, kid. We have work to do."

Numbly, I did as he said.

TWENTY-TWO

"First thing you need to do is go find a couple of ladders," Lance said.

I looked from him standing in the front yard to Lauren biting her nails a few feet away. "Okay. Then what?"

"There's some old scrap wood in my shed, should be enough to barricade the first floor. Is there a splitting maul or a sledgehammer around here?"

"I think there's a maul in the garage."

"How about a crowbar? The bigger the better."

"Not sure. I can look."

"Please do. Be back in a few minutes."

As he walked away, a thought occurred to me. "Hey, what kind of ladder? You want like a step ladder, or a roofing ladder, or what?"

He stopped. "A step ladder is too small. Something bigger, at least ten feet."

"What are we using it for?"

"Them," he said. "Plural. We need two. I'll show you later."

I stared after him as he walked over to his house. "Ooo-kay then."

Lauren stopped biting her fingers long enough to look at me with worried eyes. "What should I do?"

I looked at her, regret scouring the inside of my chest. My father had once told me a foul temper is a coward that always searches for the easiest target. I walked closer to my stepmother and pulled her into my arms, holding her tightly. The hitching in the shoulders started after a few seconds, then came the warm dampness on my chest. "I'm sorry, Lauren."

"No, honey, you were right," she said. "I've been a useless mess. I've treated you like some kind of servant, and I've taken all my worries out on your father. You both deserve better."

"Let's just forget it, okay? We're all scared, and we've all said things we regret. It happens. The important thing is we're still here, still together. That's what matters."

I felt her nod against me.

"We have to stay focused," I went on. "We have to stay alive."

"I'm worried about Joe and the others. They should have been back by now."

"There's nothing we can do about it right now."

"I know. I hate it."

I held her at arm's length. "Listen, Lauren. Those things on the other side of the lake are coming for us. I've seen what they can do. Doors and windows won't stop them. We have to barricade them out."

"Okay." There was panic at the edges of her eyes, hazel irises darting restlessly. I remembered Dad telling me the best way to keep someone from freaking out in a bad situation is to keep them busy. Left idle, they dwell too much on the danger they're in and drive themselves crazy. Which can lead to very, very bad things.

"Listen, I need you to do something for me, all right?"

Her eyes focused. "What?"

"Go in the house, find all the nine-mil and five-five-six mags you can, and load them up. I want plenty of spares on hand just in case. Can you do that?"

She nodded.

"What about me?"

The voice made me jump. I turned around to find Sophia standing in the doorway of the cabin. "Um … I guess you can give Lauren a hand, if you want."

"Caleb," Lauren said, some of the confidence returning to her voice, "I've been married to your father for fourteen years. I haven't had your training, but I know how to load a magazine. Sophia, why don't you go with Caleb and keep an eye on him?"

I looked down at her and frowned. "I can take care of myself, Lauren."

"All the same, it won't hurt to have someone watching your back."

Sophia cut in before I could say anything else. "Sounds like a good idea."

Both of them went back inside, leaving me sputtering in the yard. A few seconds later, Sophia emerged with an M-4 and three spare magazines riding her hip on a web belt. Between her slender figure, vintage Pink Floyd t-shirt, white shorts that barely touched her upper thighs, and combat boots, the rifle and tactical gear looked garishly out of place. She noticed my appraisal and frowned.

"Don't look at me like that."

"Like what?"

"Like I just grew a dick out of my forehead."

I looked away. "Sorry."

She marched down from the porch and stopped in front of me. "Where should we start?"

"Dale's ladder isn't long enough. There's a house down the street that has one the right size, but we need two."

"So let's get that one first, then look around for another one."

"Thanks. I never would have figured that out on my own."

"Fuck you."

"When did you become so foul-mouthed?"

"Hey, you're the one who just cussed out his own stepmother."

A flush crept from my neck to my hairline. "You haven't had the day I have."

Sophia stepped closer, her expression growing serious. "Bob and Maureen, are they really …"

"Yeah. They're gone."

She studied the ground between her feet. "Was it bad?"

"Bad ain't the word, Sophia. Come on, we're wasting time."

Lance's old Chevy pickup roared to life next door as we walked down the street. Sophia had to break into a light jog to keep up with my longer stride. "Hey, what about the guy that lives down the street from the Kennedys? Phil what's-his-name."

I stopped in my tracks. "Shit. I forgot all about him."

"Did you see him at all?"

"No."

"Should we go check on him?"

I thought about the swarm of ghouls skirting the edges of the lake on their way toward the cabin. "No, there's no time. He's on his own for now."

"We can't just leave him there, not with those things around."

Her chestnut eyes met mine as I squared off with her. "You want to go after him? Be my guest. But I suggest you take more ammo with you. You're gonna need it."

The gaze burned a few degrees hotter, but I didn't look away. Finally, she let out a sigh. "Fine. I guess you're right. I just feel bad, is all."

I didn't bother with an answer. It seemed obvious to me what our priorities should be, and risking my neck any more than I already had was not at the top of the list. A few weeks ago, I might have thought differently. I might have insisted we take the Jeep and bring Phil to the cabin, even if I had to drag him kicking and screaming. But the more I accepted I was living at the end of the world, the more any sense of moral duty seemed silly. This was not some Hollywood movie—there would be no shot-in-the-arm plot twist, no last minute rescue, no helicopters and sirens and flashing lights at the end, no god in the machine. Bob and Maureen had started this day like any other, never expecting it would end for them the way it did. But death had come calling, and if I wasn't careful, it could come for me just as easily.

"We need that ladder." I said, and continued down the street.

It was blue, the fiberglass kind used by electricians, extendable to twenty feet. Sophia helped me carry it the short distance back to the cabin. "One down," she said. "Where do you want to start looking for the next one?"

I looked back the way we came. A bug flew in front of my face, buzzing furiously. "Your guess is as good as mine," I said, shooing the bug away. "Let's split up, we can cover more ground that way."

"Works for me. I'll search this side of the street."

"Fine. Yell if you find one. If I don't answer, fire a shot in the air."

The sound of hammering reached my ears on the fourth house I checked. After having no luck finding a ladder there, I returned to the street and looked back toward the cabin. Lance was nailing a piece of plywood over one of the downstairs windows.

I looked to the other side of the lake to see how much time we had. The swarm was about halfway across and closing steadily. Looking away, my eyes drifted to the cabin cruiser floating about a hundred feet from shore.

I smacked myself in the forehead.

"Why the hell didn't I think of that earlier?"

I started running back toward the cabin, but then heard a single shot echo from about ten houses down. I stopped in front of the cabin and briefly debated what to do before heading in Sophia's direction. She appeared in a yard ahead of me and waved an arm over her head. I waved back.

When I reached her, she went into the house behind her and opened the garage. A ladder nearly identical to the other one we found hung from a wall on a set of hooks. "Nice work," I said.

"Thanks. Now help me carry it."

"I don't think we'll need it, but we'll take it anyway."

"What do you mean?" she asked as we took the ladder down.

"Dale's boat."

Sophia went still. "Son of a bitch. Why didn't I think of that?"

"Probably the same reason I didn't. Come on, let's get back."

Lance worked quickly; nearly all the downstairs windows had a sheet of plywood and several two-by-sixes covering them. When we returned, he was swinging a big framing hammer with deft precision, driving each nail home with no more than three swings.

"Tell me something," I said as Sophia and I dropped the ladder on the sparse lawn. "Why are we bothering with all this? Dale's boat is right there."

"I know," Lance said. "But I don't want those things getting into your house tonight. Or mine, for that matter."

Just then, Lauren came out the back door with a wheelbarrow half full of food and half full of loaded rifle magazines. "Just in time," Lance said. "Caleb, why don't you help her roll that off the porch?"

I looked at Lauren, then back at Lance, and hooked a thumb over my shoulder toward the boat. "You could have told me that was your plan all along."

His face twitched in what on another person might have been a smile. "And rob you of the joy of figuring it out for yourself?"

"Asshole." I grabbed the front of the wheelbarrow and lifted it while Lauren came down the steps. She thanked me, then began pushing it across the yard toward the dinghy. After retrieving the outboard motor from the garage and gassing it up, I attached it to the dinghy and helped Lauren load the supplies and ammo inside. Once finished, Lauren and I pushed the little boat into the water. The motor started on the first try.

"You good, or do you need me to come with you?" I asked Lauren.

"I can handle it. Go help Lance." She motored away.

Back at the cabin, I said, "What do you want me to do with these ladders?"

"Take one of them in the house and put it on the second floor landing," he said. "Leave the other one on the porch. You find a crowbar yet?"

"Be right back." I had seen one in the garage where we found the second ladder. After retrieving it, I asked Lance what he wanted me to do with it.

"Get that splitting maul and tear out the stairs below the first landing."

I stared at him for a good ten heartbeats. "I'm sorry, you want me to do what?"

"You remember fighting those corpses on the balcony, right?"

"Yeah. So?"

"You see anything from 'em to make you think they're smart enough to climb?"

I thought about it, and shook my head. "Not really. But we don't know for sure *what* those things are capable of."

"I think they're dumb as bricks," Lance said. "How many of them did we shoot down while the others just watched? No matter how many we killed, they just kept coming. That seem like evidence of high-order intelligence to you?"

Again, I couldn't argue. "No, it doesn't."

"Well there you go. Now go on, get to work."

I couldn't think of a good reason not to, so I did. While I worked, Sophia helped Lauren cart supplies, fuel, and ammunition to the boat. Lance finished barricading the downstairs portion of the cabin but left the back door open. He placed the lumber he planned to seal it with beside the entrance, then went to his house and set to work barricading it as well.

Dismantling the stairs was surprisingly easy. After clearing away the drywall with the crowbar, I used the maul to bash apart the steps and knock over the support posts. After that, it was just a question of levering the remaining boards apart with the crowbar. In ten minutes, a ragged mess of shattered lumber lay where the first eight steps of the staircase once stood. Sophia came over and stared at my handiwork, hands on her shapely hips.

"Looks like we finally found something you're good at."

"Puts me one up on you."

"Go fuck yourself."

"Again with the language." I dropped the crowbar and started toward the back door. "If anybody asks, tell them I went up the street to get Lola."

"Are we bringing her with us?"

I stopped and looked over my shoulder. "You think we shouldn't?"

"Doesn't she have her own boat?"

"Safety in numbers, Sophia."

"That what it is?"

I faced her. "What do you mean?"

"She's pretty. You think I haven't noticed you looking at her?"

I blinked twice, mouth hanging open. "Are you kidding me?"

"Do I look like I'm kidding?"

I blinked again, still not believing what I was hearing. "I don't have time for this." I walked out the back door without another word.

Lola answered on the third round of knocking, eyes glassy. She swayed unsteadily in the doorway, trying to focus her vision and not finding much success. "Caleb?"

"Yes ma'am."

"Sumthin' I'cn do for you?" Her breath reeked of wine.

"We have a problem. A big one."

The eyes settled, coming to rest somewhere around my chin. I wondered how many of me she was seeing. "Wha' problem?"

"You should come take a look."

She stepped outside, not bothering to shut the door, weaving a drunken line across the front yard. "Wha' isit?"

I grabbed her around the shoulders to keep her from falling over. "How well can you see right now, Lola?"

"Jus' fine." She tapped her glasses.

"You see that over there?" I asked, turning her to face northward.

She looked, squinting in the distance. "S'people over there."

"Not people, Lola." She looked up at me. "Infected."

She looked again and went rigid in my arms. "Oh shit. Oh fuck, ohfuckohfuckohfuck no. We hav'ta get outta here."

She struggled, trying to run away down the street. I held her by the arm. "We're going to do that Lola, but running won't help. You see that boat down there?"

Her eyes tracked down my arm to where I pointed. "We're going to take it out and wait until they move on."

"'Kay. Cn'I come with you?"

"Yes, Lola. That's what I'm here for."

I half-carried her back to the cabin. Lauren had dragged the dinghy ashore and gone back inside to retrieve more supplies. I had Lola sit down, pushed the boat into the water, and drove her to the cabin cruiser. Getting her from the dinghy to the fantail was a bit dicey, but I managed to keep her from falling overboard.

"Just stay here," I said after pushing her onto one of the white bench seats under the deck canopy. "I'll be back in a few minutes."

"'Kay."

"Don't move."

She stretched out on the seat and closed her eyes, glasses hanging askew. "'Kay."

I pulled her glasses from her face and stowed them under the opposite bench, then went to the control panel and turned the engine over. The fresh water tank was full, which was good, and the fuel was at half, which was plenty. Once out in the deep water, all we had to do was set anchor and kill the engine. Didn't take much fuel for that. The boat had a separate generator to power the electrical system, so we would have electricity without having to run the less efficient five-liter V8 main motor.

Finished, I killed the engine, climbed back down to the dinghy, and drove ashore. Lauren and Sophia were headed toward me with a final wheelbarrow of supplies while Lance nailed the last two-by-six over the plywood covering the back door.

"Is Lola with you?" Lauren asked.

"More or less." I jumped back over the gunwale and stacked the contents of the wheelbarrow so the weight was evenly distributed. That done, I drove the women to the cruiser. This time, I tied the dinghy to the fantail cleats to make unloading it easier. When it was empty again, Lauren and Sophia went up to the forward lounge, carefully avoiding Lola, who now lay with one arm hanging from the bench, snoring loudly. I untied the dinghy and said, "Be back shortly."

Back ashore, Lance had just finished the last of his preparations. I helped him put his tools away, then waited while he gathered his weapons. Finally, we made our last trip to the cruiser and secured the dinghy astern. At the controls, Lance leaned against the captain's chair, cranked the engine, and eased the boat forward to slacken the anchor lines. When they had enough play, I used the windlass to bring them up.

"Where we headed?" I asked.

"Hundred meters or so from shore should be far enough. You know what kind of anchor this thing has?"

"Thirteen-pound plow, fourteen feet of anchor chain, couple hundred feet of line. Line and chain are both half-inch."

Lance disengaged the bow thruster and eased forward on the throttle. "Should be plenty."

He steered us straight out until he estimated we were far enough from shore, then turned north toward a pair of thin islands jutting out from a shallow cove. Five minutes of putting along at seven knots brought the nearest island about a hundred meters from our port bow.

"This spot should work just fine," Lance said. "Water's about seventy feet deep, rises pretty sharp when you get close to the island. If we have to jump ship, it'll be a close swim."

I went forward and dropped the anchor. Lance reversed the propeller and eased backward until the scope of the line was forty-five degrees from the bow. The anchor dug in firmly until we stayed put with the throttle in reverse at four knots, much stronger than the Guadalupe River's lazy current as it pushed through the lake.

"So what now?" I asked, staring at the shore. It was mid-afternoon, plenty of daylight left. To the north of the cabin, I saw the horde reach the edge of the peninsula and head straight for Colleen Drive. At best estimate, we had escaped them by about fifteen minutes.

"Now we stow the supplies," Lance said. "Not a good idea to leave them on the deck."

It was the work of less than five minutes to form a human chain, hand everything down to the galley, and stash it in cabinets and stowage compartments. The only thing left out was a case of Jameson's Irish Whiskey. "Who brought that aboard?" I asked, pointing.

"I did." Sophia grabbed a bottle. "Where are the glasses around here?"

"I don't think that's a good idea, sweetie," Lauren said. "Your father wouldn't like you drinking."

"Well, my father isn't here. So unless you wanna tie me down, I'm getting drunk." She shifted her chestnut eyes back to me. "Glasses?"

"Cabinet behind your head."

She turned and grabbed two glasses, then pointed at Lance. "What about you?"

His face didn't move, just a slight head tilt to the left. "Why not? Got nothin' better to do."

"Jesus Christ," Lauren said disgustedly, standing up to leave. "You people are unbelievable."

We watched her stomp up the ladder to the main deck and slam the door behind her. I looked over at Lance.

"Think I should go talk to her?"

"Right now? No. What's her problem, anyway?" He went to the counter and let Sophia pour him a drink.

I sighed and stared at the door. "If I knew the answer to that I wouldn't be asking for advice, Lance."

"All right then," he said, handing me two glasses. "Take this to her and set it down beside her. Don't say a word. Just sit down close by and don't look at her or speak to her. Sooner or later, she'll crack. Won't be long after that she'll pick that drink up and ask for another."

"You think?"

He shrugged. "Got nothin' to lose trying."

I took the glasses.

TWENTY-THREE

She lasted five minutes.

During that time, I gassed up the generator, switched on the radio, dialed in to the frequency Dad and the others used on their handhelds, and sent ten messages at thirty-second intervals.

No response.

Frustrated and scared, I slammed the mike down in its cradle.

"They're probably just out of range," Lauren said.

I turned to look at her. She sat with her back to the sun, outlined against a tangerine sky, legs crossed and bouncing nervously. Lola snored away on the bench behind me, oblivious.

"Yeah."

"We'll probably hear from them soon."

"I hope you're right."

Silence for a while, then she said, "This is for me, I assume?" She took the drink from the cup holder on the back of the bench and held it up to the light.

"You assume correctly."

"What the hell, maybe Sophia has the right idea." She took a sip and made a face.

"Isn't this supposed to be the good stuff?"

"I guess so. I get the impression people drink it more for the effect than the taste. Kind of like coffee." To punctuate, I drained half of mine in a single gulp. My stomach was still empty from throwing up earlier, so I felt the buzz almost immediately.

"So what do you think of her?" Lauren asked.

My eyebrows came together. "Who?"

"You know who."

I looked back at Lola. "I think she needs a therapist."

Lauren gave a slight laugh and shook her head. "That's not who I meant."

"Sophia?"

She nodded.

"She's all right, I guess. Kind of a smartass."

"I think she likes you."

I stared at her flatly. "Maybe you're the one that needs a therapist."

"Call it a woman's intuition."

I turned back in the captain's chair to stare across the bow. The second half of the drink went down the hatch easier than the first. When I could talk again, I said, "Even if she does, which I doubt very much, I've got more important things to worry about."

"We all do, Caleb. But you shouldn't let that distract you from what little pleasure there is left in life."

I watched her drain her drink, then get up from the bench. "There a stateroom on this thing?"

"Down the ladder, first door to your left."

"I'm going to take a nap. Come get me if you hear from your father."

"Will do."

She opened the door and took a few steps, then hesitated, eyes fixed on her feet, refusing to look up. "Caleb … I just want you to know I love you, and I always have. I know I'm not your real mother, but I love you as much as any woman ever loved her own flesh and blood. No matter what happens, I want you to remember that. Okay?"

Something in her tone made my stomach feel heavy and my blood run slow in my veins. "I know, Lauren. I've never doubted that for a second. You're the best mother a guy could ask for. And for the record, I love you too."

She gave a weak smile, still not looking me in the eye, and went belowdecks.

A gentle breeze blew across Canyon Lake from the east, stirring the water and sending white waves lapping at the western shore. The fabric of the canopy flapped lazily as the deck rocked slowly beneath me, a strong hint of rotten fish smell lingering in the air. I turned the empty glass in my hand and wondered why people like me hung on to life so hard when we were all destined, sooner or later, to lose our grip.

*****

It became a cycle.

Crank up the generator. Wait for the little amber light. Send out the message. Wait. Curse. Put the mike down. Turn off the generator. Stew for an hour. Repeat.

Night fell. Still no contact. Finally, I ran the generator until the batteries in the engine compartment were charged and left the receiver on. It takes a lot less power to receive a signal than to transmit one, so I felt confident the batteries would hold out overnight. That done, I sat and waited.

Lance brought me a plate of food. Chili, I think; I didn't really look at it. After the tasteless mechanical function of mastication, swallowing, and the first stages of the digestive process, I went belowdecks and deposited bowl and spoon in sink and applied the necessary rinse.

Finished, I looked around. The door to Lauren's stateroom was closed. Lance sat shirtless and sweating at the table, rifle dismantled, cleaning kit on display, hands moving with the exaggerated slowness and precision of the experienced drunk. At some point, Lola had moved to one of the fold-down cots forward of the galley and resumed sleeping it off. Sophia had changed into a bikini and sat in front of an open porthole, the evening breeze blowing over her bronze skin. My gaze lingered there for longer than I wanted it to, distracted by the sheen of sweat covering her chest and thighs. Sophia looked my way and smiled, eyes more than a little glazed.

"It's a lot cooler above decks," I announced. Lance grunted. The door to the stateroom remained closed. Lola snored.

Sophia stood up.

"Fuck it. It's hot down here."

I turned, climbed the ladder, and held the door for her. She took a hand I didn't realize I had reached out and let me help her to the main deck. There was a bottle dangling from her right hand.

"Thanks," she said as she stepped up to the forward lounge, a little extra sway in her hips. I thought about what Lauren told me and wondered if that over-emphasis of stride and flex of buttocks was for my benefit, or just something girls did when they were drunk.

I sat down in the captain's chair and watched Sophia stand on the forecastle, long hair hanging loose and blowing in the breeze. She held her arms out and turned a slow circle to let the air dry the moisture from her skin.

"God that feels better," she said. When her circuit brought her facing me, she tilted her head and held out the bottle. I held up a palm and shook my head.

"Come on," she said and walked closer, that same sway in her hips, breasts shaking slightly under the fabric of her halter top. I am firmly convinced every girl in the world stands in front of a mirror and practices that bouncing walk to maximize its brain-dimming effect on the male of the species. She stopped in front of me, arm outstretched, holding the bottle close enough to my face to read *Sine Metu*.

"I'd rather not," I said.

"What's the matter, you a lightweight?"

I frowned at her. "No, I'm just not a drunk."

"Not yet. But you will be." She giggled and took another pull from the bottle.

"You're going to feel like shit tomorrow."

"Probably." She turned and hurled the mostly-empty bottle over the side. I had to give the girl credit: she had an arm. The bottle sailed high and flipped over no less than eight times before it splashed down in the lake. I watched it float through the ripples and was about to say something about her future in professional sports when I felt a warm firmness press against one hip, then the other. When I turned my head, my view was obscured by the pebbled surface of Sophia's breasts.

"Sophia …"

"Shut up." One of her hands went behind my neck while the other pulled a string and let her bikini bottom fall away. A warm heat settled over my hips as she pressed her lips against mine, gently at first, then urgent and searching, forcing my mouth open, her soft tongue touching mine. She began to rock slowly back and forth, grinding her hips in a figure-eight.

My heart sped up until I thought it would burst. Fire roared through my veins. I ran trembling hands up Sophia's back, then down to her ass and gripped her hard. She moaned against my mouth and reached down to fumble at my belt. I broke off the kiss and closed my lips over one of her breasts, sucking, swirling my tongue. She gasped and arched her back, fingernails digging into my skin, hips grinding faster and faster. I kissed my way up to her neck and bit down gently, eliciting a small, husky gasp. Seconds later, I felt her fingers wrap around me, gliding up and down, the warm wetness between her legs achingly close.

In that moment, I had a choice to make. I knew Mike would not approve of what I was about to do, nor would my father. *Don't do this*, I told myself. *This isn't right.* But her skin was so soft, and her taste sent my mind spinning, and her hand felt like magic as she kept our mouths together and stroked. Her heat was so close, all it would take was a lift, a bit of positioning, and then a warm, delicious plunge.

I wish I could say I stopped myself. I wish I could say I pushed her away and said, *Not like this, Sophia. You're drunk. If you really want to do this, come to me sober and we'll see where it takes us.*

That would have been the smart thing to do. The honorable thing.

But that's not what happened.

*****

I awoke to the sound of static.

"Fox, this is Eagle, do you read? Over."

My head rose from the bench, swirling with grogginess. I had been in the middle of a dream, a bad one, but could not remember the details. The world around me was dim gray, a cool wind blowing over my skin, and I had something firm and warm that smelled faintly of body odor and sex wrapped in my arms. Distantly, I wondered what all this talk of foxes and eagles was about.

"Fox, this is Eagle, come in Fox. Over."

There are moments when you wake up in a strange place and nothing is clear. There is no recall. You feel disoriented, wondering where you are, how you got there, and what happened beyond the gauze of unremembered time. It is not a good feeling. Then the cobwebs clear, and you remember where you are, how you got there, and you spring up in a moderate state of panic, hand fumbling for the radio.

"Eagle, this is Fox," I said in a voice thick with sleep. "Read you loud and clear, over."

"Thank God," Blake said. "Please tell me y'all ain't in the cabin. Over."

"No, we're not. We took the boat and anchored out away from shore. Over."

"Everyone all right? Over."

"Yes. Can we stop saying *over* already?"

A chuckle. "I guess there's no harm in it."

"How are you guys?"

A silence. "We'll talk about it when we get back."

"I don't like the sound of that, amigo."

"Everything's fine."

"I know when you're lying, Blake."

A sigh. "Listen, those infected still have the cabin surrounded. We're going to try something to get them out of there. Keep an eye out, but don't approach until we give you the all clear. You copy?"

"Roger that," I said. "What are you going to do?"

"Something probably not very smart. Shouldn't take us more than an hour or so. We'll be out of range for a while, but we'll be back in touch with you as soon as we can."

"Okay. I'll let the others know."

"Thanks, kid. Talk to you soon. Out."

I hung the radio on its cradle and looked down to see Sophia staring at me.

After spending ourselves the night before, she had lain exhausted against me for a while, arms tight around my neck, her labored breath warm against my neck. Then she sat up, smiled sweetly, and told me she had wanted to do that for years. We kissed, and after a few minutes I felt a certain part of me come back to life, so I carried her to one of the wide benches where we made love again, slowly this time. Afterward, I got a blanket from belowdecks and we fell asleep to the sound of wind over water.

She reached up a hand to my cheek and smiled wanly. "My fucking head hurts."

I laughed. Not just a chuckle, but a full-bellied guffaw that brought tears to my eyes and made my stomach cramp just a bit. Sophia slapped me, but without much enthusiasm.

"You're such an asshole."

I leaned down and kissed her. She smelled of sweat and sex and the whiskey she drank the night before, but I didn't care. Something inside me, something ratcheting down with each passing day, something I knew was starting to fray at the seams, to pop its stitches, to bleed through the bandages, had finally let go. It felt good, and I didn't ever want to feel any other way. I wanted to lay on that bench with Sophia and feel her soft lips against mine and forget the whole damn rest of the world.

I was beginning to consider an encore performance when Sophia gently pushed me away. Her skin was flushed, breath coming quickly, nipples erect against my chest. "Settle down, stud. We need to wake the others."

I groaned and pulled her closer. "Do we have to? Can't we just lay here for a while?"

When she looked at me, all the sarcasm and cynical mockery she'd shown over the last few weeks was gone. There was something else in her eyes, now. Something kinder, and open,

219

and warm, and it pulled me in like a singularity consuming a star.

"Believe me, Caleb, there's nowhere I'd rather be. But this is important. My Dad is out there. Yours too."

The sun chose that instant to break the horizon, piercing the clouds and lighting Sophia's face a bright shade of honey gold. I watched the way her irises seemed suspended in that burnished glow, as if floating in amber. "You're right." My thumb traced her cheek and came to rest at the corner of her mouth. "Just one question."

"Hmm?"

"Why did you wait so long?"

TWENTY-FOUR

Hollow Rock, Tennessee

"Now I know what you meant." Miranda said.

"About what?"

"About not liking what I was going to hear."

Caleb laughed quietly. After lunch, he and Miranda had gone for a walk to Stall's tavern. They had taken a table outside and ordered two tall glasses of what Mike Stall called his Special Hard Cider. Really, it was whatever fruit juice he could get his hands on laced with grain liquor.

A few high, wispy clouds had moved in, but it was still a bright, pleasantly warm spring day—not unlike the morning Caleb had woken next to Sophia on Dale's boat. He looked across the table at Miranda, at how much she resembled Sophia, the biggest differences being Miranda's curvier body and blue eyes, and wondered if his feelings for her were just a coincidence.

"Don't tell me you've never had a boyfriend," Caleb said.

"I could, but I would be lying."

"Anybody worth mentioning?"

She shook her head, eyes fixed on her glass. "Not really."

The conversation lulled for a while, and Caleb could tell she was working her way up to something. It went through a few fits and starts, until finally she said, "So what's the big mystery here, anyway?"

Caleb frowned. "What do you mean?"

"Well … you talk about your past like you're carrying some kind of dark secret. But so far, you haven't told me anything I might not hear from any number of people. I mean, the Outbreak was brutal; it took a toll on us all. And I'm not trying to downplay what happened to you, or how awful it was. But I've heard worse. Hell, I've lived through worse."

Caleb took a long sip of eighty-proof pineapple juice and sat back in his chair. "I'm getting around to it."

"I'm not trying to rush you, I just ... you know what? I shouldn't have said anything. That was stupid. What a stupid, insensitive thing to say."

"It wasn't stupid, Miranda. Tell you the truth, I've been dragging my feet."

She reached for his hand. "Not your favorite subject, is it?"

"No. It's not."

"It's okay if you want to stop. You don't need to tell me anything else."

"I kind of do, Miranda. I need to get it out."

"I'm not going anywhere."

The server came by. Caleb ordered another round, and for the next couple of hours, he kept his voice low.

*****

Canyon Lake, Texas

Breakfast was instant grits and fried Spam.

Lauren, Lance and I washed ours down with coffee, whereas Sophia and Lola fled at the sight of food. After eating, I raided Dale's liquor cabinet, whipped up a couple of Bloody Marys, and brought them topside. The girls' spirits improved dramatically.

As the sun rose higher and a fine mist began to rise from the lake, I sat by the radio waiting in vain for it to squawk again. This lasted for the better part of a half hour, until Lola and Sophia declared the hair of the dog had eased its owner's bite enough they could endure the short transit back to the cabin. Lance eased the boat forward while I used the windlass to pull in the anchor. We motored southward.

Rounding the bend in the shoreline, our view of the street was obscured by the houses lining the waterfront. Still, I could hear the unmistakable rumble of the Humvee's engines followed by several cracks of a rifle. The infected walking aimless laps around the cabin whipped their heads in the direction of the reports, sending up an earsplitting clamor of moans.

"The heck are they doin'?" Lance muttered.

I stood beside him on the forecastle and shook my head. "No idea."

A few minutes later, the strategy became clear. The sounds of engines and gunfire grabbed the undead's attention as Dad and the others slowly led the horde away. I thought back to Perry Torrance, and how he seemed to know exactly where Tyrel and I were standing despite the fact he couldn't see us, and a light bulb came on over my head.

"It's sound," I said.

Lance turned his head. "What's that?"

"The infected. They hunt by sound."

He narrowed his eyes. "I don't follow."

"Think about it. Their eyes are glazed over with that white stuff. They probably can't see very well. Back at the Kennedys' house, they didn't notice us until we were close enough they could hear our footsteps. And look at what they're doing over there on the shore. The infected can't see the Humvee any better than we can, but they're still following it. How else could they do that?"

Lance brought a hand to his chin and watched the horde wander after the Humvees. "You know, you may be on to something."

An uneasy hour went by while we watched and worried, and the lamentations of the undead grew increasingly distant. Sophia and Lola went belowdecks to clean up while Lance and I sat by the radio, waiting. Lauren paced back and forth from the forecastle to the aft part of the main deck, chewing on her nails, muttering and cursing under her breath. Finally, a crackle of static broke the silence.

"Fox, this is Eagle. Do you copy, over."

I snatched up the handset. "Copy Eagle. Everyone okay?"

"More or less. We're en route, ETA five minutes. Don't approach yet, there's still a few infected in the neighborhood."

"Copy. Standing by."

The roar of Humvee engines approached again, followed by the staccato clamor of gunfire. Several times, the thunder of M-240s pounded the air, the last of which ended with a tremendous WHUMP that sent every bird in a hundred yard radius flapping and screeching in fear.

"Jesus," Lance said, shading his eyes as he stared at the shore. "Was that a grenade?"

"I think so." I said.

"The hell did they get a grenade?"

"Beats me."

Lauren stopped pacing. "Do you think they're all right?"

224

I picked up the handset. "Eagle, Fox. What was that explosion? Over."

A few seconds passed, then Blake answered, "Frag Grenade. Can't talk." Another voice said something else, but the hammering of a machine gun drowned it out.

The gunshots and steady thrum of 400 cubic-inch V8 turbo-diesels increased in volume until they were directly in front of the cabin. The frequency of fire slowed until nearly a minute went by with no shots at all. The engines cut off, then a few seconds later, the gun-toting silhouettes of Dad, Blake, and Mike appeared in the back yard.

"Where's Tyrel?" I wondered aloud.

The radio crackled. "Fox, Eagle. You are clear to approach. Acknowledge."

I grabbed the mike. "Copy, Eagle. On our way."

Lance took the helm and guided us in, slowing down parallel to the shore and dropping anchor a hundred feet out. The five of us climbed into the dinghy and set off for shore, leaving the supplies and spare ammo aboard the cruiser. We could always come back for it later.

I drove the dinghy to within twenty feet of the shoreline, then killed the engine and let it drift the rest of the way. When it came to rest in the sand, we all hopped out and dragged it ashore.

"Everybody all right?" Mike asked.

My heart leapt in my chest at the sight of him, my mind going back to last night. I cleared my throat and took a deep breath to steady my hands lest Mike see them shaking.

"We're all fine," Lauren answered.

Sophia ran to her father and jumped into his arms. She hugged the big Marine, kissed him on the cheek, then reared back and swatted him on the arm hard enough to raise a welt. "Where the hell have you been? I've been worried sick. You were supposed to be back yesterday afternoon. What happened?"

Mike rubbed his bicep and backed away. "Listen, sweetie, it wasn't our fault. I'll explain everything later, but right now we need to start packing."

Lauren walked up to them, Dad and Blake looking on. "What do you mean, start packing?"

"We have to leave," Mike said.

"Why?" Lola asked. "What's going on?"

"There's trouble headed our way," Mike said. "Serious trouble."

*****

"San Antonio didn't make out any better than Houston," Dad said, following Mike and I as we unloaded Tyrel from one of the Humvees. "We barely made it back alive."

"What happened to Tyrel?" I asked. He was unconscious, the left leg of his pants cut away to reveal a wide swath of bandages over his thigh.

"What does it look like?" Mike said. "He got shot."

"By who?"

"Long story."

I grunted in irritation as we carried the heavy ex-SEAL around back and up the steps. "How bad is it?"

"Not too bad. Missed the bone and the femoral artery. Painkillers knocked him out."

Lance finished prying the last nail from the plywood covering the back door just as we arrived. He lifted it out of the way and stood aside, looking on mutely as we deposited Tyrel on the sofa. Lola followed us in and pushed me out of the way so she could kneel beside him.

"Is he going to be all right," she asked, voice quavering.

"As long as the wound doesn't get infected," Blake said from behind me, "he should be fine in a few weeks."

Lola stroked Tyrel's hair out of his face, her hands slow and gentle. "Who did this to him?"

No one spoke. Dad looked around at the defenses Lance had erected and nodded to himself in approval. "We should be okay for a while," he said. "Blake, Mike, let's get something to eat. The rest of you hungry?"

We said no, explaining we had eaten already. Dad grabbed three MREs from a box in the den and tossed two of them to Blake and Mike. "So we have good news and bad news," Dad said. "The good news is we got the fuel we need, and we found out why no other refugees made it to Canyon Lake."

"Okay," Lauren said. "So what's the bad news?"

"Tyrel got shot, and there's a giant horde of infected, as well as a thousand or so troops, headed this way."

The room went silent as those of us who hadn't gone to San Antonio absorbed the news. After a long pause, I said, "So that's what Mike meant when he said we need to start packing."

Dad nodded. "Exactly."

When he didn't say anything else for a while, Sophia raised her hand as though she were in a classroom. "So … you wanna explain what happened?"

Dad peeled open his MRE, sat down on the ottoman, and laid aside his rifle. "The idea was to approach San Antonio from the north, find a vantage point, and try to get an idea what was going on in the city. Maybe swing around south to Lackland Air Force Base, see what was left."

He opened a brown mil-spec pouch of five-year-old spaghetti and meatballs and dug in with a plastic spoon. "We didn't get very far."

TWENTY-FIVE

It took him ten minutes to explain.

They had headed south, intent on entering the city limits by paralleling Highway 281. There were infected in the distance, but the highway was strangely clear, abandoned cars pushed to the shoulder as if by a giant hand. In a few places, evenly slotted lines pitted the pavement, indicating someone had used bulldozers to move the cars aside.

Somewhere near the junction of 281 and the 46 loop north of San Antonio, they topped a rise and saw what looked like a roadblock up ahead. Even as far away as they were, they could hear gunfire and the unmistakable thunder of tanks and artillery. Helicopters patrolled in the distance, occasionally opening up with machine guns and rocket fire.

To be safe, they backtracked, found a water tower, and sent Blake up with his massive binoculars. A short time later, he climbed down and said the roadblock was military, and extended as far as he could see. Scattered hordes of infected were approaching from the south, obscured in the distance by the hazy smoke of the burning city beyond. He couldn't tell how many there were, but the piles of dead bodies just past the highway were enormous.

Earthmovers crisscrossed the open ground beyond the barricades pushing corpses into heaps for a small army of dump trucks to haul away. On both sides of the highway, there were earthen berms piled twenty feet high, telephone poles and fence posts and shattered remnants of cars jutting out from the hastily dug earth. Most of the fighting was happening to the south, but a few smaller hordes were filtering in from the east and west. To the north, the direction Dad was coming from, things looked clear. But there were thick clusters of trees and scattered buildings between the water tower and the roadblock. Anything could be waiting there.

At that point, they had a decision to make. It would be no trouble at all to simply fill up on gas and diesel by draining fuel from abandoned vehicles along the road. Doing so would give them what they needed without taking any unnecessary risks. But a large military force might also have information about what was going on with the rest of the country, how the fight against the infected was proceeding, and if there was somewhere we could go that was safer than Canyon Lake. They decided it was worth the risk for one of them to approach the troops and see what they could learn.

Tyrel volunteered.

The other three split up in the Humvees and found positions where they could keep an eye on Tyrel without being spotted. Blake dropped him off on River Way a mile north of the junction before falling back.

Tyrel covered the remaining distance on foot, leaving behind his gear and weapons except for a knife, a pack containing a few bottles of water, and his ever-present Beretta M-9. He made it about halfway unmolested, but as he drew closer to the roadblock, the undead began to appear from doorways and storage sheds and clusters of dense foliage. At first, he simply sped up to outpace them, but the moans they sent up alerted other infected farther down the line. Ghouls began to converge from all directions, forcing him to draw his weapon and begin taking potshots. Not enough to wipe them out—he lacked sufficient ammo for that—but enough to clear a path.

As the dead become more numerous, he had to set a harder and harder pace to keep away from their grasping hands. With over a quarter mile to go before he reached the roadblock, he found himself down to his last two magazines. At that point, he turned and signaled to Mike, who had taken position a few hundred meters away on overwatch.

From a rooftop, Mike sighted through a Leupold scope mounted to his Barrett .300 Winchester magnum and started picking off infected. After four shots, he had cleared a path for Tyrel to a house on the side of the road. Tyrel sprinted for it, kicked open the front door, and disappeared inside. Moments later, he emerged with a .22 rifle and several hundred cartridges.

.22 rifles are not very powerful, but at close range, they can penetrate a ghoul's head—or a person's—with lethal results. In many cases, the bullet enters the skull but loses the necessary kinetic energy to exit the other side. As a result, it ricochets inside the brain case, effectively turning gray matter into guava paste. Tyrel used this phenomenon to his advantage as he fought his way the last few hundred yards to the berm bordering the roadblock.

The moment he topped the rise, a trio of armed soldiers riding ATVs surrounded him, guns leveled. Tyrel tossed down his weapons when ordered to do so, put his hands on his head, and went down to his knees. The soldiers quickly bound his hands and feet with zip ties, lashed him to the back of an ATV, and drove back to camp. At this point, Dad and the others lost track of him.

"We weren't sure what to do at that point," Dad said. "For a while, we just waited and watched. Kept eyes on the camp, trying to catch sight of Tyrel. After nightfall, we set up a watch rotation and switched to night vision. Blake was on watch at about three in the morning when they finally brought him out." Dad nodded in Blake's direction.

"They'd stripped him down to just his pants," Blake said, "but other than that, he didn't seem hurt. There was this fenced-in enclosure like the ones you see on prison yards where they put guys doing time in solitary. The guards put him in there with a few dozen other people. Looked like some kind of quarantine."

"The enclosure was close to the edge of camp," Dad resumed. "They'd made a restaurant across the street into a command center. We figured if we caused a disturbance there, we might be able to sneak in and get Tyrel out."

"Now, you gotta remember," Blake cut in. "This whole time, the fightin' don't stop. Helicopters flying back and forth shootin' anything that moves, artillery blowing shit up, machine gun nests goin' crazy—I'm tellin' you, man, I ain't never seen anything like it. And the whole time, you can hear the infected getting closer and closer. Not quickly, mind you, but slow, like the tide coming in. And those soldiers knew it, too. I could see it in their faces, the way they moved, the way they talked to each other. They were nervous. Scared. Like they knew they couldn't hold out much longer. Saw a bunch of 'em sneak off in the middle of the night."

"That's what tore it for us," Mike spoke up, "the deserters. We weren't about to take a chance on that place being overrun with Tyrel still in there."

Dad nodded. "So once we had a visual on Tyrel, we moved."

"First thing we did," Blake said, "we caught up with a few of those deserters. Found a couple 'bout the same size as Joe and me and took their uniforms. As you can imagine, they weren't too happy about that. Asked us what they was supposed to do to survive. I told 'em there's plenty of houses to scavenge on the way to Colorado, at least one of 'em was bound to have some clothes. Probably weapons too. In the meantime, we needed the passwords to get into the camp. We left ol' Mike behind with 'em as an insurance policy in case they gave us bad intel."

"Turned out to be unnecessary," Dad said. "The units there were ad-hoc. Mix of Marines, National Guard, Air Force, even some law enforcement types. Nobody seemed to know anybody. All we had to do was wait until the end of watch and slip in with the guys coming off duty. Walked in like we owned the place."

"Next part was easy," said Blake. "Joe climbed on top of a truck and found an empty room in the command center while I rounded up some materials and made a napalm Molotov. Waited until I was sure I couldn't be seen, then lobbed it through a window. Made a hell of a mess."

"So the alarm goes up," Dad cut in, "this fire truck comes rolling over, everybody's looking at the command center trying to figure out what happened. Blake and I work our way over to the enclosure and catch Tyrel's attention, sneak him a pair of wire-cutters. He tells us to find a vehicle and come around to the west side. So we go over to a motor pool and try to talk our way into a Humvee, but the supply sergeant isn't having it. I'll give you one guess how we handled *that* situation."

Blake chuckled. "After we dragged him behind a stack of fuel drums, we drove back to the enclosure. Tyrel, he's got these dudes standing around him in a circle all casual like while he cuts a hole in the fence. Soon as the hole's big enough, he jumps in the Humvee and we book it for the gate at Highway 281. The rest of the prisoners run for cover. When we start getting close to the gate, one of the guards sees us coming. Steps in front of us, starts yelling at us to stop. We don't, and this guy manning a fifty-cal starts swinging it our direction. I yell back to Tyrel, and he gets on the sixty and sends a few warning shots their way, just enough to make 'em keep their heads down. We bust through the gate, but by then some dudes on a guard tower start shooting at us. Tyrel returns fire, but takes one in the leg doing it."

"I didn't know why at the time," Dad said, "But they didn't bother chasing us. It wasn't until we got back to our vehicles I figured it out." He finished his spaghetti and tossed the empty packet aside.

"Turns out, just as we were leaving, the infected breached the south perimeter."

*****

I told them what happened to Bob and Maureen. Dad listened, nodding sadly at the end. "I'm sorry you had to see that, son."

"I think I should go check on Phil," I said.

He shook his head. "Too many infected between here and there. I can't let you risk it."

"I'll take Dale's boat. All I need is one person to help with the lines."

"I'll go," Sophia said, a little too quickly.

Dad glanced at her, then back at me. "Fine. Take your rifle. Clear the yard before you make landfall. If it looks too dicey, abort. I know it's a terrible thing to say, but we barely know Phil. He's not worth risking your life over."

I smiled at my father. "It's not a terrible thing to say, Dad."

He held my gaze, eyes steady. The two of us had always been on the same page for the most part, but I think it made him feel better to reaffirm it. "Don't take too long," he said. "I want us out of here in an hour. We should be ready to roll out by the time you get back."

"Don't worry," I replied. "I want to leave this place as much as you do."

"As for you," Mike said, stepping closer to Sophia. "You stay on the boat. I don't want you getting anywhere near those infected. You hear?"

She sighed and rolled her eyes. "Okay, Dad."

Mike kissed her on the cheek and gave me a hard stare. "Be careful. Look after my little girl like your life depends on it."

I watched Sophia walk toward me, a flutter in my chest and a tightening in my stomach. She stopped close enough to smell the sweat on her skin, her fingers warm and dry as she slipped them into mine.

"Count on it," I said.

No one seemed surprised.

TWENTY-SIX

"If my theory is correct," I said, "the last thing I want to do is start shooting."

Sophia eyed the crowbar in my hands as she eased off the throttle and let the boat drift closer to shore. The water was deeper here, allowing us to pull in closer than at the cabin.

"I think you're fucking crazy," she said. "No way in hell am I letting you off this boat without a rifle."

I shook my head. "It'll just slow me down. Besides, I have my pistol."

I went to the fantail and climbed down into the dinghy. After untying it, I gave Sophia a mock salute and said, "Be back in a few minutes."

"Hey," she said, crooking a finger at me. "Come here."

I rowed until the dinghy's bow was next to the fantail and stood up, putting us at eye level. When I was close enough, she grabbed me by the front of my shirt, pulled me in, and pressed her lips hard against mine. One of her hands slipped around the back of my neck, making me break out in goosebumps. After the better part of a minute, she let me come up for air. "You be careful, you hear me? I've had you less than a day. I don't want to lose you just yet."

"I'm always careful, Sophia. And for the record, you could have had me any time you wanted." I grabbed her around the waist and kissed her again, taking my time about it. When I finally let her go, her breath was coming quickly and I could feel her heart pounding against my chest.

"For the record," she said, "I'm sorry I waited."

I pointed at the rifle leaning against the control panel. "Keep that handy. If trouble shows up, don't hesitate to get the hell out of here."

"I'm not leaving without you."

"I'm serious. I can always get back to the cabin in the dinghy. Worst case scenario, I'll swim."

"You can't swim that far Caleb."

"Like hell I can't. I've swam farther in rougher waters." It was true. Tyrel insisted I learn to swim in the open ocean, namely the Gulf of Mexico. The farthest I had ever gone in one sitting was four miles.

"I told you I'm not leaving without you," Sophia said. "And I meant it."

I wanted to argue, but the look in her eyes told me it would be a waste of time. Instead, I let out a frustrated sigh, gave her one last squeeze, and got moving.

The engine was small, but loud. I did not dare crank it lest I draw a swarm of infected. It took only a minute or two to row the boat ashore. There were no infected in Phil's back yard, but I could hear their feet crunching the asphalt in the street beyond. It struck me, then, just how different the world seemed without all the background noise: the ever-present drone of cars on pavement, jetliners roaring overhead, the rattle and whir of air conditioning units, the hum of power lines and streetlights, human voices in the distance, music drifting through open windows—all of it gone, now. Replaced by the wind, the buzzing of insects, the skittering of squirrels on tree bark, birdsong, the rustling of leaves and branches, the crackle of rodents and small lizards fleeing my footsteps in the brush. It was as if God had turned down the volume on mankind and raised it on mother nature. Even the scrub grass under my feet seemed too loud as I walked across it. I found myself holding my breath, straining my ears, and walking on the sides of my feet.

Moving quickly, I traversed the yard and went up the porch steps in two big strides. Knocking would have made too much noise, so I tried the door handle. Not surprisingly, it was locked.

Now what?

Glancing around, I saw a couple of windows on the ground floor. I walked to the closest one and peered through the glass at the little bronze clasp. It was unlatched. Using the crowbar, I wedged the flat end under the sill and levered upward.

After pushing the window up and slowly releasing it to make sure it wouldn't come crashing down, I peeked inside. A living room lay in front of me, complete with sofas, bookshelves, entertainment center, and a gigantic flat-screen TV. The bottom of the window was only waist high, allowing me to place the crowbar on the carpeted floor and step inside. Once through, I slowly eased the window shut.

Now the problem was finding Phil and not eating a bullet for intruding. Shouting for him would have been the easy thing to do, but also stupid. Announcing my presence to a swarm of hungry ghouls would not do either one of us a bit of good. So I did what I always do: I fell back on my training.

Room by room, I swept the house, starting with the ground floor. At each doorway, I gave a little tap of the knuckles and whispered, "Phil, it's me, Caleb. Are you in there? I'm going to open the door. If you're armed, don't shoot."

The living room, kitchen, garage, and downstairs bathroom were all empty. Ditto for the three bedrooms and two bathrooms upstairs. After clearing the laundry room, I stood in the doorway, shoulders slumped, perplexed.

"Did he take off already?" I muttered aloud.

Back in the hallway, I looked left, then right, wondering where he might have gone. Finally, I looked up and realized there was one place I had not yet looked.

A quick tug on the string popped the trap door to the attic. I grabbed the stairs and eased them to the floor as quietly as I could. "Phil?" I said, voice pitched just above a whisper. "You up there?"

No answer.

I set the crowbar down, drew my pistol, and eased my way up the steps. Under other circumstances, I would have led with the gun. But in this case, I had come to help Phil, not shoot him. So I kept the Beretta down by my hip. It seemed like such a small decision when I made it, but like many small decisions I've made since the Outbreak, it saved my life.

When I was halfway up the steps, Phil stood up from behind a stack of cardboard boxes and raised his right hand in my direction. In his grip was a large, nickel-plated revolver.

"Stop right there," he said.

I froze. "What are you doing, Phil?"

"I could ask you the same question." His graying hair stood around his head in a frazzled halo, framing his bald pate. His clothes were stained and rumpled, looking as though he had been wearing them for several days. He hadn't shaved in a while, and I was guessing he probably hadn't bathed either. "I'm afraid you caught me at a bad time." He gestured behind me with his gun.

I turned and looked over my shoulder. The space behind me was empty of boxes, the floor covered in blue tarps tacked down with roofing nails. At the far end, a very attractive, very naked woman was bent over a metal desk, arms and legs bound with duct tape and chained to eyebolts driven into the wall. For a moment, I thought she was alive. But then I noticed the mottled gray skin and the missing gouge of flesh on her left calf muscle. She bucked and thrashed, and made inarticulate growling noises through a ball gag. Around her feet lay several used condoms and empty foil packets.

Slowly, as if my head were on a rusty hinge, I turned back to Phil. "Listen, man. What you do in your spare time is none of my business, all right?"

He shook his head, a smile beginning to stretch his mouth. "You shouldn't have come here. I'm afraid I can't let you leave, now."

My mind raced. It occurred to me Phil couldn't see my hands. If he could, he probably would have pulled the trigger already. Which meant I had one chance, but I would have to be quick.

"Phil, I don't care what you're doing here. No one does. Maybe you didn't notice, but it's pretty much the wild west out there. There's no reason not to let me just walk away."

"I'm curious," he said, as if I hadn't spoken. "What brought you here?"

"There's a giant horde of infected coming this way. Soldiers too. The Army set up a perimeter around the north side of San Antonio, but they were overrun. My father and some of the others saw it; the troops there are in full retreat. Some of them deserted. If they come this way looking for food, I doubt they'll take no for an answer."

"So you came here to warn me?"

I nodded.

"Very kind of you. Now I need you to go ahead and step on up onto those tarps over there."

"No."

The smile faltered. "I don't think you understand, kid. I'm not asking you. If you're not on that tarp in the next three seconds, I'm going to-"

"You pull that trigger," I interrupted, "and you'll bring every infected in a mile radius down on this place."

Phil shrugged. "I have enough food to last for months." He nudged a box with one of his feet. "Water too. All I have to do is pull up the ladder. Besides, I have all the entertainment I need. Now move." He waved at the tarps with the pistol, a stupid thing to do when pointing a gun at someone. *There's your chance, Caleb.*

"My family will come looking for me," I said. "Two former Green Berets, a Navy SEAL, and a Marine. They'll kill you, Phil."

Another shrug. "I think you're full of shit, kid. But even if you're right, let them try. I'll blow a hole in 'em and feed 'em to the dead."

If you only knew. I looked behind me at the reanimated corpse and faked a defeated sigh. "Fuck it. Nothing much left to live for anyway." I looked back at Phil and said, "Listen, man, before you do it, would you mind if I ... you know? Just one last time?" I hooked a thumb over my shoulder at the dead woman.

The smile on Phil's face took on a ghastly light. "I don't see why not."

I felt a familiar coldness start in my chest and spread to my hands and face.

"You're a good looking kid."

My eyes locked to the gun, the breath slowly leaving my lungs.

"I like women, mostly, but I have a thing for fit young men too."

I kept my hand loose on the Beretta, finger looped over the trigger, arm relaxed.

"You look like you're in good shape. Bet you have a great ass, nice and firm."

He took a couple of steps forward. I watched and waited.

"Maybe I'll rub one out while you fuck her. Go on, give her a go."

He waved the revolver.

There was no thinking. My eyes shifted from the gun to Phil's chest, the world going gray at the edges. The Beretta rose, a heavy black star in an empty sky, the distilled power of death over life. Five reports crashed against my ears in the small attic, deafeningly loud. Phil jerked with the impacts, eyes widening in shocked surprise. The nickel-plated revolver clattered to the ground, followed by its owner. I stood still a few seconds, gun trained on Phil's head. His eyes remained open, fat cheeks squashed to the side, his legs locking underneath him so that his buttocks protruded comically in the air. Behind me, the dead woman thrashed with renewed violence.

"Time to go, Caleb."

My hand didn't move. I counted backwards from five and let out a long breath. The gray began to fade from my vision.

"Time to go, Caleb."

The desk rattled behind me, clanking and clattering against the wall. I imagined myself in the same situation and knew without question I would not want to be left that way. So despite the danger and my collapsing timetable, I stepped the rest of the way into the attic and approached the infected woman.

Her bite on the gag was so intense her teeth had sunk into the rubber ball clear to the gum line. The muscles of her jaw stood out in striated relief, exerting pressure far in excess of what any sane living person could have managed. She craned her head over her shoulder and glared at me with wide, red-rimmed eyes.

I raised my pistol and centered the white dots on her forehead. "I guess your friends already heard me," I said. "So one more shot won't make much difference now, will it?"

TWENTY-SEVEN

My first instinct was to run out the back door and sprint for the boat. However, when I reached the bottom of the staircase, I could see a knot of at least a dozen undead blocking the way.

"Shit."

Think, Caleb.

I knew they hunted by sound. I knew the blast of my pistol attracted them. I knew they would follow that sound wherever it led. The question was how keen was their tracking ability?

With no other option, I made my way to the front door, stepped out onto the porch, and fired a shot in the air. All at once, a scattering of more than a hundred undead looked in my direction, eyes wide with inhuman hunger. One of them opened its mouth and let out a ragged *GAAUUGGGHHGGHH,* and began lurching toward me. Another followed suit, then another, and another, until in short order, they were all headed my way. From the back of the house, I heard an answering call and the sound of dragging footsteps.

"Stay calm. Stand your ground."

I waited, although every instinct screamed at me to run. There is something about the infected, some primal response in the human brain, that incites panic in even the most rational and courageous of minds. Perhaps it is the reminder of our own mortality, or the prospect of becoming one of them, or the

241

innate homo sapiens fear of being eaten. Whatever the cause, it is powerful.

They drew closer. My hands began to sweat around the pistol and the crowbar. I thought about discarding the big hunk of metal, but decided against it. If things went south, at least I knew it would not run out of ammo.

The infected from the back yard flowed around the sides of the house like sluggish lava. I thought about all the times I had gone fishing, and appreciated how the bait worms must have felt. Nonetheless, I stood still.

The closest infected was ten feet away now. It had been a woman, once. Middle aged, long graying hair, medium height and build, bare feet torn and bloody, most of the meat of her abdomen and right leg eaten away, loops of intestine dangling from a gaping black cavity where her midsection used to be, flies and maggots swarming the blackened flesh. The smell reached me and forced me to swallow hard against a throat full of bile.

I let her get to within six feet before I raised the pistol and put her out of her misery. Not because I felt particularly sorry for her, but because I wanted her dead body to form a trip hazard for the other infected walking up the steps. After she fell, I dragged her body so it laid at the most inconvenient angle possible, then ducked through the door and locked it.

Peering through a window into the back yard, I saw it was now empty. I breathed a sigh of relief and stepped outside.

And promptly pitched forward onto my face.

Something had clamped down on my ankle with the strength of a vise. I threw my hands out to catch myself, and let out a surprised *oomph* as I hit the ground. The pistol went flying off the porch, tumbling into the grass ahead of me. I managed to hang on to the crowbar.

Recovering, I looked behind me and saw something out of a nightmare.

Its legs were gone. Not all of them—the femur bones, some muscle tissue, and a few tendons and ligaments remained—but everything from the knees down had been eaten away. It was male, dark skinned, rail thin, its scalp hairless, lips curled over bloody teeth. I let out an involuntary shout and tried to kick it away to no avail. Its grip was iron, its fingers like steel cables wrapped around my ankle. With incredible strength, it dragged my foot to its mouth and bit down on the steel toe of my boot. I stared in sick fascination as its upper teeth chipped and broke away. The spell was broken when it began thrashing its head back and forth like an attack dog.

I swung the crowbar one handed, but it had no effect. The metal simply bounced off the creature's head with a dull clunk. Sitting up, I gripped the bar with both hands, took careful aim, and brought it down on the ghoul's wrist. There was a crunch, but its grip did not let up. I raised the bar and swung again, then a third time, a fourth. On the fifth swing, there was a wet snapping sound and the pressure on my leg finally released. I scrambled up, cursing and stumbling.

"Rotten sack of shit."

Already, the crawler was pulling itself across the porch, a moan rattling in its throat, mouth gaping. I stared in horror at the pure, animal need in the things eyes—eyes that had once belonged to a man with a heart, and a mind, and a soul. I felt as though I were looking upon a profound desecration, an abomination of something once sacrosanct. I would have been less affected watching someone smear shit on the ceiling of the Sistine Chapel.

The crowbar rose and fell three times, and the crawler went still.

*****

Sophia heard the gunshots, but as requested, stayed on the boat.

243

"What happened," she asked as I hopped aboard, eyeing the gore-streaked crowbar in my hand. "Where's Phil?"

"Dead."

"Dead? How?"

I tapped the Beretta in its holster. "I shot him."

"What!"

"He tried to kill me, Sophia."

Her face froze. A bloom of anger started somewhere behind her eyes and spread in a red flush until it disappeared beneath her shirt. "Why?"

I told her I only wanted to explain it once, so she would have to wait until we got back to the cabin. The others were waiting for me on the shore, evidently having heard the shots as well. There was a cacophony of questions, everyone trying to speak over one another. I waved them into silence.

And then I told them.

Lauren put her arms around me and wept and said she was sorry I had been through so much, so young. My father looked on, and I wondered how a man as strong and capable as he was could look quite so at a loss for words.

The others left us alone.

*****

We took 2673 to 306 North.

The idea was to put the lake between the soldiers and infected headed our way. Mike drove the lead Humvee, followed by Blake in his Jeep, Sophia and I in her father's truck, Dad and Lauren behind us, and Lance bringing up the rear in the other Humvee. Lola rode in the back of the rear vehicle with Tyrel across her lap, still unconscious.

We had loaded as much food, ammo, water, and medical supplies as we could into the five vehicles, but decided to leave the stolen Army Humvee behind, figuring the big fuel-guzzler would have been too much of a strain on our limited diesel supply. However, we did relieve it of its weaponry, including an M-249 SAW, a box of frag grenades, two LAW rockets, and several thousand rounds of belted 5.56mm ammunition.

"Where are we going?" Sophia asked.

I glanced out the driver's side window at the rolling hills of burned and blackened trees. They reminded me of bristles on a giant, coarse brush. "Colorado would be my guess," I said. "I overheard my dad and Tyrel talking about Pike National Forest last week. I think the idea was to lay low in Canyon Lake until things settled down, then head north."

"Would have been nice if they had disclosed that little tidbit of information."

"I'm sure they had their reasons for keeping it quiet."

"Of course they did. The wisdom of our collective parental units is incalculable."

"Hey, we're still alive, aren't we?"

I felt her gaze on the side of my face. "I don't like being kept in the dark," she said.

"I don't either, Sophia. But what else are we supposed to do?"

She was quiet for a couple of miles, then said, "I guess we don't have much of a choice but to trust him."

"Who?"

"Your father. He seems to be the one in charge."

"Only because no one else wants the job."

"Touché."

"He knows what he's doing."

"I hope so. It would really ruin my day if he got us all killed."

I turned my head and glared. "Careful. That's my father you're talking about."

The heat in my voice made her eyes go wide. "Caleb, I didn't mean …"

"Save it." I put my focus back on the road.

We didn't speak for a while after that. Miles rolled under the wheels and the ash gray expanse of Canyon Lake grew smaller to my left. I snuck a few glances at Sophia from the corner of my eye and felt the old defenses begin to weaken. I had always been touchy when it came to my father and what people had to say about him. If the tone was negative, I was quick to mine the fields and zero in the artillery and man the machine-gun nests. In most cases, it was overkill. And worse, I was sensible enough to know it.

Sophia sat with her legs folded in front of her, arms around her knees, face turned away from me. I studied the shadow under her jawline, the grace of it, the way it flowed seamlessly into the curve of long neck and delicate earlobe. Her hair was tied back, a few unbound strands falling loose along the side of her face, the tips barely touching her flawless skin. Looking at them made my hands tingle.

"Hey," I said.

She looked at me, a vulnerability in her eyes I decided I never wanted to see again. "I'm sorry."

"It's okay."

She put a hand on the center console, palm up. I covered it with mine and squeezed. "Let's not do that anymore."

"Deal."

*****

When we drew near the 306 North junction with 281, Mike ordered the convoy to a halt. "I'm gonna recon ahead, see if the way is clear. Y'all stay here, 'cept for Caleb. Acknowledge."

I hesitated a moment, then keyed my radio. "Copy. On my way."

As I walked to the lead Humvee, I kept expecting my father to raise some sort of protest, but he didn't. I glanced back at him to see him seated in his truck. He gave me a thumbs-up and a strained smile that didn't quite touch his eyes. Lauren, on the other hand, stared blankly ahead.

She had not taken the news of our departure well. She and Dad argued. Again. He finally won by telling her if we stayed, we would die. She started to say something, then stopped, looked at the ground, and said, "Fine. Let's go." Afterward, she climbed in the truck, buckled her seatbelt, and had not moved or spoken to anyone since.

"Let's get moving," I heard Mike say. "We're burnin' daylight."

His face was impassive as I approached, dark chestnut-colored eyes so much like Sophia's focused through a pair of field glasses. He had slung his big sniper-modified M1A battle rifle across his back, barrel pointed at the ground.

It occurred to me we were about the same height, but because he had roughly fifty pounds of muscle on me, I always felt like I was looking up at him. "Got everything you need?" he asked, not lowering the glasses.

I checked my canteen was full, ammo carriers stocked, round in the chamber on my carbine, safety on, Beretta in its customary drop holster. "I'm good, as long as we're not gone for more than a few hours. Think I should bring some food?"

He lowered the binoculars and shook his head. "No. We won't be gone that long. Come on."

I followed Mike to the other side of the highway, which put us on the left of it as we headed west. The land around us was relatively flat, despite the fact we were in the Texas hill country.

247

Highway 281 lay just short of a mile from where we stood, but despite the flat terrain, there was sufficient bend in the highway and denseness of dead forest ahead to obscure our view.

As we walked through the incinerated trees, the remains of a few houses were visible nearby, the occasional charred rafter or blackened section of frame reaching up from the scorched ground. We stayed low and kept well clear of the highway, paralleling it toward the junction. We saw no movement until halfway to our destination when we came upon the remnants of two large houses, a swimming pool filled with ashes, a few burned-out vehicles, and a flame-gutted camping trailer.

The nearest house lay in a blackened pile, fire-seared boards leaning against one another, roof caved in, a refrigerator, dishwasher, stove, and some squat thing I could not identify in a cluster as if holding a meeting among the ashes. The vehicles ahead sat sinking into the ground on bare rotors, tires melted away, upholstery incinerated, paint jobs scorched down to bare metal. I looked beyond them to the camping trailer, identifiable only by its shape. Reaching out a hand, I tapped Mike on the shoulder.

"Hey," I whispered. "We should swing that way." I pointed to my left. "Might be infected in that camper up there."

He gave me a skeptical look. "Son, ain't nothing could have survived these fires. Not even the dead. Now come on."

He strode ahead, feet crunching on the crisp, dry ground. I ground my teeth and followed, eyes searching the trailer for signs of movement. Sure enough, when we were about fifty yards away, there was a thump and a clatter, and the trailer rocked on its rear suspension springs. Mike stopped and stared open-mouthed.

"Goddammit, Mike."

It took a few seconds for the creature to find the door and make its way around the camper. Mike and I both drew in a breath at the sight of it.

It's clothes were gone, burned away. So was its skin, a few outer layers of muscle tissue, and its eyes. Empty black sockets swiveled left and right as the ghoul cocked its head from one side to the other, turning first its left ear, then its right, in our direction.

"Holy shit," Mike muttered.

I did a face-palm.

The creature stopped moving, empty hollow circles of black fixed squarely our way. It opened its skeletal mouth, bereft of skin and lips, and tried to moan, but only a dry scratching sound like sandpaper over rusty metal came out. Mike raised his rifle and began to sight in, but I reached out and forestalled him.

"Wait," I said, and drew my knife.

"Why?"

"Haven't you figured it out yet?"

"What?"

"They hunt by sound, Mike."

He lowered his rifle and turned his gaze back to the ghoul. "Yeah, I kinda figured. Sorry. Wasn't thinking."

"They tend to have that effect on people."

I approached the half-roasted ghoul with my knife held low at my side. The creature moved more slowly than the others I had seen, almost like stop-motion animation. The fire must have done something to what remained of its nerves, interfered with its motor skills. I considered it a lucky break. The thing's lack of agility made my job that much easier.

The fight went quickly. I batted its grasping hands aside, stepped behind it, and stomped its right knee ninety degrees the wrong direction. There were a rapid series of dry cracks, like snapping a handful of thin carrots in a dishtowel, and the ghoul pitched over on its face.

It had not been a large person in life—and I say person because its gender was impossible to guess—and burning to a crisp had done nothing to increase its mass. Nevertheless, it was a struggle to keep its arms pinned behind its back while I placed the tip of my dagger against the base of its skull and pushed. There was resistance at first, so I pushed harder until the blade went in with a crunch. The ghoul twitched a few times, then went still.

As I stood up and placed a boot on its skull to wrench my knife free, Mike came up beside me. "Should I put a bullet in its head just to make sure?"

"It's dead Mike. Permanently this time. Besides, wouldn't that kind of defeat the purpose?"

I waved the knife in the air. He looked at it and let out a long breath. "Yeah, I guess. You sure that thing's dead?"

"Sure as I can be. We still have work to do, Mike. Lead the way."

He turned a final glance to the skeletal creature on the ground and nudged it with a boot. In a horrid sort of way, the creature blended well with its blasted, scalded surroundings. "You believe in omens?" he asked.

"Not really."

"Well I do. And I think *that,*" he pointed at the infected, "is a bad one."

TWENTY-EIGHT

"It looks like a settlement," Mike said, handing me the field glasses. I peered through them.

At the highway junction, there was a gas station, a farmers market, and an RV park, all separated from the forest by a broad asphalt parking lot. The fireproof buffer zone had kept the structures and recreational vehicles safe from the fires that had come through not long ago. From where Mike and I lay at the top of a rise near the treeline, we could see the people below had moved the RVs so they formed a ring around the two buildings. They had also packed the space beneath the vehicles with dirt and were using the wide trenches left behind as latrines.

Now that's what I call multi-tasking.

I counted a couple of dozen people, some of them standing guard, others engaged in menial tasks, and still more doing nothing much at all. There seemed to be an even dispersion of men and women, even a few children here and there. I gauged the size of the small compound and the amount of work that must have gone into securing it, and decided something did not add up.

"There's not enough people," I said.

"I was thinking the same thing," Mike replied.

"All that dirt, the number of RVs, there must be others somewhere."

"Or maybe there were, but they moved on."

I put the field glasses down. "Could be."

"Let's give it a while. Keep an eye on them, see what we see."

"Good idea."

We settled in.

It was nostalgic, in a way, lying there among the torched foliage. During the years when Mike was imparting the lessons he had learned from his days at Quantico and on the battlefield, we had spent countless hours in the wilds, lying motionless, waiting, just like we were doing then.

In the early days, my targets had been javelina, deer, and coyotes. Those initial hunts were organized so Mike could teach me the basics. He figured since animals had better senses, better instincts, and are generally more perceptive than humans, if I could get close to them, I could get the drop on a man with no problem. Mike's lessons took hold quickly, and it was not long before he decided I was ready for phase two.

Next, he began setting up targets in open fields and had me try to shoot at them while he watched for me through a spotting scope. By the time I was fourteen, I could consistently fire two shots on target undetected from two-hundred yards.

When I could do it from eighty yards, Mike decided it was time to up the ante with mock sniper duels.

I took on all of them: Mike, Dad, Tyrel, and Blake. Even a few of their students who wanted to try their luck against me. We would start on opposite ends of various landscapes in the Texas hill country, make our way to one of three pre-established destinations, and try to spot the other guy in the distance. If we did, we fired at a steel target hung above and away from them to stop the match. If the shooter hit the right target, he then had to walk a spotter via radio to where the other sniper lay hidden. If

252

he was successful, he won. If not, we reset and started over. The match went on until one of us was victorious or it grew too late and we had to call it.

Mike was the only one I never beat. He taught me, after all, so he knew all my tricks.

The others I had much better luck with. Which is not to say I bested them on a consistent basis—I didn't—but I got them enough times to know my skills were well above average.

So despite the heat, and the smell of charred wood clogging my nose, and the slowly building pressure in my bladder, I lay still and watched. Mike did the same, but he was not as still as I was. There was the occasional twitch and fidget and shift of torso, a surplus of unnecessary movement. The untrained eye would never have seen it, but to someone who had seen Mike lie still as a stone for hours on end, it was like watching him pace around wringing his hands. After a while, I grew tired of it.

"What's wrong with you?"

"Huh?"

"Something's bothering you. What is it?"

"Nothing. I'm fine."

"Bullshit."

There was a rustle of fabric as he turned his head. "I'm fine."

"Mike …"

"All right already. You want to know what's on my mind? I'll tell you." He leaned close so he was right next to my ear. "Did you sleep with my daughter, Caleb?"

My face turned to ice. "Um …"

"Well?"

"I wouldn't put it in those terms, exactly."

"You did, didn't you?"

"Mike, it wasn't like that." I met his gaze, and what I saw there made me want to back away slowly and avoid sudden movements. It hurt to see it; Mike was almost as much a father to me as my real one. I blurted out, "I love her, Mike."

He closed his eyes and shook his head. "Caleb, you're only eighteen. You don't know what love is."

"Look, maybe I haven't been around the block like you have, but I know how I feel. You talk about what's between me and Sophia like it's some sordid, tawdry thing. It's not. We care about each other. I've had feelings for her for a long time, and she told me she feels the same way. We just never said anything to each other about it."

Mike looked at me again, much of the hardness gone from his gaze. "Do you really care about her, Caleb? You're not just taking advantage of her?"

"What? No, Mike. I would never do that. You know that."

"She's been under a lot of stress lately. Stress can make a girl vulnerable, make her do things she normally wouldn't."

"I told you, Mike. I would never do that to her, or any other girl for that matter."

He sighed and turned his face back down the hill. "Sorry, son. I didn't mean to … listen you have to understand what it's been like for me all these years. Guys have been coming after Sophia since she was eleven years old. Fuckin' hordes of them. All this time, it was all I could do to keep her from ending up like my mom, barefoot and pregnant by the time she was sixteen. I don't want that to happen to Sophia."

"You don't think she's smart enough to avoid that?"

"I think she's a kid," Mike said. "I think she's made some bad decisions along the way. The partying, the drugs, the crowd she hangs out with … well, used to hang out with, anyway. For a while there, I thought I was gonna lose her."

"But you didn't, Mike. She did some crazy teenager shit like most teenagers do, and she got over it."

"You didn't."

"Didn't what?"

"Do a bunch of crazy teenager shit."

I gave a small shrug. "I'm not like most teenagers."

Mike stared at me. "Yeah. I guess not." He grabbed the field glasses and peered down the hill again, sweeping slowly from left to right. I lay next to him, chin on my hands, thinking about Sophia. Enough time passed I thought he had dropped the subject, so when he spoke, it startled me.

"I guess if there's any guy I would want her to end up with," he said. "It'd be you, Caleb. Just make sure you take good care of her."

I looked at him, surprised. I had to swallow a few times before I could speak. "Thanks, Mike. That means a lot to me."

He grunted and continued staring down the hill.

Nothing much happened in the settlement below as the sun stretched the shadows into afternoon. I was beginning to consider suggesting we head back and get the others when I heard the sound of a car approaching.

"Hand me the eyes," Mike said. He had given me the field glasses so he could take a rest. I passed them back.

We watched a car pull up to the compound: a GMC pickup, loaded with supplies, two people seated in the cab. It stopped in front of a low-rider Cadillac that served as the settlement's main gate. Two men climbed over the Caddy and approached the truck. A brief conversation followed, ending when one of the people in the truck handed something to a gate guard. The guard then ran into the main enclosure, disappeared into an RV, and came back out with a small box in his hands. After handing the box to the man in the truck, there was a quick round of conversation—thank-you-and-goodbye by the look of it—and the truck was off.

"Huh," Mike said.

"Yeah."

"Looked friendly enough."

"Sure did. I'm thinking I might have an idea."

255

The big Marine glanced at me warily. "Caleb …"

"What? These people might be able to help us. And I'm a lot less scary looking than you. Besides, if anything goes wrong, you'll be up here on overwatch."

He thought it over. "All right. But approach from the road. If things turn bad, signal me by scratching your right ear with your left hand. Got it?"

"Right ear, left hand. Got it."

*****

I let them see me coming a long way off.

After backing down from the shallow hillside, I circled around in defilade and emerged at the base of another hill onto Highway 281. The lookouts at the settlement didn't see me until I topped the rise and skylined myself.

I could see them in the distance, eyes peering through binoculars, rifles hung over their shoulders, faint echoes reaching me as they called to one another. Their posture seemed neither aggressive nor overly relaxed. They wanted to make it clear they were aware of my approach, but had no plans to get in my way.

I stopped in front of the Cadillac—a purple one, lots of after-market modifications, barely four inches off the ground—and waved at a guard standing atop an RV.

"Hello."

The man nodded in my direction. He was a little shorter than me, heavyset, late thirties, big bushy moustache. He said, "Howdy."

"Don't suppose you have any water in there, do you?"

"Depends. What you got to trade?"

"What are you looking for?"

He reached in his back pocket and pulled out a list. As he did, a light wind kicked up, sending streamers of ash across the soot-stained parking lot. "Got any feminine hygiene products?"

"Um, no."

"Antibiotics?"

"Sorry."

"Pain medicine?"

"Afraid not."

"Toilet paper?"

"No."

"Booze?"

I chuckled at that one. "No."

He stuffed the list back in his pocket. "Well, I guess that just leaves ammo."

I patted the mag pouches on my vest. "I can spare some five-five-six and nine-mil."

"How many rounds?"

"That depends. How much water are we talking about?"

One corner of the man's mouth twitched upward. "You're pretty sharp for a young fella." He made a motion over the Caddy. "Come on in. Just hop right over the car there."

As I obeyed, the guard turned and shouted to someone I couldn't see. My feet hit the opposite side of the gate just in time to see several men and two women emerge from RVs, all carrying weapons. My hand tightened on the grip of my rifle, but I stayed relaxed, letting it dangle from its tactical sling. If things went south, after I signaled Mike, the rifle would be a distraction. While all eyes were focused on it, I would quick-draw my pistol and start gunning people down. At this range, the sidearm would be easier to bring to bear.

"What's your name?" one of the men said. Tall, about my height, salt-and-pepper hair, mid to late forties, strong build,

257

moved and spoke like a cop. By the way the others gravitated toward him, I figured him for the leader.

"Caleb Hicks," I said, seeing no harm in giving my real name.

"Who are you with?" The man said, coming to a halt a few feet in front of me. His tone was not entirely hostile, just authoritarian, like he was accustomed to being answered when he posed a question, and being answered quickly.

"Me, myself, and I," I said, looking around casually. "What is this place?"

"I'll ask the questions." I returned my gaze to him. He had dark brown eyes, focused and intense.

"What are you doing here?"

"Passing through. I need some water." I lowered a hand slowly to my canteen and gave it a shake. It made a light splashing sound, indicating it was almost empty. I had actually drank most of it earlier, planning to use the empty canteen as an excuse for approaching the settlement. "Came across a house a day ago that hadn't burned down, found a few liters left in the hot water heater. But I've just about burned through it. If you have any water to spare, I'm more than happy to trade for it. Can't drink bullets, after all."

"Where are you coming from?"

I hooked a thumb over my shoulder. "San Antonio. Or what's left of it, anyway. When Houston went up like a road flare, I saw the writing on the wall. The highways were choked by then, so I left on foot. Had to hide out from the fires for a while, and now I'm trying to make my way to Colorado."

The man looked from me to the guard standing on top of the RV. "We don't normally let people inside the gate," he said pointedly.

"Aw, come on, Travis," the guard replied. "He's just a kid. Stop being so damn paranoid and let him have some water. We got plenty for Christ's sake."

The leader, Travis, glared a moment longer, then returned his attention to me. "I suppose Jerry's right. Leave your rifle and your sidearm at the gate, then go with Mabel here." He gestured to a frumpy, fiftyish woman behind him. "She'll get you some water."

Travis walked off and disappeared into his RV. The others with him cast me a final, curious glance and then did the same. Mabel stepped closer, offering a doughy hand. I shook it.

"Nice to meet you Caleb."

"Same to you, ma'am."

"You'll have to forgive Travis. He's a good man, but a bit overprotective."

Jerry climbed down from the RV and took my carbine and pistol, but didn't ask for my ammo. Mabel began walking toward the gas station in the center of the ring of campers. I followed a few feet behind.

"How long have you been here?" I asked.

"Well, let's see … it's been a little over a month since what happened in Houston. Most everyone around these parts evacuated long before then. There were a bunch of us came up from San Antonio with the National Guard. Stopped here for gas, but while the soldiers were fueling up their trucks, they got orders to head back south. Commanding officer apologized, but said he had no choice."

"So they just left you here?"

She nodded. "Sure did."

"You don't sound angry."

"My husband was a soldier, God rest his soul. I know what orders are. Besides, we had Travis. He organized us, had us scavenge around for food, medicine, weapons, things like that. It was his idea to circle the campers and fill 'em in with dirt. Does a good job of keeping the infected out."

Mabel led me behind the gas station to an old-fashioned hand pump. She put a small metal bucket beneath it and began

259

pumping out water. "Back about a week ago, some folks got together and decided they couldn't stay in this place any longer. Said it was *unsustainable*. I believe that was the word the fella eggin' 'em on used. Name was Thornton, used to be a state senator. Slimy little snake of a man. Convinced all those folks to head west for Arizona. Said there was some kind of bunker out there he knew about, place where they were taking a bunch of folks part of some secret government project. Sounded like a bunch o' hooey to me, and I told him as much. So did Travis, and those other folks you see here. But they wouldn't listen. Lit out, and took most of our food with 'em. God only knows if they made it or not."

She finished pumping the water and held up the bucket. I tilted the mouth of my canteen beneath it and held it steady while she poured. "Seen anyone else come through?" I asked. "Travelers, other survivors, the military, anything like that?"

"Had a few folks pass through, lookin' to trade. Most of 'em wantin' bullets or water or both. Offerin' food or whatever else they had. Travis don't normally allow folks inside the wall. I imagine him and Jerry will have words about it later."

When my canteen was full, Mabel withdrew the water bucket. "How about ten rounds of rifle ammo?" she said.

I cocked an eyebrow at her. "How about four. Looks like you won't be running out of water any time soon."

She smiled. "Five?"

"Deal."

I pulled a mag from a carrier, counted out the cartridges, and handed them to her. "Thanks, Mabel. Best of luck to you."

"Same to you, darlin'. Be careful out there."

"Always."

She stayed by the pumps as I walked back toward the gate. I looked around along the way, trying to get a sense of the place. There were almost as many campers forming the perimeter as people, a solid white wall dotted at regular intervals with shatterproof glass. The residents themselves milled about in various states of solemn dejection, dust in their hair, eyes squinting under the hot sun as they stared at me from under hat brims and outstretched hands, a few of them lucky enough to be sporting sunglasses. Glancing to my right, I saw the dirty faces of a few pre-teen children pressed against a window trying to get a better look at me. The closer I came to the center of the enclosure, the more acutely I felt the weight of all those staring eyes. The attention was disconcerting.

I had hoped the people here could offer us some measure of assistance, but from what I could see, they needed help more than we did. It would probably be best for my group if we just bypassed this place altogether.

About ten feet from the gate, Travis' voice stopped me. "Mr. Hicks," he said. "Might I have a word with you for a moment?"

I turned and squinted. The sun was at his back, forcing me to shield my eyes to see him. "What about?"

"Please, it'll only take a minute or two."

I didn't move. "So come out here and let's talk."

He stepped down from his RV and approached, hands held out at his sides. His gun was notably absent from its holster. A few steps brought him around so I didn't have to squint to see him. "I just have a few questions for you, and I would prefer to ask them in private. It will only take a few minutes of your time. After that, you can be on your way."

I read his face. He looked calm, radiating sincerity. But there was an intensity in his eyes I didn't like, an unblinking steadiness that made the hair on my neck stand up. Falling back on my training, I did a quick assessment.

He wasn't armed, but that didn't mean anything. He still wielded the most dangerous weapon of all—authority. All he had to do was shout, and I was a dead man. I could decline and try to leave, but if he decided to press the issue, things would escalate. And out here in the open, with only my knife and hand-to-hand combat skills, I didn't stand a chance. Not unless I got extraordinarily lucky, and I was not about to bet my life on luck.

My left hand twitched as I thought about reaching up and casually scratching my right ear. I could see where my rifle and pistol lay on the ground only a few feet away, Jerry standing next to them. He seemed oblivious to the tension between Travis and me, but he could be faking it for all I knew. If I gave the signal, it would be the end of Travis' life, and the shock factor would very likely buy me the time I needed to cross the distance to Jerry, incapacitate him, and retrieve my weapons.

But what then?

My best bet would be to run for the southeast side of the encampment, staying low and hugging the wall of campers, and serpentine my way through the dead trees there, hoping none of the residents here were expert marksmen. I knew I could count on Mike to cover me and take out anyone who stuck their head up too far once I was outside the gate.

But did it really need to come to that? What if Travis sincerely just wanted to ask a few questions and send me on my way? Furthermore, if he tried to break bad on me, we would be in the confines of his camper at hand-to-hand range. Travis was strong looking, but I am no weakling, and I sincerely doubted he could match my skill in a stand-up fight. Few people I had ever met could.

I was also still at the point in my life I thought it best to avoid bloodshed whenever possible. I have since become a far less sentimental person, but at the time, I conceded, thinking it was the sensible thing to do.

"Lead the way," I said, holding a hand toward Travis' RV.

He walked ahead of me a few feet and disappeared through the door. I followed him in, blinking at the sudden dimness of the camper's interior. If the afternoon had been overcast instead of blindingly bright, I would have noticed him hurrying to the small table in the kitchenette sooner. But my eyes were still adjusting, and by the time I blinked away the sickly green film obscuring my vision, I found myself staring down the barrel of a .45 automatic.

"Where are the others?" he asked.

I blinked in confusion. "What the hell are you talking about?"

"Don't bullshit me kid. We both know you didn't come here alone."

My hands came up to shoulder level, palms out. "Listen, I don't-"

"You wanna know what I did before all this happened?" he interrupted, tilting his head at the wasteland outside the window.

"Is that a rhetorical question?"

He frowned, shifting the gun so he held it at hip level. "I was a detective with the San Antonio Police Department."

"Okay. So if you're a cop, why are you threatening me with a gun right now?"

"Because a detective notices things. Take your boots, for example."

I looked down and felt a twist in my stomach. I knew what he was about to say, but it hadn't occurred to me until just that second what a gaping hole they put in my cover story. "They're too new," he said. "They fit you perfectly, which means you bought them from a store, not found them along the way. There's no way you crossed all those miles between here and San Antonio with no more wear and tear than that." He gestured at my feet with the gun.

There was a moment of silence. I got the impression he was waiting for me to say something, an old cop trick. I didn't take the bait. Finally, he said, "Then there's your face. You're not tan enough. If you had been out in the sun these past couple of weeks, you'd be brown as a strip of bacon. Not to mention you're clean-shaven."

He took a couple of steps closer, but stayed out of arm's reach. "Now tell me, kid. Why does a man facing the prospect of dehydration waste precious water on something as unnecessary as shaving?"

My mind raced. The barrel of Travis' gun was only forty-five hundredths of an inch wide, but from my perspective, it may as well have been the size of the moon. I kept my hands up and eased back a step.

"Don't move again," Travis growled.

"Okay, fine," I said, playing for time. "Just take your finger off the trigger, okay?"

"No. I asked you some questions, boy. If you want to leave this place alive, you better start answering them."

"Okay, I will, I'll answer all your questions. All I ask is you take your finger off the trigger. Just so you don't shoot me by accident."

I was scared at this point, and didn't have to fake the tremor of fear in my voice. Travis glared a moment longer, then eased his finger off the trigger, keeping his fingertip poised just above it. "There, happy now?"

"Thank you."

"You're very welcome. Now talk."

I took a deep breath. "When I left San Antonio, I had two pairs of boots," I said. "One of them wore out. This is my second pair. That's why they look so new."

Travis seemed to consider this. He made a small motion with the gun. "What about your skin?"

"I had a hat, but I lost it a couple of days ago. There are a couple of bottles of SPF 70 in my backpack, the spray-on stuff. It only takes a little bit once or twice a day. I put it on my face and hands. My clothes protect the rest."

It was true I had the sunblock, but I had only used a little of it. The part about the hat was a lie, but there was no way for him to verify that. My clothes did indeed cover most of my exposed skin, being that my shirt was long-sleeved.

I waited for Travis to say something, but he remained silent. His expression was stoic, but I thought I detected a hint of uncertainty in his posture. "As for my beard," I went on, "I hardly ever have to shave. When it starts to grow out, I smear it with olive oil and shear it off with a straight razor. Doesn't require water, just a cloth to wipe the razor on."

"And I suppose if I search your backpack I'll find a bottle of olive oil and a straight razor?" Travis asked.

"You will." It was true. I carried the oil as part of my fire-starting kit, and the straight razor had been a gift from Blake when I turned fourteen. I kept it for sentimental reasons.

Travis' expression softened, growing regretful. He lowered the .45 and took a few steps back until the kitchen table was between us. "Okay. Sounds plausible enough. If you would be so kind as to empty your backpack."

I almost did, then remembered the two grenades and the radio within and kicked myself for bringing them along. *Should have left them behind, idiot. What the hell did you think you would need them for?*

If Travis searched my bag, the game was up. The grenades could be explained away, but not the radio. I lowered my hands. "What the hell for?"

"So I can verify you're telling the truth."

"Fuck you, cop." I said, growing angry. "You ain't searching my shit."

His eyes narrowed, his face darkening in anger. "What's wrong, kid? Got something to hide?"

"Me? What about you, motherfucker? Why are we doing this bullshit in here and not out there?" I pointed out the window at the courtyard in the center of the compound. Something crossed Travis' face, just a flicker, but it was all the confirmation I needed.

"What's the matter, don't want those people out there knowing what you're doing in here?" I started backing toward the doorway. "Why do I get the feeling they wouldn't approve of you shaking me down for no good reason?"

Travis squared off with me, but kept the gun at his side. "Stop where you are, kid. Don't take another step."

"You know what," I said, affecting a tone of indignation, "I already answered your questions. I'm done explaining myself to you. It's time for me to go. You want to stop me? Shoot me." And with that, I turned my back and began walking toward the exit.

"Stop!" Travis shouted. I ignored him and kept walking, not hurrying my pace. The kind of thing a man would do when he felt he had done nothing wrong. As the light through the doorway grew brighter, I felt a burning, itching sensation between my shoulder blades. I wondered what it would feel like if a .45 hollow point mushroomed against my spine before blowing my heart out through my sternum. Would there be pain, or would there just be an impact, a moment of breathlessness, and then darkness?

Luckily, I didn't have to find out. The doorway came and went and there was no thunder of large-caliber death along the way. I stomped angrily toward the main gate, head down, stride determined. Behind me, I heard Travis scramble after me.

"I told you to stop!"

"I told you to go fuck yourself."

"Jerry, don't let him out of the gate."

The guard who had been so kind to me earlier obeyed immediately and aimed his rifle at my chest. I stopped. "What the fuck, Jerry?"

"Just doin' my job, kid."

Footsteps crunched behind me, then stopped. "Listen," Travis said. "Just calm down, okay? There's no need for this to go any further. Just let me search your pack. If you're telling the truth, this whole thing will be over with and you'll be free to go."

I looked around and saw people begin to emerge from campers and stand up from seats in the shade. They wandered closer, eyes wide, no doubt wondering what all the excitement was about. Slowly, I turned and faced Travis, once again forced to squint against the sun's glare. Shading my eyes with my right hand, I could see his pistol was holstered, but his fingers dangled close to the grip, the retaining strap unbuttoned.

Slimy son of a bitch.

"This is the last time I'm going to tell you, kid," he said. "Drop the bag."

I shook my head. "I'm afraid that's not going to happen."

My right ear didn't itch, but I reached up with my left hand and scratched it anyway.

TWENTY-NINE

I expected Mike to shoot Travis first.

What I failed to consider was how the situation looked from his perspective, staring through the Leupold scope mounted to his M1A rifle over a hundred yards away. As overwatch, his priority would be to eliminate the most egregious threat first—Jerry, in this case.

At that range, the impact came barely a fraction of a second before the report. The 7.62mm projectile, traveling at over 2500 feet per second, hit its target with a sharp metallic *THWACK*.

I had a scant moment to think, *Thwack?*

There should have been a meaty *WHAP*, followed by a gurgling scream, the sound of a body collapsing, and limbs thrashing in the dirt. Instead, there was a startled cry from Jerry and the sound of a large piece of metal being dropped.

Things happened quickly after that.

In the lightning rapidity of thought, I realized Mike had directed his fire at Jerry first, but whether or not he had killed him, I had no idea. Something told me he had not, but I doubted Mike would have left him in any condition to be a threat to me either. I did not dare look over my shoulder to find out, however, because I was too busy charging headlong at Travis.

One of the many lessons my father taught me about unarmed combat is the Twenty-One Foot Rule. It goes like this: If a man is standing twenty-one feet away from you, and you have a holstered sidearm, in most cases, the attacker will be able to reach you before you can draw your weapon. I did not believe my father when he first told me this, so we did an experiment. He had me wear a holstered training pistol, took up a rubber knife, backed off exactly twenty-one feet, and told me to try to draw my weapon and aim it at him before he could get his hands on me.

After the sixth time he put the tip of the little rubber knife to my throat before I could clear my pistol, I finally believed him.

Travis had a bit of an advantage: the retaining strap that normally kept his pistol from bouncing out of its holster was not buttoned down. However, when the report reached his ears—shockingly loud in the quiet of the burned-out barrens—he whipped his head in the direction of the shot.

It was all the encouragement I needed.

There were less than twenty-one feet between us, maybe twelve at the most. I covered the distance in three long strides. By the time Travis recovered and began to reach for his weapon, it was too late.

One hand grabbed his wrist and pushed it away from his sidearm while the other covered his face, blinding him, wrenching his head backward and pushing him off balance. After forcing him back two steps, I reared back with my right leg and brought a knee into his solar plexus with all the strength I could muster. The strike hit with enormous force, driving the air from his lungs in an agonized *whoosh*. He doubled over, gun forgotten, a high-pitched gasp peeling from his throat as he tried to pull air into his chest cavity.

The key to victory, once you have your opponent hurt, is to be relentless, to never let up, to hit them again, and again, and again, until they go down and do not get back up. The principle of continuous attack.

The next blow was an elbow strike to the temple. It turned his legs to rubber and made his eyes roll around independent of one another like a goggle-eyed lizard. I followed the elbow up with a spinning back fist to the jaw that spun him around, but amazingly, he kept his feet.

Tough son of a bitch.

When his back was turned to me, I stomped the crease of his knee, forcing him to the ground. He immediately tried to stand up, but again, I was on him too quickly. With the fingers of my left hand curled into a half fist, I slammed the edge of my palm into his brachial nerve once, twice, three times. On the fourth, he went down limply and did not move.

Not wasting any time, I yanked his gun from its holster and brought it up to the low ready position. The sights tracked first to the left, then right, following my line of vision. I kept my finger tight on the trigger, taking in some of the slack. I expected to see a crowd of people staring at me, maybe a mixture of shock and anger, some of them standing open-mouthed, some of them going for weapons. Instead, all of them, including Jerry, who clutched a bleeding left forearm, gaped southward at a rising plume of dust stretching skyward and approaching rapidly.

"What the hell?"

I lowered the weapon and looked around again. No one was paying me any attention. I took a few deep breaths and cleared my thoughts, focusing on my senses. The first thing that came to me was the rumble of vehicles, lots of them, diesel engines, the hum of tires, and a rapid, metallic clattering.

Treads.

Which meant ... what? Tanks? Bulldozers?

Shit.

I looked up again and saw dozens of black plumes, exhaust stacks. As the noise of them closed the distance to the compound, I heard the engines begin to ratchet down, the grinding and grunting of big transmissions downshifting as they slowly came to a halt.

Calmly, so as not to draw attention to myself, I walked toward my carbine and pistol. They lay on the ground near Jerry where I last saw them. I was a few feet away before he noticed me. When he saw me coming, he tried to step in my way.

"Hey," he said.

I raised the pistol. "Jerry, you do not want to fuck with me right now."

He paled. "Okay."

"Step away, Jerry."

He did, four steps. I motioned with my free hand for him to keep going. When he had gone far enough, I stooped to pick up my rifle, still pointing Travis' gun at him, then retrieved my Beretta. Once I had my gear sorted out, I lowered the pistol and motioned Jerry over. He complied, warily coming to a halt a few feet in front of me. I dropped the mag from Travis's gun, cleared the chamber, and thumbed out the remaining six rounds. They made little puffs in the dust as they fell to the ground. That done, I tossed the whole works at Jerry's feet. He was not bleeding too badly, telling me Mike must have shot his weapon out of his hand. The cuts were undoubtedly from shrapnel.

"I'm sorry about all this," I said. "But Travis had no right to search my things. He may have been a cop once, but he isn't any more. He has no jurisdiction here, or anywhere else for that matter. If he had just let me go on my way, none of this," I pointed first to Jerry's wounded arm, then to Travis' still prone form, "would have happened."

"I'll tell him that when he comes around," Jerry said drily. "Don't think it'll make much difference, though."

"What about you, Jerry? Are you all right?"

"My fucking arm hurts."

"You'll forgive me if I'm not terribly sympathetic. You were pointing a rifle at my chest, after all. And besides, it could have been worse. A lot worse."

Jerry cast a nervous eye in the direction the shot had come from. "Who the hell was that, anyway?"

"A friend of mine."

"What is he, a sniper or something?"

"Something like that."

Jerry looked back at me, eyes wide around the edges. "He could have killed me."

"Is that a realization, or a question?"

"He still out there?"

"I imagine so."

He held up his hands and backed away. "Tell me something, kid. Why do you need a sniper watching this place if all you wanted was some water?"

I leapt up on the Cadillac at the gate and casually strode across its hood. "Insurance, Jerry. It's a dangerous world we live in."

*****

There were thirty vehicles in the convoy.

Most of them were the wheeled variety, but there was one Abrams tank, a couple of mobile Howitzers, and four Bradley fighting vehicles. I also counted eight Humvees, six M35 deuce-and-a-halfs, five armored personnel carriers, and four HEMTT cargo trucks. The line of vehicles came to a halt in front of the settlement's main gate as I turned southward and began walking down Highway 281.

The plan was to stroll casually by and turn left at the southeast corner of the wall. I saw no reason why the Army, or Marines, or whoever it was would be interested in a lone traveler, even a well-armed one. This was Texas, after all, where firearms were as common as cowboy hats.

So when a Humvee's passenger door opened a few feet away and a soldier spilled out, carbine trained in my direction, shouting at me to get my fucking hands in the air *now*, I froze in genuine shock.

"I said get your goddamn hands up!" he yelled when I didn't move. Slowly, I did as ordered.

"Turn away from me." The soldier said. I tried to read his nametag, but his arms covered it.

"What's this about?" I asked. "Why are you-"

"SHUT THE FUCK UP!" he screamed, going red in the face. "Turn around now!"

"Johansen," a sharp voice said to my right. I turned to see who had spoken and saw a man in fatigues approaching. He had a captain's insignia on his uniform. "Lower that weapon right now."

"He's armed, sir." The soldier, Johansen, said.

"Yes, and if I were in his place, I would be too. Now lower your weapon, Sergeant."

Johansen complied, glaring daggers at me. The captain stepped closer and reached out a hand. "Sorry about that. The sergeant here is a little overzealous at times."

I shook the offered hand, not taking my eyes off Johansen. "You don't say."

Johansen's already red face darkened. Beside me, the captain said, "Name's Morgan. Insert joke here."

It was inappropriate, but I chuckled, finally looking away from Johansen. "Captain Morgan?"

The officer smiled. "Yep. I'm a real hit at parties."

"You a deserter?" Johansen growled.

I looked back at him. "What?"

"How'd you know he's a captain? He never identified his rank."

I pointed. "It's right there on his uniform."

"How do you know what a captain's bars look like?"

"My old man was in the Army."

"Mmm-hmm. And where did you get that M-4?"

I looked down. "It was a gift."

"Mind if I take a look?" Morgan asked.

I handed it to him. He glanced at the manufacturer's stamp, then handed it back. "Rock River Arms. I hear they make good stuff." He shot a pointed glance at Johansen, who looked crestfallen. If the gun had been made by Colt, it would have looked bad for me. I was in Army surplus tactical gear, after all, and was old enough to have enlisted in the Armed Services. But Rock River Arms did not make M-4s for the military, that was Colt's job, thus invalidating Johansen's suspicions.

The sound of doors opening and boots hitting the ground echoed around us. I glanced up and down the convoy to see soldiers exiting vehicles and starting the process of setting up a perimeter. A few of them started heading in our direction, no doubt intent on speaking with the captain.

"Are you in charge of all these guys?" I asked.

Morgan's expression sobered. "Sadly, yes. We're a bit of a rag-tag contingent, you might say. Came up from San Antonio, what's left of it, anyway. Where are you from?"

"Houston, originally," I said, seeing no point in lying. "Not much left there either."

"So I heard."

"How bad did San Antonio get hit?" I didn't think it was a good idea to let on that I already knew, considering the hijinks my father and the other guys got into less than twenty-four hours ago.

"Bad. We were part of a larger force along Highway 46. Tried to keep the infected from spreading north." He shook his head. "Didn't last long. What you see here is a big chunk of what survived."

"I'm sorry to hear that."

He nodded, eyes fixed in the distance. "After the retreat, we got orders to head north to Colorado Springs. Supposed to look for survivors along the way, ask them to come with us, render what assistance we can. Can you tell me anything about this place?" He pointed a thumb over his shoulder at the wall of RVs.

I thought of Jerry's wounded arm, and Travis' prone form just inside the gate, and wondered how to play it. After a few seconds, I said. "My best advice is to watch yourself around these people."

Morgan raised an eyebrow. "What do you mean?"

"I came here to trade some ammo for water. Things were friendly enough at first, but then the guy who runs the place tried to shake me down. Said he used to be a cop, wanted to search my stuff. I told him to go fuck himself and went to leave, and he had one of his guards draw down on me. I got a buddy out there with a scoped .308 watching over me. He shot the gun out of the guy's hands while I used the distraction to deal with the leader. I was just leaving when you guys showed up."

"I'm sorry," Morgan said, eyes narrow with suspicion. "Did you say there's a sniper in the hills?"

"Yep. Marine Force Recon, old friend of my father's. We've been traveling together since Houston, looking out for each other. Figured it would be best for him to hang back in case these people weren't as nice as they seemed. Turned out to be a good idea."

The captain looked at Johansen, then back at me. "I don't suppose he would mind coming down and having a talk with us, would he?"

I shrugged. "Not sure. I can go ask him, though. He might, he might not."

"Kid," Johansen said, "if we have to hunt him down, he ain't gonna like it."

I shot him a level stare. "I'd like to see you try."

"Johansen," Morgan said, glaring, "why don't you go somewhere and make yourself useful?"

The sergeant looked like he was going to say something else, but when he saw the impatience on Morgan's face, he bit down on it, gave a curt, "Yes sir," and stalked away.

"I suppose if your friend was a threat to us," Morgan said, "Johansen would no longer be among the living. Is that a fair assumption?"

I nodded. "I would have said something when he was pointing his gun at me, but to be honest, I was too surprised. What's that guy's problem, anyway?"

"I don't know. Too much testosterone? Maybe his parents didn't hug him enough? Honestly, though, he probably just had you pegged for a deserter. We've been having problems with that lately."

"Do you think it occurred to him if I was a deserter, I wouldn't go strolling by an Army convoy in my tactical gear? Wouldn't it have been smarter to—oh, I don't know—change into civilian clothes?"

"Things like that don't always occur to Sergeant Johansen. He's not what you might call quick on the uptake."

"I gathered that."

Morgan sighed, took off his helmet, and ran a hand through a thick mop of short black hair. His face looked mildly sunburned and he was sweating in the heat. "About your friend, the Marine. If he shot someone, I'm kind of obligated to investigate. Was anyone killed?"

"No."

"Any serious injuries?"

"Not sure. I put the hurt on the guy who tried to stop me from leaving."

"How bad?"

"He was unconscious last I saw him."

Morgan cursed softly. The quartet of men who had been walking toward us from the front of the column finally arrived. They came to a halt behind the captain, eyeing me suspiciously. "Okay," he said, "here's what we're going to do. Turn your weapons over to these men here. We'll conduct an investigation. If everything is how you say it is, you'll be free to go."

"Just like that?" I asked.

He nodded. "Things are pretty bad out there, kid. This is the least of the messed up shit I've seen. The way I see it, you have a right to defend yourself and your property. If you traded with these people in good faith, and they did something out of line, you were well within your rights to fight back. But you better be telling me the truth. Understood?"

I nodded. "Understood."

THIRTY

Ten minutes later, Travis was red-faced and sputtering.

"I want him arrested," he hissed, jabbing a finger in my direction. There was a large shiner on his temple where my elbow had hit him. We were standing in a ring of soldiers and curious onlookers just past the compound's gate, baking under the mid-afternoon sun.

"For what?" Morgan said. "Maybe you didn't notice, officer, but you're outside your jurisdiction. Furthermore, your department doesn't exist anymore. You have no official capacity here. Ergo, you had no right to demand this young man allow you to search his belongings, much less detain him at gunpoint. On the other hand, if Mr. Hicks here decides to press charges against you for attempted kidnapping, a federal crime, I'll be obliged to take you into custody until we arrive in Colorado Springs, at which time you will be brought up on charges."

Travis' eyes widened in sudden realization at what he had done. I felt a sort of sympathy for him; he was so fixated on surviving and protecting his little community, he had lost perspective on his actions. I stepped forward and raised a hand to get Morgan's attention.

"That won't be necessary, Captain," I said. "It was a misunderstanding, that's all. As far as I'm concerned, it's been resolved. There's no need for things to go any further."

"Misunderstanding?" Jerry shouted, standing next to Travis, holding his bandaged arm. "Look at this! Whoever's out there shot me in the arm!"

"First of all," Morgan said, "that's a shrapnel wound, not a gunshot wound. Second, weren't you *pointing a gun* at Mr. Hicks here when the incident occurred?"

Jerry worked his mouth like a fish a few times, then said, "Well yes, but-"

"And why were you pointing a gun at him?"

More fish-face. "Because he told me to." He nodded his head at Travis, who grimaced.

"Jerry, you idiot, just shut up."

"And when you pointed your gun at him," Morgan went on, "was he threatening you?"

"Well … no, he wasn't."

"Was he threatening anyone else, or stealing something, or brandishing a weapon, or doing anything that was in any way a danger to the lives of anyone in this compound, or detrimental to their property?"

"Uh … no."

"So what exactly was he doing when you decided to threaten him with a rifle?"

"He was … walking."

"Walking?"

"Yeah. Walking." Jerry lowered his head, realizing how ridiculous he sounded.

"So you pointed a gun at him. For walking. Because this guy told you to." The captain pointed at Travis, who by now looked almost as embarrassed as Jerry.

"I gotta tell you guys," Morgan said disgustedly. "You don't present a very damning case." He gestured to the staff sergeant holding my weapons. "I don't have time for this shit. Give him his property back."

I took my rifle and pistol and began walking toward the gate, anxious to be away. Morgan shouted from behind me, "Hey Hicks."

I stopped and looked over my shoulder.

"Can I talk you into hanging out for a few minutes?"

"For what?"

"Might have a job for you if you're interested."

I wasn't, but I figured it would be a bad idea to refuse outright. So I shrugged and did my best to appear as if I was considering it. "All right. I'll hear you out."

"Find a spot in the shade. I have some things to take care of, then we'll talk."

I walked over to an RV that looked empty and had one of those retractable awnings. After lowering it, I went inside and searched until I found a folding chair, then took a seat and waited.

The soldiers worked quickly, their first order of business helping anyone who needed medical attention. A few people had minor injuries, but the community was mostly healthy. Next, they assessed the vehicles at the settlement's disposal and inventoried their fuel, trying to decide how far they could go on what they had. I overheard Mabel explain that the National Guard troops who had left these people here had mostly drained the reserves in the gas station's underground tanks. What remained would not get them very far.

The few children in the encampment came out and surrounded some of the more friendly soldiers, touching their equipment and peppering them with questions. The men in uniform were unfailingly kind and patient, letting the kids look at their unloaded rifles and try on their helmets. It reminded me of YouTube videos I had seen of soldiers hanging out with children in Iraq, giving them candy bars and toys, trying to win

280

hearts and minds. It was eerie to see the same thing happen on U.S. soil.

Once finished with their initial assessment, Morgan asked Travis to gather his people in the center of the enclosure. When they had come together in a loose, anxious knot, Morgan stood on an empty milk crate and raised his voice.

"I have good news, and I have bad news," he said. "So I'll give you the bad news first. There is a swarm of infected about eight miles behind us. I'd like to tell you how many of them there are, but I'm afraid it's too many to count. Tens of thousands would be my best guess."

A chorus of worried noise went up from the gathered survivors at this. Eyes went wide, couples pulled each other into shaky arms, parents clutched their children. The voices turned toward Travis, a dozen questions at once, all with the same message: What do we do?

"All right, all right," Travis said, holding up his hands. "Don't start panicking. Let the captain finish."

The crowd quieted. Morgan nodded his thanks and continued. "If the horde follows the same patterns we've seen others follow, eventually they'll disperse. But I can't guarantee that will happen before they reach this settlement. And even if they do, the numbers of infected in the area will increase dramatically. Your defenses here will not be enough to stop them."

He paused to let the facts sink in. The crowd went quiet, absorbing the news. When he sensed it had been long enough, Morgan said, "Now for the good news. There are about twenty thousand troops in Colorado Springs as we speak. By the end of the month, that number should be up to about thirty-five thousand. Just this morning, I received word that FEMA is setting up disaster relief stations in the area, and is offering aid to anyone who can make it there. Now here's the deal, folks. I can't promise you anything. I thought we had a pretty good chance of saving San Antonio, but there were too many infected. We were overrun. But I've been to Colorado, and I can tell you the terrain there in the Rockies will give us a hell of an advantage. We'll have a lot better chance at fighting the infected there than we do here. So that's where we're headed. You're all welcome to come with us. We should have enough room to fit you on the trucks, or you can travel in your own vehicles if you want. I can't guarantee I'll get you all to Colorado safely, but I can promise you I will damn well try. If you don't want to come along, I can't force you. But be aware, if you stay here, you're probably not going to make it."

He stepped down from the crate and looked at Travis at eye level. "We move out in an hour. You have until then to decide."

With that, he walked away, motioning his troops to return to the convoy.

As the people in the settlement talked among themselves deciding what to do, Morgan looked my way and beckoned me over. I got up and followed him out of the gate and over to his Humvee. Once there, he passed a quick message over the radio and then stared at me for a few seconds, measuring me up.

"You look like you're in pretty good shape," he said finally. "That Travis guy was no joke, but you put him down with no problem. I'm gonna go out on a limb here and say you probably know how to handle yourself. You any good with that carbine?"

"I'm not terrible with it."

"Had to kill any infected yet?"

"A few."

"So you know about the headshot rule?"

"Damn near learned the hard way."

He let out a short, humorless laugh. "Yeah, me too. Listen, we're short-handed here. We have a big job ahead of us, and not enough people to get it done. I need all the help I can get. You follow?"

"I'm not interested in joining the Army."

"I'm not asking you to. I need people who can fight, and who can keep their head in a bad situation. What you just dealt with in there, most people wouldn't have had the nerve to do what you did. I could use a guy like you, assuming you can follow instructions."

"And what are you offering in return?"

"Safe passage to Colorado. As safe as I can make it, anyway. Think about it, man. What are you gonna do out here? You think you can survive in this place long term? Hell, most of it's burned to the ground. Things are better up north. And you're not going to find a faster, better way to get there than this convoy."

I thought about it a moment and realized he had a point. But I had more than just myself to think about. "I have to admit, you make a good sales pitch," I said. "But there are other people in my group."

"More than just your buddy up there in the hills?"

I nodded. "My family."

"Can any of them fight?"

"Some."

He looked at me more closely, but I kept my face blank. When he realized I was not giving anything else away, he said, "Like I told you. I need all the help I can get. You can bring them along."

"I'll have to talk to them about it. Might take a while."

"We leave in an hour. Sorry, but orders are orders."

"Do what you have to do. If they decide to come along, we'll catch up. What route are you taking?"

He took out a map and showed me. I committed it to memory, and then offered him my hand. "No promises, Captain, but you very well might be seeing me again. If you do, I'll have company."

He shook my hand. "Either way, it was nice to meet you, kid."

"Likewise."

*****

"I didn't recognize any of them," Mike said.

We had gathered in a circle back at the vehicles, all except for Lauren. She elected to stay in Dad's truck with the engine running and the AC cranked as high as it would go. Tyrel had regained consciousness and stood across from me, one side supported by a makeshift crutch, the other by Lola. His eyes were still somewhat glassy from the pain meds, but at least he was on his feet. Lance, meanwhile, leaned against the fender of my father's truck, arms crossed over his chest, keeping his distance from the conversation.

"Doesn't surprise me," Blake said. "46 is a long highway. There were thousands of troops when we left."

"But from what that captain was saying, not many survived," Tyrel said. "How many were in that convoy, do you think?"

I shook my head. "Maybe a hundred or so."

"Jesus," Dad muttered, wiping a hand across his face. "I'm not happy about what they did to Tyrel, but I didn't wish them dead."

"None of us did," Mike said. "But we can't change what happened. What's important right now is what we decide going forward."

"Are you sure they're not the same troops we ran into on Highway 46?" Tyrel asked.

"As sure as I can be," Mike replied. "Looked to me like they came from a different section of the highway than the one we tried to cross."

"Either way," Dad said, "the only one of us they would recognize is Tyrel, and even that's pretty damn unlikely."

Tyrel grimaced. "There's also the matter of my leg."

"We can explain that away," Dad said. "Tell them someone tried to rob us and we fought them off, something like that."

"Works for me."

"Then it's decided?" Mike asked. "Are we really going to do this?"

Dad searched all of our faces. "Any objections?"

No one spoke. He turned around and looked at Lance. "What do you say? You in?"

Lance shrugged. "Got nothing else going at the moment. Might as well."

"Caleb, you ride up front with Mike," Dad said. "When we catch up with the convoy, I'll let you do the talking."

THIRTY-ONE

We caught up with them on 281 just outside of Blanco.

Captain Morgan (to this day I can't say it without a smile) had stopped the convoy a mile outside of town and sent scouts ahead in Humvees. When a lookout saw us approaching, Morgan and one of his aides drove back to meet us.

"Good to see you again, Mr. Hicks," he said, stepping out of his vehicle. His aide remained behind, no doubt monitoring radio traffic. The captain eyed our Humvees skeptically. "Where the hell did you find those?"

"You might say they were a gift."

He raised an eyebrow.

"Come meet everyone. My father can explain."

We did the round of introductions. Morgan took in the other men's appearance—the weapons, the tactical gear, the familiar, confident way in which my father and his friends handled themselves—and I saw an acquisitive gleam in the Army officer's eyes. When he shifted his attention to Sophia, Lola, and Lauren, the gleam faded, replaced by apprehension.

"Nice to meet all of you," he said. "Do you mind telling me where you came across those?" He pointed to the Humvees.

My father spoke up. "These three and I used to work for a civilian-owned survival and firearms training facility, Black

Wolf Tactical. Everything you see here except the trucks and the Jeep were owned by the company."

"Even the machine guns?"

Dad nodded. "Yep."

"Aren't those illegal for civilians to own?"

"In most cases, yes. Unless you have the proper licenses, which BWT did."

"I don't suppose you have any documentation to back that up, do you?"

"I do." Dad held a hand toward the lead Humvee. "Would you like me to show you?"

"Lead the way."

I watched my father remove a cardboard box from the back of a Humvee, open it, and neatly arrange a number of files on the back seat. He pointed to each one, explaining what it contained. Morgan picked up a couple of them, half-heartedly sifted through the papers within, then shook his head and dropped them back in the box.

"Good enough for me," he said. "Honestly, at this point, I wouldn't care if you stole this stuff as long as you're willing to help me."

"What help do you need?" Dad asked.

"You look ex-military to me. These other guys too. Am I right?"

The four men took turns explaining their credentials. My father disclosed he had been a Green Beret, but stopped short of mentioning his time in Delta Force. It seemed odd to me, but I shrugged it off, figuring the old man had his reasons.

Lance revealed he had served four years in the Marines, then spent the last twenty years in law enforcement, twelve of those with the Houston Police Department's SWAT team. Figuring he was eighteen when he joined the Marines, I guessed his age at forty-two. He was in good shape, but looked older than that.

With each proffered resume, the acquisitive light in Morgan's eyes grew steadily brighter. He expressed concern about Tyrel's wounded leg, but seemed appeased when Tyrel assured him he could still man a machine gun or provide long-range fire support with his .338 Lapua magnum. Finally, Morgan returned his attention to me.

"Well, you make a little more sense now. Did you grow up around these guys?"

"All except Lance, yes. We met recently."

He chuckled. "Christ, kid. You must be a freakin' monster."

"So what do you think, Captain?" My dad said. From his expression, I could tell he was eager to change the subject. "Got a place for us in your convoy?"

"Absolutely," Morgan said. "Just hang back in the rear for now. Once we know what's ahead of us, I'll sort out where to put you." He went through another round of handshakes, this one more enthusiastic than the first. "Again, it was nice to meet all of you. Glad to have you on board."

"Same to you, Captain," Dad said. We watched the young officer stride away, climb into his Humvee, and drive back toward the head of the column.

"Well that went well," Blake said.

"Yeah," Dad said, sounding uncertain.

I looked at him, not liking his tone. He stared at the dust trail in the wake of Morgan's Humvee, his dark eyes unhappy.

"What's wrong?" I asked him.

He glanced at me and shook his head. "We'll talk about it later. Mike, take point if you don't mind."

The big man nodded once. "Not a problem."

"Everybody else, let's get out of this heat."

"Fuckin' gladly," Tyrel said, leaning on Lola's arm as he limped back to his Humvee. Sophia came to stand next to me,

288

her arm slipping around my waist. I pulled her close and kissed the top of her head.

"How you holdin' up?"

She nuzzled her face against my chest. "Better, now that you're back."

"I think things are going to be all right, now." I said. "What that guy Morgan said about Colorado Springs, he seemed pretty convinced. I think we'll be safe there."

"I hope so," Sophia said. "I hate all this running. It's only been a few weeks since Houston, but it feels like a lifetime."

"Tell me about it."

She looked up at me, her eyes like pools of dark honey. "Do you really think things will be better in Colorado? You think we'll be safe?"

The truth was, I had no idea. Nothing I had seen of the spiraling world around me gave me the slightest confidence there was such a thing as a safe place anymore. But when I looked down at Sophia, I saw hope, and I saw her confidence in me, and her trust, and there was a surge of something in my chest that made me want to be all the things I saw in her eyes. So in my foolishness, rather than reveal my doubts and my fears, and speak to her honestly of the risks we were taking and let her make an informed, adult decision, I took the coward's way out—I resorted to false bravado.

"Everything's going to be fine, Sophia," I said, and planted a gentle kiss on her lips. "I'm not going to let anything happen to you."

She smiled at me, little dimples forming in her cheeks. "I believe you."

How easy it was to make promises, then, before I understood the consequences of failure and hubris. Before I learned of the demons that come in the late hours before sleep, and the burdens of regret one carries in their wake.

Fate is a cruel teacher. But by God, her lessons stick.

*****

With the exception of a few wandering infected, the town of Blanco was abandoned.

The sun was low in the sky, wearing on toward evening. The captain decided to make camp in town for the night and move on at first light. The convoy went in first to exterminate what few undead occupied the streets. We waited in our vehicles with the windows down and the engines off to conserve fuel. Sophia sat in the passenger's seat, one hand clasped in mine, the other fanning her face with a torn-off flap of cardboard. A thin sheen of perspiration covered her skin, turning her hair dark brown where it stuck to her neck.

"How long do you think this is going to take?" she asked.

I shook my head. "No idea. Guess it depends on how many undead there are."

We didn't talk much after that, just sat and listened to the sound of distant gunfire. One of Morgan's troops made his way back to us and inquired if we had radios or not. When he found out we did, he told us what frequency to set them to so we could receive messages from Morgan and his senior staff. I turned the knob to the appropriate setting, placed the radio on the dashboard, and waited.

Not long after that, the cracks of gunfire diminished in frequency until they ceased altogether. A few minutes later, the radio came to life.

"All stations, this is Captain John Morgan. At this time, it appears the town is clear of infected. However, I urge you to proceed with caution. There's no telling where more of them might be trapped, or how many more might be headed our way. Do not, I repeat *do not* open any doors, approach any windows, or attempt to enter any buildings. I've posted troops throughout town who will direct you to the Best Western on 281, where we'll be making camp for the night. Follow their directions, and do not deviate from the path. If you do, my men will not be responsible for your safety. Please proceed ahead."

On the road beyond the windshield, two big green trucks laden with the survivors from the RV encampment and their possessions revved their motors and slowly lumbered north. We waited until they gained some distance on us, then followed suit.

The bridge on 281 leading into town passed slowly under our wheels. A thin green lake too neat and even not to have been shaped by the hand of man surrounded Blanco to the south. We rolled through the streets, first passing empty lots, then a mix of small businesses, houses, a few restaurants, and a large graying building occupying the center of an entire block proclaiming itself the Old Blanco County Courthouse. Farther on, it was more of the same. A bank, a real-estate office, a church, an auto parts store, a moving truck rental agency, and interspersed amongst it all, house after empty house.

"Looks like the people who lived here took their cars with them," I said. "What few I see are mostly junkers."

"It's so sad," Sophia replied. "Houses look different when nobody lives in them anymore. Like they're in mourning or something."

I scanned the periphery of the street, watching the forgotten mailboxes, empty windows, and yawning driveways slip by. "Maybe they are."

"I wonder where they all went."

"Colorado? Kansas, maybe?"

"Think they're still alive?"

"Who knows, Sophia?"

A soldier on the road motioned us ahead, looking bored and uncomfortable in his heavy gear. His eyes lingered on Sophia as we passed, and I shot him a hard stare. If he noticed, he gave no indication. Several minutes and a few more ogling soldiers later, the hotel rose into view and the brake lights of my father's truck flared red in front of us. I eased my foot on the brake until we came to a halt, then watched a soldier approach Mike in the lead Humvee. There was a brief exchange, followed by Mike exiting his vehicle and motioning for us to do the same.

"Let's see what this is about."

Sophia and I got out and walked over to where Mike stood. The soldier remained behind him, eyes wandering back and forth between Lola and Sophia. Tyrel noticed as well, and when he drew close, he leaned in until he was barely two inches from the young man's nose.

"You got a staring problem, boy?"

The soldier leaned away from the ex-SEAL's face, all sharp angles and heavy brows and merciless black eyes, and he took a step back.

"S-sorry," the troop stammered. "I didn't mean …"

"Don't you have somewhere else you need to be, Private?"

"Yes sir."

"Then get there."

Blake stepped up beside me, stifling a laugh as the soldier scurried away. "It's like he forgot he's carrying a gun."

"Ol' Ty has that effect on people."

Tyrel looked my way, mean-mug still in place, and winked.

"So what's going on, Mike?" Dad said, getting everyone's attention.

"We got a choice to make," Mike said. "We can stay here at the hotel, or we can find someplace else to bed down for the night. Personally, I vote for the latter."

"What's wrong with spending the night in the hotel?" Lola asked. The question startled me; it had been so long since Lola had spoken I had almost forgotten she was there.

"Well, I shot one of the folks from the RV camp earlier today," Mike said. "Not bad, mind you. Just a graze. But I doubt he's gonna be happy with me about it. And Caleb here damn near beat the wheels off their leader."

Lola swiveled her head to look at me, a new brand of regard in her eyes. I imagine her expression would have been much the same if she had been standing in the desert and suddenly realized the lumpy brown thing next to her feet was a rattlesnake. "Is that true?" she asked.

"I'm not proud of it, but yes. He didn't leave me much choice."

"How bad did you hurt him?" Dad asked.

"Bumps and bruises."

He looked skeptical. "You sure?"

"I saw him after the fact. He had a big shiner on his temple, but otherwise, he was fine."

Blake laughed next to me. "Man, I feel sorry for that guy. I've sparred with you enough to know what you can do when you play for keeps."

Next to me, I could feel Sophia's stare, and see the smirk on my father's face, and hear Mike's approving grunt, and I reddened, uncomfortable with the attention. "Anyway, Mike has a point. The two of us probably aren't their favorite people right now. And the rest of you will be guilty by association. It's probably best if we find our own place for the night."

"I agree," Dad said. "We'll head down the street to the brewery. The roof of the main building looks good and flat. We'll sleep there tonight."

"How will we get up there?" I asked.

"We'll figure something out. Let's go."

THIRTY-TWO

Blanco, Texas

Morgan waved us over as we drove by.

He was in the hotel parking lot on the roof of his Humvee, directing operations. I got on the radio and said I would handle it, and drove in his direction. The others proceeded ahead to the brewery.

"I need you to stay here," I told Sophia after stopping next to Morgan's vehicle. "This shouldn't take long."

"All right," she said. Her eyes were fixed on the massive Abrams tank squatting in the middle of the road, swiveling its turret back the way we had come. The Bradleys and Howitzers drove past us, dispersing toward the bridges on the south side of town, most likely with orders to blow them if they saw too many infected coming.

Morgan jumped down when I got out of the truck and walked over to me. "Where are you folks headed?"

"To the brewery," I said, standing close so only he could hear me. "I'm thinking Travis and Jerry probably aren't too happy with me right now. Probably best if we make our own accommodations for the night."

Morgan thought about it and nodded. "You're probably right. Infighting is the last thing we need right now. You gonna be okay on your own?"

"We'll be fine. We still have our radios. We'll call if we run into anything we can't handle."

"Sounds good. See you in the morning." He walked back toward his men.

I climbed in the truck and drove away.

"Any trouble?" Sophia asked on the way to the brewery.

"Nope. Morgan seems like a stand up guy."

Sophia tilted her head to look in the side view mirror, the image of the hotel growing smaller in the square of glass. "So far, anyway."

I turned right from Highway 281 onto the narrow, dusty street leading to the brewery. Looking around, it occurred to me Blanco had not been hit by the fires like areas farther south. When I thought about it, I remembered the prevailing winds the night of the fire had mostly been from the north, so between that and the lake protecting the town to the south, Blanco had escaped mostly unscathed. Which probably had a lot to do with why Captain Morgan wanted to stay the night here.

Up ahead, I saw the two Humvees and the other vehicles stopped. They sat across a dirt parking lot from a loading dock, a small copse of trees occupying the middle of the space. A few rusty shipping containers stood to their right, and to the left, I could see the main building and the larger brewing facility beyond.

Dad, Blake, and Mike stood in a huddle while Tyrel rested his hands on the stock of an M-240, barrel trained toward the loading dock. I had a moment to wonder what was holding them up, but then I drove closer to Mike's Humvee and the mystery was solved.

Infected.

"Shit," I muttered.

Sophia reached in the back and grabbed her rifle. "Dad said I need target practice. Guess this is as good a time as any." Before I could say anything, she was out the door and headed toward the parking lot. I grabbed my own weapon and scrambled after her.

"Sophia! Hold up." I caught her in six running strides. She had already reached Mike, who stood in her path, hand upraised.

"Whoa there," the big Marine said. "Where do you think you're going, little girl?"

She gave him a withering glare. "You know I hate it when you call me that."

"Sorry. Where do you think you're going, *young lady*?"

"I was thinking about going over there and shooting those infected."

Mike's face closed down. "Like hell you are. Get back in the truck. Let us take care of these things."

"I'm not a little girl anymore, Dad," Sophia said. "You don't get to order me around."

She went to brush by him, but Mike's hand shot out and seized her arm. "Sophia, stop it."

Her eyes tracked coldly from the hand to her father's face. "Let. Go."

"Sophia ..."

"Let. Go. Now. Or I swear to God, I will leave this place and you will never see me again."

She sounded like she meant it. I stood and stared, shocked at her sudden anger, wondering what the hell had gotten into her. Mike looked pained, mouth half-open, unsure what to say. In a flash of inspiration, I stepped up and put a hand on both of them.

"Okay, hold up a minute," I said. "I have an idea."

They both looked at me, Mike with desperate hope, Sophia blankly. "Listen, Mike. These things are everywhere. She's going to have to learn to deal with them sooner or later. There aren't that many of them. This is a good opportunity to let her get some real world experience in a controlled environment."

I could see the gears turning behind Mike's eyes. His hand loosened on her arm and fell away. Pressing my advantage, I said, "She can stay close to the two of us. Me on one side, you on the other. We'll watch her flanks while she takes out the infected ahead of us. The three of us can work one side of the parking lot, Dad and Blake can set up a crossfire on the other. If things get too heavy, we'll all fall back and let Tyrel light 'em up with the heavy machine gun. Sound good to you?"

Mike looked to the others, who gave short nods, then back to me. "Sounds like a plan."

I turned to Lance. "You mind staying here in the middle? Hang back and take out the ones that slip by?"

He checked the safety on his carbine, then slid back the charging handle to make sure there was a round in the chamber. "I can do that."

"All right then," I smiled at Sophia. She smiled back. "Let's do this."

The infected were spread out across the parking lot, perhaps a hundred of them, more emerging from a stand of trees to the left of the main building. It was roughly the same number Lance and I had faced the day we found Bob and Maureen killed in their home. If the two of us could handle that many on our own, I felt confident of our chances with Dad, Blake, Mike, and Tyrel helping out. Not to mention Sophia.

Mike led the way, walking toward the shipping containers. Looking at them, a thought occurred to me. "Hey Mike."

"Yeah."

I pointed at the closest container. "Ever heard the saying about working smarter, not harder?"

Mike looked where I pointed and grunted approvingly. "Think you can haul my big ass up there?"

"We'll manage."

We broke into a jog; the infected were drawing close enough to be worrisome. Mike slid his rifle around to his back, leaned against the container, and interlaced his fingers at hip level. I stepped into them, hauled myself up high enough to grasp the top of the container, then pushed off his shoulder with my right foot. It was enough to get me over the top, and once there, I told him to send Sophia up.

After helping her up the container, I told her to grab hold of my belt, dig in her heels, and lean back as hard as she could.

"What for?" she asked.

"So your bear of a father doesn't drag all three of us to the ground."

"You ready up there," Mike shouted, casting a worried glance at the steadily approaching undead.

"Ready," I said. "Come on up."

He backed off, took two running steps, and with surprising agility for a man his size, leapt up and seized the edge of the container. Then, feet scrambling for purchase, he pulled himself up until his chin was over the edge, at which point I was able to grip the back of his vest and haul him the rest of the way over. That done, we stood up and sorted ourselves out.

"Cut it close enough didn't we?" I said, pointing at a ghoul who now occupied the space where Mike had stood a few seconds ago.

"They're faster than they look," Mike said. "The ones that ain't messed up too bad can really move."

"Yeah, I noticed the same thing."

"Well, are we going to stand around admiring them all day," Sophia said, "or are we going to kill the damn things?"

She stood at the edge of the container, rifle at port arms, eyes bright with anticipation. It seemed odd to me that she should be so eager to kill the undead. Sure, they were a threat, but they had been people once. Human beings. I had killed a number of them, but felt no elation or satisfaction at doing so. It was a simple matter of survival, of necessity. I derived no pleasure from it.

Watching her, I was reminded of everything I had read over the years about projection and catharsis. How some people have a need to externalize their fears and insecurities and purge their inner pain. They find a target, an outlet, someone or something they can point their finger at and say, *That is bad*, and feel better about themselves. Or in Sophia's case, designate an object of contempt and diminish it so low on her scale of regard that killing it carries no more meaning than squashing a mosquito against her neck.

I have met a great many people who feel the same way. They have an unreasoning hatred for the undead and will go out of their way to kill them, even when it is dangerous or unnecessary to do so. These people see the dead, and they see the reason for everything they have lost, for everything the world has become, for all the death, and pain, and suffering, and all the shattered dreams and lives, and the screams of the dying that haunt them in the night. I can see how these people come to this conclusion, and I understand where they are coming from. But I do not agree with them.

When I look at the infected, I see victims.

When I put them down, it is not retribution. I am doing them a kindness. And God forbid, if I am ever infected, I hope some merciful soul will do the same for me.

"All right, Sophia," Mike said, stepping next to her. "Remember what I taught you now. Stay relaxed, lean into the rifle, let out half a breath before you shoot, and make sure you squeeze the trigger, don't jerk it."

"I know, Dad," she said, motioning for him to back up. She took a breath, brought the rifle to her shoulder, sighted through the red-dot scope, took aim, and fired.

And missed.

"Shit." She shuffled her feet, re-aiming.

"You're too stiff," Mike said. "It's making you jump when you pull the trigger."

"All right, all right," she huffed. "Just let me get a few practice shots."

She fired three more times. On the third, she managed to blast a chunk of bone, skin, and most of one ear from an infected woman's head, but not enough to kill it.

"Son of a *bitch*." She ground her teeth, took a deep breath, and readied herself to try again.

"Try this, sweetheart," Mike said in a gentle voice. "Move your left hand further down the forearm, and relax your shoulders-"

"Dad, just stop. Okay?"

"But I'm just-"

I decided it was time to intervene. "I noticed something that might help," I said, giving Mike a pointed look. He let out an exasperated breath and stepped back.

"Be my guest."

As I took his place next to Sophia, the difference in her demeanor was immediate. Gone was the tension, the irritation, the shallow breathing of someone about to lose her temper. When I went to move her shoulders and arms, she became pliant under my hands.

"You want to relax here and here," I said, touching the two sides of her trapezius muscles. "Just take a breath and kind of roll your shoulders around. Good. Now take this hand and move it forward. It's too close to the mag-well back here, makes it hard to switch your point of aim. Having your hand farther down the barrel makes for a faster transition."

Behind me, Mike sputtered and fumed. "But … but that's the same thing I just …"

I glanced over my shoulder at him and shook my head. His shoulders sagged. He threw up his hands, walked over to the other side of the container, aimed his carbine, and began killing infected with savage enthusiasm.

There you go, big guy, I thought. *Work it out.*

"Okay, close your eyes, Sophia. Now take a deep breath. Fill up your lungs." I kept my hand on her back, making sure she did as I said. "Now let it out slowly. When I say go, open your eyes, pick a target, and fire with both eyes open. Make sure the red dot is just a little bit high."

Her ribcage contracted, contracted, and when it was at the halfway point, I said, "Go."

Her eyes opened. They were clear, focused, no longer clouded with eagerness or frustration or anything else. The scope was slightly below her line of sight. Keeping both eyes open, she raised it, acquired a target, and squeezed the trigger slowly until the report caught her by surprise—exactly the way it is supposed to be done. Ten yards away, a splash of black and red spouted from the back of a ghoul's head, and it slumped to the ground.

"Perfect," I said. "Just keep doing what you're doing. Start with the closest targets, then try to hit a few farther away."

She spared me a glance and a white-toothed smile. "I think I got it now."

"And be careful where you aim." I pointed to where Dad and Blake had taken up position. "We don't want any friendly fire."

She nodded soberly and promised me she would be careful. I relocated to the middle of the container, split the difference between Mike and Sophia, and lay down in the prone position. The metal was hot underneath me from baking all day in the sun, but I ignored it. Firing from the prone position is the most accurate way to do business, and I wanted to conserve as much ammunition as possible. The high vantage point afforded by the shipping container gave me an excellent field of fire. It would be a shame not to take advantage of it.

I dialed the magnification on my scope down to 2x and started taking potshots at the infected closest to the main building. Mike and Sophia were doing a good job eliminating the ones closest to our side of the parking lot, while Dad and Blake were steadily mowing down the undead on their side. Despite the progress they were making, it was obvious from my perch they would have to fall back soon. It seemed that for every infected they dropped, two more emerged from somewhere to take their place. I began focusing my fire on the periphery of the horde, trying to cut their numbers before they could reach the parking lot.

The reticle in my vision found what was once a man still wearing a torn and bloody business suit, tie flapping in the breeze, one wingtip shoe missing. The uneven footing caused him to lurch dangerously with every step, looking as though he were about to fall over before wheeling his arms around and righting himself. I timed his movements, noticing that when he stood up straight, there was a second of two of hesitation before he tried to make the next step. So I waited.

Step, totter, groan, flappy-flap of the arms, next foot comes forward, pushes off the ground, torso straightens, head is up for a second and-

CRACK.

Down he goes. Next target: middle aged woman, obese, cardigan, long denim skirt, sensible clogs on her feet, most of her face missing on the right side, right arm chewed down to gristle and bone. Probably someone's grandma once. She was lumbering at a steady pace toward Dad and Blake, both of her legs still intact. I waited for her to rock left, then pause on the sway to the right before transitioning to the other foot, and *CRACK.*

The bullet struck the back of her head on the part called the occipital bunt and blew most of it off, leaving a ragged, dripping mess in its wake. The wound did not immediately kill her, but it scragged her wiring enough she did a face-plant and stayed there in a twitching, quivering heap. Rather than waste a bullet finishing her off, I moved on to the next target.

A minute or two later, the chamber locked open on an empty magazine. I dropped it, stowed it, and slid home a new one. Before I started firing, I did another battlefield assessment.

Mike and Sophia were doing a good job of reducing the horde on our side. They had widened the semi-circle of ghouls around the container by several meters and counting. Dad and Blake, on the other hand, were dealing with a far denser cluster of undead and were slowly retreating toward the vehicles, dropping corpses as they went. At a signal from Blake, Lance left his post and ran over to back them up. Tyrel, evidently tired of being left out of the action, disappeared into the Humvee for a moment, reappeared with Mike's M1A, steadied himself on the roof of the Humvee, and filled the air with a cadence of hollow booms.

From the corner of my eye, I saw a dust plume approaching from the south. I came up to my knees and peered in that direction, trying to see who was coming. A few seconds later, a Humvee rounded the corner and pulled into the parking lot. The driver slowed and conferred with the man beside him as though unsure how to approach. I saved him the trouble by standing up and waving him over.

On the way to our position, the SAW gunner standing in the roof turret opened up on the horde with tight, controlled bursts of fire. He had obviously learned a thing or two about fighting the undead because rather than aim center of mass or try for headshots—which would have been next to impossible in a moving vehicle while firing on full-auto—he aimed at the infected's legs.

Blood and bone and kneecaps and lower halves of legs disintegrated under the hail of bullets. The gunner disabled dozens of undead in the space of less than thirty seconds, and while it did not kill them, it reduced their mobility to a crawl. More importantly, it did so quickly and en masse. I found myself nodding in approval.

Have to remember that one.

The Humvee stopped below us, a few yards away. I shouted to them, "Looks like you missed a few."

The soldier in the turret turned toward me. "Sorry. Didn't search this far north, figured all the infected would be coming from the south."

"Looks like you figured wrong."

He had the good grace to look sheepish. "How about you folks back off? We'll take it from here."

"I have a better idea," I said. "How about you ride around and do your leg-shooting trick with the rest of these things, and we'll come behind you and mop up."

"Works for me." He leaned down and said something to the driver, and they were off.

Dad, Blake, and Lance abandoned their positions, double-timed it back to the vehicles, and safely ensconced themselves in a Humvee. The Army vehicle drove into the middle of the infected, laid down a broad volley of fire, then stopped and waited while the horde gathered round. The gunner turned so he was facing the vehicle's rear and let out occasional bursts of fire to keep the undead from blocking their escape route. When the undead had pressed in tightly enough to begin climbing the hood and beating on the windows, the driver put it in reverse and peeled out, running over a few infected along the way.

One of the ghouls clung to the hood and was steadily climbing toward the gunner who still had his back turned. Mike and I shouted warnings, pointing at the thing behind him. He heard us, turned, reached a hand into a pocket of his vest, and produced a snub-nosed revolver. With the ghoul almost in arm's reach, he stuck the gun in its face and pulled the trigger. Gore splashed across the creature's back as the top of its head flew apart, brain and skull spatter painting the front end of the

Humvee. From the report, I knew the gun was a .357 magnum. Hollow point slugs too, judging by the damage. At that range, he may as well have shot it in the face with an artillery piece. The creature collapsed, nearly headless, and slid from the vehicle.

The driver turned a slow circle around the now congregated infected while the gunner stashed his pistol and returned his focus to the SAW. Once again, the *ratatatat* of controlled fire rang out, and once again, undead legs flew to pieces. The soldiers worked quickly, driving four laps around the ghouls in concentric circles, gradually whittling them down. Finally, none were left standing.

The Humvee drove to where the other vehicles were parked, squelching over a few corpses along the way. One of them grabbed part of the right rear fender and was dragged along, its lower body remaining in place while the torso trailed an ever-lengthening rope of intestine. Sophia made a choking sound next to me and turned away.

"God, that is so fucking gross."

"You okay?"

"Yeah. Just give me a minute."

I watched as the Humvee stopped next to where the others waited. Mike climbed down from the container by lowering himself over the edge and then dropping the last few feet. I followed suit, then turned and caught Sophia on the way down and lowered her gently.

"Thank you," she said, standing close enough to kiss. It amazed me that even here, standing in a field of stinking, festering undead, the male sex drive was strong enough to rear its ancient, incorrigible head. I ignored it and put a hand on Sophia's lower back as we threaded our way through the corpses on the way back to the vehicles.

"Gonna be a hell of a mess to clean up," I overheard one of the soldiers say to my father. "We'll have to get some people out here. Haul those thing away to a good safe distance."

"Hey," I called, getting his attention. He looked at me. "Isn't one of those HEMTTs equipped with a shovel, or a bucket attachment, or whatever you call it?"

His eyes grew sharp. "Yes. Yes it is. Good thinking, I'll see if I can get it out here. You folks okay in the meantime?"

"We're fine," Dad said. "But we appreciate the help. While you're gone, we'll go around and make sure these things are taken care of permanently."

"Be careful doing that," the soldier said. "Those things are twice as dangerous on the ground. Don't let them get their hands on you, they're strong as hell."

"I'm well aware. Thanks again, gentlemen."

"Be back soon."

The Humvee drove away. My father looked around at the rest of us, checked his rifle, and tilted his head toward the crawling, moaning horrors in the parking lot. "The sooner we get started, the sooner we'll be finished."

I looked at the infected, their blood black and shiny in the fading afternoon light, and watched them drag their carcasses toward me, unconcerned with their injuries, shredded hands grasping at gore-soaked asphalt.

Feeling a shift in my stomach, I looked away to the north woodlands, above the parking lot, over the infected, and across the roof of the brewery beyond. Knobby treetops rustled under a sky darkening to electric purple as I thought about what lay across the Mississippi River. The last newscast I had seen before they stopped airing was from California. The talking head was relaying information from affiliates in the Midwest.

The east coast has gone dark.

Nice way to put it. The most verdant, populous region of the country, home to over a hundred and fifty million people, had been overrun. Everything east of the Appalachians was now an infested, toxic, and in many places radioactive no man's land.

Gone dark.

306

The Appalachians had not stopped them. The Mississippi River had not stopped them. The combined might of the U.S. Armed Forces had not stopped them. Nothing stopped them. Delayed them, maybe. Held them back for a while. But there was no stopping them. All we had done here was buy time, nothing more. A buffer zone, breathing room, enough space to get some rest and then move on.

I looked down at my rifle and wondered what it would be like to try to wipe out a swarm of mosquitos with it.

"I don't know Dad," I said. "As far as killing the infected goes, I'm not sure if we'll ever be finished."

THIRTY-THREE

Full dark, and the stars came out.

I lay on my bedroll, eyes open to the brilliance of the sky. Sophia was a warm, heavy weight next to me.

"I've never seen it like this," she said. "The night sky."

"You mean without a roof between you?"

She slapped my shoulder. "No, asshole. I mean bright. Like this." She pointed a finger heavenward.

"It's because the power is out," I said. "No streetlights, no city lights, no light at all. Light pollution obscures the sky at night. Drowns out the stars. Must have been very disappointing for all those photons."

"Disappointing?"

"To travel billions of years only to fizzle out in a smog-choked haze."

"You say it like the stars actually care. Last I heard, they're just big burning balls of plasma."

"We're made of them, you know. Human beings. The dust of stars given life."

"What?"

"The fundamental elements, the components, the building blocks of life. All deposited on this planet by stars, flung across the universe as they died."

Sophia was silent for a while, then said, "There's a kind of beauty in that, I think. The lifeless given life."

I turned my head and gazed over the edge of the white metal roof. The distant moans of infected drifted to my ears. "The lifeless given life. It supports the duality, I suppose."

Sophia shuffled closer, lips brushing against my neck. "Now I understand why you don't talk much. You don't make a bit of fucking sense."

There was something wildly erotic about the way she said it, our warmth nestled together under the coldness of an indifferent sky. "It's beauty and corruption, Sophia. Light and dark. Life and death. For every point, a counterpoint. We, the human race, are the defiance. The struggle of sentience in an ocean of oblivion. Those things out there, they're a corruption of us. An abomination of something beautiful."

Another silence, then she said, "You really think people are beautiful? I mean, with all the things we've done to each other? War and murder and all the rest of it?"

"I think life is beauty, Sophia. And while there are as many tragedies as there are people in the world to live them, those tragedies don't diminish the importance of our existence. Think of how far we've come. It wasn't all that long ago we were lying on bare ground, fires burning next to us, wondering what all those bright spots in the big wide dark were all about. Now we know. Now we can draw their chemical components on computer diagrams and replicate their energy in small scale. Ever seen a plasma torch cut through two inches of steel in less time than it takes to say it?"

"No."

"It's a thing to see."

I lay in the dark and tightened my arms around Sophia and wondered what was wrong with the night. The hot starkness of day no longer assaulted us; the warmth of the metal under my back had faded hours ago. There was a gentle breeze, a stirring of leaves flush with the green blessing of late spring. I listened, ears tuning out the moans, the booming snores of Mike and my father twenty yards distant, and the rumbling of a Humvee engine as a patrol checked on us. I closed my eyes against the brilliance of a searchlight playing over the rooftop, face turned into the sweetness of Sophia's scent, and the answer came to me.

There were no crickets. The fires had sent them all away.

*****

Midnight.

Had to be. Otherwise the hand on my shoulder would not have been there.

"Rise and shine, lover boy," Blake said. "We're on the clock."

I gently disentangled myself from Sophia's arms and pushed aside the leg draped over my midsection. She stirred a little, then rolled over to her other side, heaved a deep breath, and continued snoring quietly.

Blake laid a steadying hand on my shoulder as I stood up and nearly toppled over. The scant two hours of sleep I'd managed were just enough to make me truly feel like shit.

"You all right?" Blake asked.

"Ask me again in five minutes."

"Just make sure you keep your gun pointed away from me."

"Hardy-har-har."

"I'm not kidding."

I left my pack where it lay, but donned my vest, belt, drop holster, and slung my rifle. One hastily chugged canteen of water later, I felt almost human.

"Okay," I said. "Let the mid-watch begin."

Blake smiled. He had not done much of that lately and it was good to see it again. "Look at it this way. It's only four hours, then you can go back to sleep."

"Lovely."

"Your breath is wonderful, by the way."

"Duly noted."

After pissing over the edge of the roof with my eyes closed for the better part of a thousand years, I used the last splash of water in my canteen to wet my toothbrush, applied a minimum of paste, solved the problem, and spit the excess to the parking lot. To my surprise, it landed on the face of an infected wandering below the edge of the periphery. Looking around, I saw the shadows of dozens more stumbling and shambling in the light of the half-moon.

"Son of a bitch!"

"Yeah," Blake said behind me. "They wandered in over the last hour."

"Did anyone radio Captain Morgan?"

Blake snickered. "Captain Morgan. Man, I hope that guy gets promoted soon."

"Well?"

"Yeah, Joe called it in. They'll send the Bradleys around at daybreak. It's nothing a twenty-five millimeter chain gun can't take care of."

I relaxed, comforted by the idea of armored cavalry. The infected may have been legion, but they were composed of flesh, after all. And in the battle of flesh versus high-velocity tungsten, I knew where I would be placing my bets.

We walked along the rooftop, staying well clear of the edge. I rubbed the sleep out of my eyes and wondered what the hell the point of posting a watch was anyway. There were over a hundred troops nearby, not to mention the fact we were thirty feet off the ground. I had posed this question to my father after being informed I had pulled the mid-watch, and his answer was a shrug and a simple, "You never know. Better safe than sorry."

Hard to argue with that logic.

I looked down as we passed the shipping container and ladder we had used to ascend the brewery. A search of a nearby neighborhood had yielded the ladder, but it was too short for what we needed. So after the bucket-equipped HEMTT had cleared the permanently-dead infected from the parking lot, I talked the driver into bulldozing an empty shipping container next to the wall. After that, it was easy.

"So," Blake said, breaking the silence. "You and Sophia."

"Yeah. Me and Sophia."

"You know that girl done had a crush on you for years now, right?"

"So she says."

"You never seen it?"

"She never gave me the time of day, Blake."

He bobbed his head from side to side. "She always did get quiet when you were around. Then again, you did the same thing. Never tried to flirt with her. Probably what got her interested. All those boys coming after her all the time, and you barely paying her any attention. Kind of thing makes a girl curious."

"I'll be the first to admit I don't know much about girls, Blake."

"I'll let you in on a secret." He leaned in close and lowered his voice. "No one does. Not even them. It's how they keep us off balance."

I laughed, and gently slapped him on the arm. Blake was the kind of guy it was hard not to laugh around. He was always quick with a smile or a joke, or if needed, a word of encouragement. When I was about eleven or twelve, I asked him why he was so happy all the time. He sat me down and told me what it was like for him growing up.

He was from New Orleans, originally. His father died in an accident at work when he was only three, leaving his mother to raise him alone. She worked two jobs, sometimes three, to make ends meet. They used food stamps to buy groceries, bought clothes at Goodwill and the Salvation Army, and because he was black, and poor, and the child of a single mother, he was stigmatized everywhere he went.

The neighborhood he grew up in was rough. Drugs were endemic. If you were not a dealer, someone you knew or were related to was. The cops were an ever-present evil, looming over everything and everyone. Walking down the street was reason enough to get thrown up against a wall and searched, and if you mouthed off, dragged into an alley and beaten.

Blake knew. It had happened to him many times.

His early impressions of life were of white faces buying drugs down the street from his house, and white faces snarled with hate swinging a baton at his head, and white faces looking at him with fear and contempt at every turn, the whispers, the snide comments, the subtext of every interaction the same.

You are a thug, and I don't trust you.

But there was one problem.

They were wrong.

He dressed the part. He acted the part. Every young man in the neighborhood did because they had to. Failure to conform was punished harshly. You did not want to be seen as non-complicit. Savage beatings on a daily basis were a very real possibility for those who did not tow the line with the drug gangs. One did not have to participate, but you sure as hell better not get in the way or give any indication of disapproval. To do so was to invite disaster.

So Blake walked the line. He stayed out of trouble at school, quietly keeping his grades up. He steered clear of the gangs, being careful not to get on their bad side. Which is not to say he never broke the law—he did what he had to do to survive—but he was careful about it.

Then came graduation, and the recruiter's office, and the Army, and his tearful, dutiful mother telling him to shake the dust from his feet and write as soon as he got the chance.

She died a few years later from a stroke. Blake had been sending her money every month, hoping that between the two of them they could save enough for her to move to a better neighborhood. She never spent a dime of the money.

"I had a choice to make," Blake said. "I could succumb to hate, and anger, and spend the rest of my life being bitter, or I could do what my momma always told me to do when things were bad."

He looked at me then, tears in his dark, thoughtful eyes. "She said to me, 'Baby, you just got to smile. No matter what the world throws at you, you just got to smile.' So that's what I do. No matter what the world throws at me, I just keep right on smiling. I used to see it as revenge, but then I got older and realized that's a foolish way to look at things. Revenge never did no good for anybody. The world ain't got nothing against me. What happened, happened. I just got to rise above it and move on. And that's what I do."

"So where you see this going, the two of you?" Blake asked, interrupting my thoughts.

"Hell if I know, man. I'm just taking it a day at a time."

He looked out toward the hotel and the dim orange dots of campfires in the parking lot. Humvees patrolled and rifles cracked in the distance as the troops on watch kept the infected at bay. His customary smile faded, replaced by a fearful solemnity that hurt me to see on his jovial face. "Guess that's all anybody can do right now, things being the way they are."

We walked in the dark for a while, each in his own thoughts. As we passed by Sophia's sleeping form, I stopped to watch her. Blake stopped as well, back turned, giving me a moment to myself. He was good that way. Perceptive. The kind of guy who understood things without needing someone to say it outright.

"What's going to happen to us, do you think?" I asked.

I heard Blake's boot scrape the metal roof as he turned and walked over to me. His hand was warm on my shoulder as he stood beside me, voice close to my ear. "Caleb, I don't know. You're a grown man now, so I ain't gonna bullshit you. Things are bad. Real bad. Worst I ever seen."

"I know that much."

"I know you do. What I'm saying is, I think it's going to get worse before it gets better. I think we're in the early stages of something long, and dark, and terrible. If we want to get through it, we got to be strong. We got to stick together like family. You understand?"

I nodded, and did.

"Come on," he said. "Let's keep moving. Best lesson I ever learned—when in doubt, keep moving."

The half-moon was clear the next few hours. No clouds obscured its shine on an oasis of green in a sea of charred black. At four in the morning, after an impossibly long watch, I woke Mike and Lance and waited while they cleared their heads and armed themselves. Afterward, I ambled back to my bedroll, back to Sophia. She stirred as I lay down and draped an arm around her.

"Hey," she muttered. "Ev'thing okay?"

I kissed her cheek. "Everything's fine, pretty lady. Go back to sleep."

She smiled. I closed my eyes to the stars and the moon and languished in her sweet, humid, feminine warmth.

315

Even the gunshots and roar of engines could not keep me awake.

THIRTY-FOUR

"Come on," Dad said, shaking my arm. "Spear practice."

I sat up and blinked against the early light of dawn. To the east, the sun was an angry scarlet eye peeking over the hills in the distance. Low banks of clouds rolled overhead in varying shades of red, orange, pale yellow, and finally blue that darkened to steel gray in the west. The air was cool, but heavy with humidity and the promise of higher temperatures to come.

Sophia had rolled away from me in the night and lay curled up under her thin blanket. I brushed the hair from her face and kissed her cheek. She stirred, sighed, and smiled. I kissed her again before I left.

Dad had set up a fast-rope descent to the parking lot. When I arrived, he slid down it like the practiced expert he was, then tossed his harness up to me. Although I was quite a bit taller than him, we were about the same through the hips. The harness fit me just fine. I repeated the process, albeit without quite the same grace and fluidity.

The bucket-equipped HEMTT was already on site, breaking the infected's bodies by crushing them, then scraping them into a pile in the middle of the pavement. It was gruesome work, but effective. The parking lot was almost clear. Two Bradleys circled the operation, big chain-guns aimed at the thicker knots of undead.

"Let's find someplace a bit more peaceful," Dad said. I nodded in agreement and followed him to one of the Humvees. We drove back to 281 and pulled into the parking lot of the hotel where the rest of the soldiers and civilians had spent the night. Evidently, none of them were awake yet except for the guards on patrol. The place was quiet, only a few bleary-eyed troops and roving vehicles on hand to disturb the early morning silence.

Dad pulled around the back of the building near the service entrance where there was a narrow stretch of cracked asphalt, a half-full dumpster, silent AC units, and not much else. To our right was an expanse of slightly overgrown lawn roughly two acres wide.

"Looks like a good spot," I said. Dad agreed. He drove the Humvee over the curb, parked, and got out.

The old man—who really was not old at all—opened the back so I could crawl inside and dig out our two rubber-tipped practice spears. When I tossed him his full-length faux weapon, he caught it one handed, spun it deftly around his body, and assumed a fighting stance, knees slightly bent, haft close to his hips, rubber tip pointed in my direction.

My own weapon was only half as long, the handle shortened to my specifications. The blade on the end of mine was wider, heavier, and longer than the one my father wielded, although also formed of the same vulcanized rubber. I held it with my hand choked near the blade, the bulk of the handle protruding over my shoulder. In the years since I'd developed this unique fighting style, Dad had never quite sorted out all my tricks.

"You're too traditional," I said for the umpteenth time as we circled each other. "Too stiff. You need to innovate."

"Don't worry, kid," he said, a determined look on his face. "I'll figure you out yet."

"Why are we still fighting with spears anyway?" I asked. "Wouldn't knives or machetes make more sense?"

The answer was predictable; I had heard it a thousand times. "Spears were the infantry rifle of the ancient world," he said. "You've probably read volumes about swords, but the truth is spears were the deciding factor in countless battles throughout history. They're easy to forge, durable, and extend a warrior's reach by meters without requiring an undue amount of resources to manufacture. Swords, axes, and maces are pretty to look at, but spears, halberds, and billhooks were the preferred weapons of the soldiers of old. And with good reason."

I nodded along, too tired to argue the merits of modern weapons over ancient. "All right then. Let's see what you got."

I barely had time to dodge the tip of his weapon as it whipped past my head. One second my father was standing twelve feet away, and the next he had closed the distance, his spear extended in a two-handed grip. Dad was many things, but slow was not one of them.

Fortunately for me, my boxing coach always insisted I learn and practice the fundamentals of head movement. It is less about being fast than it is about understanding body mechanics, watching your opponent, and knowing where the next attack is coming from. My dad was a competent boxer, among other fighting styles, but he did not start as early as I did. The muscle memory was not as deeply ingrained in him as it was in me. So when he swept the spear to the side after missing with the initial thrust, I had already ducked it and circled away.

"Nice," he said, grinning. He adjusted his footwork and began closing in on my right. I switched my spear to the other side, having long ago learned the value of being able to fight with either hand.

Keeping my head low and my feet moving, I harassed him with eerie-looking over-the-shoulder thrusts with my spear's shortened handle, aimed at batting his weapon aside.

"How the hell do you do that?" he muttered, backing off. "It's like you have a scorpion tail or some shit."

Rather than answer, I used the distraction to aim a kick at the mid-point of his spear shaft, closed the distance, whipped my weapon forward, and let it slide through my hand. When I felt the slightly flared pommel hit the edge of my palm, I ducked, leapt forward, switched hands, and rolled to my right.

As expected, my father predicted the kick and the thrust, and was ready with a counter-attack. He let his arms go limp to absorb the blow to the spear, executed a spin move like a dancer's pirouette, and slashed at the spot where my head should have been.

But I wasn't there.

Instead, the last second dive-and-roll had allowed me to pop up behind him and gently press the blunted rubber edge of my practice spear to his kidney. "Checkmate," I said.

"I hope you enjoyed that," he said, smiling over his shoulder. "It's the last time you'll get away with it."

He whipped his spear through a blurring figure-eight motion, nearly knocking my weapon out of my hands and forcing me back a few steps. He pressed the attack, the wooden hafts of our spears clacking loudly against one another. Seven moves later I lay on my back, disarmed, the point of my father's practice weapon aimed at my throat.

"Okay," I chuckled. "Point taken."

"No pun intended?" He helped me to my feet, smiling broadly.

We faced each other, bowed, and set to in earnest.

No more messing around.

An hour later, we had fought twenty bouts. I won nine. Two were a draw. That put us even. Dad called a halt to the action, leaning heavily on his spear, breath coming quickly. I tossed my weapon to the ground and put my hands on my knees. There was a swelling over Dad's right eye where I had caught him with an elbow in an attempt to knock him off balance. It didn't work, and he had skewered me in the ribs for my trouble. The attack left a bruise under my arm I would feel for a week. Other than that, a few minor scrapes aside, we were uninjured.

"You're getting better," he said. "Or maybe I'm just slowing down."

I stood up and stretched, feeling a few vertebrae pop back into place. "If this is what you look like slow," I said, "I'd hate to have fought you in your prime."

We both jumped when we heard clapping behind us. Spinning around, I spotted Morgan standing on a second-floor balcony, applauding.

"Nice work, fellas," he called down. "That was some hard-core kung fu shit. The hell did you learn how to do that?"

I smiled and was about to say something witty, but then I caught my father's disapproving glare from the corner of my eye. "How long have you been standing there?" he asked, irritation in his voice.

Morgan held up his hands. "Sorry, man, didn't mean to snoop. The clickity-clacking woke me up. Came outside to see what the noise was all about."

Dad glared a moment longer, then motioned for me to get in the Humvee. "Come on. Let's go check on the others."

I gave Morgan an apologetic shrug, then followed.

"What was that all about?" I asked as we drove away. In response, rather than driving toward the brewery, Dad pulled down a side street and stopped. He left the engine running, the air conditioner laboring against the increasing temperature outside.

"Caleb, there are a few facts of life you need to understand," he said. "Things I've never discussed with you because I didn't think it would be necessary."

"Okay," I said warily. "Like what?"

Dad breathed out through his nose, staring frustratedly out the window. I thought about Lauren, and the trouble he'd been having with her, the tension and arguments and distance between them, and my heart went out to him.

"Dad," I said gently. "What's going on? Talk to me."

321

He kept his gaze averted for a while, then said, "Caleb, you don't understand who and what you are. What you represent. What you're capable of."

"Okay ..."

He reached out and closed his calloused fingers over my forearm with a grip like iron. My father was not a big man, but his strength was a force of nature, muscles hard as oak rippling under sun-browned skin.

"All the training you've had," he said, "the skills you've learned ... it's rare, Caleb. It makes you dangerous. People like us, people who can do the things we can do, we're going to be in high demand very soon. There will be factions vying to round up as many of us as they can get their hands on. The world we knew is over, now. A new world is being born, and it is going to be a dark and violent place. There are people out there who will try to use you if they can. You can't let them. Never let anyone know what you can do, Caleb. People will try to make a tool out of you. Bend you to their will. If they can't win you over with charm, they'll find some leverage, some way to hurt you. They will try to own you. Believe me, son. I know."

I stared at him for a long time, saying nothing. I had always known my upbringing was unique; the training I had received from Dad, Mike, Blake and Tyrel was something most people never experienced. But it had never dawned on me until that moment just how different it made me. How dangerous.

I had been trained from the age of five to be a super soldier.

I could shoot as well as any Special Forces operator. I was as good a sniper as anything the Marine Corps had ever produced. I had trained for over ten years in jiu jitsu, boxing, wrestling, krav maga, and various weapons styles. Room entries and cover and concealment and combat tactics were as familiar to me as tying my shoes. Not to mention my knowledge of fieldcraft, lock picking, explosives, and a host of other skills.

If I were looking for someone to exploit, I'd be pretty damned high on my list.

Dad saw understanding register on my face and let go of my forearm. "Do you see now, son? You have to be careful. Never reveal more about yourself than absolutely necessary. Do what you have to do to stay alive, but tell no one about your past. Understood?"

"All right," I said. "I get it, Dad. I really do."

He stared at me searchingly, and after a few seconds he said, "I believe you."

The morning sun was bright over his shoulder when I looked at him. "Really?"

"Yes. Because I know you, son, and I can read you like a book." He leaned closer, lowering his voice.

"And I can see how scared you are."

THIRTY-FIVE

Where highways 281 and 290 came together outside of Austin, the northbound lanes were a snarled mess of cars and corpses.

When the people fleeing the capital of Texas realized they weren't getting anywhere, they jumped the median and tried to use the southbound lanes to escape. The result was a wide, stalled parking lot that spilled out onto the shoulder for dozens of yards in every direction. At some point the infected had shown up, and it was all over but the dying.

I was out on point with Dad, Mike, Blake, and a couple of combat engineers when we made the discovery. Tyrel had stayed behind due to his injuries, along with Sophia, Lauren, Lance, and Lola.

Morgan had decided the best use of our skills was to have us scout the way ahead. We surveyed the scene, then radioed back to the convoy. One of Morgan's senior sergeants acknowledged and told us to stand by. Shortly thereafter, the Bradleys, a couple of HEMTTs, and the Abrams showed up, along with a dozen troops in a deuce-and-a-half in case infantry support was needed.

After they arrived, Morgan got on the radio and asked us to draw away as many infected as we could while his people worked to clear the road. The rest of the day consisted of my group off-roading in our Humvees and leading the undead

324

around in circles while the troops dragged dead bodies from vehicles, put transmissions in neutral, and stood clear as the heavy armor pushed wrecks aside.

By nightfall, we had made it all of thirty miles and the infected had bitten four troops. But we had reached a point where we could use side roads to parallel the highway, which would make for faster transit. Despite the long, hot hours the convoy had just endured, Captain Morgan elected to press on a few hours into the night.

Tired as we were, no one argued. The moans of the San Antonio horde were close enough to carry to us on the wind.

The four bitten soldiers were kept under observation in the back of a truck for a couple of hours until it became clear their condition would not improve. When the medics gave their final diagnosis, Morgan ordered the convoy to a halt and the men were led out of sight under heavy guard. Three of them looked resigned to their fate, stumbling along and convulsing in the throes of their infection. The fourth, however, struggled and screamed and kicked and begged his brothers in arms to let him go, to let him run for it and take his chances. His words fell on deaf ears.

His voice sounded familiar, so before he was out of sight, I raised my scope to get a better look.

It was Johansen.

While I had not enjoyed my first meeting with the man, I did not wish him to die as one of the infected. Come to think of it, I would not have wished that on anyone.

About a hundred other people and I, including the survivors from the RV encampment, watched in silence as the doomed men were led away. Johansen's increasingly panicked screams carried to us over the crest of a hill until the boom of a pistol echoed through the woods.

The shouting stopped.

Seconds later, there were three near-simultaneous cracks. Shortly thereafter, a few men lowered a small bucket loader from the back of a HEMTT and drove it in the direction of the shots. Half an hour later, their work finished, they returned to the convoy, faces drawn and somber. No one tried to speak to them. Morgan came over the radio in a quiet voice and ordered to convoy to get under way.

*****

We couldn't follow 281 forever, so we cut toward Highway 16 and used any flat, wide, unobstructed stretch of ground we could find to take us north until we were within four miles of Interstate 20.

Along the way, we found a gas station with diesel tanks that had not been looted, allowing us to refuel and restock our gerry cans and fuel barrels as well as supplement our meager provisions. Near where we stopped, a side road led into a heavily wooded region away from any significantly populated areas. According to the map, there was a large natural pond nearby. Morgan's senior sergeant ordered a HEMTT and a few Humvees to break off and get to work purifying as much of that water as they could. Morgan himself radioed us to wait for him and approached our position in his command vehicle.

"Got a mission for you," he said as he pulled alongside.

"Let me guess," Blake called back. "Recon I-20, see what we're up against."

"You are a man of impeccable logic."

Dad exchanged a look with his old friend, then said, "Can do. But we'll need to refuel first."

Morgan motioned to his driver. "Not a problem."

After topping off the tanks, we headed north toward the interstate. The section of highway we approached lay in the middle of a steep, broad V that had once been a hill. There were many such places along the interstate where the highway builders had blasted through the landscape in order to keep the road nice and straight. The resulting formation allowed us to park the vehicles at the base of the hill and approach the summit on foot, staying low to avoid detection. At the top we fanned out at ten-meter intervals along the hillside and surveyed the scene through our optics.

By that point, I thought I had seen some bad things. Crossing the bridge over I-35 that flaming evening had been something out of a fevered nightmare. The City of Houston in flames in the dark red distance was a sight that would haunt me for years. The 281/290 junction had been a blood-soaked cluster-fuck of epic proportions. But when I looked down that hillside at Interstate 20, for the second time in my life, I felt a sinking, bowel-constricting panic that I had died and my soul had been damned for all eternity.

It would have taken me years to count the infected. There were cars piled on top of cars on top of even more cars. Tractor-trailers and buses and RVs and every other vehicle imaginable lay overturned and crashed and burned down to skeletal husks. The stench of corpses was a living, crawling thing that reached down my throat and closed a hand around my windpipe. Dead bodies lay everywhere, some still in their vehicles, some on top of them, some on the side of the road, still others crawling, too damaged from the infected who consumed them to mount much mobility.

Organs, limbs and bloody streaks covered every surface, stained the ground red, splattered against windshields, and lay rotting in the ditches on the side of the road. I scanned left and saw a Blackhawk helicopter crashed in the middle of traffic, tail rotor pointing skyward, the skeletal visage of the pilot slumped against his restraints. I scanned to the right and saw a vintage convertible with the top down, the driver in pieces on the ground nearby, and, to my horror, a baby seat in the back. For a moment, the baby seat looked empty, then I realized the padding was beige under the red, and that lump at the bottom was-

NO!

I dropped my rifle, scrambled back down the slope, and got as far away as I could before I was violently, gut-wrenchingly sick. I heaved up everything inside me and kept going, dry-heaving, ribs cramping, abdomen trying to tear itself apart.

Finally, the seizures subsided and I managed to crawl away from my own bile before I collapsed and lay on my side, gasping for breath. A few moments later, I felt a hand on my shoulder.

"Hey," Blake's voice said. "I'd ask if you're okay, but I think the answer is pretty obvious."

"Can't ..." was all I could manage to croak out.

"Come on, Caleb. It's not safe here. Let's go back to the Humvee. We'll wait there for the others."

I followed him, barely conscious of where I was going, dimly accepting my rifle and slinging it over my shoulder. Blake helped me into the passenger's seat, then climbed in, cranked the engine, and turned the AC to its highest setting. After a few minutes, the cold air blowing in my face started to make me feel better.

"Sorry about that," I said, feeling a flush come up my neck.

Blake shook his head. "Don't be. If I'd stayed a few more seconds, I wouldn't have been in much better shape."

"That makes me feel a little better."

"Man, I've seen some things, but that ..."

"Yeah. No shit."

"How the hell we gonna get past that?"

"I'm sure the good captain will think of something."

We waited with no further conversation until Dad, Mike, and the two combat engineers came back down the hillside. On the way down, one of the soldiers hesitated, turned to the side, and heaved his guts behind a pine tree. The others waited, faces stoic, until he had mastered himself and started on his way again.

Back in his vehicle, Dad calmly and in detail explained the situation on the interstate. Morgan told him to stand by, presumably to confer with his staff, then came back on the radio and requested we return to the convoy.

"Roger that," my father said. "En route. Recon one out."

*****

The first time you see heavy artillery fire on a target at close range, you never forget it.

Like the others in the convoy, I waited at a good safe distance for the fireworks to start. Morgan's men had scouted the various access roads until they found a flat approach on a narrow two-lane. The Abrams and two Howitzers took point, the Bradleys backing them up, APCs waiting the wings in case infantry support was needed during the crossing.

I sat in a Humvee with Blake and Sophia at the rear of the column. My father, Lauren, and Lance were in front of us. Tyrel and Lola waited behind, Mike bringing up the rear in his truck. Dad had loaned his Ram to a trio of pregnant women from the RV encampment so they could escape the discomfort of the deuce-and-a-half they had been riding in.

Travis had observed the transaction, and afterward offered Dad a handshake and a tight-lipped thanks. He did not look in my direction.

Later, we sat on the road eyeing the woodlands around us for signs of infected and waited. There was just enough bend in the road I could see the armor as they rolled forward, stopped about two-hundred yards from the teeming, screeching mass of infected frothing through the twisted metal obstructing the interstate, spread out, rolled to a stop, and aimed their guns.

The radio crackled to life. "All stations stand by. Engaging in three, two, one ..."

BOOM-BOOM-BOOM

The projectiles traveled so fast there was no distinguishable difference between the thunder of shots and the detonation of high explosives. When the smoke cleared, there was a massive dent in the derelicts blocking our path, cars blown on top of other cars in twisted, broken heaps. But the way was not clear. With surprising speed, the crews reloaded, passed along another warning, and then fired in tandem.

BOOM-BOOM-BOOM

The shells pushed the wreckage back further, but not enough to allow the convoy to cross. So the crews kept at it, firing, issuing warnings, and firing again. It took eleven rounds of three-gun bombardment before they finally blasted a lane wide enough to allow the convoy to pass.

The ordnance obliterated the infected closest to the target area, while those standing farther away were either disabled or sent hurtling through the air. Ghouls poured into the gap from all directions, making it obvious we would have to move quickly to get clear.

"All stations, listen up," Morgan said over the radio. "I want Bradleys Alpha and Bravo to push up the edges of the path and make sure the heavy armor can get through. Once you're across, Alpha face east, Bravo face west, and annihilate anything undead that comes your way. All other armored units, clear the road ahead until all non-armored vehicles and civilian transports are safely through. Acknowledge."

After a hasty stream of affirmatives, the first two Bradleys behind the Abrams drove around it and shoved the few remaining cars blocking the path out of the way. Once done, they crossed the highway, drove on top of clusters of tightly packed sedans, and aimed their TOW missiles, chain guns, and M-240s toward the approaching infected.

"And to think," Blake said beside me, "there was a time people thought Bradleys were a waste of money."

The Abrams and Howitzers crossed the cratered expanse of I-20 first, Bradleys and APCs close behind, then the HEMTTs, troop transports, Humvees, and finally us civilians in our collection of vehicles.

"Doesn't it strike you as odd that Morgan chose to make sure his most valuable assets made it across first?" Sophia said. "It's like we poor useless civilians were just an afterthought."

The Humvee bounced and jumped as we floundered across the gaping holes left in the wake of the artillery shells. There were a couple of worrisome near-stalls, but finally we cleared the highway and picked up speed on the flat two-lane beyond.

"We made it across, didn't we?" I said, turning to look at her in the back seat.

Sophia looked at me skeptically, then went back to staring out her window. Looking past her, I watched the two remaining Bradleys open up on the approaching horde with their M-240s and chain guns.

The effect was devastating.

At close range, a 25mm chain gun can penetrate tank armor. During the first Gulf War, Bradleys were credited with more kills on enemy armored vehicles than their vaunted Abrams counterparts. So needless to say, firing such a powerful weapon into a mass of necrotic flesh at less than fifty yards was nothing less than gruesomely spectacular.

The dead did not simply fall down. They did not jerk a few times and continue shambling onward as they did when hit with small arms fire. Rather, they flew apart as if someone had implanted several grenades in various points of their anatomy and set them off at the same time.

An arm flew in one direction, a leg the other, a torso disintegrated into a red and black pulp, a head flew apart like a melon blasted with a shotgun at point-blank range, limbs pinwheeled through the air to land dozens of yards away. And because the tungsten rounds were so heavy, and traveled at such high velocity, they didn't just go through one infected, but several of them, their trajectories being thrown off only after bursting through a dozen or more corpses. There were hundreds of *TINGs, PANGs,* and *POCKs* as errant rounds hit doors and wheel hubs and engine blocks. Shrapnel and ricochets sent parts and pieces of ghouls flying in all directions.

The M-240s wreaked their own brand of havoc on the infected's legs, blasting them to pieces the same as I had seen in the brewery parking lot back in Blanco. However, despite the hail of lead and tungsten, only the first few ranks of undead went down. The horde behind them was so large the Bradleys' onslaught did little to halt their advance. It was like trying to hold back an avalanche with two bulldozers. Realizing they were doing nothing more than buying themselves a few extra seconds, the Bradleys reversed, turned up the road, and fled with the rest of the convoy.

By that point, Sophia had turned around to watch the show. As the Bradleys gained on the column and Morgan broadcast an order to pick up the pace, she turned and looked at me, her face pale and drawn, lips pressed tightly together.

"They just don't stop, do they?" she said. "It doesn't matter how many of them we kill, how many we blow up, nothing scares them. They just keep coming."

I reached back and clasped her hand, feeling the tremor in her grasp. "We have a few advantages over them, Sophia."

"Like what?"

"Well for one, we're smarter than they are. We're also faster, we can use weapons, and we can build fortifications. They can't do any of those things."

"But what if that changes? What if they get smarter? What if they start to remember things?"

I thought about it, and felt a cold black dread well up inside me. I let go of Sophia's hand and sat down in my seat.

"We just have to hope that doesn't happen."

THIRTY-SIX

Two days later,

Near Boise City, Oklahoma

There are times when you sense trouble coming. When you see its shadow darken your sky, and your hackles go up, and you reach for the nearest sharp object.

It happens in the sleeping mind, beneath the surface, where we understand the patterns that connect the ebb and flow of life and events. Where we perceive the symmetry of probabilities and execute the intuitive calculus of expected outcomes. Within this hidden depth, we understand the mercurial animal that is human nature and how it creates its own cause and effect. If we are careful, and wary, and keep our eyes open, we can sometimes deduce the problems before they catch us. We can strike, dodge, parry, and set traps.

There are also times when trouble catches us by surprise.

*****

The slow, tedious slog up the Texas panhandle took its toll.

It takes a lot of food to fill over a hundred hungry bellies, and we were three days into a road trip that under normal circumstances should have taken no more than two. So out of necessity, anytime we saw someplace that looked uninhabited and could potentially be a source of food, we stopped and raided it. Doing so kept us fed, but also slowed our progress and cost the lives of two more soldiers.

The deaths happened at a trailer park in the middle of a small town too insignificant to have its own sign. We passed it on the highway, and after a few minutes of observation, one of Morgan's staff sergeants deemed it abandoned. The usual crowd—Dad, Blake, Mike and I—accompanied two squads of regular infantry to the park. (Tyrel's leg was still healing, and Lance had taken it upon himself to make sure none of the soldiers got any funny ideas about our womenfolk. Consequently, the four of us had become Morgan's de facto outriders.)

The regular troops waited while we zipped through the trailer park and fired a few rounds in the air before returning to their position. That done, we gripped our weapons and watched for movement. Other than a slight breeze to mitigate the blazing midday sun and air rippling upward from the hot pavement, we saw nothing.

"All stations, Recon One," Dad said into his handheld. "You are clear to move in, but take it slow. Keep your eyes peeled, and be ready to bug out on a moment's notice."

"Copy," said the senior squad leader, a young staff sergeant named Alvarado. "Moving in."

We followed the four Army Humvees at a distance, Mike manning the machine-gun turret and Dad driving. The vehicles ahead of us stopped and the soldiers piled out, weapons up, ready for trouble. Almost immediately, I saw a profound difference between the two squads.

Alvarado's men were alert, focused, and seemed to appreciate the gravity of the situation. They moved with the skill of long practice, each man knowing his role, maintaining

334

muzzle discipline, checking their corners, communicating in the shorthand of soldiers who knew what to expect from one another.

The other squad, led by a sergeant named Farrell, strolled casually through the cracked and pitted streets, their attitudes every bit that of the conquistador. Sergeant Farrell reminded me of every rich-kid frat-boy who ever came to Black Wolf Tactical on his father's dime looking to inflate his fragile ego by busting caps on the close-quarters combat range.

His men glared around greedily, grins on greasy, dirty faces, gleeful avarice written in every gesture. I had the profound impression I was witnessing both the best and worst the United States Army had to offer.

"Take the west end, Farrell," Alvarado radioed. "We'll start from the east and meet you in the middle. Recon One, I need you on patrol."

"Wilco," Dad replied.

We drove slowly, bouncing and jostling over potholes and sending lizards scurrying through the brown grass lining the dead gray streets. The trailer park looked like any other trailer park from Texas to the Carolinas: shabby, poorly constructed rectangles squatting sullenly on tiny lots, dented mail boxes standing at vandal-abused angles, garbage lining the shallow drainage ditches, underpinning torn away to reveal collapsing insulation and cinder block mountings, sagging porches, windows covered with cheap blinds, rust marks streaking down from window-mounted air conditioners, and a general miasma of hopelessness and despair endemic of the crippling poverty so many Americans didn't want to admit existed.

I had lived in places like this. I got to know the people who occupied them. There were generally two kinds: the renters, the people who stayed for a short while and then moved on, and then there were the owners, the permanent residents. Renters were the overwhelming majority.

Most people from both categories worked their asses off at low-paying jobs that made civilized life possible for the more fortunate. They usually did not have health insurance or retirement savings. Many of them were on government assistance of one form or another. Drug and alcohol abuse were common, but no worse than anywhere else, really.

People drove past these homes and sneered or shuddered or shook their heads in pity. Many of the people living in these places had children early in life, limiting their options and giving their kids little chance of escaping the circumstances they were born into. It was a repeating cycle, generation after generation, with the occasional success story giving some aging mother or father something be proud of, or dismiss with jealousy. Those who escaped were often not welcome when they returned to visit. Perhaps not in an overtly hostile way, but behind whispers, and looks, and a deadpan stiffness to any attempt at being polite.

In its own way, these places were as exclusive as the country clubs and boardrooms of the well-heeled. If you were from here, you were one of them, love you or hate you. You had a pass. You could come and go at your leisure.

Outsiders, not so much.

I watched through the dusty window as the Humvee rumbled through the trailer park's confines, rifle between my knees, eyes searching for movement. Radio chatter rattled in my ears. Alvarado's squad cleared trailers and hastily stacked food in yards for later pickup, while Farrell's men took their sweet time ransacking the place for anything valuable and gathering non-perishables as an afterthought.

An hour passed. Since we had a surplus of fuel, we kept the AC running. Mike's bulk occupied enough space in the gunner's hatch he kept us from losing too much cool air. I pitied the Army grunts for not having a climate control option in their vehicles. When they rolled, they were forced to sweat it out under the merciless Oklahoma sun. But they rarely complained. I respected that, even though I felt no guilt whatsoever at not sharing in their misery.

After a while, I got bored. The trailers all looked the same, the junked vehicles on blocks looked like a waste of good scrap metal, the chatter was repetitive. We passed Alvarado's team, and though they were sweating in the heat and visibly tired, they moved quickly and remained focused on their mission. Farther down the road, Farrell's squad was a study in contrasts.

They had found a trailer with a generator and several gallons of fuel, and had used it to fire up the air conditioner. We heard the sounds of motors shattering the silence from over a hundred yards away and moved in to investigate. After knocking on the door, Dad and I entered the trailer to find them lounging in a cool living room drinking whiskey from a hodge-podge of collected shot glasses. The roar of the AC in the window reminded me of the dinosaur cartoons I used to watch as a child. It amazed me the soldiers were able to carry on their ribald conversations over its incessant din. Upon closer inspection, I saw they had cranked it up to its highest setting.

"Taking a break?" my father asked, not bothering to hide the disdain in his voice. Sgt. Farrell grinned and took another shot from a bottle of Bushmills.

"Yes, we are, civilian. Now kindly fuck off until the professionals are ready to resume their work." He held up a shot glass full of yellow liquor and tossed it back. My dad's flat brown eyes looked on blankly, then after a few seconds, he shrugged. "Have it your way." He motioned for me to leave with him. I cast a final contemptuous look around the room and followed.

Dad marched purposefully toward the Humvee, threw it into gear, and roared away to the other side of the trailer park. He stopped where Alvarado and his men were working and got out. I stepped out as well, curiosity piqued.

"You might want to check on your boy Farrell," he said. "Last I checked, drinking on duty was a serious offense."

Alvarado made a disgusted noise and tossed down a box he was holding, eyes squinting westward. He wiped a sleeve across his sweaty brow and said, "All right. I'll take care of it. Sergeant Gomez, you're in charge until I get back."

"Got it," Gomez replied.

A few minutes later, we made another pass through the neighborhood and saw Alvarado follow Farrell and his men out of the trailer. I couldn't hear what he was saying to them, but it was, by all appearances, forceful, one-sided, and involved a lot of gesticulating.

Farrell's squad ducked their heads and trundled down the steps. Alvarado stood them at attention and spent a few more minutes with his finger inches from each man's face in turn, ending with Farrell. For Farrell's part, the speech only deepened the condescending smirk on his face.

Finished, or at least with no further time to waste chewing asses, Alvarado got back in his Humvee and drove to the other side of the trailer park. Farrell motioned to his men, and they turned in the direction of another trailer, forming up for a room entry through the front door.

One of them hefted a sledgehammer, lifted it to shoulder height, and brought it down on the flimsy door handle. The handle shattered, and the men backed off, waiting to see if any infected would emerge. None did, so they poured in.

Before following his men, Farrell looked in our direction and glared for a long moment. Gone was the smirk, and the smugness, and the devil-may-care attitude. His gaze was flat and cold and utterly emotionless. I've seen hungry reptiles with more life in their eyes. I stared back, not daring to look away. Some instinct, some hairy-knuckled, slope-browed leftover in the deeper portions of my lizard brain warned me that to look away was to show weakness, and I was staring at a creature who would perceive any weakness as an invitation to attack.

The contest dragged on until one of his men shouted for him. Looking startled, Farrell ducked into the trailer, rifle at the low ready. Seconds later, the boom of a shotgun thundered from a room near the far end of the trailer followed by shouting and the staccato rattle of M-4s firing in a confined space.

"Shit," Dad said, accelerating toward the trailer.

More gunfire sounded, and as we skidded to a halt near the front door, a high, agonized scream came from within the trailer. Someone shouted, "Get it off him! Get that fucking thing off him!"

I entered the house behind my father. Mike and Blake were behind us. We turned left and headed toward the shouting at the end of a far hallway. The trailer was laid out like many others I had seen: the front door opened into the living room, to the right was a bedroom, bathroom, and laundry room, the kitchen was separated from the living room by a low island counter, and to my left was a long hallway with more bedrooms and another bathroom. The commotion came from the far bedroom at the end of the hallway. The four of us took a few brief moments to clear the rooms on our right—the doors were closed and Farrell's men had not used their orange spray paint to mark them as clear—then pushed on to see what the shouting was about.

On the way, we heard a guttural growling and snarling beneath the continuing high-pitched screams of one of Farrell's men. I had never heard a scream like that in my life, and hoped I never would again.

Fate, sadly, did not conspire to grant that wish.

A soldier's dead body lay in the entrance to the bedroom, no doubt the victim of the shotgun blast from a few moments earlier. The shot had taken him in the chest and splattered blood, flesh, and chunks of bone in a wide cone-like pattern halfway down the length of the hallway. Mike seized him by the handle on the back of his vest and dragged him into the kitchen, out of the way. Once there, he grabbed a blanket from one of the bedrooms and draped it over him.

The room the rest of us walked into was small, crowded with soldiers, and so thick with foul odor the smell nearly made me gag. A combination of body odor, rotting meat, spent cordite, and vomit hung suspended in the thick air. There was a final crack of a rifle, deafeningly loud in the confined space, and the

339

shouting stopped. The men in front of us went still, eyes looking down at something we could not see past them.

"All right, clear the goddamn room," my father shouted. So firm was his tone of command, no one questioned him. They simply turned and filed out, gathering in the hallway. "Go on," Dad said, shooing them along. "Wait outside."

They did as ordered, faces stunned, muttering among themselves. Farrell remained behind, squatting next to a bleeding soldier and trying to bandage a massive wound on the stricken man's forearm. A few feet away, a naked woman, mid-forties by the look of her, lay on the ground with a gaping exit wound in the back of her head. Her hands were tied behind her back, a rope trailing behind her toward the wall. By her mottled skin and milky white eyes—not to mention the gore smeared around her mouth—it was obvious she was one of the infected.

My eyes tracked the rope across the room to where a portly, middle-aged man lay slumped against the wall. A shotgun lay at his feet, and he clutched a hunting knife in his left hand. A quick glance around the room told the story of what happened.

The infected woman's bound hands were secured to an eyebolt driven into the floor. A short length of rope allowed her to move halfway toward the entrance, but no further. Flies buzzed on smears of blood and scraps of bones scattered across the bare plywood flooring.

There was a picture on the wall next to me of the two people when they were alive. It looked recent. They were standing on a pier, the bright sunny ocean behind them, holding cocktails and smiling at the camera, arms around each other's shoulders.

"Let me guess," Blake said behind me. "The wife got infected, and the husband was keeping her alive in here. Feeding her."

"Feeding her what?" Dad asked.

I bent down and examined a few bones. I recognized the shoulder blade and leg bones of a wild pig. "Looks like he hunted for it."

After poking around a little more, I moved aside a coyote skull and came across an adult human femur still connected to the hipbone by dried black tendons. Disgusted, I kicked it away. "And it looks like he wasn't too discriminating about what he shot."

My father looked across the room at the dead man, his filthy shirt dotted with at least a dozen bloody 5.56mm holes. From the look on his face, any pity he might have felt for the man had left town on its fastest horse. "Sick son of a bitch."

"It gets worse," Blake said, standing over the eyebolt. He reached down and picked up a frayed end of rope. "Looks like when he knew he was done for, he had just enough left in the tank to cut his wife loose." Blake dropped the rope and stepped away. "He turned her loose on them."

Dad looked down at Farrell. "Does that about cover what happened here?"

The young sergeant did not look up, just nodded, eyes fixed on the dead infected woman. Next to him, the bitten soldier held his arm to his chest, rocking slowly back and forth, face pale white, lips blue, eyes pressed together and streaming tears. A steady litany of whispered curses issued from his mouth, repeating to himself how fucked he was.

My father looked at the bitten man, then at Farrell, and then with the sudden, blinding speed he was capable of when roused to anger, he gripped the bigger man by the shoulders, lifted him to his feet, and slammed him against the wall.

"What the hell were you thinking letting your men drink, you idiot?" he roared. "What if they had been focused? What if they had been paying attention to what they were doing? None of this would have happened!"

Farrell's face twisted in anger, the reptilian mercilessness I saw earlier returning, and he tried to struggle out of my father's grip. His struggles quickly ceased when Dad's fist slammed into his breadbasket with the force of a battering ram. Farrell let out a surprised *OOOF* and doubled over, giving my father the opening he needed to run him across the room and slam him head first into the opposite wall. The sergeant hit with enough impact to shatter the wood paneling, his legs going limp beneath him. Dad snatched his sidearm from its holster and reared back for a pistol whip, but I got to him first and lifted him bodily.

"Dad, no. For Christ's sake, calm down before you kill somebody." He went stiff as I carried him from the room, but offered no resistance. I put him down in the kitchen and held his shoulders while he took deep breaths, eyes closed, the redness in his face slowly receding.

"Sorry about that, son," he said finally, holstering his pistol. "Kind of lost it for a minute there."

"Yeah, you think?"

He laughed shakily and wiped a hand across the back of his neck. "Think he's gonna be all right?"

"Farrell?"

"Yeah."

I shrugged. "Probably. You should go back to the Humvee, though. Alvarado will be here any minute. Let me and Blake do the talking."

Dad nodded. "Where'd Mike go?"

Just as he said it, the big Marine came through the front door with a couple of heavy-duty contractor trash bags. When he saw us looking at him, he said, "We still have a job to do. There's food in that kitchen."

Dad went back to the vehicle while I stayed behind. Blake helped Farrell to his feet and escorted him outside, then grabbed a couple of volunteers to help him drag the dead body out of the kitchen and into the driveway. Just as they were wrapping him in a sheet, Alvarado stopped out front and practically flew from the driver's side door.

He walked directly up to Farrell, who still looked a little dazed from the beating he had taken, and yelled, "What the fuck happened here?"

The sergeant explained. Alvarado listened quietly. His face slowly darkened until it was the color of stained mahogany. A single vein pulsed in his forehead. He lowered his voice and leaned in close to Farrell's ear, and said, "I hope you're happy, Sergeant. You were responsible for the safety of these men. For training them, for keeping them in line, for making sure they did their jobs they way they're supposed to. But as always, you slacked off, and half-assed, and treated a dangerous task like it was some kind of a joke. Well, I bet it doesn't seem very funny right now, does it? Not with one of your men dead and another dying." Alvarado stepped back and spit on Farrell's boot. "You're a fucking disgrace."

He turned to Blake and me. "You mind taking this piece of shit back to the convoy?"

"Not at all," Blake said.

"Thanks. When you get there, ask around until you find Master Sergeant Heller and tell him what happened here. He'll know what to do."

Blake told him we would. He and I rode in the front while Dad rode in the back with Farrell. Mike stayed behind to help out, saying he would catch a ride back with Alvarado's men.

No one spoke during the drive.

THIRTY-SEVEN

"So what's going to happen to them?" Lola asked.

I took a bite of my rice and beans, washed it down with bleach-purified, charcoal-filtered water, and said, "I don't know."

For the first time since we had left Canyon Lake, my group was sharing a meal. We lounged in cloth camping chairs around a small fire, the convoy's vehicles a broad, grimly patrolled circle around us.

Morgan had chosen an empty field about five miles from Boise City to strike camp for the night. The area around us was sparsely populated, and while we heard the occasional muffled crack from the suppressed carbines the guards carried, there were not many infected to bother us.

Dad and Mike had cooked the evening meal while the rest of us drank cheap Lipton tea and wondered how long it would be before such simple luxuries became a thing of the past. The sky above was bright and heavy with stars, the myriad campfires of the convoy helpless to drown out their brilliance.

"I talked to Captain Morgan," Dad said, and for once, no one giggled. "He took a statement from me. You other three," he pointed to Mike, Blake and me, "should expect to do the same tomorrow."

"What did he want to know?" I asked.

"My version of what happened to Farrell's squad."

"What did you tell him?"

Dad looked across the fire at me. "The truth."

Blake said, "What did he think of you beating down one of his squad leaders?"

Dad picked something off his spoon. "He said under the circumstances, he was willing to look the other way. This time. I told him that was fair enough."

We ate in silence for a while after that, each person too focused on filling the emptiness in their stomach to bother with conversation. My eyes strayed often to Lauren, the dim orange gloom of the fire framing her against the night. She sat next to my father, but despite their proximity, the distance between them was vast. And growing.

Lauren's face was pinched, the age lines deepened, new wrinkles showing around her eyes and mouth. She had lost weight. Her cheekbones stood out sharply beneath her skin. Her hair was lank and greasy. The circles under her eyes were black as new bruises, the skin puffy from too much crying. Next to her, Dad sat and ate with a desolate sadness lurking behind his confident veneer. There was a tension to his shoulders, he ate too quickly and bounced his left foot incessantly, and every so often, his right hand would twitch in Lauren's direction, then ball into a fist, relax, and go back to holding his bowl of rice and beans. Seeing it, I felt as if someone had gripped my throat and started to squeeze.

I remembered the time before the Outbreak when our life had been normal, before the infected, and the fires, and the desperation I had adjusted to so quickly it scared me. I remembered our home on the outskirts of Houston, the kitchen, the bedrooms, the living room.

Dad had a recliner in the living room he declared as His Seat. And when he was home, only he was permitted to sit in it. If he caught me sitting in His Seat, he snapped his fingers, pointed a thumb at the ceiling, and said, "Up."

That was my cue to relocate.

There was also a sofa next to the recliner, and between them, a small table complete with a lamp and coasters. Both ends of the sofa had built-in recliners, and the end closest to Dad's Recliner was Lauren's Seat. When Dad got home from work, after dinner, the two of them would watch some stupid reality show, usually involving people singing or dancing or both, and I would sit at the kitchen table, both parents within my line of sight, and read while they sat in Their Seats.

Sometimes I would take a break from my story and watch them. They smiled a lot, told jokes, made fun of each other, and occasionally Lauren would swat my father on the arm and rub the place she had hit, a sensuous gleam in her eyes. I always looked away when that happened, knowing I had at least an uncomfortable half-hour of stifled moans and creaking bedsprings to look forward to when the lights went out.

But that night, in the struggling luminescence of the small fire, the twitch in my father's hand, the hesitation, was something entirely new. Instinctively, I understood it for what it was.

He wanted to reach out and put his hand on Lauren's arm. He wanted to intertwine his fingers in hers as he had done a thousand times, but knew the gesture would not be welcome. So he resisted, and kept his eyes down, and did nothing to provoke my stepmother. I didn't blame him. In those days, it did not take much to set her off. When she became argumentative for no apparent reason, or cried without explanation, or stormed off from normal conversation as if someone had said something horrifically offensive, part of me wanted to scream at her. But another, bigger part of me wanted to hold her, and cry, and beg her to snap out of it.

All men are little boys at their core. There is an enduring place for a mother and father—or at the very least a protector—in each of our hearts. We cling to whoever fills that void, and when the tenuous balance of family, in whatever form it takes, is disrupted, all we want is for everything to be set right again. But sometimes, in the jagged arena of the heart, children fall by the wayside. Especially the grown variety.

*****

Earlier in the day, I had spotted a camping trailer in the driveway of an abandoned house that appeared to be in good working order. The propane and fresh water tanks were both full, the chemical toilet had been emptied recently, and the treads on the tires had plenty of life left in them. Figuring it beat the hell out of sleeping on the ground, I hitched it up to Mike's truck and brought it along.

It had enough room to fit four people comfortably, so Lauren, Dad, Sophia and I agreed to share it. Mike said he preferred to sleep outdoors, and Blake, ever the lady's man, had caught the attention of a rather attractive female soldier and invited her to sleep in a tent he scrounged somewhere along to the way. She accepted.

After dinner, Tyrel and Lola went off somewhere to be alone, and Lance wandered over to the other side of camp. There was a forty-something widow he had taken an interest in among the people from the RV encampment. He advised us not to expect him back that night.

"So I guess you're off for the night as well?" I asked Blake when his soldier friend, Tran according to her nametag, showed up at our camp and politely introduced herself. Her first name was Alice, she had grown up in Bakersfield California, first generation American, family originally from Vietnam, five years in the Army, and was a mechanic of some sort. When I shook her hand, it was strong, firm, and calloused from years of hard work. And she had very nice eyes.

"Yeah, I'll see y'all in the morning." Blake gave me a little wink as he stood up and put an arm around Alice Tran's shoulders. As they walked away into the night, I shook my head and shared a knowing glance with my father.

Shortly thereafter, an aging warrant officer stopped by our camp. In his right hand, he held a large metal clipboard. "Name's Grohl," he said, not bothering with military formalities. "I was wondering if you folks might be willing to help out with a few things around camp tonight."

We shared a round of looks, then Dad said, "What did you have in mind?"

He looked at the clipboard. "We're short a few people for the patrols, the supply folks could use a few extra hands doing inventory, and … let's see …" He flipped couple of pages before pointing at Mike. "I understand you were a sniper in the Marines. That correct?"

Mike nodded. "Trained at Quantico."

"Heard that's a tough one."

"It is."

"Mind taking a shift on overwatch tonight? It'd only be for three hours."

"Which post?"

Grohl pointed at a telescoping tower rising up from the back of a HEMTT. "Northwest. Shift starts at 2200 hours."

Mike glanced at his watch. "That gives me forty-five minutes to get ready. Yeah, I'll help you out."

"Much appreciated."

Sophia raised a hand. "I might be able to help your supply people."

"You have any experience managing inventory?"

"I do, actually. I was an assistant manager at a pharmacy before all this happened. Can't imagine it's all that different."

Grohl wrote something on his clipboard. "Fair enough. Gotta head that way myself here in a minute, so I'll walk you to 'em.

348

What about you two," he wiggled a finger between Dad and me. "Think you can take one of the patrols? I know you've had a long day, but even just a couple of hours would be a big help."

"What do you think?" Dad said, shifting his attention to me. "Ten to midnight be okay?"

I shrugged. "Works for me."

Grohl made another notation. "Excellent. Come see me at the command tent fifteen minutes prior and I'll show you where to go."

"Will do," Dad replied.

Grohl then glanced at Lauren, eyes flicking up and down, taking in her general state, and said, "Well that should about do it. I really appreciate it, folks." He turned to Sophia. "If you'll follow me, ma'am?"

"Sure thing." She gave me a quick peck on the cheek as she got up. "See you later tonight."

"Be careful," I said. "Keep your gun handy."

She patted the Smith and Wesson on her hip. "I'll be fine. Worry about yourself."

"Thanks again," Grohl said as he turned to leave.

"Glad to be of service," Dad replied, and watched the two of them walk away.

"Are you going to be okay here by yourself until we get back?" I asked Lauren.

She nodded slowly, eyes never leaving the fire. "I'll be fine."

"Come on, son," my father patted me on the shoulder as he stood up. "Let's get this mess cleaned up and get ready for watch."

I cast one last worried look at Lauren and said, "Yeah, sure."

*****

According to the satellite feed on Grohl's ruggedized tablet, the area of Oklahoma we were in was a massive, near-perfect grid of interconnected farm land. Many of the squares on the grid were filled with perfect geometric circles that touched the gridlines, but left curving triangles of excess land at the corners. They looked like round pegs in square holes. When I asked Grohl what the circles were, he explained they were from pivot irrigation systems—machines that run on electricity, roll on massive wheels, and spread water from a central point in the field.

Our camp was located in one such field, much larger than the square inch or so it represented on the tablet. The problem Grohl and his troops faced was they had a large area of terrain to keep watch over and not enough people to cover it all while still allowing everyone to get at least a few hours' sleep.

"I need you to set up here in this area on the southern end of the perimeter," Grohl said, "patrol between these two points here and here. It's a lot of ground to cover, so you'll have to stay sharp."

"Nothing we can't handle," Dad said.

"Do you need radios?"

"Got our own."

"You good on weapons and ammo?"

Dad patted his rifle and spare magazines. "Good to go."

"We only have enough NVGs to issue you one set. As for suppressors, let me see here ..." He began to thumb through an inventory log.

"Don't worry about it," Dad interrupted. "We have our own."

"NVGs or suppressors?"

"Both."

Grohl raised an eyebrow. "Seriously?"

"Yep. I used to work for a company called Black Wolf Tactical. Ever heard of it?"

"It rings a bell. One of those outfits like the Gunsite Academy in Arizona, right?"

"Along the same lines, yeah."

Grohl scratched at his day's growth of stubble. "Well that explains a lot. You need anything else from me?"

"Nope," Dad said. "I believe we're all set."

"Very well. Stay sharp out there fellas."

"Will do."

THIRTY-EIGHT

As my father and I approached the break between two Bradleys that served as a gate, the glare of floodlights illuminating the interior of the camp grew dim. I reached a hand back to the pouch where I normally kept my NVGs and found it empty.

"Ah, son of a bitch."

Dad stopped a few steps ahead of me, looked back, and said, "What?"

I thought for a moment before remembering unpacking my NVGs a few hours ago to swap out the batteries. I had been inside the camper at the time, sitting at the table, and must have forgotten to put them back in the pouch. *Stupid.*

"I think I left my NVGs back at camp."

"Are you fucking kidding me?"

"Afraid not. They're probably on the kitchen table."

He made an exasperated noise. "Well go back and get them, and hurry. We're going to be late for watch."

"Wait here, I'll be right back." I shoved my rifle in my father's hands so it would not slow me down, broke into a fast jog, and beelined for the other side of camp. We had parked our camping trailer on the north side of the circle away from the people from the RV encampment and the soldiers' tents. It was out of the way, relatively quiet, and aside from Warrant Officer Grohl, no one had bothered us.

After crossing the encampment, I arrived at our site and expected to see Lauren sitting in front of the fire. But her chair was empty. Stopping, I cast a quick glance around to see if she was nearby.

"Lauren?" I called. No answer.

Then I heard noise from the camper, a rattle and a squeak. The big metal box shifted on its axles. I tried the door and found it locked.

"Lauren?" I called again, louder this time. There was a thump from inside the camper, but nothing else. A cold feeling suffused my face, and I felt my heart begin to beat faster in my chest. There was no way Lauren would lock herself in unless she was using the toilet, and even if that were the case, she would answer when I called.

One of the items I usually kept lashed to my pack was a flat pry bar about the length of my forearm. It worked great for a variety of purposes, not the least of which was prying open windows of abandoned houses. Before leaving for watch, I had removed it and left it beside my chair, figuring I would be more comfortable without the extra weight. Picking it up from where it lay, I jammed it into the thin slot between the door and frame and hauled on it with everything I had.

For a couple of seconds, the latch resisted, the pry bar bending a few inches backward. I called up every ounce of strength I had, teeth gritted, blood suffusing my face, muscles standing out like cords under my skin, until finally the door came open with a metallic pop. Drawing my pistol, I dropped the pry bar, stepped through the door, and led the way with my weapon.

And nearly died.

It was dark inside the camper, the room filled with silhouettes. There was someone in there with me, tall and broad, standing on the other side of the small space with a rifle in his

353

hands. I dropped to one knee as he took aim and fired, a three-round burst cutting the air just inches over my head and shattering the window behind me.

I knew in that instant if I had been a fraction of a second slower those rounds would have killed me. Without thinking, I aimed my Beretta, popped off two shots center of mass, then shifted aim and fired a third at his head. The first two shots staggered him, but the third blew the top of his head off. Blood pumped from the wound like a fountain as the gunman fell shuddering to the ground, a black pool spreading on the floor beneath him.

For a few heartbeats, I didn't move.

I didn't have the shakes yet, but they were in the mail. The gunman's feet kicked spasmodically, and I heard his bowels let go. The stench of piss and shit mixing with the coppery, meaty scent of blood tore at my gag reflex. Fighting it down, I rose to my feet, fished a flashlight from my vest, and shined it across the room. On the bed opposite me, Lauren lay face down, limp and unmoving, a rope around her neck, pants around her ankles. She was bent over the edge of the bed, her buttocks and legs exposed, twin streams of blood trickling down her inner thighs. My mind flashed back across the years to our old house, and the closed front door, and the men assaulting her in her own bedroom, the gunshots, the cops, the questions, and the months of walking on eggshells trying not to upset her.

"Oh God. Lauren, no."

I hurried closer on numb feet and unwound the rope from her neck, desperately hoping I wasn't too late. As soon as the rope fell free, she drew a rattling breath and started coughing. Her face was battered, her left eye bruised and swollen, blood running from her nose.

Her eyes opened and stared at me in abject panic. She began to buck and thrash, pushing at me with her hands, struggling to scream but unable to do so.

"Wait, Lauren, it's me, Caleb." I took a step back, one hand raised defensively, and shined the flashlight on my face. She saw me, and after a few seconds, the panic left her eyes and she began sobbing.

"Caleb, please, turn around."

I did as she asked. The sound of her struggling to pull her pants up awakened a cold rage within me.

Since my night vision was ruined, I put the flashlight on the man I had just killed. For an insane moment, I hoped he would come back to life so I could kill him again, slowly this time. His face was a bloody, unrecognizable mess, but the nametag on his uniform was plain to see.

Farrell.

"Come on, Lauren," I said gently. "We need to get you to the medical tent."

*****

0800 the next morning.

I was in the back of a deuce-and-a-half, my hands cuffed in front of me, sitting at the end of one of the long benches near the cab. There were two armed guards by the exit, hands loose on their rifles. I had not slept. My head hung almost to my knees from exhaustion, my stomach roiled with hunger, and my throat burned with thirst. I had tried to request water, but the guards' only response was a curt, "Stop talking."

There had been raised voices in the night. I heard the angry tenor of my father, and Mike's thundering bass. As usual, Blake kept everyone from killing each other.

My eyes closed again, and this time I did not try to open them. My mind drifted back to the dead body of Sergeant Farrell, and carrying Lauren to the medical tent, and how light she felt in my arms, like carrying a child. The medics asked me what happened to her, and I told them what I had seen. Lauren gathered herself enough to explain the rest in detail.

She had been sitting next to the fire, alone. A soldier approached out of the darkness and asked if she had any coffee to spare. Said he was willing to trade for it. He offered a can of table salt in exchange, which we happened to be running low on. Lauren agreed, and went into the camper to fetch the coffee. The soldier followed her in, and when she turned her back to him, he struck her in the head.

When she fell, he hit her several more times, then forced her onto the bed, pulled her pants down, wrapped a length of nylon rope around her neck to keep her from screaming, and proceeded to rape her. He was perhaps a minute into it by the time I arrived.

After hearing her story, one of the medics grabbed a private who happened by and told him to go find Captain Morgan. The captain arrived a few minutes later, accompanied by two armed sergeants. After I explained what happened, he told me he had to place me under arrest until he could conduct a full investigation. My father arrived right about then, frantic, and things got ugly.

It took me, Mike, Lance, and four soldiers to subdue the old man. After wrestling him to the ground, I told him to calm the hell down and let Morgan do his job. He finally agreed, though he was still fuming with rage. He stayed with Lauren for a few minutes, then left so the medics could treat her injuries.

At 0900, Morgan showed up at the truck with my father. The scent of fried spam, beans, and tortillas drifted to me, making my stomach clench painfully. Morgan dismissed the guards and followed my father inside, then removed my cuffs and sat down across from me. Dad gave me a canteen of water.

"You all right, son?" he asked. I chugged half the canteen, then said, "Doing a lot better now, thanks. That for me?" I pointed at the food.

"Yeah. Eat up."

I did, then set my plate aside and looked at Morgan. "So what's going to happen now?"

"We're still investigating," he said, "but so far your story holds up."

"Of course it fucking does," Dad said heatedly.

Morgan winced as if struck, then said, "Detective Travis Holzman is assisting with the investigation. He's been a big help."

"Is that the same detective I beat the hell out of a few days ago?" I said.

"Yes. But he's been very professional about the whole thing."

"You'll have to forgive me if I'm a bit skeptical."

"I understand your concerns. But believe me, he's working hard to get to the bottom of what happened. You should have seen him after he interviewed your stepmother. I thought lightning bolts were going to fly out of his eyes."

It occurred to me then that if Travis really was a good cop, he was probably a lot more concerned about Lauren than he was with me. "Okay. I'll take your word for it."

"Listen, I need you to stay here for a while longer," Morgan said. "Just until Detective Holzman has had time to sort out all the details. Things are kind of tense out there right now. Rumors flying, that sort of thing. I'm worried some of the soldiers might try to retaliate. Sergeant Farrell had a lot of friends."

Dad said, "Well you better kick those soldiers in the ass and tell them to mind their goddamn manners. Any of them takes a shot at my boy, I'll put a bullet between their eyes and worry about the consequences later."

"Mr. Hicks, I understand you're angry, but-"

"You don't understand shit!" Dad snarled. "That son of a bitch raped my wife. He deserved to die, and he was one of your men. Your responsibility!" He punctuated the end of the sentence by jamming a hard finger into Morgan's chest.

Morgan paled, his mouth pinching down to a thin, flat line. "I'm sorry, Mr. Hicks. I can't tell you how sorry I am. But I have to face reality, okay? And the reality is, this place is a powder keg. So give me some time to defuse it before you go flying off the handle, all right?"

My father's fists balled up as his sides, muscles straining under the skin of his jaw.

"Dad, please."

He looked at me, the anger in his eyes a living thing, boiling and writhing and burning to be let loose.

"Dad, please," I repeated. "You're not making things any better." I turned to Morgan. "It's okay. I'll stay here for now. Just leave me some water, and let me know what you find out, okay?"

"I can do that."

"And Dad, just stay at the camp. Or better yet, go be with Lauren."

It was as if I had stuck a needle in a balloon. The fists unclenched, the eyes closed, the shoulders sagged. He leaned down and put his head in his hands and sighed in helpless frustration. "You're right. Are you sure you're okay in here, son?"

"Like I said, just leave me some water."

They did, and left. Morgan posted another guard, just one this time, and I had the impression he was there to keep people out rather than to keep me in. He was a young private, maybe about my age, with the big round red-cheeked face of a Nebraska farm boy. There were a few attempts on his part to strike up a conversation—a soldier's go-to method to pass the time on a boring watch—but after a few grunts and monosyllabic answers from me, he gave it up.

I did not feel like talking.

*****

I could see through the exit the sky was overcast, which explained why it didn't get too hot that day. The weak sun cast pale shadows on the ground outside the truck, slowly moving them from right to left, telling me I was facing south. The shadows began to lengthen until about 1600 when Travis showed up with my father. The guard left, and the two men stepped in.

Once again, Dad brought food. They gave me time to wolf it down before launching into the conversation.

"So what did you find out, Detective?" I asked.

He opened a notebook and said, "I need you to answer some questions first."

"Okay."

He asked me to repeat the statement I had given Captain Morgan. Then he asked me to repeat it again. He asked me questions, some of them direct, some of them obviously baited.

One of the classic methods of interrogation is to give someone enough rope to hang them with, then pull the noose tight. My father had taught me a thing or two about it, but I wasn't worried. There was no need to be. I had the truth on my side.

Half an hour later, Holzman made a final notation in his book, then set it down and looked me in the eye. "Here's what I've come up with so far. After the incident yesterday when two of Sergeant Farrell's men were killed, Captain Morgan relieved him of command of his squad and put him under armed guard pending arrival in Colorado. He was facing charges for dereliction of duty, among other things. I interviewed his men, as well as your father and those friends of yours who were there. Long story short, things weren't looking too good for Sergeant Farrell. Compounding this, there was the altercation between Farrell and your father." He gestured at Dad. "From what I gathered, he blamed Mr. Hicks for the trouble he ran into."

"That's ridiculous," I said. "My father didn't hold a gun to his head and force him to get his men drunk. Soldiers aren't allowed to drink on duty for a very good reason. You ask me, they probably botched the job clearing the trailer. Didn't follow procedure. If they had, those two men would probably still be alive."

Holzman nodded. "I stand to agree. Farrell struck me as the kind of person who likes to blame all his problems on everyone except the responsible party—himself."

"You said he was under armed guard," Dad chimed in. "How did he manage to get away from them?"

Holzman sighed and pinched the bridge of his nose. "There was only one guard on duty at the time. He tried to say Farrell overpowered him and knocked him unconscious, but the only injury the medics found was a black eye. Now I've been doing this a long time, and I've never seen someone get knocked out by a punch to the eye. So I braced the kid, and after sweating him for an hour, he finally confessed that Farrell had bribed him into letting him go."

"Bribed him?" I asked. "With what?"

Holzman let out another sigh, his jaded cop eyes red around the edges. "The location of a case of Jack Daniels whiskey stashed in one of the HEMTTs. Farrell punched the kid in the face to make it look legit, then set his escape plan into motion."

"He was going to desert," Dad said.

Holzman nodded. "Somewhere on the way up here through Texas, Farrell found a dirt bike and talked a HEMTT driver into letting him stash it with the other cargo. Near as I can tell, the first thing he did was retrieve the bike, slip past the guards on the western edge of the circle, and then hide it a few hundred yards away, along with a big can of fuel. One of the patrols found it a couple of hours ago. Afterward, he snuck back into the camp, found a can of salt somewhere, and used it to convince Lauren he wanted to trade."

"So this was retaliation," Dad said, a desolate look on his face. "For what I did to him. This whole thing is because of me."

"Absolutely not." Holzman turned to my father. "Listen, this is Farrell's fault and no one else's. He's the one who committed the crime." The detective shot me a meaningful glance. "And he paid for it with his life."

"But If I'd ..."

"No, Dad," I said. "Detective Holzman is right. What happened to Lauren was not your fault, so don't start blaming yourself. Right now you need to forget about all that and focus on what you need to do to help Lauren heal from this."

Dad nodded quietly, but he did not meet my eyes.

"What about the soldier who helped Farrell escape?" I asked. "What's going to happen to him?"

"Morgan arrested him and placed him under armed guard. You ask me, I think he's in deep shit. Desertion has become such a big problem the Army has authorized commanding officers to summarily execute any deserters they catch, as well as any active duty personnel caught aiding and abetting."

Dad's eyes widened. "Summary execution? Jesus. Back in my day, they busted you down, took half your pay for two months, gave you 45 days of restriction and extra duty, and then rolled you out of the Army. Things must be pretty bad if they're executing people."

"That's the impression I got too," Holzman said. "The soldier, a kid named Stanhouse, will be going before Captain Morgan this afternoon. We'll have to wait and see what happens."

"So what about me," I asked. "Am I free to go now?"

"You are. Farrell attacked your stepmother, then tried to kill you. Compound that with the evidence he intended to desert from the Army, and I think we have a pretty clear-cut case of justifiable homicide. But I would steer clear of any military personnel until after the trial later this afternoon. The facts will come out then, and hopefully that will calm things down."

"Understood."

Holzman stood up and led the way out of the truck. I jumped down and stretched cramped muscles, grateful to be out of the vehicle's confines. The detective shook hands with my father, then with me.

"Thank you, Detective," I said. "I know we've had our problems, but ... you're a good policeman. I'm sorry about what happened a few days ago."

"Forget it," he said. "I overreacted to the situation. I should never have threatened you the way I did." He cast a long look around the camp, the soldiers milling about, the people from the RV encampment going about their tasks, the smoke of cook fires hanging in the air. He ran a worried hand across his face. "Things have gotten pretty bad, there's no denying that. But it doesn't give me a license to take the law into my own hands. I swore an oath, and no matter how dark the road gets, I intend to keep it."

"Well, good luck to you on that one," Dad said. "I have a feeling you're going to need it."

Holzman began walking away. Over his shoulder, he said, "I have a feeling you're right."

THIRTY-NINE

The sentencing was held at 1900 hours. All military personnel not on watch, as well as the contingent of civilians, attended.

It was a simple affair. Someone rigged up a PA system using a CB loudspeaker so Morgan could bring things to order. Detective Holzman presented his findings, starting with the incident in the trailer park and culminating with Farrell's death at my hands. For my part, all I had to do was repeat the same story I had told several times earlier. Captain Morgan declared that I had acted in self-defense and would not be charged with any crimes. He then explained to his troops that my actions were justified, and if anyone so much as looked at me crossways, he would put his boot up so far up their ass they would taste shoe polish. That seemed to get the message across.

Finally, a couple of armed sergeants brought Private Stanhouse forward. Morgan told the assembled crowd that the young man had confessed to aiding and abetting a deserter, and if not for his actions, none of the tragic events that happened afterward would have occurred. Finished, he asked the kid what he had to say for himself.

Most of it was unintelligible. He was weeping and shivering with fear, but I got the impression he was trying to apologize. If the previous night's events had happened to someone else, I might have felt sorry for the kid. I might have wanted Morgan to show him mercy and find some form of punishment that would teach him his lesson, but let him continue on in life.

But it didn't happen to someone else. It happened to Lauren and me.

Lastly, Morgan asked my father and me to come forth and say what we wanted to the soldier. I declined; I had nothing to say to him. My father, however, did.

"I don't give a damn if you're sorry," he told the weeping soldier. "That bastard Farrell raped my wife and tried to kill my son. You abandoned your duties and deliberately let that happen. And for what? A box of whiskey?" He spit in the soldier's face. "Rot in hell."

To Morgan, he said, "You want my advice? Shoot the fucker. Hell, I'll even do it for you."

The captain thought it over for most of a full minute. His expression was stoic, but I could see the turmoil behind his eyes. The crowd stayed silent, waiting. Finally, he picked up the microphone.

"Desertion has become a rampant problem in the Army. Our responsibilities are now too grave to allow an offense like this to be punished lightly. For those of you thinking about striking out on your own, I would remind you of the oath you swore to defend the people of this country. To abandon your duties now, in a time of such profound turmoil, is the height of selfishness and irresponsibility. And I, for one, will not abide it."

He turned to the trembling soldier and stared at him flatly. "You knowingly aided and abetted a deserter. Worse, you allowed a criminal to harm one of the very people he was charged with protecting. Now that soldier is dead, and an innocent woman will have to live with the aftermath of a sexual assault for the rest of her life. There is a reason why desertion is a crime, soldier. And you have crossed the line."

Raising his voice, he said, "Private Lawrence Stanhouse, I hereby sentence you to death. Your execution will be carried out immediately."

A stir of whispers flowed through the crowd, the soldiers looking back and forth at each other in disbelief. Private

Stanhouse went ghost white, his mouth hanging open in raw shock. Morgan turned to my father and offered him his sidearm. Dad took it, glaring coldly at the doomed man.

The two armed sergeants half-dragged, half-carried the private outside the gate kicking and screaming and begging the whole way. Dad followed a few paces behind, his face a mask of hate.

Morgan ordered the soldiers in the crowd to remain where they were and stand at attention. To one of his aides, he quietly gave orders to arrange a burial detail once he had dismissed everyone. We all stood in silence, military and civilian alike, until a few minutes later, a single report thundered across the field. Morgan stood with his hands clasped behind his back as the echo faded, then turned smartly and picked up the microphone.

"Let me make myself abundantly clear," he said. "I. Am. Done. Fucking. Around. Discipline has been getting worse and worse since we left San Antonio, and I will tolerate it no further. Senior NCOs and squad leaders, you had better straighten your people the up, or so help me, I will come down on you like the hammer of God. The rest of you, I strongly suggest you get the fuck in line. There will be no more incidents like this one. There will be no more incidents PERIOD. Do I make myself clear?"

Stridently, in unison, the troops shouted, "YES SIR!"

"Very well. Dismissed."

Behind me, I heard Lola say, "I can't believe that just happened."

Soft hands wrapped around my arm, and I looked down to see Sophia staring up at me with tears in her eyes. "Caleb, I am so sorry. I don't know what to say."

I pulled her close, kissed the top of her head, and said, "There's nothing to say, Sophia. Now we just have to try to move on."

"What about Lauren. Is she going to be all right?"

I didn't have an answer for that, so I held her and said nothing.

*****

Lauren was doing remarkably well.

Night had fallen, and the medics finally allowed me to visit her in the medical tent. She was sitting up on her cot eating a bowl of soup when I walked in.

"Hi there, sweetheart." She put her bowl down on a small table and let me kneel and pull her into a hug.

"How are you holding up?" I asked.

"I've been better, Caleb. I've been better."

"Are you in pain?" I whispered. "I have some pain meds stashed in my pack. You can have them if you want."

The look of relief in her eyes made me want to weep. "Oh God, that would be so great. They don't have much to give me here. My … um … you know, they had to stitch things up."

This time, there was no stopping the tears. I felt them flow down my cheeks and pulled the woman who had raised me like her own into my arms and rocked her back and forth, bitterness and rage and despair warring for dominance. "I'm so sorry Lauren. I wish I had gotten there sooner."

She hugged me back, and I felt warm wetness spread on my shirt where she pressed her face against it. "Don't, Caleb. You did the best you could. You saved me. Again."

We stayed that way, holding each other. Finally, I let go and sat down on the cot beside her. We talked for a while, mostly about how Dad was doing. I asked if she wanted to see him yet, and she said she wasn't sure she was ready. I used the conversation as a pretext to surreptitiously fish the bottle of pills from my pack and stash them under her pillow. She watched me do it, and mouthed, *Thank you.*

I leaned in and whispered, "It's oxycodone, so don't take more than one every eight hours, okay?"

She hugged me again, her face turned away, and said, "Don't worry. I won't."

A few minutes later, Lauren said she was happy to see me, but she was very tired. "And I'm not going to lie," she added. "I'm really looking forward to taking one of those pills."

"I understand." I kissed her on her cheek and asked, "Anything else you need from me?"

"Just one thing. If you could send Lola by, I would appreciate it. I need her to get something for me."

"What is it? Maybe I can get it for you."

She flushed and said, "No, honey. I'd prefer if it was her. Girl stuff, you know."

"Oh. Say no more. See you in the morning, Lauren."

"Goodnight, sweetie."

I hugged her one last time and left.

*****

The next morning, I woke up to the smell of food cooking and Sophia's warm body next to mine.

While I was visiting Lauren the night before, Mike had hauled the camper outside the gate and left it by the side of the road, so we were all sleeping in tents. Not that I begrudged Mike for getting rid of the camper; blowing Farrell's brains out had made a hell of a mess. Furthermore, I could only imagine how traumatic it would be for Lauren to see the camper again and be reminded of what happened to her there. I would sleep on a bed of nails if it spared my stepmother that pain.

Lola and Tyrel were already up and busy cooking canned meat, rice, beans, and flatbread over an open fire. I left Sophia sleeping and followed my nose toward breakfast.

"Smells great," I said, sitting down in my chair.

"Thanks," Lola replied, smiling. I watched her for a moment, having a hard time believing the change that had occurred in her. She had gained weight—not much, but enough she did not look gaunt anymore—and the bags under her eyes were gone. She moved with easy grace, her eyes bright and alive. It could not believe I was looking at the same sad, sallow, booze-soaked woman we had found hiding from the world at Canyon Lake.

Shifting my gaze, I noticed Tyrel watching her as well, smiling, his dark black eyes glistening with what I could only describe as infatuation. Lola seemed to be aware of the scrutiny, but made no effort to discourage it. Quite the opposite, actually. Despite the leaden pain in my chest, I found myself smiling.

"Hey, Earth to Ty," I said, tossing a pebble at my old friend.

"What?" he grumped, throwing the pebble back at me.

"How's the leg?"

"Stiff as hell," he said, straightening it out and wincing. "But getting better. It was a through-and-through, no deformation of the projectile. I can walk on it without a crutch now, but it's still slowing me down. I'll be glad when it heals up."

There were probably only a few people in the world who could handle a gunshot wound to the leg with such aplomb, and Ty was one of them. I reminded myself never to get on his bad side.

"Glad to hear you're getting better. Now how about some of that grub?"

"How about you get off your ass and come get it?"

Good old Ty. Such a giver.

I found a clean plate, piled it with grub, and covered the whole works with a piece of flatbread. Despite the growling in my stomach, I waited a few minutes for steam from the food to soften the stiff bread. When it became limp to the touch, I piled the ingredients and gorged on what I had affectionately come to refer to as camp tacos.

Lola sat down next to Tyrel and started eating her breakfast. I asked her, "Did you go see Lauren last night?"

"Yes, I did."

"Did you get her what she needed?"

She nodded, swallowed a mouthful of beans, and said, "Yeah, but it was kind of a weird request coming from her. She doesn't normally drink."

I went still. Cold dread bloomed in my chest and spread to my face and hands. There are moments in life when seemingly unrelated events suddenly become warning signs, when a highlight reel of red flags you should have connected long ago flashes through your mind. Maybe you were distracted, or scared, or angry, or some other pressing matter demanded your attention. Whatever the case, there is an instant of clarity, and those signs suddenly coalesce into a single aggregated realization. A terrible understanding descends.

"What did you give her, Lola?"

Something in my voice made her look up, eyes wide and round. "I told you. She wanted a drink, so I snuck her a bottle of lemon vodka. What? Why are you looking at me like that?"

I dropped my plate and sprinted for the medical tent.

She wasn't in her cot. The tent was empty. I stumbled outside, heart pounding, a loud ringing in my ears. A soldier walked by whom I recognized, one of the medics from the night I had brought Lauren in. I ran to him and grabbed his arm.

"Where did she go?"

He stepped back, one hand raised defensively. "Whoa! Calm down, man. What are you talking about?"

"My stepmother, Lauren Hicks. The woman I brought in the other night. Where is she?"

The medic shrugged. "I don't know, man. You tell me. She said she was going back to your campsite when she left."

The ringing grew louder. I had to shout to hear myself over it. "What time did she leave?"

"Around midnight. Why? What's the problem?"

I wanted to gouge his eyes out. I wanted to pull my gun and shoot him in the face until the trigger clicked on an empty magazine. "You ... *let* her leave?"

"Of course. There was nothing else we could do for her. I don't have the authority to make her stay if she doesn't want to."

"Did she take anything with her?"

"Um ... a few personal items. I'm not sure what they were; she wrapped them up in one of her shirts. Oh, and she borrowed a pen and a notepad from me. If you find her, could you ask her to bring those back? We're kind of ... hey, where you goin'?"

The medic said something else, but I didn't catch it. The ringing had gotten too loud, punctuated by the timpani of my heart thudding, thudding, thudding. I walked a circle around the tent until I spotted a track that matched Lauren's hiking boots. The trail led me to a deuce-and-a-half parked on the outer perimeter. Lauren's tracks stopped at the rear bumper. I stepped up into the cargo area and shined my flashlight around.

She lay on one of the benches, slumped over as if she had been sitting down, then lost consciousness. I rushed to her side and shook her.

"Lauren, wake up." No response.

There is a stillness that comes over a person in death, an utter lack of movement, no slight stirring of respiratory action, no involuntary twitches, no thrum of pulse against the skin of the neck. Nothing.

The tears started flowing, then. What small spark of hope I had left died when I laid my fingers over Lauren's carotid artery. I left them against her cold skin for a long moment, praying I would feel a beat, a flutter, anything.

My prayers went unanswered.

*****

The troops who took her away later told me they found us because they heard someone screaming. I don't remember that part. I remember pulling her into my arms, and the dreadful realization that rigor mortis had begun to set in, and wondering what I was going to tell my father, and how the ringing in my ears became so loud I thought it would shatter the world.

The rest is a blur.

I came to my senses in the medical tent. When I sat up on my cot, I felt a hand touch my shoulder and looked up to see my father sitting across from me.

"Dad ..."

"How are you feeling, son?"

I shook my head. There was nothing to say. Dad took my hand and pressed a piece of paper into it.

"She left a note, Caleb."

I stared at it, a little white square with my stepmother's last words on it. When I looked back up at my father, his eyes were red-rimmed and bloodshot, his cheeks hollow, sunken, and covered in beard stubble. "Read it," he said.

It took a few seconds to force my hands to respond. They shook as I unfolded the paper and held it up to the light.

Joe and Caleb,

This is not your fault. I did not do this because of you.

I've had enough. I look ahead of me, and I see nothing but darkness. There is no light at the end, no hope.

I can't do this anymore.

The two of you brought me laughter, and love, and the best years of my life. You were the brightest stars in my sky. I will always love you.

We will see each other again, in a better place.

Take care of each other.

Lauren.

A sudden anger seized me. I crumpled the note and threw it to the ground. "How could she be so *fucking* selfish."

"I'm sorry, son."

"She should have said something. She should have come to us for help."

"Caleb, don't do this."

"I can't believe she would just leave us like this!"

Dad moved over to sit beside me. "There's nothing we can do now, son. Getting angry and bitter won't change a thing. And it won't bring her back."

My father put his arm around my shoulders and pulled me to his chest just as he had done a thousand times throughout my life. I sagged against him, his strength supporting me while I wept, and I remembered a smiling, auburn-haired young woman with hazel eyes and a shining smile and a laugh like the sound of bells ringing.

*****

Later, long after nightfall, after we had buried Lauren and said a few words over her and hammered a wooden cross into the ground, I sat atop a hill overlooking the convoy and stared at the fires straining against the endless dark. Part of an old poem I liked came to mind, one of Robinson Jeffers' works:

Here the granite flanks are scarred with ancient fire.

The ghosts of the tribe crouch in the nights beside the ghost of a fire.

They try to remember the sunlight.

Light has gone out of their skies.

FORTY

Six days.

Six days since the convoy left the RV encampment. Six days since we had joined them hoping to find safety in numbers. And so far, all we had done was risk our lives so Morgan's men would not have to, given up nearly all of our supplies, and lost the woman who mattered most to us in the world.

My father and I were in agreement. It was time to go.

After Lauren's funeral, Morgan waited an hour, then announced the convoy would be heading out in the morning. He had managed to arrange for a supply drop, but we would have to cross into Colorado to get it. Personally, I thought he was full of shit. There was no reason an aircraft with the range of a Chinook couldn't make it south to Oklahoma. He just wanted an excuse to get things moving. Tensions had been high in the wake of Private Stanhouse's execution, and my guess was Morgan wanted to keep the peace by keeping his troops too busy to think.

Dad and I gathered everyone together early in the morning around a low-banked campfire. There was a clear sky overhead, the air was warm and getting hotter, and a strong breeze carried dust over the hills from the north. We stood in a tight cluster while my father spoke, staring at each other in the pale dawn light.

He said if any of them wanted to come with us, they were welcome. But if they wanted to stay with the convoy, that was all right as well. No hard feelings.

"Where you go, I go," Sophia said, moving to stand next to me.

I pulled her close and looked to her father. "You're under no obligation, Mike. Sophia is an adult now. She can make her own decisions. I'll take good care of her."

The big Marine chuckled and shook his head at me. "You two have no idea how dumb you are. Don't get me wrong, I love you both, and I know you mean well. But you're stupid as hell if you think I'm gonna let either one of you out of my sight."

I smiled and acknowledged with a single nod. Dad took a moment to grip Sophia's hand, then turned to the others. "Lance, what do you say, man?"

His eyes strayed to the other side of the camp where the rest of the civilians were slowly starting their day. "I think I'm gonna stay, Joe. I appreciate everything you've done for me, and I'm glad I could help you when you needed it. But I met a nice woman, and I know she isn't going to leave this convoy. It might sound selfish, but right now, it's the only thing I have to live for."

Dad reached out and shook his hand. "Been nice knowing you, Lance. Best of luck."

"Same to you."

Blake took a step forward and said, "I'm with you, Joe. We've come this far together, might as well see it through."

Dad thanked him, then looked at Tyrel and Lola. "What's it gonna be, Ty?"

Our old friend shuffled his feet and glanced at Lola from the corner of his eye. "Well, my leg is still messed up. I wouldn't want to slow you down. And I have Lola to think about." He reached out and slipped his hand into hers.

Dad stepped closer and gripped his shoulders. "I understand, brother. Believe me, I do."

They embraced briefly, patting each other on the back, then Dad turned to Lola. "Take care of this jackass," he said, and kissed her on the cheek. "He requires constant supervision."

Lola smiled. "I'll do my best."

To the rest of the group, he said, "We leave in half an hour. Let's get to work."

While the others loaded what supplies we were taking with us into the vehicles, I made my way to the command tent and requested to speak with the captain. A hard-eyed staff sergeant kept me waiting a few minutes and glared at me hotly enough to let me know my presence was unwelcome. I glared right back. After what had befallen my family, I did not give a baboon's swollen red ass about his opinion. Finally, Morgan poked his head out of the tent and waved me in.

"What can I do for you?" he asked, moving to sit behind the folding table that functioned as his desk. He shuffled a few papers around and picked up a cup of coffee.

"We're leaving," I said.

The coffee stopped halfway to his face. He stared at me a long instant, then said "Leaving?"

"Yes, along with most of the others in my group. Lance is staying behind, as well as Tyrel and Lola. The rest are coming with us."

He put the cup down and folded his hands on the desk. "I'm sorry to hear that. I really am. When are you leaving?"

"In about half an hour."

He stood up and came around the desk to offer me a hand. "I wish we had met under better circumstances, Mr. Hicks. You're a good man. I could use a hell of a lot more like you. And for what it's worth, I'm terribly sorry about what happened to your stepmother."

"Thank you, Captain."

"Is there anything I can say to make you change your mind?"

"I'm afraid not."

"Well then, best of luck to you. I hope we meet again someday."

"Good luck to you too." And with that, I walked out.

On the way back to the campsite, I thought about the subtexts of conversations, the subtle ways we communicate on various levels when we speak to each other. There are cues you can detect in things like body language, facial expression, and tone of voice. If you live long enough, and if you are observant, you can learn to read the messages beneath the surface. Morgan had said all the proper things, made all the proper gestures, and his spoken message had been one of regret. But judging by other things, the facial tics, and inflection of voice, and the briskness of his movements—not to mention the way he seemed not at all upset by my departure—regret was not foremost in his thoughts.

If I had to guess, I would say the captain was relieved.

*****

"So here's the deal," Mike said, reading from a list scrawled in his hasty print. We were stopped on the side of the road, engines idling on a hillside a mile from the convoy. Our vehicles consisted of one of the Humvees from BWT, Blake's Jeep, and Mike's pickup truck. Dad let the folks from the RV encampment keep his Ram, and we let Tyrel and Lola have the other Humvee.

"We have enough food for two weeks if we're careful," Mike said, "and twenty gallons of fresh water. So supplies aren't a problem right now. Worst-case scenario, we can hunt or scrounge what we need. As for medical supplies, we'd all have to be shot, stabbed, drowned, blown up, beaten half to death, and partially dismembered to run out. And if that happens, we're all fucked and it won't matter anyway."

"What about weapons?" Dad asked.

"Weapons are as follows: Seven M-4 carbines, four MP-5 submachine guns, various pistols, my sniper rifles, two hunting rifles, and one M-249 SAW. As for ammo, we have three-thousand rounds of 5.56 loose, another thousand belted for the SAW, eight-hundred rounds of nine-millimeter, five-hundred rounds of 7.62, a hundred rounds of .300 Winchester magnum, and two-hundred rounds of .45 ACP." He patted the Colt 1911 on his hip. "Additionally, we have two M-203 grenade launchers, fifty 40-millimeter HE rounds, and fifty frag grenades. Equipment wise, we have our tactical gear, four suppressors for the M-4s, one suppressor each for the MP-5s, four sets of NVGs, two pairs of binoculars, and the optics for our rifles."

He tossed the piece of paper into the back of the Humvee and stared pointedly at my father. "The rest we donated to the fucking Army."

Dad shrugged. "Seemed like a good idea at the time."

"No sense crying over it now," Blake said. "We have enough to get us to Colorado. That's the important thing."

I sat on the tailgate of Mike's truck, the warmth of Sophia's thigh next to mine, and thought about all the gear we had taken from BWT. When we set out, we'd had enough hardware to outfit a small army. Now, we were down to a fraction of what we had started out with, and to make things worse, we were still at best a couple of days away from Colorado Springs. Not to mention the fact a soulless rapist had nearly killed me and driven my stepmother to take her own life. All in all, it seemed our experience with the United States Army had been a shit deal.

"Anyway," Mike went on. "We're good on food, water, and ordnance, but we only have enough fuel to get us maybe three-hundred miles if we're lucky. After that, we're on foot. Personally, I'd rather not take the chance."

"What do you suggest?" Dad asked.

"I've been monitoring radio chatter from the convoy. They got word from Colorado Springs that I-25 has been cleared all the way south of Raton, New Mexico. My guess is they're going to go south on 56 for a while, then cut west on 87 and pick up the interstate from there. They have all the fuel and supplies they need to make that trip."

"Which means what for us?" Sophia asked.

"It means if we want to stay out of the Army's way, the first thing we need to do is stock up on fuel. Best place to get what we need is Boise City. After we do that, we head north on 287 all the way up to 24 and approach Colorado Springs from the north."

"What's between here and there on that route?" I asked.

"Not a whole hell of a lot. Farms and road towns mostly. Anybody living in that area has probably evacuated already. Might be a few holdouts, so we'll have to be careful. Other than that, it should be an easy trip." He leaned against the Humvee and crossed his arms, staring in the direction of the convoy. "That said, I'd feel a hell of a lot better about this whole thing if we hadn't given away damn near all our supplies."

"Mike, we can stand around whining about what we don't have," I said flatly, "or we can get a move on. Personally, I vote for the latter."

Dad and Mike swiveled their heads in unison. Any other time, there would have been an angry retort from one or both of them. But it had been less than twenty-four hours since I'd buried a woman I loved as much as any son ever loved his own mother, and I could feel the strain of it radiating from me. Consequently, the two men bit down on whatever they wanted to say and simply nodded. Sophia's hand closed over mine.

"It's okay, Caleb," she said. "Everything's going to be okay."

"No, Sophia. It's not." I jumped down from the tailgate and opened the driver's side door. "Are we ready to go or what?"

We went.

FORTY-ONE

Hollow Rock, Tennessee

"I lost my parents a month after the Outbreak," Miranda said. She reached up a hand and swatted at a low-hanging willow branch as she and Caleb passed it. "The Free Legion killed my brother."

Night had fallen, and they were walking back to Miranda's trailer. Caleb had paced himself with the drinks, but still had a buzzy, glossy feeling in his head. He put an arm around Miranda's shoulders. "If you want to tell me about it, I'll listen. No pressure."

Miranda said nothing for a while. She held Caleb's waist and leaned against him as they ambled down the street. She'd had nearly as much to drink as Caleb, but possessed less than two-thirds of his body mass to tone down the effect. He had warned her to slow down, but she waved off his concerns with a flick of a long-fingered hand.

They passed the center of town and the general store, then rounded the corner to Miranda's street before she spoke again. "I'm originally from Nashville. Did I ever tell you that?"

"No. But then again, I never told you I'm from Houston."

"You told me today."

"Then I guess we're even."

Miranda stopped on the sidewalk and watched two small children chase lightning bugs around a well-tended yard. Their parents sat not far away in lawn chairs, the mother sipping something from a plastic cup, the father holding a rifle in his lap, eyes constantly on the move.

"People don't talk about that kind of stuff anymore," she said. "Life before the Outbreak. Family. You might hear someone mention what they did for a living, but that's about it."

"It's not surprising," Caleb said. "I've said it before but it bears repeating—those of us left are still in mourning."

Miranda turned a bleary-eyed stare in Caleb's direction. "You know Eric and Allison Riordan?"

"Of course. You know I know them."

"Oh, yeah, that's right. Anyway, did you know Eric did his undergrad work at Princeton?"

Caleb's eyes widened. "No, I didn't know that. He never mentioned it."

"Yep," Miranda said, stumbling a bit. "Majored in accounting. Then he got an MBA from UNC. Apparently they had a pretty good business school."

"UNC was one of the colleges I was thinking of applying to when I finished my high school work."

Miranda looked up at him and smiled. "It's strange to hear you say it like that. 'Finished my high school work'. Most people would just say 'when I graduated from high school'."

"It's different when you're home schooled."

"I can't imagine what my teenage years would have been like without high school. All my friends, and the football games, cheer squad, the parties, all the rest of it."

Caleb shrugged. "I don't think I would have cared for all that. I prefer my own company most of the time. Home school gave me more time to focus on the things I enjoyed."

"Like training?"

Caleb looked down at her. "Please keep that between the two of us."

"I will."

"I mean it, not a word to anyone. You have to promise."

They had reached Miranda's front porch. She climbed the first step so she was eye to eye with him, took his face in her hands, and said, "I promise." Then sealed it with a kiss.

Inside the trailer, they went to the bedroom and changed into nightclothes. Caleb lay down beside Miranda and raised an arm so she could entwine herself around him. He stared at the ceiling in the dim gloom, the pale light through the window revealing more of his surroundings as his night vision kicked in.

"I'm not tired yet," Miranda said, twirling a finger through the fine sandy-blond hair on his chest.

"Me either."

"Feel like telling me the rest of the story? If we have time that is."

"We do. It'll be late before I'm finished, though."

"If you're willing, I'd like to hear it."

Caleb turned on his side so he was looking Miranda in the eye, her leg draped over his hip, their faces inches apart. His hand moved up and down the smooth curves of her back. "It doesn't end well," he said.

"These days, sweetie, nobody's story ends well."

Caleb decided he could not argue with that.

*****

Boise City, Oklahoma

My father and I drove to a hill overlooking the highway, parked out of sight, and climbed to the summit in our ghillie suits. We watched the convoy pack up and move out, a plume of windblown dust rising from the road in their wake. When they were out of sight, I put down my hunting rifle.

"Good riddance," Dad said. "Although I will miss Tyrel."

"Lance and Lola were nice too," I said. "I hope we see them again in Colorado."

"Lord willin'. Come on, let's get back to the others."

I hesitated, and said, "Dad?"

"Yeah? What is it, son?"

"Are you all right?"

He knew better than to insult my intelligence by asking me what I meant, so he said, "I don't know, son. I guess it hasn't sunk in yet. Or maybe I'm just too focused on taking care of you. Either way, I'm functional, and I plan to stay that way. I'll have plenty of time to mourn once I get everyone to safety."

"If you ever want to talk about it …"

Dad reached out and gripped the side of my neck. "I should be saying that to you, son."

"It's just … I love you, Dad. Whatever happens, I want you to know that. I could not have asked for a better father."

The old man smiled, his eyes reddening with unshed tears. "I know. And I love you too, Caleb. I can't tell you how proud I am of the man you've become. Now come on, we need to get going."

We met up with the others back at the highway and reported our findings. Mike volunteered to take point, Blake assumed his usual role as navigator, and Dad opted to act as rear guard.

"Why don't you drive Blake's jeep so he can focus on the map?" I asked Sophia. "I'll ride up front with Mike. He might need a gunner."

"Are you sure?" she asked, stepping close and taking my hands in hers. "I'd rather you ride with me. If anything happens to you ..."

I kissed her forehead and traced a thumb down her jaw. "Listen, these guys have been training me my whole life. I can handle myself. Mike and I make a good team. We'll be fine."

She looked dubious. "Okay. I'll take your word for it."

"Just keep your radio charged," I said. "And your rifle handy. No telling what we might run into."

"Will do."

I pulled her against me and squeezed harder than I should have, but she didn't complain. She drew a breath when I let her go and pressed her lips to mine. "What is it you guys always say? Keep your head on a swivel?"

I laughed. "Yes. And I will."

We parted. On the way to the Humvee, I could swear I detected a faint smile on Mike's face. Thankfully, he said nothing as we climbed into the vehicle and I stood up through the gunner's hatch.

A thought occurred to me on the way to Boise City, and I fixed one of the M-4s with an M-203 grenade launcher, loaded several 40mm shells into a bandolier, and slung it over my shoulder. My thinking was we probably would not need that kind of firepower, but as my dad was fond of saying, it is better to have and not need, than need and not have.

We approached Boise City from the north, turning off 287 onto 385. Dad, Blake, and Sophia spread their vehicles out on the flat terrain in the fields surrounding the highway. The plan was to have them remain in reserve in case Mike and I ran into a situation we couldn't fight our way out of.

"All stations in position?" Mike asked over the radio. After a round of affirmatives, he said, "All right, moving in. Keep your ears open."

We rolled into the north side of town.

Calling Boise City a city was far too generous in my opinion. The place was brown, and dusty, and the buildings were sad and neglected, and I had the distinct impression the place was dying long before the Outbreak. It was small, no more than a square mile or two, and from the signs above doors and storefronts, it seemed the economy had primarily been bolstered by farming, ranching, and wildcat oil and gas drilling. There were the usual collections of hotels, fast food chains, strip malls, and rental agencies that were an unavoidable part of America's homogenized corporate dominance. Aside from bull's horns over the entrances of a few restaurants and stores advertising Native American artwork, if the place had any significant character or culture, I could not see it.

According to our map, the town was laid out in a simple grid pattern. We drove to the center of it and stopped. Thus far, we had seen no infected, no movement in windows or doorways or on the streets, no signs of life at all.

"What do you think?" Mike asked.

I leaned down so he could hear me. "I say we drive around a bit more, make some noise. If there are infected here, they'll come after us."

"Works for me."

The radio squawked. "Anything yet?" Dad asked. "Over."

"All clear thus far," Mike answered. "Gonna poke around a little more. Will advise, over."

"Copy."

We drove through empty streets, harsh hot winds sending streamers of dust over the sunbaked pavement. Aside from a few startled rabbits and one prowling, mangy coyote, we saw nothing. Finally, we turned down Main Street and drove past the Cimarron County Courthouse. I tapped Mike on the shoulder.

"Hold up, let's stop here."

"Why?"

"Looks like this place was the county seat. There might be info on what happened here."

As I said it, I noticed a hastily erected sign built of plywood and four-by-fours standing in the brown grass in front of the courthouse. The nails supporting one side of the sign had given way, leaving the plywood message tilted at an angle, the wind banging it against a post. I said, "Look over there."

Mike did, eyes squinting. "Can you tell what it says?"

"No. Get us closer."

He did, jumping the curb and driving straight over the dead lawn. The Humvee slowed to a halt a few feet from the sign. The words were spray painted in black over bare wood. It read:

Infected coming. Town evacuated.

If you are reading this, leave now and head for Colorado Springs.

God be with us all.

"Well, nothing surprising there," Mike said as he put the Humvee in reverse. "There's abandoned cars here and a couple of gas stations. Let's call the others in and get what we need."

I stared at the sign a moment longer, a queasy feeling in my gut. "All right. I guess so."

We drove back to the street and Mike radioed for the others to converge on our position. For reasons I did not understand at the time, I had a nearly overwhelming urge to slap the radio out of his hand and tell him to drive as fast as he could for the edge of town. Back then, I had not yet learned to trust my instincts. If I had, it would have save me a world of grief.

Dad and Blake rode to the courthouse in Blake's Jeep, Sophia bringing up the rear in her father's truck. Evidently, they had swapped out somewhere along the way. They stopped their vehicles in the opposite lane while Blake pulled up next to our Humvee and rolled down his window.

"Where should we start?" he asked.

"There's enough cars around here we should be able to get what we need from the tanks," Mike replied. "Mostly gas vehicles, but a few diesel trucks as well. We'll stick together, it'll make things go faster. You and me can fill the gerry cans while the others keep watch."

Blake gave a single nod. "Sounds good to me."

We drove a short distance up the street to where two SUVs were parked on the side of the road, one of them diesel driven. There were buildings on either side of us, two to three stories each. The only way out was a cross street ahead and the intersection of two streets behind. I looked back and forth between them from my position in the turret and felt my sense of unease begin to grow.

"Uh, guys? Maybe we should look somewhere else," I said.

"What's the problem?" Blake said as he forcefully jammed a Phillips head screwdriver into the diesel SUV's fuel tank, jerked it free, and shoved a bucket beneath the draining liquid.

My eyes darted around nervously, my heart beating faster, an inexplicable desire to flee rising within me. "I don't like this," I said. "Something isn't right."

"Settle down," Dad said, exiting Blake's Jeep and scanning the street, rifle in hand. He had also affixed one of the grenade launchers under his M-4 and wore a bandolier of shells slung over his shoulder. "It's just nerves. We'll be out of here in no time."

I looked to Sophia. "Why don't you get in the Humvee? Just in case."

She frowned at me. "Why are you being so paranoid?"

I hardened my tone. "Sophia, please."

She rolled her eyes, said, "Fine," and stepped out of her father's truck.

The big gray pickup was parked behind the Humvee. Blake's Jeep sat with the driver's side door open and the engine idling ahead of us. My father walked along the sidewalk, rifle held at the low ready, eyes scanning the distance. Mike squatted next to Blake, another bucket in his hands ready to go when the one under the SUV was full.

I stayed in the turret as Sophia climbed in the Humvee. The alarm bells in my head refused to stop ringing despite all the rationalizations I threw their way. My eyes strayed to every window, doorway, corner, and alley. There were too many to monitor all at once. A few times, I thought I caught something, a shadow of movement beyond the light. But when I looked back, I saw nothing.

Then, on the third story of a multi-use office building up the street, I saw a curtain move. The M-240 made a squeaking sound as I swiveled it and took aim. "Guys! We have company."

My father looked at me and followed my gaze to the office building. He held a hand over his eyes to block the sun. "What is it, son? I don't see-"

A shot rang out. High caliber, not more than fifty meters away. We all jumped. Dad and Mike ran around the near side of the vehicles and took cover behind the engine blocks. Blake didn't move.

"Blake!" I shouted. He looked down at his chest in shocked disbelief. As I watched, a red circle expanded on his back, straight in line with his heart, and began flowing downward. There was blood spatter on the fender of the car in front of him, an impossible amount. The surprise never left his face as he fell onto his back, arms limp. He stared at the sky blankly, all the light gone out of his eyes.

"YOU MOTHERFUCKERS!" I sprayed the wall of buildings across from us indiscriminately, triggering the SAW in short bursts, aiming at every window and doorway above the ground floor. Dad popped up over the front of Blake's Jeep and fired a grenade. It blasted the third floor of a storefront half a block up the street and reduced a car-sized section of brick wall to rubble. I was pretty sure it was the same place the shot that killed Blake had come from. I poured a dozen or so rounds into the hole just for good measure and was rewarded with a chorus of screams.

"Come on, let's get the fuck out of here!" Mike yelled. He ran for the Humvee, climbed in the driver's seat, and started the engine.

I heard the *phump* of someone across the street triggering a grenade launcher, and had barely a second to register panic before Blake's jeep erupted in an explosion of flame. The blast knocked me backward, my vision going white, then orange, then gray. A searing, scattered pain spread up the left side of my body from my hip all the way to my face.

There was a hollow pressure in my ears as hands gripped me and pulled me down into the Humvee. I think I was unconscious for a few moments. Then there was movement, and I remember groggily watching my father reload his grenade launcher and blast another section of storefront. Small clouds of dust erupted all around where he stood, holes appearing in the walls and concrete behind him. He ducked for cover and shouted something I couldn't understand at Mike. The Humvee moved and stopped next to the Jeep. Sophia fired her carbine out the passenger's side window as Mike climbed over me, grabbed the M-4 I had equipped with a grenade launcher, and plucked a couple of shells from my bandolier. I heard him stand up through the turret, launch the grenades, then take hold of the SAW and began concentrating bursts of fire at places where muzzle flashes gave away the positions of our attackers.

Dad jumped into the driver's seat, tossed his rifle back to me, and put the Humvee in gear. I tried to catch his weapon as it flew toward me, but my hands were too slow. The barrel hit me across the mouth, and I felt my lip begin to swell. Finally, I wrapped my arms around it and was dimly aware of buildings passing us by as we sped through the streets.

Ahead of us, several cars darted from alleyways and stopped in the intersection, blocking our way. Men jumped out of them

390

and trained weapons in our direction. Mike wasted no time suppressing them with fire from the SAW while dad gunned the accelerator.

Something snapped in my head, and just as quickly as my wits had left me, my mind cleared again. I took up my father's rifle, loaded it with a grenade, leaned out the window, and fired at a small sedan in the middle of the road. The explosion killed one of the gunmen ahead of us and sent the rest running. Dad swerved to the far side of the roadblock, clipped a car on its front fender, revved the engine, and pushed through. Once past, he sped up and did not slow down until the low buildings of Boise City were a speck in the distance. I kept my eyes on our back trail, grenade loaded and ready to fire, but no one followed us. When we were somewhere close to twenty miles out of town, Dad brought the Humvee to a halt.

"Mike," he said. "I need you to take over."

The big Marine climbed down from the turret and looked to his old friend. "Why? What's the matter?"

I leaned forward in my seat to get a better look. That was when I noticed the blood.

*****

During our time with the convoy, Mike had traded a Kimber .45 automatic and fifty rounds of ammo to a medic in exchange for five vials of morphine. We had retained a significant supply of pain meds, but nothing beats morphine, and Mike wanted a little on hand just in case.

For whatever reason, the Army had a surplus of the stuff, and in those days, it could be had on the cheap. I administered a shot to my father as Mike drove us north away from Boise City. After a few moments, the pain on his face faded and his eyes drooped. I had taken off his vest and cut way his shirt so he was bare-chested, then bandaged and packed his wounds as best I could. There was one bullet hole in his left shoulder that had missed the bone and gone straight through the thick muscle. If that had been his only injury, I would not have been worried. The old man had survived worse.

It was the three bullet holes in his abdomen that made me panic.

Dad wanted water, so I gave it to him. He drained both my canteens, then complained he was still thirsty. I had Sophia pull another canteen from Mike's belt and gave it to him. He drained that one too. The morphine made him drowsy, but I shook him to keep him awake, worried if he fell asleep he would not wake up. I kept him talking, listened to him tell me he had seen the man who shot Blake but was too slow to stop him. Tears ran down his cheeks as his eyes fluttered and rolled back in his head. I shook him harder.

"Dad, stay awake. Do you hear me? Stay awake."

I heard Mike turn in his seat and glanced up to see him looking over his shoulder at us. It was the first time I ever saw tears in the big man's eyes.

That was when I realized my father was dying.

We cut left and right through a maze of back roads, farm trails, and off-road two-tracks. I couldn't see anyone following us, but Mike didn't take any chances. When it got to the point that no amount of jostling kept my father's eyes open, I screamed at Mike to stop the goddamn car.

He pulled into the driveway of a farmhouse, abandoned by the look of it, the yard overgrown, weeds tall among dead crops, no vehicles in sight. When the Humvee stopped, I grabbed my father by the shoulders and began dragging him out the door. His dense musculature from a lifetime of hard training made him heavy, forcing me to strain hard to move him.

"Mike, help me!"

He got out of the car, took Dad's legs, and helped me lower him to the ground. There was blood everywhere, all over him, me, the back seat, and now pouring out on the ground through the bandages. In the back of my mind, I knew at least one of the bullets must have struck an artery. Dad's jaw was slack as I lifted him up and held him, trying to shake him awake.

"Dad. Dad! Wake up! You have to wake up!"

For just a moment, he came to, lifted his head, and looked me in the eye. A calloused hand touched my cheek, his dark eyes smiling one last time.

"It's okay, Caleb. You're gonna be all right."

Then he went limp.

I shook him. No reaction. His eyes were open, pupils beginning to dilate despite the bright sun overhead. I laid him flat on the ground and shouted for Mike to help me start CPR. He exchanged a glance with Sophia, pushed her back a step with a gentle hand, and we went to work.

A minute passed. I worked the chest compressions while Mike breathed into Dad's lungs. "Come on, come on, come on," I repeated over and over again.

Sweat poured down my face, soaked my shirt, crimson droplets fell onto my father's bloody torso. Five minutes went by. I felt Dad's ribs crack, but kept working anyway. My breathing became labored, heart pounding in my chest. Several times Mike became light-headed and had to put his head between his knees to recover.

Several more minutes went by. The grinding in my father's chest sounded like sticks rattling under a rubber mat. Finally, strong hands gripped me by the arms and pulled me away.

"Stop, Caleb," Mike said, his voice hitching. "It's over, son. He's gone."

I struggled against him for a moment, but it was no use. He was more than twice as strong as I was. He sat on the ground and held me in a bear hug until the kicking and screaming subsided into choking, racking sobs.

When he finally let me go, I pulled my father's head to my chest and cried for him under the harsh, impartial glare of the Oklahoma sun.

FORTY-TWO

After an indeterminate period of wailing and cursing God for taking Lauren, Dad, and Blake away from me, when I finally gathered myself enough to assess our situation, I kissed my father on his cooling forehead and asked Mike to help me search the property for a shovel. He told me I needed to sit down and let him look me over.

"Why? What's wrong?"

He took me to the driver's side of the Humvee and turned the mirror so I could see my face. The left side was a bloody mess, the eye swollen, my cheek and forehead lacerated in dozens of places, several pieces of shrapnel embedded in the skin. I touched one of them and felt it grind against my upper gum line. It was a miracle I had not lost an eye. Oddly, there was no pain.

"Now look here," Mike said, pointing at my torso and left arm. They hadn't fared much better than my face. My shirt was soaked with so much blood I couldn't tell its original color had been desert tan.

I sat on the front porch and let Mike and Sophia cut away my clothes and tend to my wounds. They extracted the shrapnel with tweezers, and in the case of one big shard stuck in my hip, a pair of needle-nose pliers. The pain gradually began to penetrate the haze of grief and adrenaline, but I simply gritted my teeth and took it. An hour later, the metal was out of me, the

395

wounds were cleaned, stitched, and irrigated, and I had fifteen milligrams of OxyContin in my system. The multitude of bandages on the left side of my body reminded me of a confetti-covered street after a parade. I put on fresh clothes and the three of us searched the house.

The inside was ransacked, as though whoever once lived there had packed up and left in a hurry. There were three bedrooms, two bathrooms, and a wide, spacious kitchen. The pantry was empty except for a few cans of vegetables on the floor and a burst-open sack of ant-ridden sugar. Most of the pots and pans were gone, and there were color-mismatched squares on the walls where pictures had been taken down. Others, mostly old-fashioned artist's prints, remained. I could only assume the missing frames had contained family photos.

Funny, the things people take when they evacuate.

There was a gun cabinet in the master bedroom, but it was empty. The three beds still had sheets on them, clean except for a little dust. One of the bedrooms looked as if it belonged to a teenage boy, while the third was clearly the domain of a pre-teen girl. Lots of pink, and unicorns, and rainbows, and racks of stuffed animals.

The only part of the property that seemed undisturbed was the tool shed. It had a padlock on it, but a few swings of a crowbar solved that problem. Inside the shed, we found the usual collection of yard implements—lawn mower, weed trimmer, hedge clippers, tree pruner, etc.—and a couple of digging spades.

It took the two of us most of the afternoon to dig a grave. I used the mental exercises Mike taught me about keeping my mind clear to focus on the task at hand, losing myself in the rhythmic stab of the shovel, stomp of foot, levering of dirt, and shoulder-swing throw into an ever-growing pile. The sound of rocks and earth rasping over metal filled my existence, drowning out all other voices. When the grave was deep enough, we wrapped my father in a sheet and lowered him into it. Then we filled it in again and stood for a while mopping sweat from our faces. Dad was not a religious man, so we didn't bother with a cross. He would not have wanted one.

During the process, Sophia expressed concern the people who attacked us in Boise City might come looking for us and maybe we should hurry up and get going. I told her to grab a pair of binoculars from the Humvee, climb to the balcony above the farmhouse's second floor, and keep a lookout. If anyone showed up, I would shoot them, cut out their heart, and eat the fucking thing in front of them while they died.

She paled, nodded, and backed away.

*****

Night fell.

We stayed at the farmhouse. I sat on the front porch, outfitted for battle, grenade-launcher equipped carbine between my knees. Mike and Sophia went inside to eat dinner, but I declined. I had no appetite.

There was a pair of NVGs next to me. When full dark came, and the half-moon and stars were the only light to be seen, I donned them and conducted a wide patrol, circling the property, praying I saw signs of pursuers. I wanted them to come for us. I wanted to see the outline of the suppressor through my rifle's optics, feel the stock buck against my shoulder, hear the clack of the chamber, the muted crack. I wanted to hear screams of pain as people died in the darkness. I wanted them to know they were being punished.

But no one came.

Maybe they got what they wanted from the vehicles we left behind, or maybe we killed enough of them they decided it wasn't worth coming after us, or both. Maybe they tried, but simply could not find us. Mike had done a good job of leaving a meandering, double-backed, circuitous trail for any tracker to follow. Even with a good horse and a flashlight, I would have been hard pressed to figure it out myself. Whatever the case, as dawn crept red and gold over the eastern sky, I switched off my NVGs and headed back to the farmhouse, disappointed.

Mike and Sophia greeted me from the kitchen table and offered me breakfast. I took off my gear, sat down, and shoveled food down wordlessly. I do not remember what I ate. Minutes later, I went upstairs to one of the bedrooms, took off my boots and combat gear, and fell into a dreamless slumber.

*****

Five weeks passed.

My wounds, carefully tended to by Sophia, healed quickly. Soon, all that remained of them were fresh pink scars and a few persistent aches where the shrapnel had scraped bone. I was still sore most of the time, but did not let it slow me down.

Mike spent most of his time scouting the area and hunting wild game. Sometimes I went with him, but most of the time I made some excuse to stay at the farmhouse with Sophia. I know he knew why, but he didn't make an issue of it. Not that it would have done him any good.

Sophia and I made love often, taking comfort in each other's embrace, reveling in the heated, gasping, kissing, thrusting passion of new lovers. We explored each other, teased each other, took turns reducing one another to clutching, moaning incoherence. Then we would rest for a while, talk and laugh in exhausted, throaty voices, and start all over again.

I often wondered in the months after why my sexual appetite, which had never been much of a distraction before, suddenly had so much power over me. It was not until after I joined the Army, and the battle of Singletary Lake, that I learned of the strange urges that possess a man after combat. I remember sitting with my back against a cinder-block wall, and a Navy medic coming around to check the guys in my platoon for injuries, and how pretty her green eyes were, and the roaring, burning urge to pull her clothes off and take her right then and there.

She must have seen something of it in my eyes, because she gave me a strange look. Or maybe she noticed the swelling in my pants. Either way, I cast my eyes to the ground, ashamed, willing the feeling to go away. It has happened a few times since, and for a while, I thought there was something wrong with me. But later, I learned most of the other soldiers I served with had experienced the same thing at one point or another, and it was not unique to men. Why it happens, I do not know. I am sure there is a psychologist out there somewhere who can give me a rational explanation, but I have not crossed paths with them yet.

So with Sophia at my side, and Mike the Stalwart an ever-present reassurance, the pain and anguish slowly began to fade. But I never let Boise City out of my mind for more than a few hours. The shadows behind the windows, the indistinguishable faces behind muzzle flashes, the glimpses of what I could have sworn were Army issue combat fatigues. A single word kept rattling around my mind, whispering to me, visiting me in the dark hours when I drifted off to sleep next to Sophia's warmth.

Deserters.

During those weeks, I did not spend all my time eating roasted meat and indulging carnal pleasures. I drew up a few ideas about how we might head back and recon Boise City, see what we were up against, what we could do to make them pay for what they did to us. When I thought I had worked out all the angles, or at least as many as I could see, I asked Mike to join me for a sit-down on a nearby hill.

He listened patiently, chewing on a toothpick. When I was finished, he tossed the toothpick into the brush and said, "Caleb, you have to let it go."

"It's not that simple, Mike. They killed Blake. They killed my father."

"We all knew we were taking a risk going into Boise City, son. There could have been infected, or hostile locals, or deserters holed up, or any host of dangers. We went in there with our eyes wide open—Joe and Blake included. We rolled the dice, and we came up snake-eyes. Joe and Blake were two of the best friends I've ever had. I loved them both like brothers. But they're gone now, and we ain't gonna accomplish a goddamn thing getting ourselves killed trying to avenge them. It's not what they would want us to do. I know that because if I had died and they had lived, I wouldn't want them to risk their lives the same way. There's been enough bloodshed here, Caleb. No measure of revenge is ever going to bring them back. We need to move on."

I opened my mouth to argue, but Mike interrupted. "And what about Sophia, Caleb? What if something happens to us, and she's on her own? What do you think will happen to her?"

To my shame, the thought had never occurred to me. I had been too caught up in my own anger and plotting and pain. The idea of Sophia alone in these wastelands, unprotected, sent an invisible spear through my gut. I looked down and crossed my hands in my lap. "I'm sorry, Mike. I never thought of that."

The big man reached out and put a massive hand on my shoulder. "Listen, kid. For all I know, you and Sophia are all I have left. I have no way of knowing if my wife is still in Oregon, or if she's even still alive. I think it's pretty safe to assume the Outbreak made it that far. The only way for me to find out is to get you two someplace safe and then try to find her. Maybe I can, maybe I can't. I don't know. But I can't start trying until the two of you are out of harm's way. And every day that goes by, my chances of finding her alive get slimmer and slimmer. So do me a favor, Caleb. I know you're hurting. We're all hurting. But I need you to start thinking about someone other than yourself for a while. Okay?"

I sat quietly and watched him walk down the hillside back to the house. Inwardly, I cursed myself for a fool. Mike was right. I had been a selfish idiot. I had forgotten about protecting Sophia. I had forgotten about Mike's wife, Sophia's mother, stranded in Oregon. All I had thought about was myself, and my pain, and how much I wanted, *needed* to lash out, to make someone else hurt as much as I did.

I looked down at my hands, the calloused palms, the new scars, the dark brown skin from too much time in the sun. They were not the hands of a child. They were the hands of a grown man.

It was about time I started acting like one.

FORTY-THREE

"We need to find a place to hole up," Mike said, stating the obvious.

Sunrise crested the horizon on the outskirts of Springfield Colorado, brightening the ink-black night with the iridescent colors of dawn. Through the windows, the shapes of tall grass and solitary trees moved slowly past, lonely shadows against the charcoal gray of early morning.

"Just keep following these trails," I said. "There's bound to be a house around here somewhere."

"I hope so," Sophia said from the back seat, stifling a yawn. "I'm exhausted."

I glanced over my shoulder, seeing only a dim outline of her face in the Humvee's gloomy cab. "Worst case scenario," I said, "we'll park in a hollow and hide out until nightfall."

"I'd rather sleep in a bed."

Mike said, "We'll take what we can get, Sophia."

She rolled her eyes but didn't argue.

I turned back around and stared through the front windshield, the hazy outlines of wrecked and abandoned vehicles drifting by like ships passing in a thick fog. Mike drove slowly, navigating via the Humvee's blackout lights and a pair of NVGs, maneuvering deftly around the increasingly frequent obstacles on Highway 287. We had left the farmhouse just before midnight, Mike and I having decided it would be best to travel under cover of darkness. We knew by then the infected were more active at night, and figured anyone we might encounter who had survived thus far would be aware of that fact as well. Ergo, it made sense that if we wanted to avoid other people as much as possible, we should use the danger posed by the infected to our advantage.

Sophia had not been crazy about the idea, but after I explained that traveling during the day would make us an easy target for marauders, deserters, or just plain desperate people, she saw the wisdom of our plan.

The route we chose was roughly 265 miles, a distance we hoped to cross before daybreak. But the slow speeds we'd had to maintain to ensure safe travel on the increasingly choked highway, not to mention all the times we had to drive off road to make any progress at all, had seen us cover barely more than fifty miles.

For the last two hours, we had skirted the edges of Springfield, sticking to back roads and dirt trails across empty farmland and keeping our distance from the small town. Boise City had taught us a harsh lesson—wilderness good, towns bad—and instilled within us a healthy dose of paranoia. But despite our caution, I kept expecting to hear the *thwap* of bullets striking the Humvee, or the popping of tires over hidden booby traps, or vehicles to surround us with glaring headlights and bristling weapons. Thankfully, none of that happened.

The dirt trail we followed curved eastward across the highway and led us to a narrow strip of woodland running north to south. We went off-road and turned northward, keeping the thin treeline between us and the road. After a mile or so, the trees disappeared revealing a collection of squat buildings, a few livestock trailers, and acres of empty barbed-wire corral. Mike removed his NVGs, the day having brightened enough to see without them, and backed the Humvee down a shallow embankment until the buildings were out of sight.

"What do you think?" he asked, staring out the windshield. "Small-time ranch operation?"

"Looks like it," I said. "See any movement?"

"No. But it's early. If someone is there, they might still be asleep."

"Ghillie suits?"

"Ghillie suits."

"What about me?" Sophia asked.

"Stay here," Mike said. "Stay out of sight and keep your rifle handy. If you spot trouble, drive out of here as fast as you can. If possible, pick us up along the way. If not, just run."

Sophia laughed. "Yeah, sure, that's what I'll do. Just leave you here. Great thinking, Dad. Except *hell no*, that's not gonna happen."

He scowled in her direction, then climbed out of the vehicle. I followed him to the back of the Humvee and waited while he opened the hatch. Inside was the majority of the ammo, weapons, and medical supplies we had taken with us upon leaving the convoy. There were also two five-gallon gerry cans of fuel, one of fresh water, and a few days' worth of food. More if we rationed.

Behind the cases of ammunition and cardboard boxes lay three ghillie suits, neatly rolled and tied, one for me, one for Mike, and one for my father. Blake's had been in his Jeep.

I had kept my father, as well as Lauren and Blake, out of mind as much as possible over the last few of weeks. But seeing Dad's old camouflage caused a bolt of grief to lance through me, twisting my stomach and cutting with renewed pain. Mike didn't notice and reached inside to retrieve the suits, making me grateful for the sullen, ambient grayness of the morning.

"That field over there is tall enough to hide us," Mike said. "We'll go straight at it, then turn west and work our way back to the Humvee."

I cleared my throat. "Works for me."

404

"You okay?"

"Not really, but let's do this anyway."

Mike studied me a few seconds, then handed me my ghillie suit without a word. We both attached suppressors to our rifles, grabbed a couple of grenades each, and swapped out our red-dot sights for VCOG scopes. Once outfitted, we made our way up the hill in a crouch, going to our bellies near the summit. From there it was a question of moving slowly, not allowing ourselves to rush, and being careful not to disturb the grass around us. A few minutes in, a strong wind picked up from the east allowing us to move more quickly.

Just as the sun cleared the horizon, we stopped behind a thicket of vines covering an old, slowly rotting wooden fence. I made my way to Mike's position and spoke to him in whispers. "Now what?"

"We move in," he said. "The sun is at our backs; it'll make us harder to see. Stay low and follow my lead."

The two of us crawled to the edge of the field where we came to a dirt-and-rock-strewn clearing patched with clusters of short brown grass. Although it was still early morning, the sun seared down from a cloudless sky, raising sweat on my back and warming my rifle under my hands.

Tin roofs of low buildings shimmered in the near distance, waves of undulating heat rising and dissipating, the pop and creak of expanding metal on plywood audible from where I lay. The two of us peered through our scopes, scanning. Minutes ticked by, but we saw no movement, no indication of occupants.

"I think it's safe to approach," Mike said. "But keep your eyes open."

We stood up and moved swiftly across the clearing, intent on the nearest building. Once there, we put our backs against the bricks and moved to opposite corners. Peeking around, I saw low walls with empty space above them, four-by-four columns supporting a slanted roof, and narrow doors permitting entry into wide, dirt-floored stalls. The entrances were too small for horses. Sheep maybe?

To the north, barbed wire fence surrounded about ten acres of corral. Beyond where I stood were five more mini-barns of identical construction, a shack the size of a small camper, and two open-air sheds with rusted tools dangling from wall hooks. Past these were a few livestock trailers.

Looking more closely, I saw the tires on the trailers were inflated and showed no signs of dry rot. The wire comprising the corral was well tended, and the water trough by the gate was full but not scummy. By all appearances, the ranch had been, until recently, an active operation. Whoever owned this place had not abandoned it very long ago.

Rocks crunched softly under Mike's boots as he moved closer. "Looks clear on my side."

"Same here."

"Let's split up. I'll take the buildings this way, you search over there."

"Got it."

Mike leap-frogged around me while I swept the stalls closest to us. Finding them empty, I moved on to the next building, wincing at the noise my steps made in the loose, omnipresent gravel. The vegetation immediately around the stables had been worn away by hundreds of trampling hooves, with some of the prints still visible in the hard-packed dirt.

Definitely sheep.

The door to every stall was open. I spotted a line of old, washed out tracks heading westward, indicating whoever owned this place had let the animals go free. I admired his or her decision; if I had been in their place, and all hope was lost, I would have done the same thing. Better to let the critters take their chances in the wild than doom them to starvation or death at the hands of the infected. Maybe years from now people would be hunting wild sheep and raising them for wool. It was an interesting thought.

Just as I turned to walk to the shed at edge of the field, Mike let out a startled curse and I heard the muted crack of his carbine.

Then came the moans.

It started as one, then four or five, and then I lost count as more groaning answered, coming from a stable to my left. A pair of gray hands knocked aside the door of the shed I approached, followed by a gore-streaked old man in ragged clothes. He stumbled into the brightness of early morning, head swinging side to side, ears tilted toward the sky. More infected lurched out after him, also swiveling their heads.

In the space of seconds, where there had been peaceful silence, more than a dozen undead had appeared. In the field ahead of me, I saw more emerge from the tall growth, standing up unsteadily, looking dazed as if they had been sleeping. The sound of Mike's rifle went from a slow trickle to a frenetic barrage.

"Caleb, fall back!"

I raised my rifle and fired without thinking, dropping the five infected closest to me. There was a grating, shuffling sound behind me, and I turned just in time for a ghoul to seize my arm and lunge at me. I let out a terrified yelp and pulled away, but the creature had a grip like steel. Its teeth snapped shut less than an inch from my bicep. With no time for a plan, I raised the barrel of my rifle and shoved it sideways into the ghoul's mouth. It bit down on the hardened steel, teeth chipping and cracking from the pressure.

I let go of the gun just in time for the creature to start shaking its head back and forth like a dog and crack me across the temple with the stock. Stars danced in my vision as I dropped to one knee, drew my pistol, and fired a shot upward through its throat. Red and black mist erupted from the back of its head, the painful grip on my arm releasing instantly as the ghoul slumped to the ground.

I stood up and turned a quick circle, gun at the ready, legs rubbery from the blow to my head. Another ghoul had made it within four feet of me, arms outstretched, hissing like a pissed-off cobra. My first shot missed. Cursing, I backed up a few steps, centered my aim, and fired again. This time, it went down.

Boots pounded the dirt behind me, growing closer. I looked over my shoulder to see Mike sprinting toward me, rifle slung across his back, a short, slotted metal fencepost in his hands. At the end of the post was a rough, heavy-looking cylinder of dirt-crusted concrete.

Where the hell did he get that?

As I watched, he angled toward one of the undead closing in on me, raised the improvised weapon, screwed his heels into the ground, and swung it like a baseball bat. The concrete cylinder burst the walker's skull open like a ripe melon, bone and brain fragments flying in one direction while the corpse fell in another.

"Caleb, come on!"

I had stopped moving and was staring at the corpse, its skull shattered, brain tumbling out, dirt sticking to the shriveled tissue. A large, fat fly circled down and landed among the mess, its wings buzzing as it walked excitedly over its feast. My feet felt leaden, vision gray and black around the edges, mind blank, disconnected, a numb tingling creeping up my face. Something constricted my chest, making my breath come in short, stuttering gasps. Mike yelled again, and when I didn't respond, he slapped me across the cheek hard enough to make my eyes water.

"Wake up!"

I did, blinking against the pain. "Son of a bitch."

He bent, picked up my rifle, and shoved it against my chest. "Take your gun, dammit."

I grabbed it and brought it to my shoulder, muscle memory putting my hands in the proper places.

"Back to back," Mike said. "We'll shoot our way out of here." He took a couple of seconds to raise the metal and concrete club over his head, take aim, and throw it like an axe. It spun end over end three times before striking a ghoul in the chest and knocking it to the ground. I heard ribs shatter from fifteen feet away.

Shaking the last of the fuzziness from my head, I adjusted my VCOG to its 1x setting, aimed, and began firing. My breathing was even now, hands steady, the trembling in my legs gone. I let fly ten rounds in ten seconds and dropped ten ghouls. Behind me, I heard the *shuck*, *snap*, and *clack* of Mike reloading.

We moved steadily toward the western field, keeping each other in our peripheral vision, checking our flanks and corners every few shots, dropping anything trying to angle in on us from the side. By the time I had burned through my first magazine, there were only fifteen or twenty walkers left standing. A minute later, they were all down.

Mike and I stood among the once-human wreckage, bodies strewn around us, spray patterns of coagulated blood and brain tissue contrasting sharply with the pale dirt under our feet. We gripped our rifles and looked around dazedly, hardly believing what just happened.

"We watched this place for a long time," Mike said. "I saw *nothing*."

"Neither did I."

"Not a stir, not a peep, not a damn thing. They came out of nowhere."

I looked at the stables and the fields beyond. "It's like they were waiting for us."

Mike thought a few seconds, then shook his head. "No, I don't think so."

"Why not?"

"I talked to some of those soldiers from San Antonio. The things they told me are starting to make sense now."

"Like what?"

"This one guy told me they don't like sunlight, especially when it's hot outside. Said if they can't find food they look for shelter, or just kind of drop like they're hibernating or something. Might explain why they're more active at night."

I thought of the ghouls emerging from the field and stables, faces confused, swaying and turning circles as though punch drunk, angling their heads to vector in on me. There was no way they could have known we were headed this way—*we* didn't know we were headed this way—and none of the undead's behavior thus far indicated they were intelligent enough to plan an ambush.

"I see your point. But it's early morning, Mike. Why weren't they out last night?"

"Maybe nothing worth eating came along in a while."

"So you think they were sleeping?"

"Hell, I don't know. I'm just telling you what the man said. Your guess is as good as mine." He removed the half-spent mag from his carbine and replaced it with a full one. "Think we got 'em all?"

"Could be more in the fields. Crawlers."

"Have to keep an eye out."

I turned toward the Humvee. "Yes, we will."

*****

It took us an hour to stack the bodies in one of the stables.

That done, we used shovels liberated from the tool shed to scrape the leftover gore into small piles, which we then carted away in a wheelbarrow and dumped out of sight in the fields.

Last, we made makeshift brooms with bundles of grass and erased both our tracks and those of the undead.

From a distance, our location would look abandoned and undisturbed. But up close, the striations left by the grass stalks would be a dead giveaway. All we could do was hope the weather helped us out with a strong wind or an afternoon thunderstorm.

After cleaning up, the three of us looked at each other, each one waiting for the others to speak. Finally, Mike said, "Well, anyone feel like sleeping in one of the stables?"

Sophia and I said, in unison, "No."

We looked at each other and laughed. "Kind of seems like a lot of work for nothing, doesn't it?" I said.

Mike shrugged. "I've done a lot harder work for a lot dumber reasons. At least the next person who comes along won't have to worry about those things."

"Walkers," I said, more to myself than the others.

"What?"

I looked at Mike. "That's what the soldiers called them. Walkers. Walking corpses, walking dead, you know. Like an abbreviation."

He turned his head toward the stable loaded with dead bodies. "Makes as much sense as anything, I suppose."

"Walkers, schmalkers," Sophia said. "I'm tired. Let's get out of here."

Mike and Sophia slept under the shade of a lodgepole pine near the Humvee, the engine making the occasional faint ticking as it finished cooling. I stayed close for a while, perched atop the wide vehicle, binoculars focused on the small ranch up the hill until it became clear no more infected were nearby. Thanking fate for small favors, I put my ghillie suit back on and conducted a slow, careful sweep of the surrounding area.

I'm a firm believer people overuse the word 'surreal', often applying it to situations out of context with its definition, but

411

that's exactly what the next five hours were like. Surreal. No airplanes droned overhead, no cars buzzed along the highway, no voices drifted to me on the wind, nothing manmade. The only sound was a light breeze sighing through the dry brush and the rustling of sparse evergreen limbs. Sometimes a rodent or lizard skittered away at my approach, a bird took flight with a flap of feathered wings, or a door to one of the open stalls beat against its frame. Otherwise, I heard nothing.

After a while, I realized that other than Mike and Sophia, I was probably the only living person for miles. All the sneaking and crawling and straining of ears began to feel silly. So I stood up in the middle of hundreds of acres of open terrain, made a pile of my gear, and removed my ghillie suit. Rolled it up. Tied it to my assault pack. Tilted my head back and closed my eyes to the sun.

Orange spots raced across my vision, the amber glow of faraway nuclear fusion backlighting my eyelids. The wind ruffled my hair and flapped my collar against my neck, carrying the scents of warmth, dry grass, pinesap, and the faint, earthy undertone of decay. The field around me was a static crackling of brown stalks gently colliding in the breeze, dipping and rising like the surface of a lake, flashes of white reflected at a cloudless, azure sky.

My eyes stung when I opened them, forcing me to blink to restore sight. When I could see without large, multi-colored spots obscuring half the world, I picked up my gear, finished my patrol, and headed back to camp.

It was a refreshing, clear-minded peace I felt that morning, alone in that bright field. It was pure. Undiluted. An instant of hopeful clarity amidst a maelstrom of chaos and fear.

No peace has found me since.

FORTY-FOUR

Two more days on the road brought us to the outskirts of Colorado Springs.

The first day was downright boring. We set out at night, Mike and I taking turns driving, and after seven hours of dodging wrecks, abandoned vehicles, fallen trees, dead bodies, and a crashed single-engine airplane, we spotted a cluster of buildings. Drawing closer, I could see the buildings comprised one of those parasitic road towns that once earned a bleak subsistence siphoning money from tourists and passing travelers.

Gas stations, chain restaurants, and a dry cleaner lined the road, while in the center of town was a squat strip mall, complete with coin laundry, coffee shop, nail salon, barber, used books, and the all-important grocery store. Looters had shattered the grocery store's front window, leaving broken glass glittering in the parking lot. Looking past the entrance, I could see whoever trashed the place had done a thorough job of cleaning it out. Not much point in searching for leftovers. I glanced around to see if there were any cars nearby. A nineties-model Mercedes with flat tires was the only vehicle in sight.

"How much you wanna bet there's a maintenance ladder around back?" I asked.

"No bet," Mike said. He drove to the service entrance and followed a narrow strip of gravel behind the building. The lane widened into a flat loading area. Mike parked next to one of several service ladders.

"Not much of a lock," Mike said. A metal security grate covered the ladder, held shut by a cheap bronze padlock. I grabbed a crowbar from the back of the Humvee and levered it off. While I worked, Sophia appeared with Mike's tent and bedroll and kissed him on the cheek. "Sleep well, Dad," she said. "See you this afternoon."

She grabbed my arm and started pulling me away. Mike said, "Where are you two going?"

"We'll be on the roof of that gas station over there," she replied. "Keep your radio handy."

Mike looked like he was about argue, then let it go with a sigh, looking deflated. "Fine. Just keep it down over there. Don't want to draw any infected."

"Okay, Dad."

I kept my mouth shut and followed.

While Sophia was settling in, I retrieved an empty five-gallon fuel can from the Humvee and checked the abandoned Mercedes' tank. To my delight, not only was it a diesel, but there were just over four gallons left. I thought about how long it had been since the Outbreak and wondered how much longer it would be before what limited quantities of salvageable fuel were left lying around went bad. The prospect of walking to Colorado Springs appealed not at all.

After stowing the fuel, I went back to Sophia and lay down with her in the tent. A simple kiss became two, then three, and the next thing I knew we were tearing each other's clothes off, skin hot, hands exploring.

There are few things more awkward than two people trying to undress one another in a pup tent, but somehow we managed. There was a lot of pulling and cursing and pauses to kiss whatever portion of skin one of us happened to expose on the other. Then came the clutching, and thrusting, and gasping, and heavy breathing, and Sophia's white teeth biting down on her lower lip.

We tried to be quiet. We really did.

*****

Later, as Sophia drifted to sleep next to me, I lay awake, ears straining.

A few hours passed. I heard nothing but birds, insects, and the breathing sound of the wind against our tent. I thought about Mike on the other rooftop, alone, and wondered if he was thinking of his wife, and if so, was he remembering the good times, or the bad?

I tried to imagine what would preoccupy my thoughts if Sophia were far away, unreachable, and putting my mind in that place, I knew I would remember the arguments, the harsh words, the digs we took at each other. For Mike's sake, I hoped he had enough good memories to outweigh the bad.

It is easy to be impatient with someone when they are close to you. When you can reach out and touch them, and hear their voice, and apologize for whatever stupid thing you did or said. But distance creates perspective, and when that distance is eternal, there is no salve for the regret of loved ones taken for granted.

Memories stirred of my father, and Lauren, and Blake, and I clenched my fists to keep my hands from trembling. That way held nothing but pain, regret, and sorrow, and its path ended at a cliff. Once over it, no matter how much I clutched and scrambled, there would be no coming back. So instead, I closed my eyes and focused on the immense black nothing in front of me, wondering if it was the last thing they saw before the end. If the empty dark was what waited for us all, the answer to the great mystery of life after death, the idea people had been debating and philosophizing and fighting wars over for millennia. Maybe the answer had been staring us in the face all along, every time we closed our eyes. I wondered, when my time came, if my family would be there waiting with hands outstretched to lead me home.

Sophia stirred beside me, turned over onto her side. I opened my eyes and sat up a little, the light filtering through the tent's canopy chasing away dark thoughts. The pain faded somewhat, diluted by the soft warm body next to me. I moved closer and draped an arm around her, listening to her sigh contentedly as I pulled her close.

Plenty of time to mourn later, I told myself. *For now, hold it together.*

Just past midday, I slept.

*****

The next night was more of the same. About five miles from I-40 we turned left and traveled cross-country toward Highway 24, staying well away from the interstate. The scars left over from the horrors we had witnessed on I-35 and I-20 were still fresh, and none of us were willing to bet I-40 was any better.

During the transit, I thought of how I had always imagined Colorado as a wonderland of soaring mountains, sweeping valleys, verdant forests, and flower-covered fields dotted with crystal blue lakes. That was what I had always seen in pictures, magazines, and on television—America's version of the Bavarian Alps. But the reality was far different from the idyllic setting I had dreamed up in my mind. The region we traveled over was mostly flat with the occasional lifts, saddles, and long, sloping basins.

When we could, we traveled on roads. When we couldn't, we relied on the Humvee's off-road capabilities. On four separate occasions, we got stuck and had to drive over wooden planks after digging our way free of wet, clinging mud. Out of frustration, I asked Mike why it was so fucking damp around here despite the lack of rain.

"We're in a saddle," Mike said. "A damned big one. Starts back there at 287 and goes clear to the foothills that way." He pointed east. "The water runoff between flows down here, smack dab the middle."

"So we're basically standing in the bottom of a giant drainage ditch."

"Pretty much."

"Fantastic."

At just after four 'o clock in the morning, I drove the Humvee over a rise and could see the flat expanse of Highway 24 a couple of miles below. "Not much farther now," I said.

"You see the highway?" Mike asked.

"Yep."

Sophia let out a sleepy little whoop from the back. Grinning, I angled around a stand of trees and made for the road.

The trip down the hill went smoothly, the dry dirt at higher elevation providing better traction. I glanced at the fuel gauge nervously, thinking about the last two gallons in the back and worried it would not be enough. I voiced my concerns to Mike.

"Just keep driving for now," he said. "Get a few miles down the highway, then we'll see what we can scrounge up. Worst case, we'll pull over somewhere and stash this thing. Go the rest of the way on foot and come back for our stuff later."

I couldn't think of a better plan, so I nodded.

When we reached the highway, Mike checked the map under an LED light and declared we were just over sixty miles from Colorado Springs. There was no way our fuel would hold up that long, but I could see no cars close by. All around us was mile after mile of flat, empty grassland. If it had been daylight, I would have seen the toothy line of the Rockies in the distance, but my NVGs could not reach that far.

So we drove on, the needle lowering inexorably toward empty, wheels picking up speed on the unobstructed highway. I eased the Humvee up to thirty-five and let it stay there, figuring it was the point of greatest fuel efficiency. We made it a little over fifteen miles before the engine began to sputter and cough. Thankfully, I could make out the shape of a few buildings ahead and the unmistakable outline of a tractor-trailer.

"There's a semi up ahead," I said. "A few buildings too. Might have what we need."

"Go ahead and pull over," Mike said. "Hopefully that truck has some diesel in it. Otherwise, we got a long walk ahead of us."

I tapped the brakes and eased the Humvee to the side of the road. As I did, it struck me as an odd thing to do; we had seen no other vehicles since leaving the convoy. I could have straddled the double-yellow lines if I wanted to, and it would have made no difference.

Old habits die hard, I guess.

Mike stepped out and walked to the rear of the vehicle. I heard the back hatch open, the clattering of a gerry can and funnel being removed from the cargo area, and a few clanks as Mike poured the last of the fuel into the tank.

With the absence of road noise, I also heard the sound of slow, heavy breathing. Turning around, I saw Sophia lying across the back seat, eyes closed, mouth hanging slightly open. Even through the grainy green image of the NVGs, she was a beauty. Smiling, I waited until Mike climbed back in.

"Good to go?" I asked.

"As good as it gets for now."

I put the Humvee in gear and headed for the truck.

FORTY-FIVE

"Should we wake up Sophia?" I asked.

"Nah," Mike said. "This won't take long."

I stopped the Humvee on the road adjacent to the truck. Its previous driver had backed it off the highway and parked in front of a massive red barn the size of an airplane hangar. Looking to my left, I saw the property was not a farm, but an estate. There was a mansion set back off the road that could not have been less than ten-thousand square feet, a cottage with an empty swimming pool out front, several outbuildings, and at least a hundred acres of fenced pasture. The doors to the giant barn were open, there were no lights visible, and I saw no sign of any horses.

Then there was the semi.

"What the heck is that thing doing here?" I asked.

"Maybe it's stopped here for the night."

"Should we look around or just move on?"

"Move on? Why?"

The same uneasiness I felt at Boise City had returned, albeit not as strong as before. "I don't know," I said, "but I don't like this place. There's no reason that truck should be here."

"There's no reason it shouldn't be, either. Look, it has a sleeper cab. The driver probably stopped to catch some shuteye. Might be he'll trade us for some fuel."

Logically, what Mike said made sense. Still, I couldn't shake the feeling we were headed for trouble. Mike noticed my tension and said, "Tell you what, Caleb, let's just take a look around. If we don't like what we see, we leave."

My instinct was to say no, screw that, let's get out of here. But the fact was we needed fuel, and there was no way to know if we would find any more on the way to Colorado Springs. The roads had been remarkably empty the last few miles—no wrecks, no cars on the side of the road, no dead bodies, nothing—and I was certain I had spotted the even, parallel markings of heavy equipment treads creased into the asphalt. The most likely scenario was the government had sent crews out to clear the highway, as doing so would certainly make life easier for any refugees approaching from the east. But if that were the case, where was everybody? Surely we couldn't be the only people headed this way.

I continued staring at the truck, fingers drumming on the steering wheel. Finally, I said, "Okay. We'll check it out. But let's stash the Humvee first."

"Fair enough."

I put the vehicle in gear and drove on, going a mile down the road around a bend in the highway. When I felt confident it looked as if we had moved on, I doubled back and angled the Humvee off-road on a vector that would take us a few hundred yards behind the mansion. Once there, I drove down the back of a hill leading away from the property, turned the Humvee so it was facing the highway, and killed the engine.

"We should wake up Sophia," I said.

"Sophia's awake."

I turned to see her sitting up in the back seat. "This field has so many holes in it I thought my brain was going to bounce out of my head. Where the hell are we, anyway?"

I explained the situation and then waited while she thought it over. Her eyes turned toward the mansion as she grabbed a canteen and took a long pull. "I'm coming with you," she said, wiping her mouth.

"Good idea," I said. "Mike?"

"Fine by me."

Sophia made a disgusted noise. "For Christ's sake, Dad, I … wait, what?"

Mike turned, smiling. "I said it's fine by me. I'd rather have you close by where I can keep an eye on you."

Her eyes widened, mouth open in surprise. "Oh. Okay, then."

"Don't forget your rifle."

Mike and I exchanged an amused glance, then got out of the Humvee.

I fitted suppressors to all three carbines, gave Mike and Sophia each a pair of NVGs, and swapped out my VCOG for our sole night vision scope. Mike attached a PEQ-15—an infrared laser sight visible only through night vision optics—to his weapon, and another to Sophia's.

"So let me get this straight," she said, after we explained to her how it worked. "I can see the laser, but no one else can?"

"Unless they're wearing NVGs," I said. "Also, don't think just because it's dark they can't see you. The human eye is attracted to movement, even in low light situations. So move slowly and be as quiet as you can."

She gave a mock bow. "*Hai*, sensei. Can we go now?"

"In a minute, smart ass."

Out of habit, I tilted my rifle, checked the safety, tugged the charging handle to make sure there was a round in the chamber, leveled the scope to make sure it was activated, and clicked the button on my radio transmitter.

"Check, check."

"Copy." Mike said.

Sophia ran her fingers along the cord connected to her earpiece, found the transmit button, and said, "I can hear you."

"Try pushing the button," I said.

She did, and I heard a click.

"Say something, Sophia."

Another click. "You're an annoying shit when you get like this."

"Okay, we're good to go."

Mike grunted.

We fanned out and crossed the field, staying low and quiet. Sophia turned out to be surprisingly stealthy. When we were a hundred yards from the back of the mansion, I clicked my radio. "Stop. Time to come up with a plan. Over."

"Copy, over."

"What he said."

We crawled through the tall brush and met at the top of the rise, heads low, eyes scanning for movement. "Here's what we'll do," Mike said. "Caleb, you work your way around to the barn. If it's like most barns it'll have a hay loft. You've got the scope, so climb up there and provide overwatch."

"Okay," I said. "What about you and Sophia?"

"I'll approach the truck and have a look around. Sophia, you see that tool shed up there, the little square one to the left of the cottage?"

"The one with the wind vane on top of it?"

"That's the one."

"What about it?"

"I want you to take cover on this side, facing back toward the Humvee. Stay low and watch my back while I'm checking the truck. Can you do that?"

"Sure."

"Let's go then."

I swung around to my right, staying well clear of the mansion. Ten minutes later, I walked through the open doors of the barn, found the wooden ladder to the loft, and climbed up.

Each side of the loft was huge, easily the same square footage as my old house. A wide gap separated the two halves, and there was a thirty-foot drop to the ground between. The barn housed two rows of more than a dozen stalls each, all standing open. The scent of urine and horse manure was faint, but still strong enough to reach my nose. What little hay remained in the loft reeked of mildew, telling me this place had been abandoned for at least a few weeks.

I made my way to the wall facing the semi and carefully pulled open the shutters on a window. The window had no glass, just two pieces of plywood hung from hinges with a hook-and-lanyard to secure it shut. I had seen the same setup before. The idea was to open the shutters during good weather to let air flow through and keep the hay dry, and close them for the same reason when it rained.

The height of the window required me to stand in order to see through it, so I backed off a few feet to conceal myself, set my feet, bent my knees a little, and waited. A few minutes passed. No sign of Mike.

Concerned, I shifted a few steps to my right, looked toward the mansion, and saw Sophia creeping closer to the shed where she was to take position. Reassured Mike as still out there somewhere, I swiveled the gun back to the semi and waited for him to show up.

Another few minutes passed before I saw Mike's bulky form step away from the barn and approach the truck. He began a pattern of walking a few steps, examining the ground, glancing up, checking his surroundings, and walking a few more steps. Realizing I was on overwatch and not there to observe Mike's activities, I began moving the scope from building to building, watching for movement, ears straining.

Sophia had reached the tool shed, a sliver of leg just visible around the corner. Confident no one would spot her in the dark, I did another sweep, letting my gaze linger on each outbuilding, then the mansion, and finally back to Sophia's hiding spot.

Just as I began to turn away, I realized I could not see her leg.

Must have stepped to her right.

I was about call her on the radio just to be on the safe side when I heard raised voices and looked back to see three men emerge into view. One of them stepped out from a tack shed next to the barn, while the other two emerged from a small bunkhouse on the opposite side of the truck. They approached Mike with their weapons up, two of them carrying shotguns, the third a lever-action repeater.

"*Fuck*," I whispered.

"Drop the gun," one of the men shouted, the one from the tack shed.

Mike unslung his rifle and eased it to the ground, then did the same with his .45 automatic. "Okay, I'm unarmed," he said.

Mike was lying; he always kept a .380 revolver in a concealed holster at the small of his back. I had personally witnessed him snap it out and hit a target center of mass at twenty-five yards faster than most people could clap their hands. But he sounded earnest enough, even managing to force a little manufactured fear into his voice.

Worried someone might be coming up behind me, I turned, knelt, and swept the loft, carbine just below my line of sight. Nothing. This meant one of two things: either they didn't know I was up here, or whoever they sent after me was extremely stealthy. For the moment, all I could do was keep my ears open and hope it was the former, not the latter.

Returning my attention to the situation on the ground, I saw the two men from the bunkhouse closing in on Mike, one on either side. *Stupid*, I thought. *If they shoot, they'll hit each other*. Mike recognized this, and I saw a slight tension gather in

424

him as he prepared to make his move. But before he could, the third man, who had stopped ten feet in front of him, said, "Caul, move a few steps towards me you fucking idiot."

The man looked up, realized his mistake, and scrambled to his right.

"What do you want?" Mike asked.

"Where are the rest of you," said the man in charge, the one who had yelled at Caul.

"It's just me."

"Bullshit, Fed. There's always more of you."

I looked more closely at the leader. His hunting coveralls looked too big for him, his face sunken and gaunt, skin loose from rapid weight loss. The other two men didn't look much better, dressed in filthy, billowy rags that probably fit not so long ago. The Outbreak and the hardships it caused were having that effect on most people, myself included.

"Fed?" Mike asked, genuinely confused. "Wait, you think I'm with the Army?"

The leader—who I dubbed Henry because of his lever-action rifle—started to say something else, but a shout from where I had last seen Sophia interrupted him. "Hey, I got another one!"

Henry grinned viciously, staring Mike in the eye. "Is that a fact?"

I felt cold, like someone had dumped ice water over my head. Shifting my aim, I saw a man nearly as big as Mike emerge from the side of the shed, one brawny arm around Sophia's neck, the other holding a revolver to her head. She had a gag in her mouth, hands bound behind her back, one eye swollen nearly shut.

The sight shocked me into stillness. A grinding sound grated in my ears, and for a few seconds, I wondered what it was. Then I realized it was my own teeth.

I knew there wasn't much time. Now that they had Sophia, there was no reason to keep Mike alive. My only hope was they would be less anxious to kill Sophia, for obvious reasons.

Henry, the leader, was the biggest threat. The others clearly deferred to him, so taking him out first would cause the most confusion. At least I hoped it would.

Steadying myself, I put the reticle just under Henry's right arm, centered it on his ribcage, let out half a breath, and squeezed the trigger three times. The only sounds were a series of muted cracks, the clank of the chamber opening and closing, and three low thumps as the 5.56 rounds went straight through Henry and kicked up little puffs of dust a few feet to his left. He stiffened in shock and tried to scream, but all that came out was a high, strangled whine and a spray of blood.

The other two gunmen looked to their leader in confusion. One of them said, "Hey, you all right?"

Mike made his move.

One second he was standing with both hands in the air, the next his right arm was outstretched, pistol in hand. The gun barked twice. Without waiting to see what effect it had, Mike dove forward with surprising speed, rolled, and came one knee with his gun leveled. The two of us fired on the third man at the same time, Mike aiming at his chest, me aiming at his head. The poor bastard died with an almost comical look of surprise on his face. He did not even have a chance to shift his shotgun in Mike's direction.

As Mike turned to cover the first man he had shot, I shifted my aim to the man holding Sophia. His mouth was a wide circle of shock, eyes bulging from his head. Mike's gun rang out one more time, and in my peripheral vision, I saw the second gunman's head snap back. He turned to his right and fired his last round at Henry, also snapping his head back.

Not wasting any time, Mike dropped the .380 and snatched up his rifle, then sprinted to the back of the truck. Crouching behind one of the axles, he sighted in on the man holding Sophia.

"Let her go," he shouted, "and I'll let you walk out of here."

"Fuck you!" the man yelled back, pressing his revolver harder into Sophia's temple. "Drop that gun or I'll blow her fucking brains out."

"You do that and I'll kill you where you stand."

I keyed my radio. "Mike, do what he says, but stay behind the truck. Ease to your left slowly, try to get him to point the gun away from Sophia. Don't worry, I've got a clean shot."

Mike nodded once, not looking over his shoulder. The last gunman shouted, "Do it now, fucker, or the bitch dies."

"Okay, okay. Just don't shoot, all right?" Mike made a show of holding up his rifle, switching it to safe, and tossing it aside. "I'm coming out now. Just don't shoot."

He was wasting his breath. Hostage situations are not like they make them out to be in the movies. If someone has a human shield, even an expert marksman would be hard pressed to shoot them without running a serious risk of hitting the hostage. Which is why, in real life, cops almost never try it. Furthermore, if you step out of cover to confront a hostage-taker, you are at the disadvantage of having to aim carefully. The other guy has no such problem. All he has to do is point the gun at you and fire until you go down. And it's not like television where the bad guy just shoots one time. In real life, they spray bullets at you rapid fire, figuring at least one of them will hit you.

Consequently, Mike stayed behind cover as he stood up and raised his hands. "Okay, I'm coming out."

He had taken no more than four steps toward the end of the truck's bare chassis before the gunman pointed his revolver. Mike must have been watching the man's shoulder because as soon as he twitched, Mike hit the ground.

My first shot hit him in the shoulder, the same one attached to the arm holding the gun. He cried out and fired wildly, the bullet bashing through the wall of the barn beneath me. By its report it was powerful, maybe a .357.

Sophia, clever girl, used the distraction to snap her head savagely backward into the gunman's nose. From where I stood near the window, it sounded like someone hitting a melon with brick. The gunman cried out in pain, loosening his grip enough for Sophia to fall down and roll away.

I fired seven more times.

The first six riddled the man's torso, causing him to drop his weapon so he could clutch at his ruined insides. He stumbled backward and fell, a ragged scream escaping his lips.

Once again, I thought of the difference between movies and reality. In the movies, when the hero shoots the bad guy, he jerks to the side and falls down dead. In reality, people rarely die instantly from gunshot wounds. Even with a direct shot to the heart, it takes a few seconds to lose consciousness. During that time, the victim is awake and relatively alert, and can feel the pain of the wound.

I had deliberately missed his heart.

He lay on his side, feet kicking uselessly, mewling, mouth stretched in agony. I watched him suffer for a few seconds, jaw set, a cold flower of hate blooming in my chest. I knew I should feel sorry for him—that would have been the human thing to do—but at the moment, I felt nothing. Just a grim, distant satisfaction he was no longer a threat.

"Caleb," Mike shouted, looking at me through the window. "What are you waiting for? Finish him off."

I didn't want to. I wanted to stand there and listen to him scream, to hear the terror in his voice, to watch the blood pour out, to see the look on his face when the cold grip of oblivion closed around him and squeezed. After what he had done to Sophia, and what he would have done if I hadn't stopped him, he deserved no better.

"Caleb!"

"All right!"

With my seventh shot, I put him out of his misery.

FORTY-SIX

A search of the semi found the tanks empty, so after dragging the marauders' dead bodies out of sight, we scoured the rest of the property. The four-car garage attached to the mansion yielded diesel pickup with a full tank, which I assumed belonged to our attackers. Mike volunteered to siphon the fuel and asked me to go check on Sophia.

I found her standing on the metal steps attached to the passenger's side of the semi, staring at her reflection in the mirror, fingers gently probing her swollen eye. "Those assholes leave us any fuel?"

"Yeah, they did."

She stepped down and came to me, arms slipping around my waist. I held her gently, careful not to touch her face. "I can't believe I let that son of a bitch get the drop on me," she said.

"How did it happen?"

"I turned to look for Dad, just for a few seconds. Next thing I know my rifle is on the ground, there's an arm around my throat, and everything went black. I woke up while he was tying my hands and tried to scream, but he hit me. That's all I remember until I saw you shoot from the barn."

"You remember head-butting the fucker?"

"Yeah. I remember that part. But it shouldn't have come to that, Caleb. If I had kept my eyes on the house like you told me to, I would have seen him coming."

Her voice began to break as she spoke, so I held her tighter and kissed the top of her head. "It's okay now, Sophia. They're all dead. They won't be hurting anyone ever again."

"I could have gotten us all killed."

"Actually, I had a clean shot at him the whole time."

"That's not the point."

"I know." I put my hands on her shoulders and held her at arm's length. "Look at it this way, it's a lesson learned. Next time, you'll be more careful."

She reached up and thumbed a tear out of her good eye. "Yes, I will."

I heard footsteps approach and turned my head to see Mike rounding the corner, shoulders bent under the weight of two sloshing gerry cans. "Let's get out of here," he said. "If there are any walkers close by they probably heard the commotion."

Mike refueled the Humvee, climbed in the driver's seat, and we got under way. I sat in the back with Sophia, her head in my lap, carefully stroking her soft blond hair. The stress of the last half-hour took its toll and she was soon snoring gently, a small trickle of drool expanding in a warm wet spot on my thigh. I smiled, deciding not to say anything to her about it. She'd been through enough lately.

Leaning back in my seat, I fought against the lead weights pulling down on my eyelids. Sleep had been a bit of a problem lately. Most of my downtime was spent wide-awake, mind racing, hands never far from a weapon. When I did manage to drift off, nightmares I could not remember were never long in waking me up.

I told myself I was going to relax a little while, just long enough to clear my head. The road drifted by outside the window, grassy plains reflecting pale silver under a full moon. Both front windows were down, letting a cool wind dry the sweat on my skin. I closed my eyes, head rocking back and forth as we rode over bumps in the pavement, concentrating on the steady hum of tires speeding over asphalt.

431

At some point while I was drifting, I heard the sound of gravel crunching and looked out my window. Mike had pulled the Humvee to the side of the road and got out. I opened my door and said, "What's going on?"

"Don't worry about it. Get some sleep. We'll talk when you wake up."

That sounded like the best advice ever given. I did as he suggested, closing my eyes and letting sleep claim me. Approximately four seconds later, a hand grabbed my arm and shook me.

"Caleb, wake up." It was Sophia's voice.

I blinked rapidly and sat up straight, eyes stinging from the bright sunlight streaming in through the windows. "I was barely asleep," I said. But even to my own ears, my voice sounded groggy.

"Kid, you've been out for almost two hours," Mike said.

I rubbed my eyes and looked around blearily. "Where are we?"

"Where do you think?" Mike turned in the driver's seat, eyes red with exhaustion but smiling nonetheless. "We made it. Welcome to Colorado Springs."

*****

It was just after six in the morning.

From the heat of the sun on my back, I knew we were facing west. Ahead of us, a line of vehicles—mostly military by the look of them, but a few civilian ones as well—rose toward a heavily guarded checkpoint at the intersection of highways 24 and 94.

In the distance, the sawblade peaks of the Rocky Mountains soared over hazy rooftops, the city squat and puny by comparison. Smoke from hundreds of fires plumed toward the sky, forming an oblong cloud that stretched flat and gray under a southerly wind. The smell of burning wood stung my nose, along with the scent of diesel fumes and my own unwashed body.

Looking left and right, I saw heavy equipment and construction workers crawling like ants across the landscape, busily erecting a fence with steel I-beam posts and pre-formed slabs of concrete. I had seen a fence like it before and stared, puzzled, until memory pierced the fog of sleep.

"It's a sound barrier," I said.

Sophia turned her head, the swollen eye surrounded by an angry purple bruise. "What's that?"

I pointed. "That fence they're building. It's just like the barriers you see along interstates and bypasses near residential neighborhoods. They work like baffles, supposed to reduce road noise."

Sophia peered out the window. "Looks like they're building it to keep the infected out."

"That would be my guess too."

We made slow progress toward the checkpoint, rolling a few feet at a time as guards in Army ACUs either waved vehicles through the gate or directed them to park in the open stretches of field lining the highway. As we drew closer, I saw there was a chain-link fence topped with razor wire stretching north to south that curved along the outskirts of town. Across the field to my right, the peaked roofs of suburban homes poked their heads over a low brick wall. To my left, signs welcomed visitors and service members to Peterson Air Force Base.

From the south, the rapid thrum of spinning rotors grew steadily louder until a Blackhawk passed lazily over the checkpoint, a minigun manned on the starboard side. Moments later, an Apache gunship armed with two canisters of Hydra 70 rockets and a chain-gun drifted by, the long barrel of the gun swiveling in tandem with the pilot's line of sight. My heart caught in my chest as the cannon seemed to point right at me for a moment, then moved on.

"Security looks pretty tight," Mike said, squinting through the windshield. "Guess that's a good thing."

I watched the helicopters float away and said nothing.

An hour later, we reached the checkpoint. A harried-looking sergeant waved us forward to a painted red line and signaled for us to stop. He approached the window, rifle slung across his chest, sweat pouring down from under his helmet. "What are you doing out of uniform?" he demanded.

Mike blinked. "Excuse me?"

The sergeant narrowed his eyes. "You're not military." A statement, not a question.

"Not for about ten years now," Mike replied. "If you're wondering where we got the Humvee, I have papers for it."

The guard looked the Humvee over, noticing its modifications. "Civilian owned?"

"That's right."

His eyes drifted up to the turret, and for a moment, I was worried what he would think of the M-249 mounted there. But when I looked up, the gun was gone. I almost asked Mike where it was, but stopped myself when I remembered Mike pulling over by the side of the road the night before. It was not hard to put two and two together.

"Do you have any weapons?" the sergeant asked. I caught a glimpse of his nametag: Dillon, it read.

"Three carbines, three pistols, a hunting rifle, and a few boxes of ammo."

"Anything else? Bombs, grenades, rocket launchers, nuclear warheads?"

Mike chuckled. "No, nothing like that."

Sergeant Dillon's comment had not been a mere passing jest. I had heard of cops using the same tactic, making a joke to see

434

how a person reacted. If they laughed, it usually meant the person in question was nothing to worry about. If they didn't, it meant they were nervous, which was always a bad thing during a traffic stop.

"This your first time in Colorado Springs?" Sergeant Dillon asked.

"Yes it is."

"We're going to have to search your vehicle."

"Not a problem," Mike said. "You do it here, or should I pull over somewhere?"

"Follow that young lady over there," said Dillon. "She'll direct you where to go."

A private, who could not have been a day over twenty but had the eyes of a much older woman, waved us off the road and pointed to another uniformed soldier standing in a field. He motioned us closer, then had us turn left along a line of cars parked outside the fence. We drove to the end of the line where another soldier pointed us to our parking spot. The troop made a cutting motion across his throat. Mike killed the engine.

"Wait here," the soldier said. "Stay in your vehicle until one of us tells you to get out."

We all acknowledged politely and made ourselves comfortable.

The air warmed as the sun rose, forcing us to open the windows to stay cool. While we waited, teams of soldiers worked their way through the lines of parked cars, trucks, and SUVs, each receiving a thorough search.

ATVs towing plastic carts followed each team, the carts filled with dirty bandages, bloody strips of cloth, used diapers, and a variety of other unappetizing things. It occurred to me after several carts trundled by that the contents all had something in common—bodily fluids. The guards were looking for anything that might transmit blood-borne pathogens. I also noticed the guards all wore rubber gloves and cotton masks, and made it a point not to touch their faces.

Several times, soldiers found people with illegal drugs in their possession. Rather than make arrests, they simply confiscated the drugs and warned the offenders if the police caught them holding in the city proper they would be arrested and prosecuted. I got the distinct impression it was more of an annoyance than anything else. The troops had bigger problems to deal with.

Behind us, an argument broke out between two soldiers and a middle-aged woman. The shouting was close enough I could make out what they said.

"I will *not* take this bandage off," the old woman yelled, red-faced with indignation. "And you have no right to ask me to."

"Ma'am, we have every right," a soldier told her patiently. "This town is under martial law. We have to check everyone who shows up for signs of infection. All we need to do is examine the wound. That's all."

"I said no, and that's final. Wait … what are you doing? Get your hands off me!"

The woman tried to fight, but it was no use. Her cries became panicked as two brawny young troops wrestled her to the ground and cut the bandage from her forearm. One of the troops, the one in charge I was guessing, shot the other a meaningful look.

"Ma'am, this is a bite wound," he said, looking calmly down at the still struggling woman. "What happened? How did you get this?"

As quickly as the fight started, it ended. The woman went limp and began sobbing, begging the soldiers not to kill her. She offered no resistance as they cuffed her with zip ties and radioed for one of the transports. A short time later, a Colorado Department of Corrections truck pulled up and the soldiers loaded her inside.

"What's going to happen to her?" Sophia asked as the truck pulled away.

I said, "What do you think?"

She was quiet for a few seconds. "That's horrible."

"What are they supposed to do?" Mike asked from the front seat. "If she's infected, she's a danger to everyone. They can't just let her wander around until she turns."

"I know that," Sophia snapped. "But still, it's an awful way to go."

No one spoke again until a team of soldiers surrounded our Humvee and ordered us to step out. We complied, following a woman in civilian clothes carrying a medical kit, and stood waiting while they rooted through our belongings.

The woman with the medic's kit looked us over, checking our skin for bites. She noticed Sophia's black eye, frowned at Mike and me, and asked if she could speak to Sophia alone.

"It's not what you're thinking," Sophia said irritably. "This is my father, and this is my boyfriend. Neither of them have ever raised a hand to me."

"Then what happened to your face?" the medic asked.

"We stopped to siphon some gas last night. A guy came out of nowhere and hit me, tried to drag me away. These two stopped him."

The medic gave us both a skeptical glance. "And where is this individual now, the one who attacked you?"

"Dead," Mike said flatly.

The medic stared. "Dead?"

"Didn't I just say that?"

"So you killed him?"

Mike's expression turned to granite. "He hit my daughter and tried to kidnap her. Of course I fucking killed him."

The medic looked like she wanted to say more, then let out a weary sigh. "Fine. Good enough for me." She turned and began walking away.

"That's it?" I said before I could stop myself. Mike shot me a daggered glare as Sophia's elbow dug into my side.

The medic stopped and turned, eyes narrow, hands out at her sides. "What the hell do you want, an investigation? Listen, we hear a hundred stories like yours every day. If we looked into every one of them, we'd never have time for anything else. Just don't go shooting anyone in town without a reason, and you won't have any trouble."

"We'll keep that in mind, ma'am," Mike said, eyeing me pointedly. I looked down and kept my mouth shut.

"See that you do."

A minute or two later, the soldiers motioned Mike over and asked him about the Humvee and our guns. He showed them the paperwork from BWT, then handed over all three of our IDs.

"It checks out," one of the soldiers said, a young lieutenant with the word Hammett on his nametag. "Paperwork's not in any of their names, but it's definitely a civilian vehicle. Which puts it squarely in the category of not my problem." He handed Mike the stack of papers and our IDs.

"What about their weapons, sir?" a sergeant asked.

"Civvie guns," Lieutenant Hammett replied, then turned to address us. "You can keep them, but put the safeties on before you go through the gate and make sure they stay that way." To his team, he said, "Let's go. We're done here."

One of the sergeants wrote something on a piece of paper with an official-looking seal on it and handed it to Mike. "Put that on the dashboard in plain sight," he said, "and don't lose it. If you do, you'll have to come back through here and do all this shit again. What you do now is take that road there and follow the signs to the north side of town. Show this pass to the guard at the gate."

Mike took the slip of paper and looked at it. "Then what?"

"Then you go in."

"What about after that?"

"That's up to you," the soldier spoke over his shoulder as he turned to follow his lieutenant. "My suggestion? Get a job."

FORTY-SEVEN

Over two years have passed since I left the Springs, and I know for a fact it has changed dramatically since the early days. If you go there now, the eighty-plus mile protective wall is complete, the population has increased to over two hundred thousand, volunteer militias keep the Denver hordes mostly at bay, and civilian police have taken over day-to-day peacekeeping duties. The president and her staff still spend most of their time in Cheyenne Mountain, but the majority of other political types now reside in the city proper. There are even working electrical and water utilities, albeit limited. Not a bad place to live by today's standards.

But the day we arrived, things were much different. The wall covered the entirety of the north side of town, but only curved a few miles to the east and west. Military vehicles patrolled in the distance, the crack of faraway gunfire and artillery echoing over the plain. I looked northward through Mike's binoculars and saw soldiers in Humvees, Bradleys, APCs, and tanks engaging thousands of infected, helicopters swooping in occasionally to drop crates I could only assume contained ammunition. The undead seemed to be getting the worst of it.

We drove toward the gate under constant scrutiny from guards in wooden towers who scanned the road diligently with binoculars. Only once did we see someone pull over to the side of the road, and they were quickly surrounded by soldiers on ATVs and motorcycles.

"What's that about?" Sophia wondered aloud as we passed.

"Looks like they don't want folks stopping," Mike said.

"Why not?"

"It's a hole in their security. People might try to smuggle in something, or someone, the Army doesn't want getting in. I'll bet you this place is on lockdown at night."

We continued to the gate, which consisted of several rows of barbed wire, sandbags walls, and heavy concrete traffic barriers. The approach was arranged so that vehicles had to move in a serpentine pattern to reach the gate, ostensibly to keep anyone from trying to crash their way through.

Twelve feet of concrete and steel rose up behind the defenses with guard towers positioned at regular intervals, each tower boasting a machine gun and a sharpshooter. Between the towers, soldiers patrolled with grenade launchers mounted under their rifles, many of them also carrying LAW rockets.

A narrow gap allowed traffic to flow into town, and about a hundred yards down from us, another gate with a similarly tiny gap allowed traffic out. The intake side was much busier.

Attached to the wall itself were heavy doors on rollers welded from thick steel plates, each with a soldier standing by ready to close them. At both stations, I saw forklifts parked next to concrete traffic barriers, operators in the seats, ready to block the openings. I later learned the guards conducted random drills where they had thirty seconds to move the barriers into place, retreat inside the wall, and close the gates. I am sure the people waiting impatiently in traffic really appreciated that.

Lucky for us, they did not choose to run a drill upon our arrival. The line was much shorter here than at the highway junction, and there were no pedestrians, which meant the guards could focus on vehicle traffic rather than checking hundreds of refugees for contraband.

Ahead of us was a guard shack at the midway point of the perimeter defenses, and behind that, two Bradleys sat with their chain-guns aimed at right angles to each other. I imagined those guns spitting tungsten at the speed of sound, ripping through sheet metal and flesh like tissue paper, and felt sick to my stomach.

We wound through the defenses until it was our turn to stop at the guard shack, where a tall, brawny, well-armed private in full combat attire stopped us and coldly ordered Mike to hand over our entry pass. He did, then waited while the young man looked it over. "Thank you, sir," the private said, handing the slip back. "Please proceed." He turned away and waved at the car behind us.

Mike drove us the rest of the way through the perimeter, keeping his speed in check and examining the defenses. "I can't imagine how much manpower it takes to patrol this wall," he said. "If they plan on building this thing around the whole city, they're going to need more people."

As we cleared the wall and drove into the town proper, traffic ahead of us began picking up speed and turning off onto other roads. Sophia said, "Where to now?"

I pointed at a sign ahead of us that read: NEW ARRIVALS PROCEED SOUTH ON HWY 21 TO PETERSON AIR FORCE BASE. "Does that answer your question?"

She stared at the sign and did not reply.

I turned to Mike. "So what did you do with our grenades and machine guns?"

"Remember when we stopped last night, when I told you to get some sleep?"

"Yes."

"There's an electrical substation off the side of the road right where we stopped. I wrapped all the gear in trash bags and buried it a hundred yards away, due west. I'll show you on a map soon as we get the chance."

A flock of birds took flight at our passing, little black shapes turning and wheeling through the air, graceful and effortless, so many of them they blackened the sky. I craned my head to watch and said, "That was smart thinking. The guards probably would have confiscated that stuff at the gate."

"Yep," Mike replied. He stared at the birds as well. "And I doubt they would have stopped with the military gear."

"You think they would have taken it all?"

"Likely so."

"But that's stealing."

When Mike turned to look at me, there was a gentle contempt in his eyes. "Look around, Caleb."

I opened my mouth to ask him what he meant, thought a moment, and closed it. I am a lot of things, but I like to think I am not stupid. Mike nodded, satisfied he had gotten his point across, and focused on the road.

*****

We learned a lot in the next few hours.

The first indication of the city's condition was the people we passed on the streets: threadbare clothes, parents clutching children with dirty faces, hands close to weapons, haunted eyes with thousand-yard stares, hostile gazes peering around corners and from alleyways—people did not greet one another, did not even acknowledge each other, and gave everyone they passed a wide berth.

Then there were the buildings themselves. I could have counted the number of unbroken windows I saw on one hand and had fingers left over. Anything resembling a business of any sort had been broken into and thoroughly looted. Most of the houses we passed weren't in much better shape, occupied or otherwise, and those were the parts of town not ravaged by fire. There were entire blocks burned to the ground, ruins of blackened brick walls and incinerated roof struts jutting toward the sky, piles of refuse left to molder in the open. In some places, there were craters that could only have been caused by bombs or artillery.

I looked at Mike and said, "What the hell happened here?"

"I don't know, but whatever it was, it was bad."

We continued following the signs until we reached another gate at the AFB, showed our pass again, and proceeded to the parking lot of a large, empty storage building. There were about a hundred other cars already there, a few more streaming in behind us. A wooden sign at the entrance read: NEW ARRIVAL ORIENTATION: 1130, 1400, 1600.

Mike glanced at his watch. "11:15. Looks like we picked a good time."

We locked up the Humvee and walked toward the storage building. It was beige in color, four stories tall, and made of prefabricated metal. By its domed roof, I figured it must have been a hangar once upon a time. A polite airman greeted us at the door and directed us toward several dozen rows of metal chairs arranged in front of a low stage.

As tends to happen in uncomfortable social situations, the people who arrived before us had scattered throughout the room, putting no fewer than two chairs between groups. The front three rows were empty, and there were at least twice as many seats as people. Mike walked ahead of me and picked three unoccupied chairs a few rows forward of the middle. We drew looks from a number of people on the way in, Sophia especially, but no one tried to talk to us. It was strange to be around that many human beings in complete silence.

At precisely 11:30, a door behind the stage opened and a gray-haired Air Force officer took brisk strides up to the stage. A sergeant followed him out a moment later and began checking the sound equipment. He flipped several switches and fiddled with a few plugs before giving the old man a thumbs-up. "Ready to go, sir."

The aging officer tapped the microphone eliciting a puffing sound from the speakers. He cleared his throat and said, "Good morning."

No one said anything. The officer looked around to make sure he had everyone's attention before continuing. "My name is Lieutenant Colonel John Sherman. Welcome to Colorado Springs."

Another pause. More silence. He cleared his throat again. "I don't want to keep you all in suspense, so I'll get straight to the point. As you may have noticed on the way in, the city around us is in severe disrepair. I can only imagine what you all must have gone through getting here, and I understand if you're a bit underwhelmed at the state of things."

He got a few nodding heads. It was at this point I noticed the dark circles under his eyes, the tired stoop to his shoulders, the slight tremor in his hands, and I wondered how much of that gray hair had occurred during the last few months.

"Before you judge the place too harshly," the colonel went on, "you need to understand that things were much worse up until a couple of weeks ago. You see, despite the best efforts of this city's law enforcement agencies and emergency response services, as well as intervention on the part of the Armed Forces, the infection found its way into Colorado Springs."

He stopped again to let his statement sink in. A low murmur of alarm rippled through the scattered audience. "Now let me assure you," the colonel held up a hand, "at this point, we have the problem firmly under control. We removed the last of the infected four days ago. But as I'm sure you have noticed, the battle to take the city back from the infected was a bad one. Nearly two-thirds of the population died in the fighting, and much of the city was rendered uninhabitable. That's the bad news."

He waited, letting anticipation build. "The good news," he said, "is we are better prepared now to deal with any further incursions from the un- ... from the infected. You no doubt saw the wall on the way in, as well as the large number of troops providing security. There are, at this time, more than fifty-thousand troops stationed in the city, as well as armored cavalry and air support. We have infantry, artillery, and a host of support troops, vehicles, and equipment. We have enough fuel to last us several months, and access to vast strategic reserves. This includes ammunition, medical supplies, food, clean water, and the materials to build new shelters for you and any other refugees who may arrive."

There was a collective sigh of relief. I felt tension release from my shoulders and let out a breath I did not realize I was holding. Sophia and I smiled at each other and reached out to hold hands.

"Now before we go into all that," Sherman went on, "there are some things you need to know about life here in the Springs. You'll find out most of this for yourselves in due course, but I want to give you a heads-up so you know what to expect."

He spoke for another hour, stopping occasionally to answer questions, but the gist of his speech was as follows:

The first thing all of us would be doing upon leaving orientation was driving to The Citadel Mall, part of which had been repurposed into the Colorado Springs Federal Refugee Intake Center, where we would present our entry passes and apply for housing assignments. After that, those who wished to do so could apply for a job with the city, speak to an Army recruiter, or submit an application for a business license. Skilled tradespeople such as carpenters, masons, welders, mechanics, medical professionals, electricians, and plumbers were in high demand, as were engineers, doctors, scientists of all stripes, and anyone with military or law enforcement experience.

The colonel warned us that water and sewer services as well as electrical utilities were extremely limited. The city's residential areas were divided into small districts, each one assigned a manager who oversaw health and safety duties such as distributing fresh water and ensuring proper waste disposal. We would be briefed on our responsibilities in this regard upon arrival at our housing districts, and we would all be required to do our part to keep our area livable. Additionally, if we had any questions regarding the location of medical facilities, law enforcement, fire, or other services, we were to direct them to our district manager.

Toward the end of the speech, Sherman explained that while weapons were allowed in the city proper, we were expected to conduct ourselves responsibly. Any violence perpetrated for reasons other than self-defense and defense of others would be punished to the full extent of the law. Additionally, he warned us if any infected found their way into the city, or if there was an outbreak, we should report to the nearest military personnel as soon as possible. We were not to engage the infected unless we had no other choice. Any person killed on suspicion of being infected would be tested by medical personnel, and if the victim was not infected, whoever killed them would be charged with murder.

Thinking it over, I understood why the military did not want civilians killing walkers. If they allowed it without restriction, anyone involved in a dispute could simply shoot their antagonist in the head and claim they were infected. Not the kind of thing that contributes to a peaceful society.

Last, he explained the rules and regulations all refugees were expected to follow, which boiled down to treating each other with respect, avoiding violence, not robbing, raping, or defrauding one another, and staying the hell out of the military's way. All things I intended to do anyway.

Finished, he bid us good luck and retreated through the same door he had entered.

"Maybe it's not as bad as we thought," Sophia said, the light of hope in her eyes.

"Don't say that," Mike intoned. "You'll jinx us. Bad luck is the last thing we need."

I have never been superstitious, but in light of everything that happened after, I cannot help but wonder if Mike's fear of bad luck had been well placed.

FORTY-EIGHT

A month later, on my way home from work, I stopped at the mouth of my street and stared blankly ahead and felt a black depression sink past the weariness in my bones.

The refugee camp had been a neighborhood, once. There had been houses, and cars, and families, and people who had not known what it was like to live without electricity or running water. People who cooked indoors, and greeted each other in the morning, and held block parties, and smiled at the sounds of children laughing in the streets. People who had never had to chop wood for cooking fires, or mark the days on their calendars when the waste truck would come around to collect stinking buckets of filth, or remember that only gray water and piss went into the latrines.

They could take a bath whenever they wanted, not just wipe themselves down with a damp cloth. They did not have to stockpile clean water because the municipal supply only allowed two gallons per person, per day. They did not have to stand at the head of their streets every morning with empty jugs and wait with the other grim, silent, stinking people for the water truck to come around. They did not have to buy their food from a government commissary, or go to sleep at night to the sounds of gunfire, artillery, and moans, or live with the constant fear that the hordes sweeping down from the north would someday overwhelm the soldiers holding the line.

Life had been better then, when the houses still stood.

448

But the houses were gone now, burned down during the fighting, most of their former occupants dead, the remains bulldozed aside to make room for the refugee camp. Only the foundations remained, flat gray squares like tombstones marking the graves of a more hopeful time.

I did not see much hope as I stood there, gazing down the rows of multi-colored shipping containers. I saw smoke, and dirty people in ragged clothes, and children with gaunt, wary faces, and outhouses made of scavenged plywood and corrugated tin. I saw mud where there had once been green lawns, squat metal boxes where there had once been Tudors and colonials, and empty driveways that would probably never see a car again. I saw thousands of dirty footprints overlapping one another on the pavement, some from shoes, some from bare feet.

I clutched the cold handle of my empty lunchbox and thought about the bland meal of flatbread, canned vegetables, and beans that waited for me in the rectangular blue box less than a hundred yards away. My stomach wanted building materials, but I was not sure if I could work up the energy for an activity as vigorous as chewing.

I knew if I didn't, I probably would not have the strength to get up and go to work the next day. If I did not go to work, I wouldn't earn the little paper markers I took to the commissary once a week to purchase food. If I did not buy the food, I would not have the strength to work for another slip of paper and another trip to the commissary so I could endure another day of brutally hard work and poor rest and bad food and another slip of paper and another shopping trip and more work and more eating and more wondering what the hell it was all for.

Sophia. Do it for Sophia.

I put one foot in front of the other and trudged ahead.

*****

Where the shipping containers came from, I had no idea.

Like most of the materials and supplies that came into town they arrived with military convoys under heavy guard, the containers full of food, medical supplies, ammunition, building materials, and myriad other things. Once unloaded, they went to the camps where teams of workers installed modifications so people could live in them.

The box I called home boasted a metal ladder welded to one side, which led to the roof and a heavy steel hatch. The hatch had a rubber seal on the bottom that overlapped the edges of the hole to prevent flooding. A sturdy steel hinge connected it to the roof, and it could be locked from either inside or outside by use of a chain and padlock.

The two doors at the front of the container had steel brackets welded to them which, when secured with a heavy iron bar, prevented entry from ground level. The bar itself was also welded to the wall by a length of chain—ostensibly to keep us from losing it—the idea being if the infected attacked the camp, we could lock the front doors and climb in through the hatch, thus preventing the undead from reaching us. At least until we ran out of water. Then we were screwed.

Inside, at the back of the container, was a metal box with a grate on the bottom that functioned as a fireplace. Metal tubing ran upward through the roof, a little cone of sheet metal on top to keep the rain out and a stretch of wire mesh around the whole works to keep birds from nesting there.

Mike had found some freestanding metal shelves in the back of an abandoned restaurant, which we put up near the fireplace. We kept our food there, as well as the precious jugs that held our most valuable possession—clean water.

Our belongings occupied wooden boxes next to a pile of firewood. We slept on bedrolls. Our cleaning supplies consisted of one broom, no dustpan. Our only furniture was the folding lawn chairs we had brought with us. Sophia rigged a clothesline for the days when it was our turn to wash our clothes at the only working laundry facility in the city.

I was seriously considering trading my Beretta for a new pair of boots.

This was my life.

I had only been living this way for a month, but it felt like an eternity. I knew I had lived better once, with a family, a home, and a future. But when I remembered those days, it was like the memories happened to someone else. Someone dead.

So I walked down the street, eyes down, sweating in the heat, ignoring the bleak people shuffling around me, and turned into the empty driveway. The container sat atop a concrete slab that used to be someone's home. A real home, not the dingy, rusty excuse for an abode in which I now dwelled. The front doors were open, which was not unusual, but what *was* unusual was the man sitting across from Mike. He held a cup of water in his hand and squatted on a three-legged camping stool.

I stopped and stared, watching the man as he kept his voice low and punctuated his speech with open hand gestures. His hair was shaved down to a quarter-inch of stubble, as was his beard. Considering how expensive razors had become, seeing any man clean-shaven was enough to make people stare. He was dressed in work clothes that may have had color once, but sweat, dirt, and not enough cleaning had turned them dull brown. His boots were muddy, his hands were the color of pecan shells, and his face could have been carved out of wood. He noticed me standing there and turned his head. That was when I saw his eyes.

A person can do a lot to change their appearance, but the eyes always stay the same. For the first time in weeks, I smiled.

"Tyrel."

He grinned and stood up. "It's good to see you, kid."

I walked past his outstretched hand and pulled him into a hug. He laughed and patted me on the back. "All right, all right, knock it off."

I released him and slapped him on the shoulder. "Where have you been? Where's Lola and Lance?"

451

His smile faded. "Why don't you sit down, huh? We'll talk."

I grabbed a chair, unfolded it, and sat down. Mike poured a small amount of water into a metal cup and handed it to me. "Ty was just telling me the convoy got here four days after we left."

"Run into any trouble on the way?" I asked.

Ty looked down and sighed, his expression troubled. After a pause, he said, "No. The rest of the trip was pretty uneventful."

I almost said, *Well that's good*, but then a gear turned over in my head and the thoughts of my father, Blake, and Lauren that I had kept tightly under wraps all this time finally broke free. My feet went numb. A weight pressed against my chest as if to smother me. Someone could have poured ice down my back and I would not have noticed. I placed the cup on the ground in front of me so my shaking hand would not spill the precious water.

I said, "Is that right?"

"Yeah."

My ears rang. The same ringing I had heard when I found Lauren's cold body. The ringing I heard after the firefight that claimed Dad and Blake. The ringing that stayed in my ears for days after Mike and Sophia pulled enough shrapnel out of me to cover a dinner plate.

"Mike, did you tell him?"

The big man nodded. "Yeah. I told him."

The shaking spread from my hands to my arms and onward to the rest of me. I could hear each individual heartbeat, the pressure building to a crescendo behind my eyes. I felt like a ship tied loosely to a dock that finally slipped its moorings and began drifting inexorably out to sea.

I looked at Tyrel. "So if we'd just stayed with the convoy …"

He spread his hands and said nothing.

I started laughing. I don't know why. It grew louder and louder until I fell out of my chair and lay on the ground rolling back and forth, holding my sides, tears pouring down the edges of my face. Mike stood up and closed the front doors.

Tyrel got his hands under me and tried to sit me down, but I shoved him away and walked over to a little square mirror mounted to the wall. I put my hands on either side of the glass and looked at the man staring back. He had a blond beard, hair flopping down in greasy strings over bloodshot eyes, grin like a skull, livid red scars marring the left side of his face, and I hated every inch of him.

I raised a fist and smashed the mirror once, twice, three times, and then strong hands hauled me to the ground and held me there until I screamed and thrashed myself to stillness. Someone dragged my boots off, laid me on something soft, and put a blanket over me. I stared at the roof of the container, voices speaking close to me but at a great distance, like an echo across an ocean. Some part of me told me I should respond, but I could not work up the willpower.

Later, when the darkness came, it was overwhelming, and complete, and I welcomed it and let it take me under and begged it to never let me wake up.

*****

Morning.

It was Sunday, my day off. I pushed my blankets aside, sat up, and looked around. Sophia was asleep beside me.

Mike had charged his windup survival lantern and sat in front of his pack, weapons and equipment laid out before him in neat rows, hands busy in the hazy white light. I got up, grabbed a chair, and took a seat across from him.

"Sorry about yesterday," I said.

"How's your hand?"

Puzzled, I looked down. There was a swath of gauze wrapped around my knuckles like a boxer's fist wraps. I flexed my fingers a few times, wincing at the pain. "How bad is it?"

"You bruised your knuckles pretty good, and there were a few cuts. Nothing that needed stitches, though. Sophia cleaned the wounds and wrapped your hands."

I looked at her. "I'll have to thank her when she wakes up."

Mike grunted. We sat in silence for a while, the big Marine packing his rucksack and me watching him, until I asked, "You're leaving, aren't you?"

He stopped and put his hands in his lap. "Yes."

"Oregon?"

A nod. "I hate to leave you kids, but ..."

"You need to find your wife."

Another nod.

"It's okay, Mike."

He looked up at me. "Is it? I mean, after what happened yesterday ... are you sure you're gonna be all right?"

"I think it's out of my system now. Besides, now that Tyrel knows where we live, I figure he'll look in on us from time to time."

He looked relieved. "I was thinking the same thing."

"So when are you heading out?"

"There's a caravan leaving tomorrow morning. Salvage merchants. I signed on as a guard. They're headed north to Wyoming, then west across Idaho."

"Isn't that the same path as the Oregon Trail?"

"Close to it, yeah."

I heard a rustling to my right and turned to see Sophia sitting up in her bedroll, hair tousled, face puffy with sleep. "What time is it?" she asked.

I glanced at my watch. "Just after eight."

Her eyes scanned the two of us in the gloom, then settled on Mike's belongings arranged on the floor. A few still seconds passed before she stood up, stepped around us, and opened the front doors. I winced at the invasion of harsh yellow light.

She said, "I'll make breakfast."

FORTY-EIGHT

Later that morning, Tyrel met us at our place. He walked with us to the caravan district, formerly known as the Colorado Springs Country Club.

Gone were the expensive manicured grass, sand traps, and putting greens. All trod under by boots, hooves, and off-road tires. Where golfers had once whiled away afternoons and weekends whacking away at little white balls, traders and merchants now camped surrounded by trailers, horses, jeeps, Toyota Land Cruisers, 4x4 pickups, wagons, RVs, and even a few Humvees.

One of the Humvees belonged to Mike, parked along with several other vehicles and a collection of pilfered U-Haul trailers. He had agreed to take his payment in the form of diesel, and would follow the caravan as far as I-5. There, he would turn north to begin his search.

We stopped outside the caravan's picketed area and waited while Mike went to talk to the trail boss. The camp was abuzz with activity, rugged-looking men and women rolling up sleeping bags, striking tents, cleaning cookware, packing things away, and a few teenagers fueling up the vehicles. A couple of minutes passed before Mike came back.

"Bossman says they'll be ready to go in ten. I better get my gear squared away."

Sophia wiped her face and put her arms around her father's neck. "You take care of yourself, old man. Don't do anything stupid."

"Don't you worry, darlin'," he said, hugging her back. "With any luck, me and your momma will be home by Christmas."

I am sure Sophia knew it was wishful thinking, but she smiled anyway. "Just be careful. I love you, daddy."

Mike's big arms bunched as he squeezed tighter, eyes closed, mouth curved in a beatific smile. The wrinkles and stress lines on his face relaxed, and I got the feeling that for a bright, happy moment he let the pain fall away, held his little girl, and was a man at peace.

It's what I like to tell myself, anyway.

Finally, he said, "I love you too, sweetheart."

Tyrel and I shook his hand, said our goodbyes, and used silence and steady eye contact to say all the things men hate saying to each other but feel nonetheless. This unique language has a way of baffling women, but men understand it perfectly.

"Y'all look after each other, now," Mike said, stepping toward the camp, his voice harsh. "I'll be back as soon as I can."

We waved as he walked away.

*****

"So how are Lola and Lance doing?" I asked Tyrel.

We were walking westward on Acacia Drive, back toward our little corner of the refugee camp. People walked by us on the other side of the road, some going to work, others headed to the market or the commissary. There were no shouted greetings, no festive atmosphere, and precious few conversations occurring, ours among them. A woman in her early twenties brushed past me, eyes fixed straight ahead, feet wrapped in strips of thick red cloth bound with shoestrings.

Tyrel rubbed a hand along is jaw. "Things, uh … things didn't work out between us."

I looked at him. "Sorry to hear that, Ty."

"It happens."

"She doing okay?"

"Yeah. After we parted ways, she started shacking up with some Air Force type. A captain, I think. Lives on base with him now."

I thought about asking him what drove the two of them apart, but decided against it. Instead, I asked, "What about you? Where are you living?"

"Over in Tenth District, just south of the university."

"Oh. So you're not far from us then."

"Nope. Sorry it took so long to track you down. You know how long it takes the intake center to update the roster."

I nodded. The 'roster' he referred to was a central directory of refugees who made it to Colorado Springs maintained by the people working at the refugee intake center. They also kept a list of the missing and deceased (M&D), all gleaned from information taken from refugees upon arrival. Any day of the week, the former department store housing the roster was awash with worried relatives anxiously searching for the names of loved ones on the refugee list, and if not there, the M&D list. It was a place of joy and tears. But mostly tears.

I remembered reporting my father, Lauren, and Blake deceased when I arrived, speaking in a dead monotone, vaguely hoping Tyrel or one of the others would see it. "Did you find us on the roster?"

"Yeah. You, Mike, and Sophia anyway. When I didn't see the others' names, I checked the M&D."

I swallowed and cleared my throat. "So you knew before you came to see us."

"Yeah. I took it pretty hard at first."

"At first?"

His skin color darkened. "Sorry, Caleb. I waited a while. Two weeks, in fact. Had to get my head straight. Didn't want to show up a blubbering mess."

I wondered if I should be angry, but then decided I did not have the energy for it. "It's okay, Ty. I understand."

We said nothing else about it.

The street parted ahead of us. An Army Humvee came rolling slowly through with a gray-haired, stony-faced general sitting in the passenger's seat. There was a livid scar above his right eye, and as the Humvee passed, I could not help but feel like I had seen the general somewhere before. Dismissing the thought, I said to Tyrel, "So what are you doing for work these days?"

He watched the Humvee drive away. "I was working with a salvage crew for a while, but they disbanded. General partners had a falling out, split up the business and went their separate ways. So I filled out a resume at the intake center and took a job with one of the volunteer militias. That was about three weeks ago. What about you?"

I grimaced. "Civil Construction Corps."

"Shit. You're not working on the wall, are you?"

I nodded.

He shook his head angrily. "Caleb, that ain't no kind of a job for you, and you know it."

"What else am I supposed to do? Join the Army?"

"It's not a bad option."

I glared at him from the corner of my eye. "No, Ty."

459

"Well, what about the militias? You're perfect for that sort of work."

"Like hell," Sophia said, speaking up for the first time since we had left the caravan district. She slipped her hand into mine. "I'd rather have him dead-tired than just plain dead."

Tyrel gave her a hard look. "Did you ever bother to ask *him* what he wants to do?"

She ground her teeth, but said nothing. I let out a long sigh. "Okay, kids, no fighting. Today's been hard enough without you two going at each other."

By Ty's face, I surmised he remembered Sophia saying goodbye to her father less than twenty minutes ago. He had the good grace to look chagrined. "Sorry, Sophia."

"Don't be. I'm in a mood today."

"And you have every right to be."

We walked a little farther in silence, then out of curiosity I asked, "Ty, what happened to your hair?"

He chuckled. "Head lice. You believe that shit? My first week in the field with the salvage crew, and I come down with fucking head lice. Had to shave it bald and douse my head and all my clothes with powder. Had to buy a new bedroll too."

I couldn't help it, I laughed. "Talk about kicking a man while he's down."

Tyrel smiled.

"Heard anything from Lance lately?"

"Yeah. He's back to being a cop again, works on the south side of town. Haven't seen him in a couple of weeks, but last I heard he's doing all right."

"Glad to hear it."

A short time later, we arrived at Ty's street. "I'm up this way," he said, pointing down a row of shipping containers virtually indistinguishable from the street I lived on.

I said, "Don't be a stranger, Ty. You know where we live, now. You're welcome any time."

"Duly noted. Y'all take care."

I put my arm around Sophia, feeling the tension in her shoulders, and held her tight against me on the walk home. When we arrived, I opened the padlock, unwrapped the chain from the front doors, and swung them wide. The two of us sat on the floor, drank tepid water, and stared at nothing. The place seemed too quiet, too empty, and even more squalid than usual. It is not until someone is gone that you realize what an influence they have on your life, and your home. There is an energy to each human being, to each life, and it affects the people around them whether they realize it or not.

It was mid-afternoon before Sophia spoke again. "He'll be all right, won't he?"

I glanced up at the soft chestnut eyes, full lips, and the delicate fall of hair. My heart constricted at how beautiful she was, even dirty and dressed in clothes little better than rags. The fact I could not provide a better life for her made me want to break something. "He's a smart man, Sophia. He knows how to take care of himself."

"Just tell me he's going to be okay. Please."

"He's going to be okay."

She pushed her hair out of her face, and said, "You know what? Don't. It sounds like you're bullshitting me."

I did not know what to say to that, so as usual, I didn't say anything.

FORTY-NINE

The warmth of summer faded into the chill of autumn.

We passed the days as best we could, living and working and hoping that someday, somehow, things would get better. It was the same hope people had before the Outbreak when they climbed in their cars, or public transportation, and whisked off to jobs they hated in order to pull in a paycheck and keep the fire burning for another day. There are no promises, and some days it seems pointless, but what else are you supposed to do?

In the mornings, I would go to the end of the street and get our water, carry it back, and then we would have breakfast. Afterward, I left for my job building the wall, while Sophia left for hers on a cleanup crew. We had to make sure the place was locked up tight before leaving, as theft was rampant in the refugee districts. Leaving a door or a hatch unlocked was as good as throwing your possessions into the street.

Sophia's job, from the way she described it, mostly consisted of tearing down buildings with heavy equipment and then loading the refuse into large trucks. My job involved walking an hour to the job site, engaging in backbreaking labor for ten hours, punctuated by a thirty minute lunch break, and then enduring the long slog home.

Some days it rained, and the job site shut down. The rest was nice, but the government docked our pay.

In the evenings, either Sophia or I would heat some water in a metal pot and wash one another with damp rags. I found it amazing how little water it takes to wash when you have no soap, and consequently, do not have to worry about rinsing.

Sometimes, when we had the strength, we made love. Most nights, however, we ate a bland meal, read books from the public library (delivered to the refugee districts by volunteers), and slept. The next day, we got up and did it all again.

The fighting north of town never stopped, but it did slacken in pace. There were trenches, miles and miles of trenches, dug along the northern perimeter a few miles from the city. The Army crouched behind these trenches at night, and during the day, they made forays in armored vehicles. They located hordes, lured them to various killing grounds, and waited while fortified bulldozers, bucket loaders, and other heavy construction equipment squashed the infected into paste. With the undead immobilized, the troops dug enormous mass graves and pushed the bodies in by the thousands. Something close to half of them were still kicking and biting when they went over the edge, but the troops buried them anyway. It was easier and less dangerous than finishing them off, and used less ammo.

Tyrel came around to visit once a week, usually on Saturday evenings when we did not have to worry about getting up for work the next day. He always brought dinner from one of the few restaurants operating near the refugee districts, a luxury Sophia and I could not afford. But for Tyrel, being in a volunteer militia meant he had ample opportunity to scavenge the countryside and loot the bodies of infected he killed. A lucrative, if dangerous, line of business.

When Sophia wasn't around, which was not often, he tried to talk me into leaving the Construction Corps and joining up with his militia. Due to his advanced training and combat savvy, he had been promoted to a senior leadership position within the ranks.

"I'm in charge of hiring," he told me often. "All I have to do is say the word. You wouldn't have to break your back anymore, and you'd make a hell of a lot more trade." (The word 'trade' had come to replace 'money' in casual conversation.)

My usual reply was, "Yeah, and Sophia would cut my balls off."

"No, she wouldn't. She'd just be pissed, and you wouldn't get laid until you started bringing home food worth eating and some nice furniture. Then she'd get with the program."

I resolved not to test Tyrel's theory, and I didn't. At least not until a Tuesday evening in late September when I found Sophia crying and everything changed.

I came home from work the same as any other day. My feet hurt, my back was a wreck, and I had the beginnings of a headache riding over the horizon. I wanted nothing more than to let Sophia wipe the dust from my skin, eat something warm, and sleep for ten hours. But when I turned up the driveway and saw the doors open, I went on my guard.

"Sophia? You home?"

Her voice, tearful. "Yes. I'm here."

I walked up the drive and stepped through the door. Sophia had started a fire and sat next to it, face in her hands, wiping tears from her cheeks. I hurried over and knelt beside her. "Hey, what's wrong?"

She didn't respond, just kept sobbing. I pulled her hands down and tilted her face up. "Sophia, look at me. What happened? Did someone hurt you?"

When I walked in the door, my mind immediately went to Lauren and the attacks she had endured. If someone had hurt my Sophia, they were dead. There would be no remorse, no hesitation, no mercy, just a movement at the corner of their eye and then nothing. My teeth ground together as I tried to remember where I had put my fighting dagger.

"No, Caleb. No one hurt me."

I blinked a few times, let out a breath, and released Sophia's wrists. My fingers left red marks. "Okay. Can you to tell me what's going on?"

"Sit down, Caleb."

I was getting very tired of people telling me to sit down, but I did it anyway. "Sophia, you're freaking me out."

She took my hands and held them. "Caleb …"

"What?"

She looked up, and the fire caught in her eyes, and they gleamed like stars in the winter sky. My breath caught in my throat and I wondered if I would ever breathe again. I leaned closer, brushed my lips against her cheek, and pulled her close to me.

"Sophia, whatever it is, you can tell me. I'm not going anywhere. Not today, not tomorrow, not ever. I'm right here."

She put her face in the hollow of my shoulder, took a long, shaky breath and said, "Caleb, I'm pregnant."

*****

The next day, I traded my Beretta for a new pair of boots.

After months of mixing concrete, shoveling dirt, and exposure to wind and sun, my old clothes were just about done for. I picked out five new outfits of sturdy outdoor wear and paid for them with four boxes of nine-millimeter cartridges. Everything else I needed was waiting for me at home.

Done with shopping, I left the market, walked to the offices of the Civil Construction Corps at The Citadel Mall, and turned in my resignation. The clerk looked hard at me across the table.

"You sure you want to do this?" she said. "It's getting harder to find jobs with the city these days."

"I have something else lined up."

465

She shrugged and stuck my form in a box. "Well, best of luck then."

Next was a visit to Tyrel. I wasn't sure if he would be home, but luck was with me. He opened the door, took a moment to read my face, and knew exactly what I was there for. "About damn time," he said. "Come in and have a seat. I'll put on some tea."

The tea tasted better than anything I had ever drank. Tyrel didn't have any sugar, just the artificial stuff, but considering my options over the last few months had consisted of either cold water or hot water, it was heaven in an enameled cup.

Tyrel sat down across from me, a satisfied smirk on his face. His chairs were proper chairs, complete with foam and cloth and springs. I leaned back and tried to remember the last time I had sat in a comfortable chair. Sophia and I often joked to one another that we lived like the Japanese, most of our time spent sitting on the floor.

"So," Tyrel said, "what changed your mind?"

I sipped my tea, let it rest on my tongue a few seconds, and swallowed it gratefully. "Sophia is pregnant."

His cup stopped halfway to his mouth. "Seriously?"

I nodded.

He put his cup down on a little wooden table. The presence of such luxury made me feel like a peasant in a lord's manor. "I don't know what to say, Caleb. Congratulations?"

"I'll take it."

My old friend smiled. "Congratulations, then. You're gonna be a daddy."

I ignored the flip-flopping in my stomach at that statement and smiled back. "I'll do my best."

"Does Sophia know?"

"Well, being that she's the one who told me …"

"Hardy-har, smart ass. You know what I mean."

I sighed and held my tea in my lap. "No. I haven't told her."

"She's going to be pissed."

"Yes. Yes she will. But she'll get over it."

"Well, I think this calls for more than just a cup of tea." Tyrel stood up, lit an oil lamp, closed and locked the front doors, and started digging through a box behind his chair. A few seconds later, he returned with two small glasses and a bottle of Buffalo Trace. While he poured, I gulped down the rest of the tea, not daring to waste it.

I accepted a glass of amber liquid and gave it a little swirl in the golden lamplight. Tyrel raised his in the air and said, "To fatherhood, prosperity, and better days ahead."

"Cheers." We clinked glasses and drank.

FIFTY

Sophia did not take the news well at all.

In fact, I'm reasonably certain she was just next door to a rage blackout. And that was *before* she began throwing random missiles at my head. Lucky for me her aim was off, although there were a few near misses.

I explained myself in a reasonable manner. I told her we could barely feed ourselves, much less a baby. She countered that other people had kids and seemed to be getting by just fine. I told her that was true, but those kids were all toddlers or older. I had not seen a baby since arriving at the Springs. She told me she had, perfectly healthy ones.

I asked her what she planned to do after the baby was born. It was not as if there was a plethora of childcare options to choose from. She glared angrily and said we would figure something out.

Sensing an opening, I said, "Sophia, you're going to have to stay home with the baby. Without the food your job brings in, we'll go hungry."

"No," she replied firmly. "We won't. We'll just have to make due with less."

My temper began heating up. "Listen. I'm not going to raise a child half-assed. I have valuable skills. I'm going to use them.

I'm going to provide for this family by doing what I do best, and that's it. End of discussion."

Wrong. Thing. To say.

I slept on the roof that night and spent the rest of the week at Tyrel's place.

Early Monday morning, when I knew Sophia would be home, I went back to get my things. There was a very shrill voice in my head worried that Sophia had thrown my belongings in the street, but when I turned into the driveway, there were no signs of anything having been discarded. The smell of flatbread and boiled potatoes wafted through the half-closed doors. I knocked and poked my head in.

"Sophia?"

She adjusted the light on a wind-up lantern. "Right here."

I stepped inside. My possessions were exactly where I had left them. I wanted to talk, but I didn't have time for another argument, so I said, "I just came to get my things."

She gestured to an old wooden crate containing my weapons and tactical gear. "It's right there."

The M-4 was still clean and well oiled. The spare ammo in the P-mags had not left the pouches on my MOLLE vest. I detached the holster for my Beretta, regretting I'd had to trade it away. The knife, multi-tool, crowbar, hatchet, and all my other equipment were in their places. I suited up, put on my hat, hung a pair of goggles from my vest, and wound a scarf around my neck.

Sophia kept her attention on the tiny pot and small frying pan on top of the fireplace. I turned to leave, hesitated, and said, "Should I find another place to stay?"

She did not look up. "Do you want to?"

"No."

"Then come home."

A breeze could have knocked me over. "I don't know how long I'll be gone. Probably overnight at least."

"I'll be here."

Not wanting to push my luck, I walked toward the door. As I pushed it open, I heard Sophia say, "Caleb?"

I turned to look at her.

"Be careful."

"Always."

I left.

*****

It was not until I exited the north gate that I realized I had not been outside the wall since arriving in Colorado Springs.

It was cathartic, in a way. I had been so constrained by my limited, miserable existence, scraping and breaking my back and struggling to get by from one day to the next, I had nearly forgotten there was a world out there. A dangerous world, granted. A world not possessed of the relative safety and security of life behind the wall, but one with open spaces, salvage free for the taking, and no one to stop you and challenge you if you were out past curfew. The only curfew in the wastelands was nightfall, enforced by the dead, and if you were quick and smart and handy with your weapons, you could challenge that authority without reprisal. For a while, anyway.

On the way out, we passed a column of men marching in identical orange coveralls, their ankles tethered together with leg irons. Two policemen on horseback armed with shotguns watched them trudge wearily away from the gate. I nudged Tyrel on the arm and said, "That what I think it is?"

He glanced toward the prisoners. "Yep. Going out to work on the west side of the wall. Poor bastards."

"Takes something serious to be sentenced to hard labor, right?"

He shrugged. "Serious is a relative term. I know a fella got ten months for stealing a sack of potatoes. Just depends on what mood the judge is in, I guess. Show up on the wrong day, and you might find yourself looking at a few years. Best to stay on the right side of the law around here."

I watched one of the men stumble and fall, then roll onto his back and stare at the sky. His chest heaved, eyes closed, mouth hanging open like a tired dog. One of the cops gestured with his shotgun and shouted something I could not hear. The man behind the fallen prisoner reached down and hauled him to his feet. The cop snarled something else, nudged the prisoner in the back with the barrel of his gun, and the column started moving again.

"Seems like a shitty thing to do to a man, regardless of his offense."

"Maybe," Tyrel said, "But you don't see too many repeat offenders."

I lingered a moment more, watching the prisoners march westward. Everyone in town knew what happened to people who ran afoul of the law. There was too much work to be done and too little food to allow convicts to languish in prison cells, so they were forced to work on the wall from sunup to sundown, fed once a day, and given barely enough water to stay alive. No one liked it, but it made for a hell of a criminal deterrent.

Before that moment, I had harbored a vague, self-centered disregard for the suffering of the convicted. But there is a difference between hearing about a thing and seeing it for yourself. The suffering of others loses its abstract distance when you add a human face. It bothered me.

"Come on," Tyrel said over his shoulder. "Long walk ahead of us."

Our destination was a neighborhood on the outskirts of Monument, about twenty miles to the north. One of the squad leaders in Tyrel's platoon had scouted it a few weeks ago, and after deliberation, Tyrel and the platoon commander, a man named LaGrange, decided it was worth investigating.

LaGrange was short, stocky, had a face like a frying pan, and a nose that had been broken no less than five times. And that's being conservative. He ran first squad, Tyrel second, while third and fourth were headed up by a couple of hard-cases named Henning and Caraway.

Rather than march single file, we spread out at squad strength over an area roughly half a mile long. One of the earliest lessons Tyrel and LaGrange had learned was it was better to disperse their lines than congregate in one place. Keeping the squads separated meant if a squad found themselves surrounded by infected, they could radio for help from one of the others. The best way to deal with hordes was to give them multiple targets to pursue, break them up, and once divided, run far away. But to do that, we had to maintain a minimum distance.

Additionally, spreading out distributes searching eyes farther afield, increasing our chances of finding salvage worth carrying back to town. We were not above saving the trip to Monument for another day if we found easier pickings.

Tyrel's squad—me included—pulled 'rabbit' duty, which meant scouting ahead and setting the pace for the rest of the platoon. We covered eighteen miles before sundown, making me grateful for all the long, hard days spent working on the wall. It might have been hellish work, but it kept me in shape.

We stopped at the now-abandoned Air Force Academy and made camp on the rooftop of a service building. The building itself had been stripped long ago by the Army, along with the rest of the academy. First squad joined us a short time later, while third and fourth made camp on the other side of the campus.

The sun slid low behind the peaks of the Rampart Range behind me, painting the sky in blues and reds. The colors were richer and darker than I had ever seen them, and there was a sharp chill in the air. I thought about reports I'd heard of a nuclear exchange in the Middle East and wondered what color the sky was in Pakistan.

"Gonna be a cold winter," one of Tyrel's men said. Billings was his name. Late thirties, average height, lean build, brown hair and eyes, a well-tended beard. By the way he ran his fingers over it, I knew he was proud of that beard.

"You from around here?" I asked.

"Pretty close, yeah. Grew up down in Pueblo."

"No shit?" Tyrel said. "I lived there 'til I was eleven."

Billings grunted. "Small world."

Being the new guy, it was my job to prepare the evening meal. I boiled rice and dried venison over a small propane stove and served it on cold pre-made flatbread. The men in the squad were quiet as they ate, worn out by the day's long hike. When we finished, I wiped the plastic dishes and aluminum cookware with a wad of boiled cloth and put them away. The other men bedded down for the night, but since I had the first watch, I took a few minutes to fix my suppressor to my rifle and attach my night vision scope. The man on watch with me, a short Mexican named Rojas, eyed my gear jealously.

"You could get a good price for that silencer," he said.

"Suppressor. And it's not for sale."

He smiled like he knew something I didn't. "Sooner or later, kid, everything's for sale."

The first two hours passed mostly in silence. Rojas held a crossbow in one hand and rested the other on a quiver of bolts hanging from his belt. A few times, he began singing softly to himself in Spanish, then stopped and shook his head ruefully, calling himself a few not-so-nice words in his native language.

He seemed like a man trying to break a bad habit. Or not a *bad* habit, necessarily, but definitely a dangerous and unwise one.

We walked the perimeter of the rooftop, scanned the distance for infected, and conducted radio checks with the other squads across campus every half hour. Near the halfway point of our watch, a knot of four walkers heard our boots crunching on the tiny rocks covering the roof and wandered close. To Rojas, I said, "What should we do about those things?"

He looked at me from the corner of his eye. "What do you mean? We draw 'em close and kill 'em."

"Won't they start making noise if we do that?"

"You never seen a walker up close at night, have you?"

I shook my head.

"See man, at night they don't make noise until they get right on you. Makes it easy to take 'em out if you can spot 'em in time. Here, watch this."

He tapped his foot a few times, sending muted thumps out into the night. I watched through my scope as the walker's heads snapped up and they increased their shuffling pace in our direction. Just as Rojas predicted, they made no sound.

"Son of a bitch."

"Told you, man," Rojas said. "When they're close enough, take 'em out."

I let the undead approach to within fifty yards. By that point, I had lain down on the edge of the roof so I could fire from the prone position. The undead were a mixed group: one white guy in his twenties, a black girl no older than twelve or thirteen, an Asian woman who must have been in her nineties when she died, and a middle-aged Hispanic man with a great bushy moustache. Their wounds showed up black against the grainy green night-vision image. I let my breath ease out and squeezed the trigger. The little girl fell. The rest of the ghouls marched on heedlessly.

I kept the reticle on the girl for a few seconds, thinking about how long it had been since I'd shot a walker, and after everything I had been through, how little the killing affected me. It was as if the part of me that used to feel sorry for them, some kind of emotional sympathy gland, had atrophied during the long months in Colorado Springs.

"Nice shot," Rojas said.

In response, I cracked off three more rounds in less than four seconds, each one finding its mark.

"Damn, kid." Rojas' teeth flashed white in silver of the moon. "You're not a rookie, you're a killer."

I stood up and brushed myself off. "Something like that."

FIFTY-ONE

We marched parallel to I-25 until we reached a road that ran under a highway overpass. It was early morning. The yellow circle of the sun was hazy and muted behind a gauze of powdery gray clouds. A bracing chill in the air kept us cool as we set a hard pace.

Rojas marched ahead of me as we turned off the highway and followed an access road up the slope of the Rampart Range. The altitude increased sharply for half a mile, then the lead squad turned right onto another road marked by a green sign gilded with ornate black ironwork, reading Aspen Applause Way. Another sign with tarnished brass letters announced we were entering Aspen Acres Luxury Homes.

LaGrange called the platoon to a halt and radioed for his squad leaders to meet him at the head of the column. While they talked, the rest of us sat down and drank some water. During the march, I had noticed a long, cylindrical bundle wrapped in brown canvas lashed to Rojas' pack. Curious, I asked him about it.

"That's my pride and joy," he said, grinning. "You'll see it when it's time to kill some walkers."

I raised an eyebrow, but let the matter sit. A few minutes later, Tyrel came back over.

"Okay, here's the plan," he said. "Third and fourth squads will head north and set up overwatch on the far side of the development. First squad will head east and hang back in reserve. LaGrange will monitor comms and direct operations as usual. Our job is to approach from the west and find out what we're up against. Henning saw infected in the neighborhood when he reconned the place, but he didn't get an accurate count. So keep your eyes open and stay on your toes. Rojas, I want you and Hicks on point. Show the new guy how we do business."

"Works for me," said Rojas.

"Caleb," Tyrel continued, pointing at me. "Follow the man's lead. He's a pain in the ass sometimes, but he knows his job."

I acknowledged with a single nod. Tyrel said, "Any questions?"

Silence.

"All right then. Let's do this."

The other squads broke off in their various directions. By Tyrel's reckoning, we were directly south of the development, which meant we would have to turn left off the highway and travel upward through dense woodland to reach our destination. As we walked, Rojas told me climbing the side of the mountain was a good thing despite the effort involved.

"The walkers don't like climbing," he said. "They'll do it if they're chasing something, but otherwise, they follow the path of least resistance."

"You seem to know a lot about the infected," I replied.

"In this line of work, you have to. Keep your eyes open. You might learn something."

We passed signs informing us we were entering the Aspen Acres Nature Trail. Tyrel turned onto a dirt path that took us east down a set of long switchbacks, then up again over a ridge.

As we topped the ridge, I stopped and stared at the valley below. Nestled in the bottom were clusters of what my father would have called McMansions, big ostentatious monstrosities of homes lacking in character or charm, completely incongruous with their natural surroundings. They sat on half-acre lots with paved U-shaped driveways boasting four-car garages and swimming pools choked with leaves, algae, and debris. Infected wandered the streets, tiny as ants in the distance. Rojas stopped beside me and raised a hand to shield his eyes from the sun.

"Looks good," he said. "Nothing burned down. Should be plenty of salvage."

"Quite a few infected down there."

"You wanna earn, you gotta take some risks."

A quarter of a mile from the tall metal gate surrounding the development, Tyrel held up a hand for the squad to stop, signaled for silence, then pointed at me. I took the hint and moved up until I was close enough to kneel beside him.

"Fix your suppressor," he said in a low voice.

"What's wrong?"

He pointed ahead through the woods. I followed the line of his finger and saw the problem.

"Shit. Infected."

He withdrew his suppressor from his vest and tightened it down over the muzzle of his M-4. I did the same. "Had to happen sooner or later," Tyrel said. "Let's try to do this quietly."

Tyrel ordered the rest of the squad to fan out in diamond formation and watch all approaches. While they obeyed, the two of us worked our way down the hill, watching the infected the whole way. The ghouls moved in our direction, heads turning and twitching like deranged birds. I guessed they heard us, but had not pinpointed our position yet. This meant we would have to work quickly; if the infected got a fix on us, they would start squawking and bring every walking corpse in the valley down on our heads. When we were about fifty yards from the closest of them, Tyrel signaled a halt.

Leveling his rifle, he held up two fingers and made a go-forth motion over his shoulder. Taking that as a cue, I peered through my scope, sighted in on what had once been a fifty-something man with a bushy white beard, and squeezed the trigger. To my right, the muted crack of Ty's M-4 broke the silence.

Wasting no time, I picked another target and fired. Before it fell, I caught sight of its eyes through the magnified view of my scope. Its milky gaze was fixed firmly in my direction, looking right at me. Or so it seemed, anyway.

Half a magazine later, the infected were all down. A couple of them started making odd chuffing, croaking noises, but we shot them before they could work up a head of steam. Tyrel glanced back at me, gave a thumbs-up, and signaled to fall back with the rest of the squad. On the way, he radioed third and fourth squads for a status. They were in position, so Tyrel asked them to fire a few rounds to get the attention of the infected in the streets below. Seconds later, three sharp cracks echoed from the north.

"That ought to buy us some time," said Tyrel. Back with the rest of the squad, he said, "Rojas, I want you to take Hicks and move straight down the hillside." He pointed due east from where we sat, directly toward the development. "Radio when you're close enough to make an assessment."

Rojas stood up. "Will do. Come on, new guy. Class is in session."

I got to my feet and began following him down the hill. Behind me, Tyrel said, "Head on a swivel, Caleb. Got it?"

"Got it."

*****

Rojas put his back to the wrought-iron fence and laced his fingers at groin level. "Up you go."

I stepped into his hands, gripped the cold black fence poles, and levered myself up until I could put a boot on his shoulder.

Once there, I stepped up, grabbed the support crossbar ten inches below the spear-shaped tips of the fence, and pushed until I was lying halfway over. The thick material of my MOLLE vest kept me from being skewered.

Throwing my legs over, I planted my boots against the fence and slid down. "Okay," I said to Rojas. "Your turn."

Leaning against the poles, I reached my hands through and laced my fingers as Rojas had done for me. He climbed up nimbly, pushed off my shoulder, and threw himself over the spikes.

I said, "Looks like you've done this before."

He looked smug. "Once or twice."

As I turned toward the street leading into the neighborhood, Rojas hissed for me to stop. He dropped his pack, unlashed the bundled cylinder, and carefully rolled it out onto the dead brown grass. When he stood up, he was holding a three-and-a-half foot double-edged sword.

"Hicks, meet Penelope."

I stared. The sword looked nothing like what I had seen in books and museums. Its blade was wide and thick like a Roman Gladius, but much longer. I could have called the leather-wrapped hilt two-handed, except it was far more than that—four-handed, maybe. The crossguard was a simple rounded rectangle of aluminum, just wide enough to keep the wielder's hands from slipping up onto the sharpened edge. The blade's color was a dark reddish-black, like something forged from the leaf springs of a large truck. I had a feeling that was probably not far from the truth.

"Jesus Christ," I said.

A grin. "Ain't she a beauty?"

"I don't know which is more worrisome. The fact that you named it, or that you think it's a girl."

He laughed. "She's named after the first girl that ever gave me a blow job and swallowed. We take good care of each other."

"What a beautiful story."

"Don't be jealous."

"The hell did you find that thing?"

"Had it custom made. Cost a small fortune, but it was worth it."

I thought about the rubber-tipped spears my father had trained me to wield, and asked, "Who made it for you?"

"I'll introduce you to him when we get back to town. For right now, we got work to do. Let's go, new guy."

We crossed a hundred yards or so of grassy downslope leading to pavement. The asphalt was dark black, free of potholes, the center and shoulder lines vivid yellow and white as though recently painted, the kind of road a wealthy HOA had once paid good money to maintain. I wondered how long it would be before it cracked and crumbled and gave way to trees.

The neighborhood was laid out in a cloverleaf pattern consisting of four concentric circles, each circle lined with houses that grew larger as they wound toward the center. The one we approached was on the southwest portion of the development where the flat valley began sloping up into the mountains. Ahead of us, we saw infected milling about in the yards between houses, slowed down by dry grass nearly knee deep. As we drew closer, the ground began to level out until it was flat and even and the outer row of houses loomed ahead. We stopped at the intersection and dropped to one knee.

"Okay professor," I said, scanning ahead with my scope. "What's the plan?"

Rojas pointed to a three-story beast directly across from us. "There. We'll go in through the back door and clear the place. See if there's a way onto the roof."

"Think the infected have seen us yet?"

"Doubt it. They can't see for shit, but they'll hear us soon enough. Mark my words."

We covered the distance at a jog, slowing down as we drew closer to stifle our footsteps. I stopped twice to fire at infected I knew would detect us long before we reached the house. When we reached the back yard, a trio of walkers rounded the corner, snapped their faces toward us, and opened their mouths. I would have shot them, but Rojas took off in their direction, sword raised. I cursed and followed.

The first one began to croak as Rojas swept his massive blade from right to left, sending the top half of the walker's head spinning into the grass. Without missing a step, he pivoted on one foot and brought his sword down in an overhead chop at the second ghoul, splitting its skull down the middle. Now that he was out of the way, I had a clear shot at the third infected. I took it.

Rojas jerked his weapon free and looked over his shoulder, irritated. I nodded toward the house as if to say, *let's go*. Rojas mouthed, *Asshole*, then joined me by the door. I reached out and turned it slowly. Locked. Rojas rolled his eyes. "Fuck's sake."

I held up a finger, took my lock picks from a vest pocket, and went to work. Ten seconds later, the lock turned and I opened the door.

"After you," I whispered.

Rojas nodded appreciatively and went inside.

FIFTY-TWO

We swept the house. Empty.

Kitchen: untouched. Lots of canned food and non-perishables. Bedrooms: mostly guest rooms, one master with a full wardrobe that had not been disturbed in a while. Garage: a Cadillac Escalade with a full tank, a live battery, and keys hanging from a hook on the kitchen wall. Standard stuff in the living room.

The bathrooms turned out to be a gold mine, lots of toilet paper. Rojas said we could split the TP fifty/fifty. I asked if LaGrange would have a problem with that, being that I was only a probationary militiaman and only entitled to a half-share of the profits. Rojas said it was the reward we got for going out on point. First pick of the spoils, even for newbies. The only rule was whatever we took had to fit in a trash bag.

It is amazing how much one can fit in a trash bag when properly motivated.

There was a locked door in the kitchen. I picked and opened it to find a set of wooden stairs leading down into darkness. Rojas clicked the button on an LED tactical light and shined it around. The walls were concrete, a single bulb dangled from the ceiling, and a heavy-looking steel door stared at us forbiddingly from the bottom.

"What do you think?" Rojas asked.

"We've come this far. Might as well."

He put his sword down on the kitchen counter and drew a Sig Sauer pistol from his belt. "Let's go."

As expected, the door at the bottom was locked. I borrowed Rojas' flashlight, stared at the lock a few seconds, and selected a couple of tools from my set of picks. It took me a while to line up the tumblers—this lock was much more robust than the one at the entrance—but finally, they clicked into place. I turned the knob.

"Take it easy, now," Rojas said. "Sometimes we find booby traps."

"Really?"

"Yeah, man. Lost a guy about a month ago. We were raiding this trailer park, right, and the guy, Simmons was his name, opens a door with a shotgun wired to it. Blew a hole in his guts the size of a grapefruit. Bled out before we could get help."

I let the knob ease back. "Jesus."

"No shit. So take your time, homes. No rush."

Using the flashlight, I checked the door the way my father had trained me to, first going around the edges and looking for anything out of the ordinary like wires or electrical contacts. Just because the power was out did not mean there couldn't be some kind of backup.

The seal looked normal, so I began easing the door open a centimeter at a time, hands sensitive to any resistance. Feeling none, I opened it wide enough to poke my head inside.

"Holy hell."

"What?" Rojas asked.

Grinning, I opened the door the rest of the way. "Take a look."

He grabbed the light and shined it into the room. "Holy hell."

Beyond the threshold was what I could only describe as a survival bunker. The steel door I opened was one of two doors, the second looking like something taken from a bank vault. It was open, telling me whoever built this place was not expecting trouble when they left, however long ago that was. Which meant they had not been here since the Outbreak, or any time reasonably close to it.

The room was roughly thirty feet square, had shelves lining the walls all the way to the ceiling, a table, two chairs, a recliner, and a single bed. The furniture was arranged in the center, the shelves laden with boxes, crates, bottles, buckets, and every container in between. White stenciling on a green metal cabinet at the far end of the room read: ARMORY. Rojas and I looked at each other.

He said, "I'll radio LaGrange."

*****

"So here's how we do it," Rojas said. "You probably figured out by now the walkers hunt by sound. Right?"

I nodded.

"Right. So the way we get them out of here is to make them chase something, wait until they're out of sight, and then we clean up. Simple enough?"

"In theory, yeah. I'm guessing the practical application is more complicated."

He smiled in approval. "Yes, it is."

I shifted, resettling my rifle in an effort to get comfortable, boots digging against asphalt shingles for purchase. After radioing LaGrange we had broken the lock from the gun cabinet, taken what we wanted, and stashed the weapons, ammo, and pilfered toilet paper in the attic. That done, we used Rojas' sword to bust out a window and climb onto the roof.

"How are you going to draw them away?" I asked.

"Remember that Escalade in the garage?"

I turned my head and looked him in the eye. "You better make sure you have plenty of running room."

"Don't worry, new guy. This ain't my first rodeo. Now here's your part, man. If I run into any trouble I can't get out of, I'll fire three shots in the air. You hear that, you come running. Try to draw off the infected. That's your job. Got it?"

"If I hear three shots, come running. Got it."

"If you have trouble finding me, fire a shot in the air. Just one. I'll fire again to lead you in. All right?"

"One shot. Understood."

He climbed back through the broken window. A minute or two passed before I heard the Escalade roar to life and the sound of the garage door going up.

"Here we go," I muttered.

The key now was to stay calm and be patient. I put my cheek against the M-4's stock, dominant eye two inches from the scope's rear aperture, finger off the trigger. The lines of the reticle were comfortably familiar as I scanned right to left, doing a mental count of the infected. There were dozens lurching toward us, drawn by the noise we had made climbing onto the roof and the sound of the Escalade idling in the garage.

"Go time, Rojas."

The undead coalesced into a loose congregation, the least injured leading the way. Those with disabled legs moved slower, some crawling on hands and knees and some slithering on their bellies. Rojas backed the Escalade out to the street, cut the wheel, and began rolling slowly toward the undead. The sound of the engine was enough to keep their attention, but just for good measure, he laid on the horn. I wasn't expecting it and jumped, nearly dropping my rifle.

The air filled with moans and screeches as the living dead emerged from yards, open doors, broken windows, and the hills surrounding the development. A few of them got close enough to slap at the Escalade's windows, not a danger really, but worrisome enough Rojas increased his speed. When he reached the end of the street he cut through two front yards to get around the biggest knot of infected, then headed toward the street connecting the four quadrants of the neighborhood.

Twenty minutes later, he had made a full circuit of the development, visiting every street and laying on the horn to draw out the dead. I had to admire his work; he managed to congregate the infected in the central plaza without cutting off his own escape route. And he was patient about it, not hurrying or rushing, but taking his time and doing the job properly.

When it was clear he'd drawn out as many infected as were capable of following him, he angled toward the main road leading out of the neighborhood. I lost sight of him after that. My guess was he would take them back to the same stretch of highway our platoon had followed to get here, then double back. My intuition turned out to be correct when, an hour later, the Escalade sped back into the neighborhood. Only now, instead of just Rojas on board, it was filled with the men of first squad. I climbed down and went out the front door to the yard.

There was a crawler with one leg torn in half and the other totally missing dragging itself toward me across the street. It was an older white man, dressed only in a shredded black terry-cloth robe. The torn remnants of his thighs fluttered behind him, writhing like snakes in the long grass. He arched up and reached a clawed hand in my direction, gnashing his teeth and snarling. The milky eyes were red-rimmed, the face twisted with hunger and blind, unreasoning rage. I held out my carbine one-handed, put the barrel a few inches from his forehead, and pulled the trigger. A red mist erupted across his back. He gave a shudder and collapsed.

"Rest easy."

Behind me, I heard LaGrange say, "If only they were all so easy to kill."

I turned and began walking toward him. His men were already out of the Cadillac, two of them with ratchets and heavy-duty bolt cutters hard at work removing the seats.

"Nice work, new guy."

I shrugged. "I didn't do much. Just killed a few walkers. Rojas did the hard work."

"He told me you're pretty handy with a lock pick."

"Product of a misspent youth."

He grinned. "Tyrel said you'd be useful. Looks like he was right."

A croak split the air to my left. I leaned around the SUV and spotted a walker with a broken leg rounding the corner, maybe sixty yards away. Casually, I raised my rifle and cracked off a single shot. The walker dropped.

"Tyrel also said you could shoot at least as well as him. I didn't believe it. Looks like I was wrong."

"So did I pass the interview?"

The smile widened. "Consider it a probationary offer. Don't fuck up too bad for the next thirty days, and I'll sign you on as a full member."

I held out a hand. "Good enough for me."

We shook on it.

FIFTY-THREE

Tyrel was right. Sophia got over it.

Which is not to say she was happy with the situation—she was not. But when I showed up from my first salvage run with a trash bag full of toilet paper, a few guns and some ammo to sell, and a voucher for my share of the profits, her disapproval cooled.

Our new prosperity made the hardships of pregnancy, always difficult for a woman even under the best of circumstances, easier to bear. She still suffered from morning sickness, strange cravings, fatigue, tenderness and swelling in the breasts, and the burden of a next-to-clueless significant other, but at least she did so with comfortable furniture.

I did as much of the housework as she would let me and strictly forbade her from heavy lifting, but other than that, I was at a loss. The fact she was carrying my baby made me treat her like she was made out of porcelain, much to her irritation. Consequently, she spent a good deal of those months barking at me for fussing over her and insisting she did not need me following her around with a pillow and a worried face. It didn't do her any good.

Through incessant doting, I finally convinced her to quit her job on the cleanup crew and stay home. I don't think she really wanted to, she just wanted me to shut up about it.

By the seven-month mark, her belly had swollen noticeably, as had her ankles, a fact she bemoaned constantly. She also complained her joints felt loose in their sockets and the swelling in her stomach made her feel like she had to pee every ten minutes. I nodded in sympathy, made comforting noises, and fervently thanked whatever deities rule the universe that I was born male.

The concept of a baby and the very real fact I would soon be raising one finally jelled the first time I felt the baby move. It was past midnight on a Tuesday, no lamps burning, dark as the bottom of the ocean. The wind howled over the containers lining our street, vibrating the metal and making eerie keening sounds in the wintry night. A rustling like windblown sand grated against the steel walls, but I knew it was snow, not sand, torn from the high shoveled banks piled in the spaces between lots. Sophia was sleeping quietly, her breathing inaudible against the ruckus outside. I lay behind her on our new bed, the fabric of her shirt soft against my bare skin, the two of us nestled deep, deep beneath a comforter that had cost me a jar of unopened peanut butter and a roll of paper towels. Her hair smelled of floral-scented shampoo, a rare luxury item I had found on my last salvage run.

The roundness of her stomach was warm under my hand as sleep began to pull me under, the wisps of dreams dancing at the edges of consciousness. I had almost gone beneath the waves when I felt something press against my palm.

I snapped awake.

For a long space of heartbeats, I thought I had imagined it. But then I felt it again, a little bump, the impression of something sliding under skin and muscle, and then it was gone. Sophia mumbled something and stirred, but did not wake. I waited and waited, but nothing else happened. Finally, I let my head sink back onto the pillow and lay in the darkness, smiling.

Those were good months. I spent a lot of time away from home, but I did my best to make up for it when I was around. We lived better than most of our neighbors, a fact that rankled with more than a few of them, but I didn't care. They knew who I ran with, and they knew to stay out of my way.

I thought we were cruising. I thought after all the universe had thrown at me, the pain and loss and bloodshed, things had finally balanced out. The lives of my old family were gone, but there was a new life on the way. Sophia and I would be our own family soon, and who knew, maybe we would not stop at one child. Maybe we would have two, or three, or however many we wanted. I thought about coming home from work to the smell of food cooking, and the patter of children's feet running around the neighborhood, and going to sleep at night surrounded by my wife and kids, and I pulled Sophia closer to me.

My woman. My life. My world. Maybe it was God's apology for taking Dad, Lauren, and Blake away from me. Maybe He wanted to fill the void with something new and bright and good. Maybe after all the suffering He had allowed to befall me, He was trying to set things right. If that were the case, then apology accepted.

It was arrogant thinking, of course. It is easy to bask in the warm glow of the things you value in life and think you are somehow special. That the rules do not apply to you, that you have something the others don't, that you are smarter, tougher, more resilient than the rest. If you survive enough bad things, enough injuries and emotional trauma, it can make you dumb enough to think that nothing can knock you down.

We are all the heroes of our own stories. We all think we are the exception. And all too often, by the time we realize that there are no exceptions, it is too late.

God may give, and God may take away, but one thing He never does is apologize.

FIFTY-FOUR

Disasters always happen in threes.

I'm jumping ahead by stating that, but in this case, it's warranted. The universe may be vicious and fickle, and life often seems like a random confluence of uncorrelated events, but there are some patterns too obvious to ignore.

When Sophia hit the seven-month mark, a few of the women from her old job conspired to throw her a baby shower. In keeping with tradition, my presence, while not expressly forbidden, was strongly discouraged. The platoon was not scheduled to go on another salvage run for two weeks, the baby shower falling squarely in the middle of this timeframe. So I stopped by Tyrel's place a few days before and asked if he was up to a little freelance work. Being just as bored as I was, he readily agreed and suggested I see if Rojas wanted to come along.

Rojas and I had grown close during that time. We were LaGrange's go-to point men, and after months of working together, had developed a kind of non-verbal shorthand that allowed us to operate quietly, efficiently, and most importantly, profitably.

I wrote a brief note on a wooden slat, wood being far cheaper to come by than paper, and paid a courier to deliver it to Rojas' apartment. He sent it back that afternoon with a note on the back that read, succinctly, *FUCK YEAH*.

So the morning of the baby shower I woke up early, made myself a cup of instant coffee, and took a moment to admire my most recent purchase: the custom-forged spear I still carry to this day. Made from a length of hickory and a half-inch-thick piece of spring steel, it is sharp, perfectly balanced, and by that point in time, had already split the skulls of quite a few infected. It hung from a set of hooks over the fireplace, proudly displayed when not in use. I took it down, passed a stone across the blade even through it was not necessary, and slipped it into its harness.

"Where are you going," Sophia asked sleepily. She sat halfway up in bed, her blonde hair falling across her eyes.

"Up into the mountains," I replied. "Toward Woodland Park."

"That's pretty far. How are you getting there?"

"Tyrel hired a wagon to take us as far as Cascade. We'll hike the rest of the way."

"Isn't Woodland Park still overrun?"

"Last I heard, yeah."

She frowned. "Then why are you going there?"

"LaGrange knows a guy pretty high up in the Army. Feeds him info in exchange for a cut of our profits. His informant says they're sending three whole companies to Woodland Park next month to clear the place out."

"And you want to raid it before they get a chance?"

"Won't be much salvage left if we don't. I respect what the troops do, but they're like fucking locusts. Take anything not nailed down and half the shit that is."

"I thought they weren't supposed to do that."

I barked out a laugh. "They're not. Doesn't stop them."

She put her head back on the pillow and sighed. "So when will you be back?"

"Tomorrow most likely. Maybe the day after."

"I hate it when you leave. I like having you at home."

I leaned down and kissed her. "I know. But the salvage isn't going to come to me, and I'm not going back to being broke."

"Be careful out there."

"I love you, pretty lady. Enjoy the shower."

She groaned and pulled the blanket over her head.

*****

Raiding Woodland Park was something we never would have attempted during the warmer months. There were just too many infected. However, by then we had learned how the cold slowed the infected down, and if the temperature got low enough, stopped them altogether. The icy chill and deep snowdrifts of winter made the raid feasible.

It was sunny and bright that morning, a cloudless blue sky stretching from horizon to horizon, the ambient temperature at just over thirty-two Fahrenheit. Not cold enough to freeze the ghouls, but enough to slow them to a crawl.

Tall snowbanks lined U.S. 24 leading out of the Springs, shoveled aside by snowplows commandeered by the federal government. They had opened the road as far as Cascade, which the Army had cleared out and thoroughly looted months ago. Beyond that, the road was impassable except on foot.

The wagon we rode in was one of a very few transportation options available to civilians. The months since the Outbreak had seen gasoline supplies dwindle, then grow increasingly unreliable as the untreated fuel civilians once consumed expired. The military seemed to have ample quantities available, trucked in from places unknown, but troops were not allowed to use it for trade. Of course, as with most rules imposed on military personnel, the moratorium against said activity did nothing to curb its occurrence.

494

As the road stretched under the wagon's wheels, I stared at the mountains rising up on either side of us, snow-capped peaks ascending majestically, pine forests marching up the slopes in loosely-ordered rows. I thought if a man could find a flat spot near a source of water and wild game, a little space where he could grow vegetables in the summer, he could make a go of it out there. From what I had seen, the infected generally stuck to the lowlands, that being the path of least resistance. It was rare to hear of them climbing to the higher elevations except in pursuit of prey. Nothing a sturdy palisade wall around one's home couldn't fix.

When we neared the terminus of the accessible part of the highway, the driver tugged the reins to bring the wagon to a halt. Turning in his seat, he said, "End of the line."

I looked at the snow piled ahead of us, a wall of it nearly eight feet high, and knew the next part of the journey was not going to be easy. "Thanks for the ride," I said, grabbed my gear, and climbed out of the wagon. The driver grunted and said, "Be back tomorrow at noon. I'll wait one hour. If you don't make it, I'll be back the same time the next day. After that, your trade expires and I leave with or without you."

"Understood," Tyrel said.

As the clip-clop of iron-shod hooves faded into the distance, the three of us put on snowshoes and began the long walk to Woodland Park. Tyrel went out on point since he was the most experienced mountaineer among us. Rojas watched our six, leaving me monkey in the middle. A half-mile of slogging over hard-packed snow saw the mountain pass widen. We arrived at the small town of Cascade, site of the North Pole Home of Santa's Workshop, an amusement park billed as 'A Vibrant Christmas Themed Playland!'

Only there would be no children or costume clad workers in Santa's Workshop this year, no screaming voices on the rides, no smells of carnival food and hot chocolate, no magic shows, no hollow commerce. Cascade was under at least eight feet of snow, much like the highway ascending it. The towering granite walls surrounding the place ensured it would remain thusly encased until the spring thaw.

We passed the peaked roofs of houses and flat buildings and the triangular boughs of evergreens as we moved through town. The lower half of every building was invisible under a brilliant, reflective lake of white. But even with only half the town visible, the marks left by the Army's visit were still plain to see.

Here, a mortar had shattered the upper windows of a three-story office building. There, bullet holes riddled the side of a tattered house. To my left, a fire had burned a restaurant until most of the roof collapsed, while to my right, a scorched black hole big enough to drive a car through marred the side of a pre-fab metal storage building. I wondered if there were any infected trapped beneath the ice, and if so, were they still conscious? I imagined their white eyes fixed and staring, hands outstretched, mouths frozen open in a silent scream, hunger gnawing at them while they lay motionless, unable to move. I shivered, and not from the cold.

We hiked five more miles in silence, the midday sun beating down from overhead. It had been frigid in the shadow of the mountains in the early morning, but now, without shade in the thin high-altitude air, I began to regret wearing so many layers. Just as I was about to voice my concerns, Tyrel turned and suggested we slow down. The last thing we wanted in this weather was to break a sweat. He heard no argument.

The next community we passed through was Green Mountain Falls, little more than a sparse collection of structures paralleling the highway. The Army had not made it this far out, but the buildings were not in much better repair than Cascade. It struck me once again how quickly manmade things deteriorated when there was no one left to look after them. Maybe it was my imagination, but I could not shake the feeling that once the intent of human minds was absent, all the things once upheld by that intent went into an advanced, accelerated state of decay. Law and order not the least among them.

It was roughly five more miles to the outskirts of Woodland Park. My thighs burned and my breath was ragged from the effort of the climb. Walking in snowshoes was better than stomping through snow taller than my head, but it held its own difficulties. When the buildings were in visual range, Tyrel stopped, lifted a pair of binoculars, and studied what lay ahead. A few long, silent minutes passed, and then he said, "Let's move off the highway."

Rojas and I exchanged a glance, but did not argue. When we were under the shelter of pines north of the road, I asked, "What did you see, Ty?"

"Can't say for sure," he replied. "But it looks like somebody got here ahead of us."

I looked at Rojas again. His dark eyes were narrow and cloudy.

"What makes you say that?" I asked.

"Furrows in the snow, for starters. Not random like what the walkers leave, but neat, like people walking single file. I looked close at some doors on an apartment building, and the ones on the upper floors looked like they'd been forced open."

Rojas thought about it, finger tapping against the side of his jaw. "It wouldn't be the first time."

Tyrel looked at him. "First time for what?"

"Back in the early days, before the Army commissioned the militias, we used to have trouble with other groups out looking for salvage. That was why they started the whole program in the first place, to stop the fighting. Once there was a system in place that only allowed registered militias to trade in town, the fighting stopped. AORs, and all that."

By 'AOR' he meant areas of responsibility. LaGrange's militia, by merit of him being a former Army officer, had been assigned the lucrative territory north of the Springs. The lines were clearly delineated, and the other militias knew to stay within their sandbox. Woodland Park, however, was not included in that division of spoils, making it fair game. I had thought the three of us were the only idiots crazy enough to come out here looking for salvage, but it looked like I was wrong.

I said, "So what do you want to do about it?"

Muscles twitched in Tyrel's jaw as he stared toward town, eyes flitting from one side to the other. He picked up a handful of powdery snow and let it run through his gloved fingers. "You bring your ghillie suit, Caleb?"

I nodded. "I always do."

"Rojas?"

"I ain't no sniper, homes. Don't own one."

"All right. We'll figure it out. Caleb, you're with me. Rojas, I'll set you up under cover until we can put things in motion."

Rojas said, "What's the plan?"

"Recon," Tyrel replied. "See what we're up against. That'll determine how this goes down. If we're outnumbered, we'll sneak around whoever's out there. If not … I don't know. Maybe we can negotiate."

The Mexican laughed. "Out here, there's only one kind of negotiation, homes." He tapped his rifle.

I felt my lips pull away from my teeth.

FIFTY-FIVE

With Rojas ensconced and camouflaged on a mountainside overlooking town with orders to wait for us to give him clearance to proceed, Tyrel and I put on our winter-pattern ghillie suits and entered Woodland Park from the east. We left our gear behind except for weapons, ammo, radios, vests, a pair of bolt cutters, crowbar, and a couple of empty duffel bags.

Houses lined the streets west and south of us, while a school building lay to the north. It would provide the best vantage point to observe the immediate area, so we headed in that direction. I stayed low behind Tyrel, the two of us literally crawling on our bellies across the snow. We set an agonizingly slow pace, a necessity when trying to avoid detection. Tendrils of my camouflage dangled in my vision, allowing me only a narrow sliver of obscured sight. The cold seeped upward through my clothes, seeming to radiate into my very bones. My scarf kept my breath from fogging in the air, but a crust of ice had formed over my mouth.

The sun had moved far to the west by the time we reached the open space between the end of the neighborhood to our right and the school ahead. A wind picked up from the north, sending streamers of white powder scuttling across the flat valley floor. Despite the wind chill, I was glad for it; the extra concealment would work in our favor. Anyone looking in our direction would have a hard time making out our shapes.

I risked lifting my face to gauge how far ahead Tyrel was. At first, I could not see him at all, then the wind shifted and I picked out a barely discernable lump about twenty meters ahead. *Good*, I thought. That meant I was keeping pace.

We crossed the clearing and met on the eastern side of the school, sheltered from the wind by a high wall. The snow was so deep the only part of the building accessible was from the second floor up. I rose to my feet and went to stand beside Tyrel as he peeked around the corner farthest from us. I was tempted to ask him what he saw, but I knew better. Best to remain silent and wait. Finally, he turned toward me and motioned me close.

"I don't see any service ladders," he said. "But we can go in through one of these windows and use the stairs."

"Won't that be loud?"

He dug into a pocket of his vest and produced a roll of cloth tape. "Caleb, you know me better than that."

I followed him around the back of the building and waited while he applied the tape to the smallest window he could find. It was enough to cover it, but just barely. When he finished, I handed him the crowbar.

He used the hooked end to tap the window left to right, top to bottom. Gently at first, then with more force as he gauged the strength of the glass. The tape muffled the noise, but did not eliminate it. I glanced around, worried as much about attracting walkers as about alerting other living people to our presence. I was not sure which one was the bigger threat.

At last, the window collapsed. Tyrel caught it with the crowbar and dragged the glass aside. I watched his back, rifle at the low ready as he crawled through. When he was clear, I followed.

I stood up in a dusty classroom, desks lined up in straight rows, the scents of cold and dust heavy in the air. Pale light filtered in through the windows, illuminating yellow squares on the white tile floor. Floating dust motes swirled through the geometric beams, disturbed by our entrance. Tyrel pointed behind me and said, "Pull that glass back in here."

He handed me the crowbar and I did as he asked, hooking the cloth and drawing it through the opening. When I had it inside, I dropped it behind the length of cinder-block wall between windows. The tinkling and scraping of shards on concrete was shockingly loud in the frigid silence.

"Let's see what we can see," Tyrel said. He went to the door and peered out the window. I stacked up on the wall behind him, rifle at the ready. Almost a full minute passed before Tyrel held up a hand, counted down three, two, one, and then opened the door.

In the hallway outside, he broke left and I followed with my back to him, weapon up. There was very little light. The walls, floor, and ceiling all looked a uniform gray, the monotony broken by doorways and dark blue lockers. We moved to the end of the hall to a door marked: STAIRWELL. Ty tried the door and found it locked.

"Shit. Hand me the crowbar."

"Come on, Ty," I said, breaking a smile. "Remember what you taught me about not using a battle axe for a job that requires a tack hammer?"

He looked at me quizzically, then nodded when I removed my picks from my vest. "Right."

I went to work on the door and said, "Where are your picks? You're the one who taught me how to do this, after all."

"Lost them somewhere along the way. Haven't found new ones."

"Now I know what to get you for Christmas."

"Just get the door open."

A few seconds later, the lock clicked and I turned the handle. "Done."

"Nice work."

I opened door and came face to face with a gray-skinned teenage boy with pale white eyes. I had half a second to register surprise before its hands shot out and gripped my arms, mouth open in a savage snarl, a guttural hiss pouring out of its throat. I scrambled backward, cursing in terror, pushing against its chest with my rifle.

The strength of the thing was enormous. Its hands dug painfully into my arms like steel talons. The ghoul lunged and I reared back, a set of snapping teeth missing my nose by less than an inch.

"Ty, help!"

An arm snaked around the dead boy's throat and pulled it fiercely, drawing its head back, but the hands held on relentlessly. Remembering my training, I let go of my rifle, grabbed one of the boy's wrists, and levered my arms against the weak point of his grip: the thumb. It took far more effort than would have been necessary with a living person, but the hand broke loose. Not wanting it to get another grip, I pivoted on one foot, used my shoulder as a fulcrum, and broke the arm at the elbow. If it hurt the creature at all, it gave no indication. The other hand continued to hold the fabric of my jacket, ripping and straining to pull me closer to the gnashing mouth.

"Ty, let it go."

Without hesitation, he took his arm from around the ghoul's neck. It immediately surged forward, teeth bared. I gripped the hand still holding me, held out one foot, and twisted. The infected boy tripped over my leg and hit the floor, still holding on. I followed it down and put a knee on its chest.

Now I had the mechanical advantage. The ghoul's grip was strong, but not stronger than my entire body. With my free hand, I drew my knife, lined the tip up with the ghoul's eye, and plunged the blade sharply down. When I felt it hit the back of the skull, I gave the handle a twist. The ghoul shuddered, let out a groaning gurgle, and went still.

"Son of a bitch."

My breathing was ragged and fast, echoing in the still air. The ghoul's hand loosened and tumbled from my arm. I stood up and backed away, checking myself for injuries. Tyrel's hands landed on my shoulders to steady me. "Easy now," he said.

A thought hit me and I spun to look back at the stairwell. The door stood open, the interior lit by a window higher up on another floor. I saw no other infected. Stepping closer, I looked up, then down, ears straining. Nothing.

"How in the hell did that thing get in there?"

Tyrel stepped up behind me. "Must have got bit, then crawled in here and locked the door. Turned later on."

The explanation made sense. I put my back to the wall and slid down to the floor. "That was too close, Ty."

"Take a minute. Get yourself together. We still have work to do."

I nodded, heaving a deep breath. Ty stood patiently, eyes watching the dead walker. It lay on its back, my knife protruding from its face, the arm I broke lying at an awkward angle beside it. There was no sound in the hallway.

Standing up, I retrieved my knife, cleaned it on the ghoul's shirt, wiped it down with a homemade alcohol-soaked sanitizing cloth, and returned it to its sheath. The dead boy was maybe sixteen or seventeen, probably a junior in high school, not much younger than I was. There was a patch of denim missing from his jeans low on his right calf muscle, and beneath, a mouth-shaped circle of ragged, bloody flesh. I dropped the bloody cloth on its chest.

"Poor kid. Probably got bit by a crawler."

"Don't," Tyrel said. "You'll drive yourself nuts. Come on, let's get moving."

His footsteps echoed up the stairs behind me. I looked at the boy for another moment, wondering what kind of man he might have turned out to be if given the chance. But that would never happen, now. Such a waste, and so many others out there just like him.

I bid him a silent farewell and left.

*****

On the third floor, we watched in alarm as a column of a dozen men, all dressed for the weather and carrying M-4s, marched on snowshoes toward the schoolhouse.

"This is not good," I said.

Tyrel stared out the window and said nothing.

"We should radio Rojas."

He stepped away and checked his rifle. "Do it, then meet me in the hallway."

I turned on my handheld and keyed the mike. "Rojas, Hicks. How copy?"

"Loud and clear, Hicks. Over."

"You see what's going on out front? Over."

"Yep. I got my scope on them, but I think they're out of range. Over."

"Probably so. Keep your eyes on them and let us know if anyone else shows up. Over."

"Wilco. Make sure you switch to your earpiece. Over."

"Acknowledged. Hicks out."

I fished a wireless transmitter/receiver from my vest, stuck it in my ear, flipped a switch on the radio, and went outside to find Tyrel. He had taken cover behind a doorway twenty feet from the stairwell. When he saw me, he said, "Go cover the other stairwell."

I moved down the hall double-time, boots squeaking on the dusty floor, picked a doorway thirty or so feet from the stairwell

504

entrance, opened it, and took cover. Anyone coming out of the stairwell would see only the barrel of my rifle and a small fraction of my face. They, on the other hand, would have no cover once in the hallway. I did not plan to let them get that far.

My father had taught me the Fatal Funnel of Fire concept. The most dangerous thing a person can do in close quarters combat is go through a door. Doors are chokepoints, and anyone with a weapon capable of a high rate of fire and sufficient ammo can devastate large numbers of people pouring through them. Essentially the same concept the Spartans used in the battle of Thermopylae: force your enemy to concentrate their numbers at a single, defensible point, thus eliminating their numerical advantage.

The sound of boots clomping up stairs reverberated in the hallway. I keyed my radio. "Ty, you think they know we're in here?"

"I'd say it's a possibility. If they're smart, they have someone on overwatch. There's a chance they spotted us coming in the building."

Just as he finished his sentence, a voice called up to us from the stairwell on my side, "We know you're up there. Put down your weapons and come out with your hands in the air."

I turned and looked down the hallway at Ty. He shook his head and held a finger over his lips, then pointed two fingers at his eyes and turned them toward the doorway. *Stay focused.*

The voice spoke again. It was deep and rough, older sounding, resonant with the confidence of a man used to being obeyed. "This doesn't need to turn ugly, gentlemen. You're trespassing here. All we want is to escort you out of town. Don't resist, and nothing will happen to you."

Tyrel spoke up, "Trespassing? Last I checked, this is unincorporated territory. Also known as *fair game.*"

"Listen smart guy, I'm not going to argue with you. This is our town. Our salvage. You can leave on your feet, or on your back. Your choice."

505

Tyrel didn't respond. I had no confidence the man in the stairwell was telling the truth about letting us go, and I knew Ty did not either. What these men were doing, forcibly chasing off salvage hunters in unincorporated territory, was illegal. The military took this kind of thing seriously—they didn't want civilians battling it out on the outskirts of town—and after we filed a complaint, they would undoubtedly send an expedition to investigate. If the investigators found sufficient evidence to support our claims, these men would be tracked down and brought up on charges. Very serious charges.

Salvage hunters are notoriously territorial. They do not like sharing their loot with outsiders. Treading on someone else's turf is a very good way to end up with a bullet in your head. Which led me to an inevitable conclusion: these men had no intention of letting us leave this place alive. They would not have bothered coming here at all if they did. It would have been far easier to let us take what we wanted and leave. But if we made it back to the Springs and told the rest of our militia that raiding this place was feasible, they would be outnumbered and forced to cede territory. It was far more profitable for them to simply kill us and leave us for the undead.

Or so they thought, anyway.

I had been in some bad situations, but this one was looking like the worst. We were outnumbered six to one, facing a well-armed, highly motivated enemy, and we had nowhere to run. Keying my radio, I said, "Ty, did you notice they didn't search the lower floors? Just came straight up the stairs."

"Yep."

"I'm thinking we should stay away from the windows."

"I believe that would be prudent," Tyrel said. "Rojas, you have a visual on any of these assholes?"

"Negative," Rojas replied. He sounded winded. "Hang tight brother, I'm on my way."

"Be careful. They probably have a sniper somewhere."

"I served three tours in Iraq, homes. I know how to watch out for snipers."

"Great. Then hustle your ass up," Tyrel replied. "I think this is about to get ugly."

The voice from the stairwell spoke again. "I'm going to give you to the count of five to come out, then we're coming up after you."

Neither of us spoke. My heart began to beat faster as I adjusted my shooting position and focused on the doorway, finger over the trigger, muscles tightening to take in the slack.

"One."

A cold feeling started in my stomach and spread to my face and hands, a rhythmic *thud-thud-thud* hammering in my ears.

"Two."

I took a deep breath, held it, and let it out.

"Three."

A hand appeared in the doorway, tossed something through, then disappeared. I heard running steps pounding down the stairs. The thrown object was small, green, and oblong, its exterior comprised of a honeycomb of tiny interconnected squares.

"Grenade!"

The voice sounded like mine, but I did not remember telling my lungs, mouth, and vocal cords to form the words.

The world slowed down, the edges of my vision going gray and narrowing down to a small, pulsating point. The grenade rolled into that point, rotating lengthwise and skittering across the slick tile floor. I had a vague sensation of movement as I darted out the doorway, took two huge running steps, and kicked the grenade toward the door of the stairwell. I had just enough time to hit the floor and curl up in the fetal position before there was a tremendous *BANG*.

The force was incredible. I felt my body come off the ground and slide backward. A shockwave poured over me like the hand of an invisible giant, knocking the breath from my lungs. My ears rang from the impact, and I dimly wondered how much permanent hearing damage I had just endured. I put my hands over my ears hoping it would help, but it did not, at least not until another slightly less powerful blast hit me from behind.

Something flew over me at tremendous velocity, tearing a hole in my sleeve and carving a shallow furrow in my upper arm. The pain was immediate and intense, and I hissed in agony. My vision dimmed, went almost completely dark, then opened up like the beginning of an old black and white movie. I saw my rifle, and beyond, the shapes of people moving in the stairwell. I thought I heard screaming, but I couldn't be sure. The ringing in my ears was too loud. I reached for my gun, grabbed it, and pushed off the ground until I was sitting upright.

Behind me, I heard gunfire.

"Shit!"

The last place I wanted to be was alone and exposed in the hallway with no cover. I scrambled backward like a crab, fired a few blind shots through the stairwell opening, and pushed my way back through the door of the classroom.

Remember your training, my father's voice told me. *Stay in the fight.*

I got up to one knee, leaned a little way around the wall, and trained my weapon toward the stairs. The gunfire behind me continued unabated, but I ignored it. I would have to trust that Tyrel had survived the grenade thrown at him and was holding his own. If not, I was as good as dead, and the only thing left for me to do was to take as many of these sons of bitches with me as I could.

The hallway was filled with smoke, the air sharp with an acrid scent I could not identify. As I watched, a man-shaped gray thing stepped into the swirling dust, weapon blazing. His shots cut the air in front of me, making little *thwap-thwap* sounds as they passed. I adjusted my aim slightly upward and

508

fired three times. The man jerked, screamed wetly, and fell. It was in my head to make a follow up shot, but then I saw two more men emerge behind him.

I focused on the closest one and fired, finger working the trigger as fast as I could. I don't know how many times I shot him, but it was enough that he dropped to the ground. The man behind him saw my muzzle flash and aimed in my direction.

We fired at the same time.

I knew my shots would hit; the reticle of my VCOG was centered squarely on the upper portion of his chest. His weapon flashed twice, and I had a brief moment of panic as I expected to feel impact, and heat, and pain. Instead, I felt a scalding sting on the right side of my face, screamed, and fell over backward.

I put my hand to my face, blinking furiously. The eye still worked, which was a good sign. My cheek was wet with blood, but not much of it, just a trickle. I sat up and moved my head, my arm, felt around on my torso. Everything seemed to be in good working order. I had a fevered remembrance of a quote from Winston Chuchhill, one I had always found amusing: *Nothing in life is so exhilarating as to be shot at without result.*

It did not seem very funny anymore. Whatever I was feeling, it was pretty damned far from exhilaration. As I sat there, it occurred to me the hallway had gone silent. I keyed my radio and whispered, "Tyrel, you still alive over there?"

"Pretty sure I am."

A wave of relief poured over me strong enough to make my eyes sting. "Glad to hear it."

"How'd you make out on your end?"

"Shot three of them."

"Dead?"

"They look pretty dead. Can't say for sure if there are any more. You?"

"Four down, and at least one more wounded. I think I heard the rest making a run for it."

"Rojas, you got anything?"

No reply. I waited a few seconds, then keyed the mike again. "Rojas, do you-"

Gunfire interrupted me, sounding like it was coming from outside the building. I belly crawled into the hallway and peered through one of the shattered windows overlooking the courtyard out front. Two men lay face down in the snow, firing toward the southwest side of town. I followed their trajectory and saw muzzle flashes at the treeline. *Rojas.*

I leaned out the window and sighted in on the men below. I knew I was taking a huge risk, but I could not just sit there and do nothing while Rojas fought for his life. The reticle settled where I wanted it to go, half a breath fogged the air in front of my face, and I squeezed the trigger. The man lying closest to me jerked and cried out in agony. The man beside him looked startled for a second, then stood up and began running away in a serpentine pattern. I moved to adjust my aim, but something whizzed past my ear close enough to feel a tug of wind on my skin, and a thudding *whack* hit the wall behind me.

"*Fuck!*"

I spun away from the window, went flat on my back, and kicked my feet until I slid back into the classroom. From outside, there was a burst of fire, a scream, and then silence.

Static. "Rojas?" It was Tyrel.

Nothing.

More static. "Rojas, you still there?"

"Yeah, man. I'm here."

I let out a breath. Ty said, "What's the situation?"

"Both bad guys are down. Caleb got one, I got the other while he was running for cover. You two all right up there?"

"More or less."

"All right. I'm on my way."

"Copy."

"Stick to the treeline," I said. "That sniper is still out there somewhere. He just took a shot at me."

"Acknowledged. Out."

"Hey Caleb," Tyrel said over the radio.

"Yeah."

"Unless my math is wrong, that's nine accounted for. Right?"

Tyrel got four, I got four, Rojas got one. "Yep. Four plus four plus one equals nine."

"Good. That grenade blast knocked the shit out of me. My head's all loopy."

"What do you want to do?"

A moment of silence, then, "I'm thinking they split their forces evenly, six on each side. We know three on your side are dead, which leaves three more."

"I'll wait until you get here."

A minute later, Tyrel crawled to the doorway, his rifle held in front of him. "Let's go."

We stayed low until we cleared the last window on the way to the stairwell, then stood and edged our way toward the door. Tyrel went first, using a technique called 'cutting the pie', which basically meant aiming your weapon around a corner in such a way as to present a small target profile. I waited behind him, holding my breath, until he relaxed and lowered his weapon.

"Jesus," he said.

"What?"

"I found our other three hostiles."

"And?"

"I think the dumb sons of bitches missed the door with that grenade they threw. Looks like it blew up on the landing. Ripped 'em to pieces."

"They didn't miss."

"What?"

"They didn't miss. It came through the door just fine. I kicked it back at them."

Tyrel turned to look at me, eyes white around the edges. "Are you serious?"

"Yes."

He stared a moment longer, then tossed his head back and laughed. "You crazy-ass motherfucker." His hand bounced off my shoulder.

I said, "What happened with the one they threw at you?"

"Didn't toss it far enough, blew up a few feet shy of the doorway. Saw it coming and jumped back. Still hit me like a fucking hammer, though."

I peered down the stairway, caught sight of a ragged, bloody stump of leg, white bone protruding through flesh, and stepped back quickly. "Shit."

"You all right?"

"Man, I've seen some things, but that …"

"Don't feel bad about it. They tried to do the same thing to you."

I was about to say something else, but Tyrel stiffened and turned his ear toward the window. "You hear that?" he asked.

"I can't hear shit right now."

Tyrel fished a telescoping mirror from his vest, edged over to the window, and held it out. I noticed it was pointed down, as though he were trying to look at the ground. I watched his eyebrows come together and his mouth tighten into a hard, flat line.

"We got trouble."

"What trouble?"

He looked disappointed. "What just happened here, Caleb?"

"A firefight."

"And firefights are ..." He held an open hand in my direction. I blanked for a few seconds, then had a flash of insight and slapped myself in the forehead.

"Loud," I said. "Firefights are loud."

"And who likes loud noises?"

I dropped my magazine, stowed it, and popped in a full one. "Infected."

"Here's what we'll-"

A crash and a scream echoed from downstairs, making us both jump. Tyrel keyed his radio. "Rojas, you all right?"

No response.

"Rojas, can you hear me?"

Silence.

"Rojas?"

FIFTY-SIX

"We have to go down there," I said.

Tyrel pointed his rifle down the stairwell. "On me."

As I followed him down, I did my best not to look at the shredded limbs and gutted torsos littering the stairs, or slip in the disturbing amount of blood. The air in the narrow passage smelled of copper, raw meat, and shit. I had to bite down hard to keep from gagging. Finally, we emerged at the second floor exit.

In the hallway ahead of us, Rojas sat with his back to the wall holding his mid-section. He turned his head when we opened the door.

"Stay there!" he shouted.

"What happened?" Tyrel replied, although I am certain he already knew the answer as well as I did.

"Goddamn sniper."

"Can you crawl over to us?"

"Probably." He sighed and winced. "But I don't see much use in it."

Tyrel blinked. "Are you insane? The infected are coming!"

Rojas, his face twisted in pain, moved his hands. A torrent of blood spilled from his midsection. "Don't worry," he said. "I won't let them get me." He patted his pistol.

"Oh no ..." I muttered, staring at the gunshot wound. My stomach felt like it weighed a hundred pounds. If my recall of Gray's Anatomy was correct, the bullet had hit one of the large arteries running near the centerline of Rojas' body.

"Rojas, I want you to listen to me," Tyrel said. "I can treat that wound. There's still a chance you can survive. But that's not going to happen if you stay there."

The man I had come to know and respect over the last seven months turned his head and smiled. "You a doctor now, Jennings?"

"No, I'm a SEAL. I have medical training, you ass. Now get the fuck over here."

Rojas chuckled. "SEAL, schmeal. Y'all ain't shit. Buncha spoiled, overrated glamour boys. You wanna be a real man, be a Ranger."

"We can argue about it upstairs. Come on, man, you can't stay here. If you don't start moving, I'm going to crawl over there and drag your sorry ass."

"Nah, man. Don't bother. It's over."

"Don't talk like that. Nothing's over."

Rojas leaned his head against the wall and closed his eyes. "You wanna know something? I'm not scared. I always thought I would be, but here at the end of it, I think I'm just relieved."

Tyrel's fists balled up. "Rojas, stop it. I don't want to hear any of this all-hope-is-lost bullshit. I'm coming over there to get you."

"I was married. I ever tell you that?" He rolled his head to look at us, eyes glassy, tears running down dark cheeks. "Had me a pretty wife and two little girls. Still got a picture of us all together." He patted his chest pocket. "Take it with me everywhere."

The tension went out of Tyrel. He sat down and leaned against the doorsill. "I didn't know that, Miguel," he said, using Rojas' first name. "You never told me."

"Yep. Met her not long after I graduated AIT. Got married down in Rosarito, near where I grew up. You ever been down there, by any chance?"

"Lots of times." Tyrel said.

"Oh yeah, that's right. You were in Coronado. That's where they send all you SEAL pussies."

Tyrel smiled with red-rimmed eyes. "Fuck you."

"Best thing ever happened to me, homes. I loved that woman, those girls. I was in Afghanistan when the Outbreak hit. Took three weeks to get us home. Shit was crazy, man. You think things were bad here in the States, you should have seen what it was like over there. Fucking pandemonium."

Tyrel nodded. "I've been there. I can imagine."

"When I got back, I deserted. Ain't ashamed of it either. Soon as my feet hit American dirt, I stole a car and hauled ass to Baja. I knew that was where they would go, to my family's place. Somebody got there first, though."

At this admission, the trickle of tears became a flood. Miguel Rojas sobbed, one bloody hand covering his face. "The house was burned down. They took everything. My wife, my girls, my parents, they were all just these black burned things."

I could not see any more at that point. I sat down beside Tyrel and leaned my forehead on his shoulder.

"I buried them there on the beach, slept the night next to their graves. Left Baja the next morning and didn't look back. Wound up in Colorado Springs. Hid in plain sight, didn't tell anybody I was in the Army. Fell in with the militia. Been living day to day ever since, trying not to think too much about the past." He looked around and let out a bitter snarl. "And here it ends. Fuck it. I guess this place is as good as anywhere. I'm ready to be done, amigos. I'm ready to see Veronica and the girls again. Been too long. Way too long."

He reached a hand down at his side and began fumbling at his pistol holster. "It's strange, losing everything. You think your life is over, but it's not. You just have to find something else to hold onto. Something else to live for. Me, I've been living for the militia. For money, for booze, for women, for whatever distracts me. But now I know I wasn't really living. I was just waiting. Passing the time the best way I knew how. My wife would be ashamed of me."

Seeing he didn't have much left in the tank, I moved past Tyrel and crawled to Rojas' side.

"Caleb!" Tyrel hissed.

I ignored him and put my back against the wall next to Rojas. "Shit, man," he said. "Help me out here?"

The moans of the infected became loud enough I could hear them past the ringing in my ears. I could even hear the crunch of their footsteps in the snow outside. I reached down and drew Rojas' pistol. He looked at me and said, "You mind?"

"No. I'll do it."

He nodded and patted me weakly on the knee. "Thanks, man. I'm glad it's you. We had some good times these last few months, huh? We made a good team."

"Miguel, it's been an honor," I said. Then I raised the gun, closed my eyes, and pulled the trigger.

FIFTY-SEVEN

I did not leave him for the infected.

The manufacturer of his MOLLE vest had installed a handle on the back so a soldier's comrades could pull him to safety if he was too wounded to walk. I gripped it and began tugging him across the floor, head bowed, teeth clamped shut. When I had to cross a window, I dropped to my side and pulled with one elbow on the ground. Outside, the infected drew closer, their moans pouring into the hallway like a flood.

"Come on," Tyrel hissed. "Move your ass."

I redoubled my efforts, drawing deep breaths and surging forward. Rojas was not very tall, but he was solidly built and heavy with muscle. My breathing soon became labored from the strain. Finally, I crossed under the last window and stood.

I said, "Help me pick him up."

Tyrel gripped Rojas under the arms and laid him over my shoulder. I bounced a few times to balance the weight while Ty hastily locked the stairwell door.

"Go on ahead," I told him. "I"ll carry Rojas upstairs, you go lock the other stairwell."

Tyrel nodded once and pounded up the stairs. A few seconds later, I heard his footsteps over my head as he sprinted across the third floor hallway.

The climb was not an easy one. The stairs were slick with blood and gore, the stench making breathing difficult. I focused on taking one step at a time, not thinking about the end goal, just the task immediately in front of me. Like that old joke:

How do you eat an elephant?

One bite at a time.

I made each surge of thigh muscle and stiffening of back a mission unto itself. Plant the boot, lean forward, flex the core, push. Now repeat. Again. Again. Again. Finally, I reached the third floor landing and emerged into the hallway. The bodies of the men who attacked us were still there, still dead. I had not noticed it before, but a thin film of blood covered the floor from wall to wall. The cold had coagulated it, turning the pool into a thick, gooey mess. There was no way I was going to cross that while carrying Rojas without slipping, so I set him down gently.

The door opened at the other end of the hall and Tyrel emerged. "All secure?" I asked.

He nodded and came over to stare at Rojas. His face was blank, the piercing black eyes steady and intense. "We need to strip his gear."

Before the Outbreak, I would have been horrified at the suggestion. I would have stared angrily at Tyrel and asked him what the hell was wrong with him. But you do not survive the end of civilization by being sentimental. You do not survive by ignoring the reality of your situation. You survive by being able to turn off your emotions and do what is necessary, no matter how unpleasant. I may not have liked it, but Rojas' gear was valuable. We could not afford to leave it.

As I thought this, Tyrel said, "You know we have to leave him here, right?"

I nodded slowly. "I know. We'll never make the rendezvous in time if we take him with us. He's too heavy."

I felt a hand on my shoulder. "You did the right thing."

"I know."

The hand left. "No man should have to kill himself when he has friends around."

I nodded, wondering what the future held for a world that viewed such grim sentiments as kindness.

"That sniper is still out there." I said. "He has to know by now his friends are all dead."

Tyrel looked toward the window. "Maybe he has more friends."

*****

Night fell.

The moans of the infected grew steadily louder as they converged on the schoolhouse. Hundreds of them packed the second floor until no more could fit. The late arrivals began squeezing together in the courtyard and other areas outside, and in less than an hour, they had packed themselves tight as sardines, standing room only, an undulating sea of grasping hands and twisted faces. There was no way we were getting out of the building until the cold immobilized them. In the meantime, we had to hope the heavy steel doors barring entry to the stairwells held up under the pressure.

Making things worse, we had no way of knowing how long the sniper was going to wait for us. A military-trained sniper can remain in one spot for days without moving. But I doubted that would be the case this time. If the cold did not force him to move, the infected eventually would.

When the sun was well behind the horizon, we put on our NVGs and moved into the hallway. The moon was still behind the mountains, making it pitch dark in the building. We laid out the empty duffel bags and filled them with the gunmen's weapons, ammo, and equipment. Then, staying low, we dumped the bodies out the shattered windows. Even with my ears still ringing somewhat, I could hear the infected in the courtyard tearing into them.

Rojas, we dragged into a classroom. After stripping him of his gear, I unrolled his sword, laid it on his chest with the blade pointed at his feet, and positioned his hands around the hilt. We said a few words over him, then covered him up with his jacket. I hated the thought of leaving him there, but he knew the risks when he agreed to come with us. In my place, he would have done the same thing.

Our loot was seven serviceable rifles, three damaged ones we could strip for parts, nearly a thousand rounds of ammunition, five pistols of varying calibers, and the gunmen's tactical vests and their contents. We even took their boots. A decent haul, but hardly worth a good man's life.

Staring at the black bags bulging with salvage, I was once again struck by the nature of the world I now lived in. Before the Outbreak, if we were caught with any of this stuff, we would have gone to prison. But now, no one would question where it came from. Abandoned military equipment could be found anywhere, making it impossible for anyone to say for certain where a particular item in a market stall came from. Bloody boots were barely worth batting an eye at. Bullet riddled tactical vests were sold at a discount, an additional ten percent off if you couldn't wash out the stains. Throw in a box of 5.56 ammo, and it was worth a gallon of purified water and half a pound of venison jerky. Squeamishness has no place in the scarcity of the new barter economy.

Later, we searched the rooms on our floor looking for something to use for bedding. We had cached our sleeping bags, along with the rest of our gear, on a hillside where they weren't doing us a damn bit of good. If we wanted a decent night's sleep, we would have to improvise.

One of the doors we opened revealed a teacher's break room, complete with two vinyl sofa's, a blank television, and a vending machine. Neither of the sofas were big enough to sleep on, so we drew knives, cut out the padding, and laid it on the floor. My legs dangled over the edge from the knee down, but it was better than nothing.

Most of the food in the vending machine was inedible, but at the bottom were two rows of little cans of Vienna wieners. We busted the glass and devoured them greedily, undeterred by the coagulated fatty goop they were immersed in. My father once told me you would be amazed what you will eat if you are hungry enough. As usual, he was right.

Afterward, Tyrel said he would take the first watch. Too tired to argue, I gratefully lay down on my makeshift mattress, covered myself with my ghillie suit and a long wool jacket taken from one of the dead gunmen, and focused on clearing my head. Too much had happened that day. I needed time to process it, put it into perspective. But that would have to wait. Exhaustion had come calling, and it was not going to leave until I paid the rent.

I watched Tyrel pull a chair up in front of the door, sit down, and lay his rifle across his lap. Looking over his shoulder, he said, "I'll wake you up in four hours. Get some rest."

I closed my eyes and slept.

*****

In the halfway space between awake and asleep, I felt warmth on my face and heard the sound of boots with dirt in the treads grating over tile.

Startled, I reached for Rojas' pistol. I had placed it next to me before lying down, arranged so I would not fumble for it in the dark, the grip turned toward me, the top of the barrel pointing at my feet. All I had to do was lay a hand over it, and muscle memory would do the rest. But muscle memory is useless when a size twelve boot comes down and arrests your efforts.

"Easy, Caleb. It's me."

Tyrel's voice. I blinked at the brilliant sunlight pouring in between the blinds. The boot took its weight off my hand.

"What the hell?"

"Sorry," Tyrel said. "Didn't mean to scare you."

His silhouette sat down in front of the window. I blinked rapidly, trying to force my eyes to adjust to the light. "What time is it?"

He held up his wrist. "Just after eight."

"What!"

"Relax. I've been up all night."

I looked around, eyes toning down the glare to something manageable. The room was the same as I had seen it last night, stripped sofas pushed into the corner, shattered glass from the vending machine kicked against the wall. I sat up and looked at what Tyrel held in his lap.

"Where did you get that?"

He leaned forward, holding the object out so I could see it. It was a rifle, but not an ordinary one. There was no wood in the stock or foregrip, only composite plastic with shock absorbing springs in the butt plate. A Leupold scope sat atop a rail mounted over the barrel. It was bolt action, and, judging by the barrel, large caliber. A bloodstain covered the chamber, stock, and a section of Tyrel's right sleeve. I knew immediately what I was looking at.

Sniper rifle.

"This is the weapon that killed Rojas," Tyrel said.

I went still. A quick examination of my old friend revealed ice on his Army surplus fatigues, dirt and pine needles stuck to the fabric, and dark face paint with unwashed brownish-red spatter staining his cheeks.

"Ty, where have you been?"

He laid the rifle across his legs and patted it as if I had not spoken. "Took me a while to find the piece of shit. Had to wait until you were asleep and the infected were frozen."

I stared, eyes finally adjusting to the light. There was some kind of sticky, rusty brown matter encrusted in Tyrel's knuckles and matted in the hair on his fingers. My eyes moved to the Ka-Bar dagger on his vest, the stains on the sheath, the smudges on the handle. I said, "Ty, where did you go last night?"

"Hunting. I went hunting."

The next question was obvious, so I didn't bother asking it. We sat in the cold silence of the room, Tyrel's fingers drumming on the rifle's foregrip, until finally he said, "The Rot finally stopped crooning about 0100. Gave 'em another hour just to be sure, then went down to check out the hallway where Rojas got shot. Found the slug in the wall; a .308, or maybe a .300 Win mag. By the size of the hole in the wall, it had to have come from less than 300 meters." He shook his head. "Went straight through him, the poor bastard. Never had a chance. Round like that, at that range, doesn't much matter where it hits you. Anyway, it gave me a good idea where the shot came from. Weren't too many angles a sniper could have used, not with all the other buildings in the way. So I worked my way to the north side of town, used the buildings for cover. Took a while. Finally got to where I was pretty sure the shot came from and started searching with the night eye."

He patted the night vision scope on his carbine. "Spotted him on the third floor of an office building. Had a nice setup, rifle rest on top of a desk, nice comfortable chair to sit in."

His hand strayed to his Ka-Bar and touched the blood smudges. "Took me about half an hour to sneak up on him. Grabbed him from behind before he could do anything about it. Told him, 'You killed my friend, you son of a bitch. Now you're gonna die.' Then slit his throat."

Tyrel made a cutting motion across the front of his neck. "You wanna hear some shit, though?"

I did not like the look on Tyrel's face. "What?"

"It wasn't a *him*. It was a *her*. The sniper was a woman." He laid the rifle on the ground with shaking hands and stared at it. "Wouldn't have changed anything, though. Even if I had known, I still would have done it."

The room was silent for a time. Birds welcomed the dawn outside, chirping and whistling back and forth, oblivious to the doings of man, alive or dead. The sun coming in through the window grew brighter until I felt warmth through the leg of my pants. I picked up the sniper rifle and said, "Tyrel, it's warming up. We have to go."

He nodded and stood, hands balled into fists at his sides. "I still would have done it."

"Tyrel, we need to move."

He looked up, eyes bloodshot, marked underneath in shades of black, "But if I *had* known, I don't think I would have cut her throat."

I studied the flint-sharp lines his face, half illuminated in gold, the other half in shadow, and wondered which one of us he was talking to.

FIFTY-EIGHT

The wagon was moving away from us.

I drew my pistol and fired a single shot into the trees. Even from a hundred yards, I could see the driver jump. His initial reaction was to lay flat against the bench, snatch a rifle from the buckboard, and take aim in our direction. Tyrel and I both raised our hands and waved them over our heads.

The driver's face was bright red when he reached us. "What the hell is wrong with you two? There's infected all over the place."

"Relax," Tyrel said. "If they were close enough to be a problem, they'd have heard your wagon. You hear any moans?"

The driver's anger dimmed somewhat. "No. I guess I don't."

"Then why don't you hop down and help us with the bags?"

"I ain't no goddam porter," the man said. "Move your own cargo."

"You just used a double negative," I replied. "Which means you *are,* in fact, a porter. Now if you want any more business from us in the future, my friend, you'll hop your ass down here and get to work. You might be cheap, but you're not the only game in town."

He looked confused for a moment, shook his head, said something unpleasant, and set the brake.

When we had left Woodland Park, we knew our bags of salvage were too heavy to carry more than a few hundred yards. We also knew it would not be long before the infected thawed out, so after retrieving our gear from where we had cached it in the hills, we liberated a tarp from an abandoned house and used sticks and paracord to improvise a sled. What followed was a long, difficult hike, and we were both exhausted by the time we reached the rendezvous.

Overhead, clouds began to gather. Low, dark, gunmetal gray clouds born along on a high, speeding wind. On the slopes above us, snow blew down in swirling plumes, scattering on the surrounding pines and cedars. The wind funneled down into the valley, and by the time we finished loading the salvage, we had to cover our eyes against the stinging ice and lean forward to keep our footing.

"We need to move," the driver shouted over the howling noise. "Bad weather coming in."

No shit, detective. "Let's go then," I said.

As we hurried back toward town, the horses tossed their heads and whinnied at the storm. The driver leaned over to Tyrel and asked, "Where's that Mexican fella that was with you?"

Tyrel set his jaw and shook his head.

"What happened?"

"None of your goddam business."

The driver looked offended. He started to say something else, but Tyrel turned his flat black-eyed glare toward him, and the driver snapped his mouth shut.

The wind blew strong and cold on the way back to the Springs.

*****

The headquarters for the Colorado Springs Volunteer Militia Corps occupied the gutted remains of what had once been a big-box retail store.

Outside was an empty parking lot, the cars abandoned there long since hauled away for scrap. On the inside, shelves and display stands had been cleared out and replaced with rows of desks, file cabinets, and locked storage containers. The containers covered two-thirds of the floor space and were where the militias kept the majority of their after-tax wealth.

After putting our salvage in storage on the west side of town, Tyrel and I hired a carriage to drive us to headquarters to deliver the bad news about Rojas. When we arrived, LaGrange was at his desk, as usual. Sometimes I wondered if the man ever left the building when not on a mission. Maybe he slept and took his meals there and only went outside to use the latrine.

He looked up when he heard us coming, his face its usual mask of barely concealed irritation. His eyes flicked back and forth between us.

"I don't like the looks on your fool-ass faces," he said.

Tyrel and I sat down in two of the three chairs facing him. He put down his pen and stared at us. "Well? What is it?"

I looked at Tyrel, who nodded to me. "We ran into some trouble in Woodland Park," I said, not meeting LaGrange's eyes. "Rojas ... he didn't make it."

The irritation left LaGrange's face. His cheeks sagged and the lines around his eyes seemed to deepen. "Shit. What happened, infected get him?"

I shook my head. "No. Salvage hunters. Rogue group, never seen them before."

The sagging cheeks began to darken. "Where are they now?"

"Dead," Tyrel said. "We killed them."

"All of them?"

Ty nodded.

LaGrange heaved a sigh. "Any indication of where they came from?"

"No," Tyrel said. "We searched, but all they had were clothes and weapons. That was it."

No one spoke for a stretch, the noise of the other militias doing business around us a low din of voices and chairs scraping over concrete. LaGrange opened a desk drawer, removed two forms from a binder, and held them out to us. We took them, and he shoved a cup full of pens in our direction.

He said, "Start from the beginning."

I spent the next hour describing what happened, leaving out the incriminating parts and omitting certain items of salvage we recovered, such as a dozen grenades. Tyrel and I had gotten our story straight on the way over, so I knew his account would match up with mine with no discrepancies. When we were finished, LaGrange read both our reports and nodded in satisfaction.

"I'll turn this in to the police in the morning. Shouldn't be any trouble for you two. Looks like a clear-cut case of self-defense. Regardless, it's not like the other guys are around to tell their side." He set the papers down. "You ever find the sniper that got Rojas?"

Tyrel said, "Officially? No."

A slight smile creased LaGrange's face. "Unofficially?"

"I took care of it."

"Good." LaGrange sat back in his desk and rubbed his hands over his tired face. "Damn shame about Rojas. He was a good man. He'll be missed." Our platoon leader stood up and stretched and picked up a stack of papers. "I'll let the rest of the men know what happened. We'll put together a memorial service. Think there's any chance of recovering the body?"

"Maybe," Tyrel said. "If it stays cold and the infected don't get to him we might be able to send a few guys. If so, I'll go with them."

"Me too," I said.

"I'll see what I can do. In the meantime, you two go home and get some rest. You look like shit."

The two of us nodded and stood up to leave. LaGrange began to walk away, then stopped in his tracks and turned around. "Wait, Hicks, I almost forgot." He opened a drawer and pulled out a letter in a sealed envelope. "This came for you yesterday morning. Courier said it was urgent."

I took the envelope. "He say anything else?"

"Nope. Try reading the letter." With that, he left.

I stared at it for a few seconds, brows close together. There was nothing written on the outside, no indication of who it came from. I opened it and took out a small scrap of paper. It read:

Caleb,

Sophia went into labor last night. She's at the hospital. The doctors said there's something wrong. Come to the maternity ward as soon as you get this letter. Ask for doctor Caligan.

It was signed by one of Sophia's old co-workers. I stared at it for several long seconds willing the words to change, hoping if I wished hard enough the letters would rearrange themselves and tell me everything was all right. Tyrel broke the trance by putting a hand on my arm.

"Hey, kid, you all right? What does the letter say?"

I handed it to him and sprinted for the door.

*****

Dr. Caligan was a short red-haired woman in her late forties. She stepped into the waiting room and stood in front of me under fluorescent lights. The hospital was one of the few facilities in the Springs with electricity, powered by fuel brought in from some strategic reserve or another. She introduced herself and asked me to have a seat.

I said, "Where's Sophia?"

"Sir, please don't shout."

I ground my teeth, took a breath, and said, "Please, doctor."

"Would you take a seat?"

I didn't move. A grinding sound reached my ears, and I felt a terrible pressure behind my eyes. The doctor looked down, wiped her mouth, and said, "Last night, your wife went into labor. There were complications."

My legs began to feel weak. "What complications?"

"Sir, you're shaking. Please sit down."

This time, I did as ordered. The doctor took a seat beside me, her eyes filled with genuine sympathy. "She was in labor for two hours. She delivered the baby, but suffered severe hemorrhaging in the process. We did everything we could for her, but ... Mr. Hicks, I'm afraid she didn't make it. She lost too much blood and passed away during surgery."

The floor disappeared beneath my feet.

I knew it was there, but could not feel it. My ears rang, sounds coming to me as from a great distance. I broke out in a cold sweat. My hands went numb. A hot tingling roared around my cheeks and in my chest. I was not hearing this. This was not real. I was not in this hospital, this doctor was not talking to me, and none of this was happening. It was a nightmare, and I would wake up soon. Sophia would be beside me in bed, and Rojas would still be alive, and Lauren, and Dad, and Blake, and the living dead would never have devoured the world and destroyed everything *and it just all had to stop.*

Closing my eyes, I said, "Where is she now?"

"She's in the morgue. I'll need you to identify the body."

I nodded numbly. "What about the baby?"

Some questions, you ask them and you already know the answer. It is intuition. It is instinct. It is the subtle inferences one can make in the course of conversation that reveal a truth without actually saying it. We convey these truths by tone, by body language, by the prerequisites of human experience, and by the things not said in their correct places. Such as telling a man the mother of his child died in childbirth and not immediately salving the wound by mentioning the child survived. So the next sentence out of her mouth was no surprise.

"I'm sorry, Mr. Hicks."

The doctor told me Sophia held her before she died. My daughter. Before the end, she had enough time to give her a name.

Lauren.

I leaned my head back against the wall, felt warmth pour down my cheeks, and remembered the picture in the locked chest in that shithole shipping container I lived in, and the beautiful blue-eyed blonde woman holding a wrinkled little baby, and her pale face, her blue lips, the sadness in her smile, and all the years of watching my father try to put himself back together.

My life had finally come full circle.

And now it was over.

FIFTY-NINE

Six weeks later, I woke up in the street.

It was night. I had no idea what time. A howling wind roared through the streets, hurling loose snow and ice like a frozen sandstorm. A hand shook my shoulder, trying to roll me over.

"Hey, mister, wake up. You can't sleep out here."

I rolled to my back. The sky above was black, starry, and clear, the streets and buildings around me illuminated by the full moon. I sat up and looked down at myself. My jacket was missing, as were my boots. Whoever robbed me had left my socks, although they weren't doing me much good. I could not feel my feet.

I looked up at the person who woke me. He was a soldier about my age, maybe eighteen or nineteen, the visible part of his face ruddy and windblown. A scarf covered his mouth and nose.

"Sir, it's freezing out here. We have to get you some place warm. Can you stand up?"

"I can try."

The soldier wrinkled his nose as he helped me stand. I managed about four steps on the wooden blocks attached to my legs before the world began to spin and I went down to my knees and was violently sick. Not that there was much in my stomach to throw up. A few minutes of dry heaves later, I staggered up.

"Okay. I think I'm a little better now. Where are we going?"

"There's a place up the street. You can warm up there for a while."

"Where are we?"

He told me. I said, "Well, at least I'm not far from home. Must have been on the way there when I passed out."

The place the soldier mentioned turned out to be a tavern built on the foundation of a building that burned down during the Outbreak. It looked like something out of the mid nineteenth century: plank floors, wooden tables and chairs, dark paneling on the walls, a long polished bar to the left of the door, and a roaring fireplace in a brick chimney on the far side of the dining room. Upstairs, a railed walkway encircled three sides of the tavern, doors spaced every eight feet or so. The soldier helping me eased me down into a chair near the fire.

"Wait here a minute," he said.

I leaned against the table, laughing to myself. I could not have gone anywhere if I had wanted to. The fire was warm and inviting, and I turned so I could rest my feet on the hearth.

Looking across the room, I saw the soldier talking to the bartender. There were only a few other patrons scattered about, all of them staring at me. The noise was low enough I could hear the conversation.

"The hell you bring him in here for?" the bartender demanded. He was a stout man with thick arms, a shaven head, and a face like a bulldog.

"Found him in the street. If I'd left him out there he would have frozen to death."

The bartender eyed me skeptically. "Probably would have been a kindness. *Look* at him, for Christ's sake."

There was a mirror on the wall at the coat rack. I turned and looked at myself and almost cringed at what I saw. The blond

534

beard was so stained it was almost brown, matted and crusted with dried vomit. My eyes peered out from sunken sockets, ringed in black, the cheeks beneath them hollow, the bones of my face standing out sharply against dry, cracked skin. My lips looked like pink grub worms. My clothes were beyond filthy, stained so badly I could not tell what color they had originally been. There was a rip in my shirt at waist level through which I could see a long expanse of gaunt, scarred rib cage. It would not have surprised me if someone mistook me for a walker and put a bullet through my head. And honestly, I don't think I would have tried to stop them.

"I know he looks bad, but he's a human being, Dave," the soldier said.

"Barely."

"Can I get some water and a bowl of soup?"

The bartender, Dave, turned his big ball of a head my way, then looked back at the soldier. "You payin'? I don't run no charity."

"I can pay for my own food," I said, raising my voice to be heard. The money belt beneath my pants was still in place. Whoever stole my jacket and boots must not have thought to look there. I dug a hand in it, came out with a small plastic zip-lock bag filled with sugar packets, and shook it where the bartender could see. A few sets of eyes focused greedily on the bag.

Money, or trade rather, was not a problem. I still had most of what I had earned with the militia in storage. But after Sophia died, I stopped showing up for work, and despite Tyrel's best efforts, had no intention of going back. The only thing I cared about anymore was pouring as much alcohol down my throat as I could manage before passing out. Because when I drank, I forgot. I forgot the blue eyes, and the long blonde hair, and the soft skin, and the musical laughter, and the shared meals, and touches, and comforting each other when things looked bleak. Most importantly, I forgot the night I felt my daughter move in her stomach.

The daughter I would never know.

As I sat at the table, my eyes stung from the memories. My heart sped up, and I knew the withdrawal symptoms were coming. The speedy heartbeat would soon become a painful pounding, my hands would shake, there would be nausea, cold sweat, and labored breathing. If I waited too long, the auditory hallucinations would start. Better to order a drink, something strong to take the edge off, and then follow it up with as many as I could buy. And since I was paying with sugar, arguably the most valuable trade item next to toilet paper and feminine hygiene products, I could afford a lot.

The bartender stomped over to my table, put his hands on his hips, and said, "If you got trade like that, what the hell you doin' runnin' around lookin' like a bum?"

"None of your fucking business, friend. You take the trade or not?"

His eyes shifted to the bag on the table, and he looked almost contrite. "Sure."

"Double whiskey, and keep 'em coming." I withdrew a packet from the bag and slid it across the table.

"Ain't got no whiskey. Just grog."

Grog was a clear liquor brewed from whatever fruit or vegetable matter a distiller could get his hands on. It tasted like turpentine and sweat, but it was strong and it got the job done.

"Fine," I said. "But since it's grog, that packet is worth two doubles."

"For five more packets, you can have a whole damn bottle."

I handed them over. "Done."

He took the sugar, started to walk away, and then looked over his shoulder. "We got a bath in the back if you want to use it, fella. I can smell you from over here."

"Maybe later."

"Suit yourself."

He returned with a bottle and a glass, his attitude toward me much improved. Leaning down, he said, "You should probably stay the night here. Some undesirables across the room are giving you the glad-eye. Probably try to rob you the minute you step out the door."

I shrugged. "Let 'em try."

"You might also have noticed it's cold outside and you ain't got no shoes or jacket."

"I do, actually, just not here. I'll be fine."

Dave the bartender shook his head and walked away. "Your funeral."

I poured my first drink since passing out in the street and downed it gratefully. The taste was terrible, and it burned my stomach like someone had poured gasoline down my throat and lit it, but it slowed my heart rate almost immediately. I thought back to the days before the Outbreak, and how heavily bartenders could be fined for serving people under the age of 21. Now, no one seemed to care. If you could reach over the bar, you were old enough to drink.

The soldier who had helped me inside finished his mug of hot herbal tea and stopped by my table. "You going to be okay?"

I nodded. "Doing much better now, thank you. Care for a drink?"

"Can't. I'm on duty."

"You see any uniforms around here?"

He smiled. "How are your feet?"

Now that I had warmed up some, I could feel them again. They had not been exposed long enough for frostbite to set in, but they still ached. "Hurts, but I'll survive. Come on, let me pour you a drink."

He shook his head, still smiling. "I can't stand that stuff. Grog, I mean."

I looked down at my glass. "It's not so bad once you get used to it."

"I have to go back out on patrol. You have a good evening, sir."

I watched as he walked out the door and held it open while another man walked in. The newcomer thanked the soldier politely, walked up to the bar, and ordered water and a bowl of soup.

The dining room was not large. Maybe thirty feet by twenty feet, not including the bar. From where I sat, I could see a glint of metal around the newcomer's neck, a necklace with a gold medallion that looked familiar. I tossed my drink back, poured another one, and tried to remember where I had seen it before. With all the drinking I had been doing lately, my brain was in a constant fog. The only modes I operated in anymore were drunk, hung over, or suffering from withdrawal symptoms. Cognitive gymnastics that were once easy now took time and great effort to accomplish. So I sat, and drank, and stared, and halfway through the bottle, I remembered where I had seen the medallion.

I could not move for a while. The rage was too intense. I did not dare look in the direction of the bar lest I alert the man eating his soup. But my mind was moving, and moving quickly. I put the cork in the bottle and carried it across the room in my stocking feet.

"I think I've had enough for tonight," I told Dave the bartender. "Mind keeping this behind the bar for me?"

He took it and placed it on a shelf under the bar. "Not at all. What name should I put it under?"

"Bacchus."

He grabbed a notepad and pencil. "How do you spell that?"

I told him, then asked if the offer to utilize his bath was still valid. He said it was, and offered to have someone wash my clothes for me.

"You got a runner around here?"

"I do."

I handed him the key to my shipping container. "Send him to get me some new clothes and a pair of boots. Shouldn't take him more than about ten minutes. I live close by here."

"Will do." He shouted for someone named Nicky, and a moment later a skinny kid no older than thirteen showed up at the bar. He took the key and the instructions, and turned to leave. I grabbed him by the arm on the way by and informed him I knew exactly where everything was in my home, and if anything went missing, I knew where to find him. "I ain't no thief," the kid said defiantly. "I earn my way."

"Keep that attitude and we'll get along just fine."

As the kid took off, I motioned the bartender to lean closer. He held his breath, but complied. "That guy at the end of the bar? Keep him here. Offer him a drink, tell him … tell him a guy was in here a little while ago, paid for the drink, then got in an argument with his woman and left before you had a chance to serve it."

Dave's eyes narrowed. "I ain't lookin' to get myself in no trouble, kid."

"No trouble, mister. It's just I think I know him from back before the Outbreak, and I don't want him to see me like this. I doubt he'll recognize me in this condition."

The eyes stayed narrow. I reached in my money belt, took out a plastic bag full of instant coffee packets, palmed it, and slid it across the bar. "For your trouble. And there's more where that came from."

After a moment's hesitation, he took the coffee and whispered, "Anything happens to that guy, and people come around askin', I'm gonna tell 'em the truth. You hear?"

"Understood."

He grunted and moved away. At a signal from Dave, an older woman who had been wiping tables came over and told me to follow her. She led me into the back and set two metal buckets of water on a pot-bellied stove, then handed me a washcloth, a dry towel, a comb, and a ball of homemade soap. I sponged myself down with warm water, wet the rag and the soap, and spent the better part of ten minutes scrubbing myself from head to toe. I even managed to get all the crust out of my beard. The comb looked clean enough, but just to be sure, I cleaned it in one of the buckets before running it through my hair. I had just finished toweling off when the old woman knocked on the door.

"You decent?"

I wrapped the towel around myself. "Come on in."

She came inside and retrieved the two buckets, the soap, the comb, and the washcloth. "What do you want me to do with your old clothes?"

"Burn them."

A nod. "Probably for the best."

A minute or two later, the runner boy, Nicky, knocked at the door. I let him in, and he handed me my clothes and the key to my home. His eyes widened as they roved over the scars on my torso. A few seconds passed while I waited for him to leave, but he didn't budge. I snapped my fingers in his face. "Got a staring problem, kid?"

He flushed, said, "Sorry sir," and ran off.

A quick peek in the mirror told me I had accomplished my goal. Anyone who saw me walk out the front door would not recognize me as the same man who went in.

I dressed hurriedly and went back into the dining room. The newcomer with the medallion was still seated at the bar nursing a glass of grog. I nodded to the bartender on the way out, walked a block down the street, and ducked into an alley.

Now it was a waiting game. If the table of men who eyed my trade so jealously were really going to rob me, they would not wait long to come out. Too much chance of losing my trail.

Perhaps a minute ticked by, and sure enough, I saw all three of them emerge from the tavern.

"Which way you think he went?" one of them said. He was short, older, thick beard, stocky build.

"There's his footsteps," another said, pointing at my tracks in the snow. "Come on."

I eased back into the alley and waited.

SIXTY

They were good at their work, I'll give them that much.

One of them did the tracking while the second scanned ahead, the third watching their six. They moved up the street quickly, following my footprints in the dim silver light. Finally, they reached the alley. I stood back in the shadows near a big green dumpster, hidden from sight.

The first of the three men, the short one, drew a pistol from under his coat and started slowly into the alley. By the way he held it, moving the barrel with his line of sight, I knew he had some measure of tactical training.

"You want a light?" the third man asked, taking an LED flashlight from his belt. I tensed, making ready to leap out and cross the distance.

"No. I can see just fine. Don't want to make a target." He took a few more tentative steps forward.

"I don't like this," the second man said. "Too dark, too many places to hide. Use the flashlight."

Your friend is smart.

Three more steps. He was less than six feet away now. I held my breath.

"Okay, fine. Give me the-"

He diverted his attention for just a second to reach for the flashlight. It was all the time I needed.

Two steps brought me to his side. My hands flashed out and stripped the pistol from his grip. He stepped back in surprise, one hand reaching for another weapon. Rather than shoot him, I bashed him in the face with his own gun. When he stumbled back, I kicked him squarely in the balls.

As he collapsed, I trained the gun on the other two. "Hands in the air. Do it now."

Slowly, they did as I said. The man I put down took a hand away from his groin long enough to try for his weapon again. I raised a boot and stomped on his throat—not hard enough to kill him, but enough to stop him from breathing for a while.

"Don't try that again, asshole. I've been nice to you so far, but I'm just about out of patience."

The man gurgled and sputtered, one hand on his groin, the other on his neck. A cut on his cheek spilled dark black liquid onto the snow.

"You two," I said to the others, "take off your jackets. Do it slow. Your life depends on it."

They removed their jackets and let them drop. I kicked them to the side of the alley and ordered the men to put their hands on the wall. When they did, I made them step back and separate their feet so they could not turn on me too quickly. Leaving them there for the moment, I grabbed one of the first man's hands, put him in a wristlock, and forced him over onto his face. A search revealed a knife and a small .380 revolver, but no other weapons. I tossed them into a pile a few feet away and told him to join his friends against the wall. He whimpered and coughed while I searched the other two and tossed their weapons in the pile as well.

Like most citizens in Colorado Springs, the men had IDs on them. One was an old Texas driver's license, and the other two were simple government issue IDs distributed at the refugee intake center. When out in public, civilians were required to carry their IDs on their person at all times. Tonight, that rule played to my advantage.

"I'm going to keep these IDs," I said. "I know your names, and I know where you live. I could report you to the police, but it would be your word against mine, so here's what's going to happen. I'm going to let you go. Your weapons belong to me now. If I ever see you again, I'll shoot first and worry about the consequences later. Are we clear?"

They uttered a frightened chorus of assent.

"Good. Now get the fuck out of here."

They got.

*****

After caching my newfound loot in a nearby abandoned building, I found a rooftop from which to watch the tavern's front door. I did not have to wait long. The man wearing the medallion stepped out into the frigid night, turned his collar up around his face, pulled his knit cap down tight over his ears, and started walking northward. I slipped down from the rooftop and followed.

The first half-mile or so was difficult work. It is not easy to trail a person on empty streets without being spotted. My father and I used to make a game out of it in our neighborhood, him trying to spot me, and me trying to sneak up close enough to touch him without being detected. It took until I was about fifteen before I could beat him more times than I lost. Considering Dad was ex-Delta Force, it was an accomplishment.

Finally, the man turned onto one of the main thoroughfares connecting the refugee districts. Even this late at night there were a large number of people moving back and forth on the street, most of them third shift people. They made it easier to follow my target.

He reached a row of shipping containers perhaps two miles from where I lived and turned down a side street. I slowed my pace and watched him from the corner of my eye. The street was not long, only ten or eleven containers arranged around a cul-de-sac. I walked past, waited a five count, then turned and walked the other way. This time, I saw him climb a ladder, open a roof hatch, and disappear inside.

Looking around, I committed as much information about the area to memory as possible. The first smooth, uncoiling tendrils of a plan begin to stir.

It was long past time to pay a visit to Tyrel.

*****

After nearly two weeks of diligent surveillance and very little sleep, the time had come to make contact.

The target's name was Tom Dills. I sincerely doubted that was his real name, but the Army was still prosecuting deserters, so it made sense for Dills to assume a new identity. Another three months would pass before the president would realize the stupidity of what the Army was doing and issue an amnesty decree.

Dills worked as a laborer on a construction crew on the south side of town; brick masonry, for the most part. He was a creature of habit, always walking the same route to and from work, occasionally stopping in for food and drinks at the tavern where I first saw him. He had very few friends, mostly just people he worked with, and occasionally visited a widow with a ten-year-old son who lived a few streets over. He was not the only man who visited her, and she did not appear to have a day job. It did not take much imagination to figure out what she did for a living.

He seemed to live a mostly solitary life, almost enough to make me feel sorry for him. Almost. I'm sure he thought keeping his head down and minding his own business would make it tough for anyone to figure out who he really was. I did not know all of his story, but I knew one small, extremely important detail of it.

I knew where he got that medallion.

It had belonged to Blake, once. His mother sent it to him for his nineteenth birthday, a plain gold disk inlaid with a silver cross surrounded by delicate ivy and roses in white gold. Blake was rarely without it.

Now that is was in Dills' possession, he wore it everywhere. Made no attempt to hide it. I even heard a few people comment on how nice it was. An Air Force officer tried to buy it from him, saying he wanted to give it to his nephew for his birthday. Dills politely refused. Why it meant so much to him, I could only guess.

The setup was simple. Tyrel rented a horse and wagon from a man who knew better than to ask questions. We loaded it with a few relatively non-valuable salvage items: bundles of cloth, scrap wood, lawn furniture, empty buckets, and, most importantly, several large tarps. Ty parked the wagon not far from Dills' container on an empty side street and pretended to brush down the horse while he waited.

For my part, I walked slowly from one end of the main road to the other, eyes roving, waiting for the now familiar shape of Tom Dills to appear.

True to his pattern, he showed up just after ten at night, head down, hands in his pockets, trudging wearily toward his favorite watering hole: the same tavern where I first saw him. I tailed him from a safe distance and waited at the end of the street until he went through the door.

"Moving in," I said to my radio.

"Copy. Advise when en route."

"Wilco. Out." I turned off the radio and hid it in my jacket.

I waited a while longer. Dills usually spent an hour or so eating and nursing a few drinks before walking home for the night. When I thought he would be halfway done, I turned down the street and entered the tavern.

It was much more crowded this night than the first time I had come here. It was also much earlier in the evening, and I was not waking up from my second drunk of the day. Despite my recent efforts at sobriety, which is to say, weaning myself off the booze, I could feel the first tremblings of withdrawal kicking in. Not as bad as a couple of weeks ago, but enough I felt compelled to have a drink to settle my nerves. It would not do to let the anxiety and paranoia that came in absentia of alcohol rattle me into making a mistake.

Dave the bartender did not recognize me. A shave and a haircut and a couple of weeks of not trying to drink myself to death had altered my appearance. I had gained back some of the weight I lost, and my eyes no longer looked like dim blue lights at the end of a long dark tunnel. So when I gave him the name Bacchus, he blinked a couple of times.

"Well I'll be damned. You're looking a hell of a lot better."

"Semi-clean living, my friend. You still have my bottle back there?"

"Sure do." He retrieved it and brought it to me.

"Thanks." I took the bottle to a table on the other side of the room and sat down near the fire. From there, I could watch the bar without arousing suspicion.

It is difficult to explain what that first drink feels like when you have been abstaining for a while. I was at the point if I did not drink at all for two or three days, the withdrawal would cease to plague me. Not the cravings, mind you, just the worst of the symptoms. But when I poured a glass of grog and sipped it a few times, and the burn hit my stomach, and the pace of my heart slowed, and heat spread through my limbs and face, it was like a warm hug from a dear old friend. A tension I did not realize I was feeling began to ease.

The urge to empty the glass quickly and pour another tall one was strong. It would have been very easy to pound the half-bottle, order another one, and see how fast I could drink it. Tom Dills was not going anywhere, after all. I could take him any time I wanted, and-

NO.

The time for waiting was over. No more drowning myself. I had a purpose now. And besides, Tyrel had paid good trade for the horse and cart. If I screwed this up because I got drunk, he would probably shoot me. Or at the very least dole out a sincere ass-kicking.

I nursed my drink, felt it settle my nerves, and waited. If anyone sitting at the bar had turned and looked at me, they would have seen a young man sitting alone staring at the fire. Several other people at nearby tables were doing the same thing, further reinforcing the illusion. But the fire was the last thing on my mind.

Tom Dills, or whatever his name was, finished a bowl of stew and ordered a drink. He sipped it slowly until it was empty, then ordered another. I palmed the Rohypnol pill in my pocket, dropped it into the last of the grog in my bottle, let it dissolve, and carried it to the bar.

All the stools were taken, a few patrons standing behind them waiting for drinks. Dave worked busily to fill the orders, sweat standing out on his bald pate. I pushed in next to Tom Dills, bumping into him a little to get his attention.

"Hey Dave," I shouted, slurring my speech. "I'm done with this shit. You want it?"

He looked up, flipped a hand at me, and went back to what he was doing. I looked at Dills. "What about you man? You want the rest of this? I'm done with it."

He blinked at me, eyes going to the bottle. "You sure, man?"

"I gotta quit drinking this shit. It's fuckin' killing me."

Dills shrugged. "Yeah, sure. I'll take it. Thanks." He took the bottle. I backed away, shouting something about the dangers of grog to Dave the bartender, who studiously ignored me.

From the corner of my eye, I watched Dills uncork the bottle, sniff it, shrug, and pour himself a glass. He tossed it back in a single gulp. Inwardly, I laughed.

Perfect.

There was only enough left for two drinks, so I probably would not have long to wait. I went outside and took position across the street, leaning against the side of a building. A few minutes later, Dills emerged from the tavern looking unsteady on his feet.

Time to move.

I tailed him for a couple of blocks, threading through the crowd, staying close. His steps began to waver, leaving a serpentine trail in the snow. Finally, he stopped to lean against a doorway. He shook his head a few times and tried to move on again, but lost his balance and fell over.

"Hey, easy now buddy." I grabbed him under the arms and hauled him to his feet. He turned to look at me with bleary, unfocused eyes.

"S'wa doon?"

"Come on man, you can't pass out here. Let me help you."

I put one of his arms over my shoulders and gripped him by the belt. He offered no resistance. A policeman up the street took notice of us and made his way over.

"What's going on here?" he demanded.

"Sorry officer. My friend here had a few too many. I'm gonna walk him home."

He eyed Dills with a mixture of pity and irritation. "See that you do."

"Yes sir."

As we stumbled away, I smiled.

SIXTY-ONE

I let Tyrel handle the unpleasant part.

The Navy trained him for that sort of thing, after all. Interrogation was a particular skill he and the others never went into with me. I did not blame them. It is not exactly the kind of thing you teach a young child. "Here, Caleb. This is how you heat an iron over a fire. This is how you drill a hole in someone's kneecap. This is how you twist skin with a pair of pliers until it bleeds. Tomorrow, we'll do an introductory course in waterboarding."

Not that I was above it. If I was right about Tom Dills, and where he got his medallion, those were the least of the agonies I would inflict upon him. It was not squeamishness that kept me from participating. Tyrel knew me well, and he did not want me doing something drastic unnecessarily. We needed Dills alive for the moment.

There was not much screaming. A little, but not much. Ty had to make sure Dills knew he was not messing around. He wanted answers, and if he was not satisfied with what he heard, consequences would follow. That was the key. Consequences.

I sat on the ground in front of a round stone fire pit and poked the coals with a stick. The cabin behind me had once belonged to Tyrel's grandfather. Ty supplemented his income by renting it out as a hunting shack before the Outbreak. We were on the side of a mountain somewhere west of Pike's Peak.

If I had paid more attention, I could probably have memorized the route we took to get here. But on the ride over, I had been too preoccupied with the unconscious man under the tarps, and what he knew, to concern myself with logistics.

Presently, Tyrel emerged from the cabin and took a seat next to me. It was dark outside, and cold, the stars shining brightly above. The hanging road of the Milky Way was a broad swath of purple-white cosmos floating against the endless black of the sky. Ty poured some water over his hands and I watched red stains sizzle into the coals, turning them dark, extinguished. The wind shifted direction, blowing smoke into my eyes. My breath steamed in the air when I said, "What did you find out?"

The firelight cast shadows under the crags and valleys of Tyrel's sharp face. "You were right."

"So he was part of the group that ambushed us in Boise City?"

A nod.

"Where are the rest of them?"

"Didn't get that far."

"Are we sure he's telling the truth, and not just saying what he thinks we want to hear?"

Tyrel took a sip of water from his canteen. "He knows details. Stuff you told me about. He was there when it happened."

I drew my knife and stared at its black blade in the orange glow of the fire. The steel felt cold in my hands. "I want to know where the others are. All of them."

Tyrel stood up. "Let's see what we can find out."

Dills looked terrified. He sat in a pool of light thrown by the room's single dim lantern. We came through the door and shut it behind us and stood staring stone-faced at the doomed man. The naked blade of my knife dangled from my right hand.

Dills' boots scrambled across the wood-plank floor as he struggled to push himself further into the corner of the cabin.

Not that it would do him any good. The chains restraining him to the thick support posts were anchored by deep-driven eyebolts. He was not going anywhere.

"You have a choice." My voice came out flat, harsh, and cold as the winter wind. "Die quick, or die slow. Tell me what I want to know, and you'll go fast. Make me work for it, and you'll die screaming until you can't scream anymore."

I waited a while. When you tell a man he is going to die, and you want information from him, you have to give him time to accept it. He begged for a few minutes, but when he figured out it was having no effect, he began spitting and cursing.

"Fuck you bastards," he said, eyes aflame with defiance. "I ain't telling you shit."

My smile felt dry and dead, and I watched some of the fire leave Dills' eyes. His snarl sagged and grew brittle.

"We'll just see about that."

*****

Every man has a breaking point. Dills took less time than expected to reach his.

There are certain pains you can inflict that leave a person intact, physically speaking. Others do permanent damage, something from which a person will never recover. It happens, and they know they will never be the same again. There is no healing from this.

I took no pleasure in it. Much like killing the infected, it was a means to an end. But unlike dispatching the undead, I did not consider it a kindness. Quite the opposite, in fact.

Small droplets of blood spattered my pants and the legs of my chair. Three fingers and a thumb lay on the ground in front of me, neatly arranged. It was important he see them lying there. Dills huddled over his ruined hand, moaning. The smell of burnt flesh was heavy in the air.

"I'm going to leave you here with Tyrel," I said. "I'm going to check out what you've told me. If you told the truth, you'll die quickly. If you lied to me," I pointed to his severed fingers, "those are just the beginning. So if you've lied to me at all, unless want to die knowing what your own dick and balls taste like, now would be the time to confess."

"I swear to God," Dills sobbed. "I told you everything."

"For your sake, I hope you're right."

Outside, Tyrel grabbed me by the arm and walked me away from the cabin. "Caleb … you sure about this? I know a thing or two about revenge, son. It leaves you empty and cold and you get back nothing you lost. And it's a damn good way to get yourself killed."

"Doesn't matter now."

He stepped closer, looking me in the eye. "It matters to me, Caleb."

I almost pulled away until I saw the concern in his eyes, the affection he had invested in me since I was seven years old. You do not simply dismiss someone who has cared for you for that long. A lump rose in my throat and my eyes stung in the chill night air. "Ty, I have to do this. I can't live with it. The anger. I have to do something or it's just going to burn me up inside until there's nothing left."

An understanding passed between us, then. Tyrel still had the bloodstains on the sheath of his knife. I had seen the sniper rifle hanging in his home above the fireplace. There were no words necessary. We shared the simple acknowledgement of two people who had been in the same place and knew what it had cost them. And when you find yourself there in the depths, down in the darkest place, you make a light any way you can. Even if it means burning down the world.

"Take the horse," Tyrel said. "He'll let you know if there's infected nearby."

"Thanks," I whispered.

He let go of my arm. "Ride fast, son. And if it comes to it, shoot straight."

I embraced my old friend, and then set off down the mountain.

SIXTY-TWO

A wave of murders struck Colorado Springs.

The first of them I caught up with on the way home from a drinking hole I heard about when I worked for the Civilian Construction Corps, a place called Flannery's. It was a dingy, stinking bar made of two shipping containers with the center walls cut away by an acetylene torch, a foot-wide length of steel welded over the top joint to keep the rain out, and it had cheap grog, a tiny stage, and a few desultory strippers. It did a good turn of business.

I hung out in the place downing drinks that tasted like turpentine and nightmares and listened to the mark get rowdy with his friends. The description fit, and he lived in the part of town Dills said he did, but I needed the name to be sure. It did not take long to get it.

"Hey Ryan," one of the roughnecks at his table said. "You got the next round or what?" He held up his empty glass and shook it.

The mark, Ryan, held up a hand. "Fine, fine, you thirsty fucker. Be right back."

When he bellied up to the bar, I turned to him. "Your name Ryan?"

He eyed me suspiciously. "Who's asking?"

"Dan Foley, out of Austin. Your last name Bromley?"

555

He shook his head. "No. Martin."

I feigned a look of disappointment. "Dang. Sorry to bother you. You look like someone I knew from … before. When I heard your name was Ryan, I thought …" I looked down into my glass.

"Don't sweat it," Ryan Martin said. He patted my shoulder with genuine sympathy. "I got one of those faces. Hope you find your friend."

The bartender brought him his drinks, and he went back to his table. I stayed in my stool, nursing grog and pretending to enjoy the gaunt, limp-breasted women gyrating on stage. At an hour before curfew, the bartender turned off the cell phone connected to a small speaker playing old hip-hop songs, plugged the phone into a solar trickle-charger that would do absolutely no good at all until morning, and announced the bar was closed. The last dancer picked up her tips—a collection of small but fairly valuable trade—and tiredly left the stage.

The few remaining patrons complained loudly, but finished their drinks quickly. Minutes later, Martin and his group got up and walked out. I paid my tab with four .308 cartridges and followed.

My hands were steady. The few drinks I'd had kept the shakes away, and probably would continue to do so for at least another hour. I had a pistol and a knife under my coat, but contrary to my normal operating procedure, the knife was primary and the pistol was backup. I wanted to do this quiet, but I would take it any way I could get it.

Martin's two friends broke off from the pedestrian road at separate intervals, leaving the ex-soldier walking alone toward his corner of the refugee districts. I kept my distance until he turned down his street, then I sped up. If he had been less inebriated, he probably would have heard me coming and I would have had to resort to the pistol. As it was, I managed to sneak up behind him just as he was about to climb the ladder to his roof hatch.

At the last instant, he either heard me or sensed something was wrong, and half turned in my direction. There was an alarmed question on his lips, but he never got a chance to ask it. My feet were set, heels dug in, hips twisting, arm following through with the momentum of a right hook that clipped him squarely on the chin, my fist striking with only the first two knuckles to avoid breaking my hand. I put everything I had into that punch, and I am fairly certain it would have dropped a rhino.

Martin's head clanged off a ladder rung as he went down. I glanced around to see if anyone had seen. The district was dark and quiet, the residents huddled next to their fireplaces or resting up for the long workday ahead. That is how you know you are in a working class neighborhood: the wood smoke is heavy, and people go to bed at a decent hour.

A quick search turned up his keys. I unlocked his front doors, dragged him inside, then closed and re-locked them. Seconds later, I climbed down through the roof hatch and locked it as well.

Martin was beginning to come around, moaning groggily on the floor. I did a quick search of the room with my tactical light and saw a gallon jug of water on a shelf. Perfect. I set it on the ground and put my tactical light next to it, bathing the room in dim white luminescence. That done, I drew my pistol, sat Martin up, and slapped him awake. When his eyes finally focused, they saw the pistol and widened in alarm.

"Look man, take whatever you want," he said. "I don't have much, but-"

"I'm not here to rob you."

He blinked in confusion. "Then what do you want?"

I pulled Blake's medallion from my jacket pocket.

"Recognize this?"

He looked at it blankly. I held it closer, but still nothing.

"I've never seen that before."

"Ever been to Boise City, Oklahoma? Some people were ambushed there a while back. Lots of shooting and grenades. Ugly business."

Now his face changed and all doubts drifted away like smoke on the wind. "Wait, man," he said, hands upraised. "You don't understand."

"Oh, I understand perfectly. You and a bunch of other deserters thought we were there to find you. You thought we had been sent by the Army to root you out. So rather than, you know, *ask* us why we were there, you shot first and didn't bother with questions."

The fear now took on a shade of confusion. "How did you …"

"Tom Dills," I said. "Or as you know him, Clayton Briggs. You two served together, right? He's not doing so well right now. He's chained to a wall in a cabin missing a few teeth and a few fingers. But that's not your problem. In fact, you don't have problems anymore."

I drew back the hammer on the pistol. It was a .38 revolver I had taken from one of the men who tried to rob me a few days ago. Martin cringed and opened his mouth to scream for help, eyes pinned to the steel against his forehead. In his terror, he didn't see what my other hand was doing.

At least, not until he felt the blade slide between his ribs and enter his heart.

He gasped, mouth opening and closing, going stiff with pain. I gripped him by his chin and said, "Consider yourself lucky. I can't afford too much noise."

His eyes dimmed, and with the last air in his lungs, he said, "Why?"

"My father. And a good man named Blake Smith. That's why."

And then he died.

*****

The next four were far less dramatic.

I realized I had been stupid. I had acted out of anger, out of a need to make the kill personal. It did not need to be that way. When I had followed Ryan Martin into that shitty bar, if someone had suggested I do the job from a rooftop a hundred yards away, I would have laughed in that person's face. But after two nights of sleeping in the bed Sophia and I once shared, and seeing Martin's face in my nightmares, and the regret in Martin's eyes as he breathed his last, I knew there needed to be a distance. A disconnect. Look too deep into the abyss, and the abyss looks into you.

Like Dills and Martin, I exercised due diligence. I would not kill the wrong people. There is a difference between retribution and murder, although I doubt the law would agree with me on that. Maybe I was right, maybe I was wrong. I don't know. I'm no philosopher. I just knew I could not stand the thought of Blake and Dad being dead and gone while their murderers lived free, unconcerned with punishment. Even if I went to the police, I could not prove anything. Not enough evidence. And they would want to know how I got my information, a question I could not answer.

Justice may wear a blindfold, but I do not.

I verified who they were. I drank just enough to keep myself steady without dulling my perceptions. My father's lessons in tradecraft served me well. I followed them one by one, arranged meetings, determined their identities beyond doubt, then handled things the smart way.

A sniper's bullet kills a man just as dead as a knife. And when you have a suppressor to mask the report of your rifle, avoiding detection becomes a simple matter of careful planning and camouflage.

By the fifth kill, the city was apoplectic. All anyone talked about was the psycho murderer randomly killing people in the refugee districts. Was it a disgruntled soldier? A serial killer? Someone driven mad by the horrors of life after the Outbreak? No one knew.

Except me.

After the last kill, I sat on the roof of my container drinking an insanely valuable bottle of Pappy Van Winkle, the M-4 I did the deeds with scattered in various dumpsters throughout the city. I watched people hurry home, eyes watchful, parents clutching their children protectively.

Worry not, I thought, drunkenly tipping my glass in their direction. *The threat has passed.*

A few alert police and military patrols rolled past my street, eyes on the rooftops. A soldier on top of an APC spotted me, told the driver to stop, and put a pair of field glasses on me. I pretended I did not see him and poured myself a tall one, singing a slurred, nonsensical song. A few moments passed, and his posture changed. He had dismissed me as just another harmless drunk. God knew there were plenty of them around these days.

Nevertheless, I decided tomorrow would be a good day to get out of town.

SIXTY-THREE

I arrived back at the cabin none too soon. Tyrel was low on food, and had been seriously considering putting a bullet in the head of Clayton Briggs—also known by his alias, Tom Dills— and leaving his body for the infected and heading back to town to look for me.

"You would have done that on foot?" I asked him.

He looked up from the outdoor fire pit where he was boiling water in a kettle and heating potatoes and canned vegetables in a skillet. The horse was picketed a few yards away, snuffling through the snow for bits of dead grass. Brilliant sunlight poured over the white mountain peaks, bathing the pines on the slopes in polished gold.

"Damn right," Tyrel said. "I've hiked farther through harsher territory."

I sat down next to him and opened a jar of instant coffee. "Well, the deeds are done."

"You get all of them?"

"Yes."

"Leave anything behind to tie it back to you?"

"No. I was careful. No witnesses, and the murder weapon is probably scattered all over the landfill by now."

"What about your knife?"

"Cleaned it and soaked it in bleach. Even a forensics lab couldn't get anything off of it."

Tyrel nodded, satisfied. "So what do you do now?"

I thought about the interrogation of Clayton Briggs. How he had remained defiant until the second finger came off and the hot iron touched the stump. Then off came the third finger, and his resolve began to waver. When I severed his thumb, leaving only a pinky finger protruding from the blistered ruin of his right hand, he finally broke.

He told me there had been eleven of them, initially. They had all left together from the San Antonio quarantine in stolen Humvees and decided to hole up in Boise City. They knew it was abandoned, and it seemed like a good place to hide. A logical enough conclusion.

The retreat from San Antonio was so disastrous they did not think the Army would send anyone to look for them. For all the chain of command knew, they had been killed like most of the other soldiers holding the line. The horde that overran their defenses had been enormous. They figured they would not be missed in the confusion.

Things were all right the first few days, but then one of them, Sergeant Falcone, thought they should move on. Find some civilian clothes, grow their hair and beards, and head north. He had two supporters, but the rest disagreed. He said he wanted to take some supplies, weapons, and ammo, and leave the group. A lieutenant by the name of Guernsey, who had been in charge up to that point, said the men were free to leave, but they would not be taking any gear or weapons with them. Or food.

The next day, as they sat in an office building arguing over what they should do, one of them heard the unmistakable drone of Humvees approaching. All conversation stopped. They fell back on their training and took up defensive positions in separate rooms, close to the windows on the upper floors so they would have the high ground.

Then the Humvees came down the street along with a couple of civilian vehicles, all occupied by men in combat fatigues.

They stopped and got out, moving like professionals, like Special Forces types. There was a girl with them, probably someone they rescued.

The lieutenant told everyone to stay low and quiet. There was a chance these people did not know about them. It could just be a coincidence. Hold your fire until I say otherwise.

Briggs did not know why the man who shot Blake, a sergeant named Prater, decided to open fire against orders. He had always been trigger happy, and sometimes had trouble keeping his cool in combat. He was his squad's designated marksman, armed with an M-110, a high-powered semi-automatic sniper rifle.

I put myself in his place, staring through the crosshairs, heart racing, finger taking in the slack on the trigger, and then, out of nowhere, *CRACK*. A moment of shock, and then the realization that he had squeezed too hard. An accident.

But at that point, there was no turning back. The people in the streets returned fire, so the other deserters opened up on them. From then on, it was all yelling and fire and confusion and explosions. Lieutenant Guernsey had the presence of mind to send three men to take the civilian cars they had hidden in a garage nearby and cut off our escape route to the north. Those would be the cars I fired a grenade at, killing one of the soldiers.

I understood why Guernsey did it. He did not want us revealing their location to anyone if we escaped. Cold, but logical. Thankfully for us, it did not work. We got away, and they were left spitting, cursing, and trying to figure out what to do next.

In the aftermath of the fight, only eight of the original eleven deserters were left. The man who had shot Blake was one of the casualties. I took a small measure of comfort in that. The other two were the man I blasted with a grenade and Lieutenant Guernsey. The lieutenant caught a burst from our SAW that stitched him from neck to abdomen, killing him before he hit the ground. I did not know if it was me or Mike that killed him.

Could have been either one of us. It did not matter. He was dead. That was the important thing.

After we escaped, the deserters knew they could not stay in Boise City. Sergeant Falcone took over and they headed north for Colorado Springs. True to his plan, they ditched their uniforms and tactical gear, searched around until they found serviceable civilian weapons, and set about the task of blending in.

"So let's do the math here," I said to Tyrel. "We killed three of them in Boise City, leaving eight. I killed five of them in the Springs, and there's one more in that cabin over there who won't live to see another day. That makes nine dead. They started out with eleven."

Tyrel looked at me. "Two left."

I drew my knife and walked into the cabin.

Briggs looked resigned. He knew he would not leave this room alive.

"There's something I forgot to ask you about," I said.

He did not look up. "What?"

"I've only accounted for nine of your group. Where are the other two?"

He shrugged his shoulders. "I don't know where they are, and that's the truth. They didn't like the Springs, didn't want to take a civilian job, and left a couple of weeks after we got here. I haven't heard from them since."

"What if I don't believe you?"

He turned his face up, eyes tired, empty, and devoid of fear. "You can torture me all you want. I can't tell you something I don't know."

Sometimes, you know the truth when you hear it. I let out a sigh, shook my head, and drew my pistol.

Briggs said, "For what it's worth, I'm sorry. I'm sorry about your friend, and I'm sorry about your father. It shouldn't have

564

happened, none of it." He leaned his head back against the wall and closed his eyes. He swallowed once and said, "Tell me, what did your father look like?"

I described him. Briggs wiped his good hand across his face, chains rattling. I watched tears fall down his cheeks. "I think it was me. In fact I'm sure it was."

My face went cold. "What are you saying?"

"I'm the one who shot your father. He was firing at the far end of the building after he launched that grenade that took out Prater, the sharpshooter. Your father was too far back from cover, so I got a bead on him and fired a burst. I saw him flinch, saw the pain on his face. He was a tough man, though. He kept fighting. So like I said, for what it's worth, I'm sorry."

Without a word, I raised the gun and squeezed the trigger until the slide locked open on an empty chamber.

*****

As the wagon creaked down the mountain on a switchback trail, I thought about Briggs, and his lieutenant, and Prater, and all the men I had killed in my life. Not even twenty years old yet and I had already racked up a body count to make a combat infantryman blush.

I began to doubt my actions. The cold fingers of regret slipped slowly into my chest, recriminations whispering in my ear. There had not been a lot of thinking involved except for how I was going to kill them. I did not take time to question my motives or the justice of my actions. From everything I had learned by talking to Briggs, the fight that killed Blake and Dad was nothing more than a misunderstanding that got horrifically out of hand. One man made a mistake, and it sent bloody ripples flowing outward across the great ocean of time and consequence. And now, all but two of them were dead.

Only at this moment, when it was too late, did I realize that Tyrel had been right. Revenge had availed me nothing. The deaths of those men would not return my lost family to me. I felt no satisfaction, no comfort, no sense of closure. Nothing had changed except a few more people who might have gone on to do good things with their lives were gone from the world. People who, when I thought about it, might not really have deserved to die.

I thought about when I first met Ryan Martin at that shitty bar in the refugee district. How when I told him I was looking for a friend and was disappointed Martin was not him, he offered a few comforting words, a pat on the shoulder. Physical contact and a sincere offering of sympathy for a stranger. Could a man capable of basic human goodness, even such a small gesture of it, really be irredeemable? Despite what he had done, what he had been a part of, I began to think perhaps not.

I knew, then, I would not pursue the last two deserters. There was no point. The man who killed my father was dead, and so was the man who killed Blake. That was enough. I had done too much killing, and I wanted no more of it.

I had hoped that seeing this thing through would put an end to this chapter of my existence, a chapter awash with grief and loss, and let me move on. But life does not happen in chapters. It happens in long, seemingly endless verses, like an epic poem, something Homer or Dante would have written. Maybe that is why their work remains compelling so long after their deaths. It has an undefinable resonance that we all understand instinctively, if not intellectually.

The first time I took another person's life, when those two men attacked Lauren, I felt like I had crossed a line. There were people who had never killed, and people who had, and I was now one of the latter. And there was no going back. But then time passed, and I rationalized things, and I knew there had been no choice. My mind puzzled over the permutations of alternate courses I could have taken, and I decided I had done the best I could. Any other path would have resulted in further injury or death to both myself and Lauren. I did what I had to do.

So I went back to feeling like a good person. Then came the Outbreak, and Canyon Lake, and that crazy perverted bastard who thought screwing a ghoul was a good idea, and again I chose to pull the trigger. It was easier the second time, and the third, and the fourth, and all the deaths thereafter.

That's the thing about crossing lines. It is only hard the first time. After that, it gets easier and easier until eventually you forget there was ever a line to begin with.

At the bottom of the mountain, we unrolled Briggs from a big blue tarp and left him in the open. His body was still warm, the blood not yet coagulated. Tyrel drew his pistol and fired a single round in the air.

"Won't be long," he said. "We need to move."

I heard moans and hisses cut the air less than two-hundred yards away. We got in the wagon, Tyrel snapped the reins, and we took off at a brisk trot.

The infected would make it easy for us. They would dispose of the body neatly and effectively, leaving nothing to tie us to the dead man on the road. Disposing of bodies was one of the few things the undead were useful for.

I wished then, and still do now, that the infected could eat more than just flesh. I wish they could eat our demons. If people could reach into themselves and pull out their regrets, and anger, and the suffered indignities of the past, and feed them to the undead, those of us still alive might have a higher opinion of the pathetic creatures.

And the ghouls would be very, very well fed.

SIXTY-FOUR

There are two methods of being an effective drunkard in the new barter economy. Both depend on what commodity you are exchanging.

In my case, I had in storage a significant amount of the two principle types of trade goods: large items, and what I call divideables. The big stuff consisted of things like guns, furniture, generators, propane grills, propane tanks, mattresses, horses, cows—things that, generally speaking, cannot be easily broken down into smaller component parts. Well ... except the horses and cows, of course. But hardly anyone butchers those kinds of animals unless they are desperately hungry. Draft animals are simply too useful for general consumption unless they are injured or too old to work. Then they are fair game. Especially cows.

Divideables are the opposite: cans of instant coffee, bags of sugar, boxes of ammunition, toilet paper, food, tampons, toothbrushes, etcetera. These are easy to trade, as just about anyone will accept a plastic bag filled with coffee, a few sugar packets, a handful of ammunition, or a couple of yards of toilet paper in exchange for a drink. You can even trade high-quality pre-Outbreak booze for large quantities of the poorly made, but very effective, post-Outbreak stuff. Sure, it might destroy your liver and make you go blind, but when the goal is to drink yourself to death a la Nicolas Cage in *Leaving Las Vegas*, what difference does it make?

Which brings me back to the topic at hand: the two methods of being an effective drunk.

You see, large trade items, while valuable, are generally exchanged for other large items. So to keep yourself in booze, you trade the big stuff for commodities you can divide up. Venison jerky, for example. This is the first method of practical drunkery.

The second is to find an establishment that will let you buy drinks on credit, keep an honest ledger, and accept large trade items as down payments against future alcoholism. This method may seem like a good idea in theory, but in practice, it is difficult to pull off. The problem is finding an honest businessman.

Lucky for me, I knew one. His name was William. I have no idea what his last name was, as he never gave one, and I'm fairly certain William was not his real first name. I did not care. He ran an honest business, kept his books with thorough precision, and offered fair value for trade.

And that is as much as I remember from that period of my life.

My next clear memory is of waking up in a jail cell feeling like I had just been run over by a truck made of hatred and knives. I tried to sit up on my cot, but my ribs screamed at me and demanded I lay back down. I complied.

Lying there, I decided that someone needed to come up with a stronger word for hangovers. The hangovers I woke up to, especially that morning, were much too powerful for the common definition to suffice. They should be called death-overs, or annihilation-overs, or I-just-got-eaten-and-shit-out-by-a-tyrannosaurus-overs, or something.

Turning my head, I thought something was wrong with my vision, but then I raised a hand to my face and understood the problem—one of my eyes was swollen shut. The rest of my mug was not in much better shape.

Then came the headache, the nausea, the shakes, the clenched bowels, and the *thump, thump, thump* of my pounding heart. The usual suspects.

Worse, there was always a delay after I woke up, just long enough to make me feel like I had become inured to the abuse I was heaping upon my body. But then the package would arrive and detonate on my proverbial doorstep, and I would be reduced to a moaning ball of agony. Most mornings, the best I could do was crawl to the nearest bottle and pour it down my throat and wait for the symptoms to abate. Repeat as necessary.

There were no windows in the cell, so I had no idea what time it was. I also had no idea why I was in my own cell and not in the tank with the rest of the drunks. Whatever the reason, I had a feeling I was not going to like it.

I searched my hazy memory, trying to remember what happened to me the night before, but mostly drew a blank. I remembered waking up in my own bed the previous morning— a rare occurrence in those days—having my first five or six drinks, and then stumbling down the street to The Amber House, the establishment ran by William No-Last-Name, owner and proprietor. But that was all. Meaning I had, as usual, blacked out.

Not for the first time, I wondered at the fact I was still alive.

An agonizing eternity passed, which was probably not more than an hour, and then a voice spoke to me through the bars of my cell.

"You awake in there?"

"Unfortunately, yes," I croaked. *Christ my throat is dry.*

"Then get up, Caleb."

Jeez, I've been here enough times I'm on a first name basis? I turned my head to see a uniformed sheriff's deputy standing at the door. I did not recognize him.

"I'm not sure if I can, officer."

A shake of the head. He looked both ways down the corridor to make sure no one was coming, then unlocked my cell and stepped inside. From his jacket pocket, he produced a small flask. "Here. This'll help get you moving."

"God bless you, you beautiful man."

It was grog, but did not taste half bad. The deputy helped me sit up far enough I would not choke on it. I took two long pulls and felt the old familiar burn in my stomach, a delightful comfort only those who have endured severe alcohol addiction can fully appreciate.

"Thanks," I said, sitting up the rest of the way. "I think I can move now."

"Good. The judge wants to see you right away."

I looked at the deputy, and the expression on his face was not a happy one. "Oh shit," I said. "What did I do?"

"You don't remember?"

I shook my aching head.

"Don't worry. You'll find out soon enough."

*****

The Honorable Judge Jack MacGregor was not what I was expecting.

When you hear a name like Jack MacGregor you think of a stern old Irishman with silver hair, eyes the color of the sea, and a South Boston accent. But that was not what I saw when I stepped into the large office that served as one of the building's courtrooms.

For starters, Jack MacGregor was neither old nor white, but a smallish black woman. I guessed Jack must have been short for Jaqueline or some other similar name. She was sitting down, not on a platform like you see in the movies, but behind an ordinary-looking desk. She was, however, wearing the black robe of her office.

I could tell she was sturdy of build, pretty in a severe sort of way, and could have been anywhere between thirty to fifty years of age. A pair of intelligent brown eyes peered out from behind wire rimmed glasses. She did not smile. The eyes appraised me coldly and thoroughly, peeling away my defenses and laying the entirety of my existence bare with one sweeping glance. My legs felt weak, but I met her gaze anyway.

Hers were the eyes of someone who had seen and heard too much, of a woman who understands the dark motivations of the human heart and can no longer be dismayed. There would be no lying to this woman, and no talking my way out of whatever trouble I was in.

In a calm, even voice dripping with authority, she said, "Sit down, Mr. Hicks."

I complied. The deputy had put me in irons before bringing me to see the judge, making sitting uncomfortable. But I did not dare complain. Not in front of this woman. A young man who I assumed by his demeanor to be my public defender was already seated to my left. An older man with graying hair, a patrician nose, and a hard flat line of a mouth sat to my right. He did not look at me.

"Do you know why you're here, Mr. Hicks?"

"I'm afraid not, Your Honor," I said. "I don't remember much from yesterday."

The eyes flicked down to a piece of paper, and I realized she was wearing bifocals. "According to those who witnessed the incident, at approximately 10:30 pm last night, March the 24th, you had a verbal altercation with a man named Alex Cannon. The argument took place in a tavern registered under the name The Amber House. The argument between the two of you escalated until the owner of the establishment had his security personnel escort the both of you from the premises." She looked up again. "Any of this ring a bell?"

I swallowed. "I'm sorry, Your Honor. I don't remember any of that."

"Once outside," she continued dryly, "you and Mr. Cannon engaged in a fistfight. Several witnesses reported that despite Cannon being significantly larger than you, you managed to get the better of the altercation, although you did suffer a few minor injuries." She flicked a hand to indicate my battered face. "Mr. Cannon's injuries, however, were not so minor."

My heart sank. The room was cool, but sweat broke out on my forehead anyway. I looked down and closed my one good eye. "What did I do to him, Your Honor?"

A shuffle of papers. "One crushed left orbital socket, four missing teeth, a jaw broken in two places, several fractured ribs, and a dislocated right shoulder." She put the paper down and glared sternly. "And he will most likely lose his left eye."

I groaned. I wanted to sink down through the floor. I wanted lightning to strike from the sky and burn me to cinders. I wanted to climb down a hole and pull it in after me. It was bad enough what I was doing to myself, but now, I had ruined someone else, maimed him for life. I thought about my first day with the militia, and the prison labor detail, and the man who fell to the ground exhausted and gasping like a fish, and I imagined his face as mine. I hung my head and said nothing.

The judge gathered the papers in front of her, tapped them on the desktop a few times to straighten them, and returned them to a manila folder. She set the folder aside. "To be honest, Mr. Hicks, Alex Cannon was no better than you. But he wasn't any worse, either. According to your record, you're simply a useless drunk who occasionally urinates in places where such actions are forbidden by city ordinance. A nuisance to be sure, but until now, a mostly harmless one."

I could find no fault with her assessment, so I stayed quiet.

"Cannon, for his part, is simply a man who lost his job as an engineer for the Civilian Construction Corps and decided to drown himself in a bottle, much as you have been doing. However, despite his current low station in life, he comes from a rather prominent family within the community. His father, who is very angry over his son's injuries, is a member of the new city council." At this, she leaned forward and pointed at the older man seated to my right. "And a friend of District Attorney John Crouch."

My guts turned to water as I looked to my right. The DA's face was impassive, his eyes focused on the judge. I did not want him to look at me, so I followed his example.

"Let me make this as clear and simple as I can, Mr. Hicks," Judge MacGregor said. "There are three ways we can handle this. Only one of them is to your benefit." She held up a finger. "One, you plead guilty to aggravated assault and resisting arrest, face six months of hard labor, and forfeit all of your registered salvage as restitution." She held up another finger. "Two, you plead not guilty, we go to trial, and you wind up facing a *year* of hard labor, and we seize *all* of your property."

She paused to let the words sink in. A year of hard labor. I had once met a man who had spent only four months in one of the prison camps. He had been a broken, hollow-eyed, starved thing. A shadow of a man. I shuddered.

"Or," she went on, putting her hand down, "you enlist in the United States Army for a period of no less than four years. If you serve out your time and receive an honorable discharge, the charges against you will be dropped. If you do not serve the full term of the enlistment and are subsequently apprehended, you will be brought back into this courtroom, and if that happens, there will be no more deals. As it is, you're lucky our docket is overly full and the Army so desperately in need of personnel, otherwise the court would not even be offering you this opportunity."

The judge sat back and rested her hands on the arms of her chair. "So what's it going to be, Mr. Hicks?"

I looked over at my defender, who had not said a word. He looked back at me and shrugged. "I've seen what happens to guys in the prison camps," he said. "I'd take door number three if I were you."

I stared at the floor for a long moment. The two swigs of liquor I had drunk earlier were wearing off. My hands shook, but not from fear. I knew I would not survive a year of hard labor in a prison camp. Death no longer had the power to frighten me, but deep down in a place I had forgotten existed, I felt a spark of something. A stirring I had not felt for so long it took me a few moments to identify it.

Hope.

It's a hell of a carrot, hope. Put it on a stick and dangle it in front of someone, even someone as low as I was, and you can walk them for miles. My dad served in the Army. So did Blake. They had never talked about it much, but how bad could it be?

I looked up and said, "Your Honor, is there a recruiter in the building?"

*****

The Army could not take me in my current condition, so the judge ordered me into a treatment program. And by treatment, I mean they locked me in a cell, fed me two Xanax a day—one in the morning and one at night—to deal with the withdrawal symptoms, and an Ambien in the evening to help me sleep. This went on for five days.

The Xanax helped, but it could only do so much. I was in agony. I could not hold down food. Horrible black bile poured out of me every hour or so, until I began to ponder where it was all coming from. I was not eating, and so wondered if I was shitting out my internal organs. It would not have surprised me.

After the first five days, my heart stopped trying to beat its way out of my chest, the flow of high viscosity motor oil stopped, and I felt something I had not felt in months—hunger. Actual 'I could seriously eat food right now and not puke it up' hunger. The spark of hope in my chest burned a little brighter.

Near the end of the second week, I felt almost human again. To my surprise, there were no cravings. When I thought about booze, I just got mildly nauseous and that was it. Now, two years after recovering, I can drink without feeling the urge to get wasted like I used to. I have a theory about this.

Some people have a switch in their brains. When they take a drink, the switch closes, a circuit is completed, and they immediately want another drink. It is a phenomenon I have seen many times. For these people, once the booze train gets rolling, there is no stopping it.

I do not think I have this affliction. I can have two drinks and call it a night. I think for me, the drinking was a deliberate thing. I did not particularly enjoy it, but it took less courage than putting a bullet in my head. So once I decided I wanted to live, the problem solved itself. Well ... that and two weeks of being locked in a room with no access to booze.

I doubt Judge MacGregor will ever know it, but I am grateful to her. She could have laid the hammer down, but she chose to give me a second chance. If I am ever back in the Springs, I will make it a point to find her and express my gratitude.

Near the end of my treatment/incarceration, Tyrel came to see me. He seemed reluctant and surprised I had accepted his visit. The guard put a chair in front of my cell door so Ty could have a seat and walked a respectful distance away.

"How's it going, man?" I asked with a smile, my hands around the bars. "You doin' all right?"

He looked confused a moment, then said, "I could ask you the same thing."

"I don't think I'm a hundred percent yet, but I'm a hell of a lot better than I was."

"You look it."

"Thanks. Where have you been? I figured you would come to visit before now."

Again, the confusion. "You don't remember, do you?"

Now it was my turn to be confused. "Remember what?" The memory of waking in my cell with a swollen eye came back to me, and I groaned and said, "Oh, jeez, what did I do?"

"We had a bit of a falling out."

"How bad?"

"You took a swing at me."

My stomach dropped. "Did I connect?"

"No, but I did. That was the end of it."

"God, Ty, I am so sorry. I was out of my head, man. Please don't hold it against me."

He stood up and shook hands with me through the bars. "Water under the bridge, son. I'm just glad to see you're doing better."

"I'm glad to be feeling better. You hear about what happened to me?"

He nodded. "It's a good thing the Army is so hard up for people. Otherwise you'd have ended up in a labor camp."

"No shit." I sighed and looked down at my hands. "Looks like I'm gonna be a proper soldier soon."

"So I hear."

I looked at my oldest and best friend and gave a wan smile. "Any advice?"

"Keep your mouth shut, do what you're told, and don't let your drill instructor learn your name. Aside from that, just remember the training we gave you and you'll be fine."

A memory sparked in my still marginally dulled brain, and I said, "Speaking of my training, have you heard from Mike? Letters or anything?"

Tyrel's face took on a sad cast. "Got a letter about a month ago dated from December. Said he'd found his wife, but heard some disturbing rumors he wanted to investigate before he came home."

"What kinds of rumors?"

A shake of the head. "He didn't say."

"Does he … does he know about Sophia?"

Tyrel shrugged. "I sent him a letter after I got his. The address was a trading post in Western Oregon. No telling if he got it or not. Those caravans that travel between here and the west coast lose as much cargo as they deliver."

I nodded, my heart aching at the thought of Mike learning of his daughter's death. I wondered if he would blame me, if he would hate me for what happened, his daughter dying giving birth to his grandchild, my daughter.

As if reading my mind, Tyrel said, "Son, it's not your fault. What happened to Sophia was an accident. It ain't nobody's fault. We live in hard times, son. Bad things happen to good people. Sometimes you just have to accept it and move on. There ain't always a moral to the story. Most of the time, there's just what happens and how you deal with it."

I nodded, thinking about Sophia's chestnut eyes and the daughter I would never get to hold. My throat tightened, and I felt the old despair begin to burn within me. There was a vise around my heart, squeezing tighter, and tighter, and-

NO!

You think you're the only person to lose a child? When you get out of here, take a good hard look around. Everybody has lost someone. Everybody is hurting. You think you're special? You're not! Suck it up and get on with your life, you wimp. If Sophia is watching, she's probably pissed at you for acting like such a whiny asshole. So summon your strength, firm your resolve, and for Christ's sake, fucking live. *It's what she would want you to do.*

The voice in my head sounded so much like my father's, I actually looked around my cell to see if he was in there with me. But he was not, of course.

I think.

Shaking myself to clear my head, I said, "Thanks for coming by, Tyrel. It's good to see a friendly face."

He smiled and we shook hands again. "Take care of yourself, son. I know the Army will probably have you travelling all over hell and half of Georgia, but if you get the chance, look in on me."

"I'll do that."

As my old mentor began to walk away, I said, "Hey Ty?"

He half turned. "Yeah?"

"Just in case I don't get another chance to say it, I love you, man. You're the best friend I've ever had."

He stared a few seconds, and if I did not know him better, I would say his eyes reddened a bit. "I love you too, kid. You watch your ass out there, you hear?"

"I'll do that. Goodbye, Tyrel."

"Goodbye, son."

He left, and I stayed in my cell another day until it was time for a sheriff's deputy to escort me to my container to retrieve my personal effects. I took Blake's medallion, the picture of my mother holding me as a newborn, my father's and Lauren's wedding rings, Sophia's locket containing a picture of her with her mother and father, and my spear. Afterward, I checked my things in with the quartermaster at Peterson AFP, took the oath of enlistment, signed the paperwork, and started my new life.

The government seized everything else I owned as restitution for my crimes.

I have not seen Tyrel since.

SIXTY-FIVE

Hollow Rock, Tennessee

"You were right," Miranda said. "That did not end well."

Caleb glanced out the window. It was nearly dawn. "Took a lot longer to tell than I expected. Sorry."

Her hand caressed his face. "You're the one deploying today. Apologize to yourself."

"Won't be the first time I've had to function on zero sleep."

A silence stretched between them as the light through the window grew brighter. Caleb gripped Miranda's hand and said, "So now you know all of it."

"Not all of it. What happened after you joined the Army?"

A shrug. "Basic training wasn't so bad. Had a hell of a time getting back in shape, though. I'd really let myself go."

Miranda's fingers traced the ridges of his abdomen. "I never would have guessed."

"You didn't know me back then. I've gained twenty-five pounds since I enlisted."

Her eyebrows shot up. "Yikes."

"Yep. I was in pretty bad shape for a while there. As for what's happened over the last two years, well … let's just say it's been ninety-five percent boredom and five percent abject terror."

Another long silence. Caleb knew he had to get up soon and get into uniform, but he was loath to leave the bed. Finally, he said, "So what do you think? You gonna run for the hills, knowing everything I've done?"

"I'll admit," Miranda said, "some of it gave me pause. Especially the thing about the deserters that attacked you in Boise City. But honestly, I've heard of people doing worse. Much worse. And I'm not so innocent myself. People do what they have to do to survive. I know I've done some pretty messed up things since the Outbreak."

"That's different. The Free Legion-"

"I'm not talking about the Legion."

Caleb met her eyes. She looked away. "I don't want to talk about it."

"You don't have to. Ever."

Miranda rolled onto her back. "I might someday, just not today. I'm not ready."

"Well, when you are …"

A smile. "You were right about what you said before, Caleb. The past doesn't matter. I still love you. Some of the things you told me … I'll need some time to process. But as far as you and me, we're good. I'm glad you shared with me, and I'll keep my mouth shut about all of it. Fair enough?"

He kissed her on the tip of her nose. "Fair enough."

"And about Sophia and your daughter … I'm so sorry, Caleb. No one should have to go through that."

Caleb sat up in bed and stared out the window. Across the street, a man stepped out of his trailer and began walking toward the north gate, a tool belt hanging from his right hand. "Miranda, so many people have lost children since the Outbreak it'll be a wonder if the human race survives at all."

He felt her move behind him and slip her arms around his chest. "We will. Somehow, one way or another, we'll find a way. And if we don't, there's no one else I'd rather live out the end of the world with."

EPILOGUE

"I'll give you one thing, you're a hustler," Caleb said. "How you convinced Captain Harlow to let you come along with us, I'll never guess."

Eric Riordan grinned. Hicks sat beside him, the truck they rode in following behind an Abrams battle tank heading northeast toward Kentucky. As usual, he had fallen in with Delta Squad. Behind them, visible through the canopy's aperture, lay Hollow Rock. In another half-mile or so, they would be too far away to see it.

"I prefer to think of myself as a taker of carefully measured risks," Eric said. "Nothing ventured, nothing gained, and all that."

"Keep spouting clichés and it's gonna be a hell of a long ride. How'd your wife take the news about you coming with us?"

Eric's smile faltered. His wife, who until a short while ago had been the town's only medical doctor, had not taken the news well at all. He thought about the baby growing inside her, his first child, and wondered if he was doing the right thing.

"About as well as can be expected," he lied.

Caleb shot him a look from the corner of his eye, but did not press. "What about Gabriel? When there's trouble afoot, you two are never far apart."

"He's in the command vehicle with Captain Harlow. You believe that shit?"

Caleb laughed. "Doesn't surprise me."

Eric heard the distinctive thrum of a Chinook fly overhead, followed by the lighter drone of an Apache Longbow attack helicopter. The Apache was to leapfrog the convoy and land far ahead of them, close to where they would be meeting up with Task Force Falcon. The Chinook carried troops tasked with protecting the Apache while it was on the ground.

For a significant portion of the ride to Kentucky, the convoy would be without air support. Eric was not worried. First Platoon rode in the company of an Abrams, two Bradleys, several Humvees equipped with heavy machine guns, and two big green HEMMTs carrying their gear. If that was not enough to handle whatever lay in their path, they were all dead men anyway.

Eric sat up when he heard a thundering boom from somewhere in the distance ahead. He looked around, confused, as it was followed by the piercing sound of something approaching and descending at incredible speed. Beside him, Caleb's eyes went wide.

He drew a breath and shouted, "INCOMING!"

The soldiers around them echoed the cry as they ducked and covered. Eric felt the truck's brakes lock and the sound of gravel rattling against metal as it went into a controlled skid. He could not see for the press of bodies around him, but heard several booms and felt a series of hard vibrations thump his chest through the bed of the truck. In a flash of panic, he remembered a stretch of road not far from where he lay and the *crack-BOOM* of a LAW rocket detonating less than two-hundred yards away. The hollow feeling in his chest was nearly identical.

"What the hell was that?" he shouted.

"Get out of the truck!" Caleb answered. "Move!"

Several more thunder claps echoed, followed by more thumps to the chest. To his right, he heard Ethan Thompson shouting at his men, and then was hauled to his feet and dragged along.

"Come on!" Caleb shouted. "Run!"

He hopped to the ground and followed the other men of First Platoon. They sprinted in the direction of the treeline, trying to get as far away from the truck as possible. As he ran, Eric spared a glance over his shoulder and nearly skidded to a halt. Had Caleb not been there, he would have reversed direction and ran back toward his home as fast as he could.

"Eric, come on! We have to move!"

Caleb's iron fingers gripped his arm and dragged him along. Eric picked up his pace and felt tears sting his eyes as he looked away from the main gate. *Please God, don't let anything happen to Allison.*

In the distance, Hollow Rock was in flames.

The saga continues in Surviving The Dead Volume 5: Savages.

Coming soon …

About the Author:

James N. Cook (who prefers to be called Jim, even though his wife insists on calling him James) is a martial arts enthusiast, a veteran of the U.S. Navy, a former cubicle dweller, and the author of the Surviving the Dead series. He hikes, he goes camping, he travels a lot, and he has trouble staying in one place for very long. He lives in North Carolina (for now) with his wife, son, daughter, two vicious attack dogs, and a cat that is scarcely aware of his existence.

Made in the USA
Lexington, KY
07 November 2015